Wonderland

AN ANTHOLOGY

Also available from Titan Books

Cursed: An Anthology of Dark Fairy Tales (March 2020)

Dark Cities: All-New Masterpieces of Urban Terror

Dead Letters: An Anthology of the Undelivered, the Missing, the Returned...

Exit Wounds

Invisible Blood

New Fears

New Fears 2

Phantoms: Haunting Tales from the Masters of the Genre

Wastelands: Stories of the Apocalypse

Wastelands 2: More Stories of the Apocalypse

Wastelands: The New Apocalypse

AN ANTHOLOGY OF WORKS INSPIRED BY

ALICE'S ADVENTURES IN WONDERLAND

WONDERLAND

Edited by

MARIE O'REGAN

and PAUL KANE

TITAN BOOKS

Print edition ISBN: 9781789091489
Electronic edition ISBN: 9781789091496

Published by Titan Books
A division of Titan Publishing Group Ltd
144 Southwark Street, London SE1 0UP
www.titanbooks.com

First edition: September 2019
2 4 6 8 10 9 7 5 3 1

Names, places and incidents are either products of the author's imagination or used fictitiously. Any resemblance to actual persons, living or dead (except for satirical purposes), is entirely coincidental.

A CIP catalogue record for this title is available from the British Library.

Printed and bound in the United States.

Table of Contents

Introduction

MARIE O'REGAN and PAUL KANE

Wonderland.

That one word conjures up all kinds of mental images, from the tea party with the Mad Hatter to the grinning Cheshire Cat, from the White Rabbit to the giant chess game and the Queen of Hearts. And Alice, of course. Always Alice.

Ever since their publication back in 1865 and 1871, Lewis Carroll's *Alice's Adventures in Wonderland* (originally called *Alice's Adventures Under Ground*) and its follow-up *Through the Looking-Glass, and What Alice Found There* have captivated readers of all ages, providing the source material for countless movies and TV shows. Beginning with the silent adaptations of 1903 and 1910, by directors Cecil Hepworth and Percy Stow, and Edwin S. Porter, then carrying on through the TV incarnations of George More

O'Ferrall in 1937 and 1946... From the classic and beloved Disney animated version of 1951 to, most recently, the Tim Burton takes of the twenty-first century, starring Mia Wasikowska in the title role, our obsession with this mythos seems to know no bounds.

Alice's adventures have been turned into a ballet, countless comic strips (we'd highly recommend picking up Dynamite Entertainment's *The Complete Alice in Wonderland*), they've inspired parodies such as *The Westminster Alice*, an opera, a popular song by Jefferson Airplane, a theme-park attraction (based on the Disney version) and even video games! References to—and the influence of—the original works can be felt across the board, and our interest extends as much to the story *behind* Wonderland as it does to the study of the place itself.

In terms of fiction, novels inspired by the works started appearing as early as 1895 with Anna M. Richards' *A New Alice in the Old Wonderland*, and have continued right up to the present with interpretations such as A.G. Howard's *Splintered* trilogy, *The White Rabbit Chronicles* from Gena Showalter, and Christina Henry's *The Chronicles of Alice*.

The originals are very special stories that have stayed with us both since childhood, and which have subsequently led to putting together this anthology you now hold in your hands. But, of course, if you are going to gather a range of tales that also take as their inspiration the world of Wonderland, including drawing on the real-life circumstances surrounding its creation, then you have to be sure you're doing something very different from what has gone before… not easy when you consider just how much of it there has been. Thankfully, the talents contributing to *Wonderland* are very special themselves, and their unique approaches have resulted in some of the best fantastical fiction we've ever read! Within these pages you'll find poetry by Jane Yolen—and the imagination on display here would put some novels to shame—while Jonathan Green uses the "Jabberwocky" poem as the jumping-off point for his story. There are historical approaches to Alice from the likes of Juliet Marillier, Genevieve Cogman and L.L. McKinney (this takes place in her own Alice-inspired monster-hunting *A Blade So Black* universe). There's even a Wild West tale from Angela Slatter and a story by Laura Mauro which presents us with a very different Wonderland, inspired by Japanese folklore.

Authors such as Alison Littlewood, Cavan Scott and Catriona Ward make the more outlandish elements their own, while James Lovegrove draws on the supernatural for his entry. Cat Rambo takes us to a part of Wonderland we haven't seen before and Lilith Saintcrow gives the mythology a science-fiction spin. The nightmarish reaches of the imagination are the breeding ground for M.R. Carey's visions, while Robert Shearman, George Mann, Rio Youers and Mark Chadbourn's tales have a deep-seated emotional core which will tug at the heartstrings as well as shock and surprise.

So, it's time now to go down the rabbit hole, or through the looking-glass, or… But no, wait. By picking up this book and starting to read it you're already there, can't you see? You don't need to do a thing because it's already surrounding you. You're not late at all; it's perfect timing, in fact! You've already begun your journey of exploration. You're already in the place that they call…

Wonderland.

Marie O'Regan and Paul Kane
Derbyshire, 2019

Alice in Armor

JANE YOLEN

She dashed from the house,
Reverend Dodgson lingering at the door.
Never again. Never again, she thought.
She knew he would not follow.
He was too timid for the chase.

She found the armor
where she'd stashed it, by the old hedge.
The hole in the root, unused for years
still gaped like a giant's mouth.
That armor had twice served
as one of the costumes
she wore—then un-wore—
for the old don's photographs.

She slipped into it, feeling a bit
like a sardine in a tin, but safe,
with a bit of borrowed power.
Curiouser and curiouser, she thought,
before plopping down at the hole's edge,
contemplating her next move.
She could hear Dodgson calling.
Her answer lay unspoken between them.
Never again. Never again.

Hands trembling, she pushed off the edge,
dropped into the hole,
going down and down and down
much heavier than before,
the armor more than doubling her weight.

She passed the familiar shelves.
Instead of empty marmalade jars,
instead of maps hung up on pegs,
she found a sheathed sword on one shelf,
a fillet knife on another, and three cannon balls.
She managed to kick the balls into the hole
and they plummeted before her.

When she finally reached bottom,
the welcoming heap of sticks and leaves,
a medal snapped perkily onto her chest plate.
A helmet topped with feathers,
red and white, settled on her head.

Spit and blood, she thought,
hefting the sword with a firm hand.
She stuck the knife into her belt.
They gave her courage for what lay ahead.
In Wonderland.

Wonders Never Cease

ROBERT SHEARMAN

I

It should go without saying, but not all the Alices survived. Some fell foul of the Red Queen, and had their heads chopped off. Some didn't respond well to the drugs: "Drink Me", and the Alices shrank and shrank until at last they winked out of existence; "Eat Me", and they grew so fast that they snapped their necks on the ceiling. And many fell down the rabbit hole and never quite managed to find the bottom. They just kept on falling, and no one knows where they might have ended up.

Let's not waste any time on them. Or any sympathy either. These are not the good Alices. These are the failures. The truth is, we wouldn't have much enjoyed their adventures anyway. Better that we get rid of them quick, so another Alice, a better Alice, can come along.

This is not their story. Tell you what, let's just pretend I never mentioned them. My mistake. Forget I spoke.

2

All the time she had been down the rabbit hole, and encountering all manner of weird and perplexing creatures, Alice had worried that the experience would change who she was beyond all recognition. But in fact Alice managed to confound the pressures to transform, and held on to her identity very well indeed. Yet something had to give. If Alice wouldn't change, then something else would have to change in her place. And as she crawled out of the earth, and saw once more a daylight she feared she'd lost forever, as she smoothed the dirt from her pretty blue dress, and spat out the soil, Alice realised that the entire world had altered whilst she had been gone. There were flying machines up in the clouds and tall grey buildings scraping the sky, and all around were cars, and concrete, and computers, and cashpoint machines. And the grassy bank on which she had begun her grand adventure was now the central reservation of a roundabout off the A1.

Alice had left her sister reading, and she went to her now to ask what had happened, and what her sister made of it, and whether her sister thought it could be put right, but her sister was dead, she was dead. Alice touched her on her shoulder and she toppled over and she wasn't breathing and she hadn't breathed for years, and maybe she'd died of old age waiting for Alice to return, or died of boredom reading a book without pictures or conversations in it, or she'd had her head chopped off by the Red Queen, yes, that was the one. Alice touched her on her shoulder, and over she toppled, and the head toppled too, it came off nice and clean, Alice didn't think it would have hurt a bit.

Alice had never had any family worth mentioning—just a sister without a name, and a cat called Dinah. She picked up Dinah, and put her under her arm, and set off into the city to find herself a new life.

She determined to find employment. At the job centre she was asked whether she could type, and Alice didn't know but said yes anyway, and it turned out she *could* type, so that was all right. She worked in an open-plan office and she had a desk just two aisles away from the window, and Alice sometimes liked to look over the other typists' heads and wonder what marvels the windows might reveal if only she were close enough to see through them. A man who was a clerk at the Ministry of Agriculture, Fisheries and Food kept giving her lots of typing to do, some days Alice felt the only typing she got to do was his. Some days he came to her desk and stood over her even though he didn't have any typing to give her at all. And eventually he told her he had fallen in love with her and wanted to marry her, and he was so very earnest about it that Alice didn't feel she should refuse. She asked him his name. It was Dom.

On their wedding night Dom got into bed beside her and turned out the lights and climbed on top of her. He was there for a good minute or two, Alice didn't quite like to ask what he was up to, she didn't want to break that very earnest concentration of his. At last he rolled off, and panted for breath, and lay beside her, and asked her whether she had enjoyed the adventure. Alice was very polite, and said it had been no more unedifying than playing croquet with flamingo mallets, and no more uncomfortable than drowning in her own tears, and mercifully briefer than either.

And then she said, into the darkness:

"I don't love you, Dom. I don't think I could ever love you. What are you? You're a talking man, but we expect men to talk, so where's the magic in that? To meet a man who wouldn't talk, now there would be a thing! And the thing I've learned about talk, is that so much of it is nonsense. To me you're like a black hole, Dom, but not a rabbit hole, Dom, not a hole down which I can find adventure, not a hole that will challenge me or perplex me or make me think. You're a void of a man, Dom. You're nothing." And she said all of this perfectly nicely, because Alice was a well-brought-up sort of girl, and had excellent manners.

It was so dark and so still that Alice thought her husband wasn't there any longer, and that he had just disappeared, and there would be some relief in that. So she reached across to see if she could prod him, and she *could* prod him, his body was solid and thick and cold. Alice said to herself, "There's nothing for it but to sleep, and see if things may be better in the morning!" And in the morning she woke up and looked to her side and Dom had gone, and his clothes were gone from the wardrobe, and his toothbrush was gone from the bathroom sink.

For a while things were much simpler. It was just Alice,

and Dinah the cat, and the other girls in the typing pool. She didn't even have to type all that much now that Dom had disappeared. But presently she began to get the funniest notion that she was never alone. There was someone else there, just out of the corner of her eye, and no matter how hard she'd turn her head she could never get a glimpse of them. And then, curiouser and curiouser, her body began to grow in different directions, and she wondered why, for she was certain she hadn't lately drunk any strange potions or eaten any strange cakes or nibbled any strange mushrooms marked "Eat Me". Her stomach distended and her belly button popped out and she felt very, very sick in the mornings.

Alice was always practical, and she soon realised what the matter was. "I will not let my body be used by a stranger for temporary accommodation!" she said firmly to her fat belly, and she rapped on it with her knuckles to get the occupant's attention. "Come out of there at once!" And out it popped, she dropped her baby right there and then in the open-plan office, she had to take an early lunch break to give these new circumstances frank and considered attention. Alice didn't know whether it was a boy or a girl, and she decided she'd think of it as a girl for the time being, and that should ever any further evidence come to light to convince her to the contrary she'd deal with it then. She chose to name it after her sister, and so didn't name it anything at all. "How very lovely you'll turn out to be," said Alice to the shrieking lump of flesh, "just as soon as you're finished!" She wasn't quite sure that the baby *would* be lovely, not particularly, but she was a good-hearted girl, and she wanted to give the baby something positive to aim for.

Alice had learned all about babies during her time down the rabbit hole, and knew that the trick was to hold its arms and legs out in all directions and wait for it to turn into a pig. The baby bawled no matter how hard and long its limbs were stretched, and by nightfall Alice began to despair it would ever become a pig at all. "Just my luck the first baby I get is defective!" thought Alice. She shook it fiercely from side to side, just to see if she could shake the pigginess to the surface, and within the blur of motion she would think she could discern the baby's nose flatten to a snout. But every time she stopped shaking and the blurring came to a halt, she'd see to her disappointment that the child stubbornly remained no more porcine than before.

"Bother!" said Alice. She took the baby home. It never stopped crying, and Alice supposed that not only was her baby broken but it also was rather unhappy. She asked Dinah her opinion, but Dinah wouldn't reply, either because she was offended by the noise the baby made, or because she was a cat. "What to do!" said Alice. She took the baby out into the garden, and she considered each and every rabbit hole there, she wanted to find one that was just right. The rabbit hole in the very centre of the lawn was cosy and snug, and the baby would fit into it perfectly. "What adventures you'll have!" said Alice. "I really am most jealous!"—and she dropped it into the hole, *plop*, and down it fell, out of sight, deep, deep, until even the bawling could no longer be heard, and Alice wondered whether her baby would ever reach the bottom.

That really ought to have been the end of it, but the next morning Alice woke to find new squirming in her stomach and new nausea in her throat. "I'm having no more of this nonsense," Alice addressed herself sternly. She phoned up Jackie, who worked on the switchboard, and told her she wouldn't be coming into the office today, she'd come down with a bug, and Jackie didn't care, because Jackie was a bitch. And then she set to work on her belly, and this time the baby was reluctant to come out and she had to prise it free with a spoon. She couldn't tell whether this was the same baby from yesterday, and that it had climbed out of the rabbit hole and crawled back inside her, or whether this baby was brand new. All she *could* tell was that it was just as noisy and as broken as before. This time she had to throw it down the rabbit hole quite forcefully—not to be cruel, but so the baby might take the hint.

But it was no good. No matter how fast she'd rip them from her womb, by the time she'd dropped them down the hole there'd be another baby inside squawking and wriggling and waiting to pop out. There were large babies with small heads, there were small babies with large heads, babies with hair and babies with teeth and babies with claws. Alice began to bag them up in batches of a dozen before taking them out to the rabbit hole, otherwise she was rushed off her feet going outside and inside and outside, being a mother was exhausting!

By night-time Alice was tired and out of sorts. "Come on, little one," she said to her latest child, and she said it as kindly as she could: it wasn't its fault it was a parasite to be disposed of. As she carried it out into the garden it occurred to Alice this one wasn't even crying, and her heart softened towards it a little. She stared down at the rabbit hole. It was full to the brim. Out of the top poked a mass of arms and legs, some of them were still writhing—not, Alice thought, in distress, but in a matter-of-fact fashion, the way Dinah did when she was asleep and dreamed of catching mice. Alice stomped hard to flatten the babies down, but that didn't work—she tried to wedge the baby into any cracks, but the wall of compacted infant just wouldn't budge.

"No room!" said Alice. "No room!" And she dared at last to look down at her daughter, and she saw its little hands, and its tiny feet, and a face shining up towards Alice with hope and wonder and love. It was *smiling.* It was smiling, and of all the children she had ever given birth to, it was the least pig-like yet. Alice sighed. The baby sighed too, as if in imitation of its mother. And Alice held her up to her face, and gave her a kiss, and took her inside away from harm.

3

Of course, that's not how the story really goes.

The divorce is amicable—or, at least, as amicable as divorces can ever be. Dom had plenty of money, and the maintenance he offered was fair. He insisted that Alice found another job—he said it was irksome to have an ex-wife in the typing pool, and he wasn't going to be the one who disappeared. Why should he disappear? He would contribute to childcare. He had no interest in child custody, and made that very clear.

And Alice was happy with that. She didn't want to share her daughter with anyone. She loved her with all her heart, and had loved her from the first moment she'd been born and the nurse had held her up to show her. As a little girl trapped down a rabbit hole she'd spent an inordinate amount of time worrying about her identity—who was Alice, what sort of person was she like? And it turned out that Alice was a mother, and she had always been a mother just waiting to happen. She went from typing job to typing job, and she never stayed for long, and she never cared—she didn't need to make friends, because she had a little daughter at home waiting for her.

She'd wanted to name her after her sister, but people told her that that was silly, she'd have to name her *something*—and she'd bought a big book of names, and some of the names were very beautiful, and in spite of that she eventually called her daughter Trish.

Trish was a good girl who worked hard at school. The teachers liked her, and she never got into trouble, and she always kept away from the bad girls who hung around the bike sheds and dated older boys and smoked. Trish told her mum she wanted to go to university one day and study Psychology and Social Sciences, and Alice thought that sounded very impressive, and wondered what it was. She looked through Trish's school textbooks, and she couldn't make head nor tail of them. There were no pictures or conversations, and what was the use of a book without pictures or conversations?

Alice watched as her daughter grew up, and how every step took her further away. She was pleased that Trish was clever, but did she have to be *so* clever, and so much cleverer than Alice? The way she talked, using long words she knew Alice wouldn't understand—the way she gave that sad sideways tilt of the head when Alice asked her to say everything again more simply and slowly. Trish was patient, but Alice didn't want her daughter being patient. Trish was kind, but who wants the person you love to be *kind* to you, always having to be *kind*? Alice wanted to grab hold of Trish and dig her nails in, right deep into her skin, and keep her pinned down like that forever, so she would stop fast, she'd stop right there and she'd never age and the gap that was widening between them would at least never get any wider. And she wanted to burn all her Psychology and Social Sciences textbooks.

And yet, it was all right. It was all right, because whenever Alice felt small, or scared, or lonely, she would stare into Trish's face. And Trish would smile, and the smile showed all her teeth, and it stretched wide so that it lit up her skin and flared her nostrils and made her eyes sparkle—and it was the same smile Trish gave when she was a baby. And Alice knew that the Trish she'd fallen in love with was still inside there somewhere, and she would never lose her, not really.

One day Trish said, "It's my birthday soon. And there's something special I would like." And Alice said yes, yes, anything, of course she'd give her anything. And Trish smiled, and the smile was a little shyer than usual, so Alice knew this had to be something she *really* wanted. Trish said, "May I have a rabbit hole, all of my own?" Because it turned out that all the other girls had rabbit holes, rabbit holes were all the rage—Wendy had got a rabbit hole, and so had Brenda, and so had Cath. Alice felt her heart sink, because weren't rabbit holes terribly expensive? And maybe Wendy's parents and Brenda's parents and Cath's parents had lots of money and it didn't matter to them, and Trish said it needn't be a *very* big rabbit hole, it didn't even have to be the latest model. She just wanted what the other girls had. Couldn't she feel normal, just for once? Alice had often wondered too what it must be like to feel normal. She said she'd try. She said she'd find the money somehow. Even if she had to work longer hours at the office, even if she had to take out a loan. And Trish suggested they could ask Dad for help, and Alice said they needn't go that far.

Alice asked the accounts department whether she could have next month's pay packet early, and the woman behind the big desk took pity on her, she had a teenage daughter too. And Alice trawled through all the small ad magazines looking for rabbit hole bargains, and at last found a second-hand rabbit hole on eBay. She pulled a sickie from work the day it was delivered, whilst Trish was still at school, and they set it down where she told them, right in the centre of the garden lawn. And it was a little smaller than the ad had suggested, and the sides were chipped, but Alice knew Trish would love it anyway. And she decided she'd do it up nicely, she'd go down it and take banners, and glitter, and a big birthday cake. No, even better, she'd buy lots of party food, she could throw a birthday party for Trish in her new rabbit hole, just the two of them! Not so much mother and daughter but best friends—sandwiches and sausage rolls and Kettle Chips and cheese-and-ham quiche. And as Alice fell down the hole she began to wonder whether she'd made a mistake with the food, was Trish still going through her vegetarian phase? She said to herself, "Does Trish eat quiche? Does Trish eat quiche?" And sometimes, "Does quiche eat Trish?" For, you see, as she couldn't answer either question, it didn't much matter which way round she put it.

She worked all afternoon making the rabbit hole the very best it could be. When Trish came home she greeted her at the door with a big hug, and told her she had a surprise for her, and as she led her out to the garden she was skipping from foot to foot, it was hard to tell who was the most excited! They went down the rabbit hole. They reached the bottom. Trish looked around. And right away Alice could see she'd made a mistake—the banners were too much, "Happy Birthday Baby Girl!" No one wanted to be called a baby when they were fifteen. The colours were too bright, it was all loud pinks and wild oranges. And the cake was decorated with cartoon animals, a Dormouse and a Mock Turtle and a Snark. Alice asked whether she liked it, and Trish tilted her head to one side and did the kind and patient thing. "You've tried so hard!" And Alice *had* tried hard, so it was nice that Trish had noticed, but it somehow wasn't quite the answer she'd been hoping for.

Trish had a single slice of quiche. She ate it slowly. Alice had some quiche too. "The hole's bigger than it looks," enthused Alice. "The banners are getting in the way."

"Yes."

"We just need to take down the banners. And, look, see there in the corner, there's a tiny door! Too tiny to fit through, or so you might think!"

"Yes, I see the door."

"But there's probably a solution somewhere. And, what's this on the table? A bottle marked 'Drink Me'!"

Trish confirmed that she'd seen the door, and she'd seen the bottle, and she'd got the general idea.

"The adventures that are in store for you! For *us*, because I could come too, if you like! I don't mind. Shall we drink together, shall we see what's behind the door?"

"Maybe later," said Trish. "I think I'd like to try it out by myself first. Would that be all right?"

"Of course," said Alice, and tried not to sound disappointed. "Do you want me to wait here, or, or shall I go back to the house, or, or...?"

"Go back to the house."

"Of course," said Alice.

In the sitting room Alice waited all alone for her daughter to return. She tried to wait with Dinah, but Dinah was old now, and didn't like people, and when Alice put her on her lap she struggled off and spat.

She wondered what Trish would make of the Mad Hatter's Tea Party! Or whether she would solve the riddle of the raven and the writing-desk. Or whether she would survive her encounter with the Red Queen—but Alice supposed she would, because after all *Alice* had survived it, and Trish was far better and far cleverer than Alice was.

And she wondered what sort of Trish there'd be at the end of it all—because sometimes it seemed to Alice that her own little adventure down the rabbit hole had been the most formative part of her entire life, and that everything that had ever happened before had been leading up to it, and that everything that had happened since had been leading away, and that maybe it was the only thing that had ever defined her and made her important and made her real. She couldn't guess how long Trish's adventure would take, but she determined to wait for her, even if Trish were gone years and years, she'd wait the rest of her life if necessary. Trish came back a little over half an hour later. "Oh, that was quick," said Alice. "Did you have fun?"

"Mum," said Trish, "we need to talk." And Trish looked so sad and so grown-up, and told Alice that she wanted to move out and live with her father instead. "Just for a while," added Trish. "Not forever, probably."

"Oh, my poor dear," said Alice, and she tried to put her arms around Trish, but Trish pulled away. "But your father doesn't want you. Don't you see? I'm the only one who wants you. I'm all you've got."

"I've been meeting up with Dad for a while," said Trish. "After school, when you think I'm at hockey practice. I'm sorry I didn't say anything. We didn't think you'd understand." And Trish said she had to find out who she was, she couldn't be just a little girl forever.

"I love you," said Alice.

"I know you do," said Trish. And again, it wasn't quite

the answer Alice was hoping for. But then Trish smiled, and the smile was spectacular—all the teeth, flared nostrils, sparkling eyes, the full works—really, it was one of Trish's all-time bests. So Alice couldn't be unhappy.

And Trish went to bed, and the only thing she left behind was the smile. "I've often seen Trish without a smile," thought Alice, "but never before a smile without a Trish! How absurd!" And she stayed up all night to watch the smile of the daughter she loved so much, until at last it faded and was gone.

4

Of course, that's not really how the story goes either.

Trish never finished her Psychology and Social Sciences degree. She met a boy called Paul who was studying Geology, and they fell in love, and then both dropped out of university to get married. She didn't even complete the first term. Alice was furious. She'd tried to argue it out over the phone, but Trish kept hanging up on her. In the end, she'd had to leave a message on the answering machine. "You're cleverer than me. You're better than me in every way. And I just want you to do better than I did, when the best part of my life was when I was seven years old and fell down a rabbit hole. Everything I have done since, *everything*, was for you. Don't you dare fuck it all up now!"

She wrote to Dom, "Could you please behave like a responsible parent, and talk some sense into your daughter, you're the one she listens to." He didn't reply.

Trish told Alice she needn't come to the wedding unless Alice apologised. Alice told Trish she wouldn't come unless Trish apologised first. Nohow and contrariwise! So, mother and daughter were in perfect accord, making sure neither got what they wanted. On the morning of the wedding day Alice woke early with a start, and she realised with cold horror that she was making a terrible mistake. She took a blue dress from her wardrobe, it wasn't new but it was the best she had; she flung it into a suitcase, flung the suitcase into a car, and then flung herself one hundred and fifty miles up the M4 breaking the speed limit all along the way. She made it to the church in time to collapse into a pew and watch as Dom led her daughter up the aisle. The bride and groom exchanged rings and vows, and when it was all over and she was properly grown-up Trish turned around and saw her mother gazing at her with pride and love, and she burst into grateful tears. Alice did the same.

Alice drank a lot of wine at the reception, and that may have been the reason she started to find Dom so suddenly attractive. She almost resented him for it, he was still slim where now she was podgy, his hair rich brown and thick without a trace of her grey. He asked her to dance, and she agreed to do just the one, and they spent the next hour and a half on the dance floor, swaying slowly from side to side. And he was whispering jokes in her ear, and being charming, and Alice thought, is he *flirting* with me?

Dom asked if he could talk to her somewhere private. She met him outside on the patio. "I don't think we should do this," she said. "I think this is a big mistake." Her heart was pounding, and she was ashamed how good that made her feel.

"I need to tell you," said Dom. "Face to face. I'm afraid I've got the big C."

It took Alice a few moments to realise what he meant. He was smiling ruefully, the way he used to do, caught out doing something wrong and knowing his charm would see him through. She'd always found it annoying until now.

"But there are things you can do...?" said Alice. Dom was shaking his head.

"Already done them," he said. "Look. Look. It's all right."

And Alice found that her sympathy and her embarrassment gave way to her famous childlike curiosity. "What does it *feel* like?" she asked. "Knowing you're going to die?"

Dom blinked at her, surprised. But he told her.

There was a hole in front of him, he said. It wasn't a very large hole, but it was always there. And all he had to do was walk towards it, and he'd drop in, and it'd be over. It didn't frighten him. The hole seemed cosy and snug. It was all right. He wasn't going to walk into the hole just yet, but it was getting harder to sidestep. It was all right, it was all right.

Alice said, "But you look so *good*." Because he did, his body lean and firm. And his wig, she could now see it was a wig, the wig suited him.

"I know," he said, and grinned. "It's a bugger, isn't it?"

They could have made love that night, and maybe they should have, but neither of them quite asked the other whether they'd like to. And six months later, when Trish phoned her up, and she wasn't crying, she was being surprisingly adult about it all, Alice wondered whether she regretted it, and couldn't quite decide.

It was only three weeks later that Alice saw the very first hole of her own. It wasn't where she'd expected to find one. She was in the supermarket, buying ready meals for one, and there it was right by the queue to the checkout. No, it wasn't frightening. It wasn't large enough to be frightening—she couldn't have fallen down it, she'd have had a job squeezing her head through it, and all the other customers stepped over it and wheeled their shopping trolleys through it with no difficulty at all. Still, she decided to stop using Sainsbury's for a while, and thereafter got her groceries from Tesco instead.

And after that, for the longest time, nothing—and Alice started to relax, to think the hole had been a one-off, or an accident, or a glitch. Her birthday came and went, and then Trish's birthday, and then Christmas—and she stopped even looking for the hole, she began even to doubt she'd seen one in the first place. Which is why that spring morning when she opened the front door to set off for work and saw it there, gaping at her on the front step, she shrieked out loud the way she did. Unexpected, and so *rude* too, to invade her personal private property like that.

It wasn't there when she returned home that night, and that was good. But after that Alice started to see the hole regularly—if not quite *every* day, then at least three or four times a week. Never in the same place, which was irritating, because it meant Alice always had to be on her guard. In the car park, on the pavement, just outside the bank. One time she found it in the lift at work, slap bang in the middle like an oily stain, and leaving her nowhere to stand—and that was annoying because she had to climb the stairs for seven floors, it quite wore her out.

Still, she wasn't frightened. She could see what Dom had meant. Cosy and snug, the hole was always cosy and snug. And *warm* somehow—Alice never wanted to get close enough to check, but she detected a warmth from it anyway. Or maybe she just felt warm inside when she saw it, a happy warmth that spread through her from top to toe, like when she had a nice hot soup, like when she took a nice hot bath. It was comforting.

And yet, something was wrong. She couldn't sleep well. Her stomach would suddenly clench painfully. She found herself short of breath, and it'd make her dizzy, and she had to stop and calm down and force air in and out of her lungs so she wouldn't pass out. She couldn't work out whether these symptoms were a consequence of the hole—or whether the hole was a consequence of them. Which would be worse? She didn't want to blame the hole. She liked the hole. She'd decided to like the hole. But she thought she should take further advice.

She went to the doctor. She asked for a full check-up. She was going to be very brave, whatever bad news he had to give her. He told her she was fine. She could drink a little less, and smoke a little less, and a spot of exercise now and then wouldn't do her any harm—but, for her age, for her size, for her condition, she was in rude health. "But how are you feeling otherwise?" he asked her gently. "Are you happy in yourself?" Alice just stared at him blankly.

Alice supposed she was happy, or happy enough. She'd go to work, she'd come home, she'd feed herself, feed the cat. Dinah was now so old, impossibly old. Dinah couldn't walk any longer, she was a spider dragging herself across the floor, and she'd glare at Alice balefully and ask to die, why wouldn't Alice just let her die? And sometimes Alice would watch the telly, if there was anything good on.

One night Alice wakes with a start, and there is the hole, mere inches above her face. Defying gravity, hanging over her. And at first she can't actually *see* it, she just knows it's there, she can feel the inviting warmth, can feel the now familiar clench of her stomach. Her eyes adjust. She can make out its shape. Its contours. How *black* it is, oh, it is so black, blacker than the easy darkness of the room, blacker than all the black there ever was.

If she were to raise her head, just a fraction, she thinks her nose would scratch it. If she sat upright—she mustn't, she *mustn't*—if she were to take leave of her senses and sit bolt upright, then her head would be absorbed, and she'd be lost, she'd be lost forever.

She takes a deep breath. Tries to calm herself. Another breath—not too deep this time, she doesn't want to suck the hole closer.

She decides to slide out from under it. If she does it carefully, maybe the hole won't even notice. Maybe the hole is asleep. (The hole is not asleep.) If she shuffles gently to the left. (The hole is not asleep! The hole is watching her. The hole is smiling down at her, all that's there is the smile.) She shuffles, and then stops dead. There is another hole. There is a hole on the pillow, it's almost kissing her cheek. She'll shuffle to the right. Don't look up. Don't look at the smile. ("I've often seen a hole without a smile," thought Alice, "but never before a smile that is a hole! How absurd!") She can't shuffle to the right. She can't shuffle to the right, because all of the right is a hole, everything around her for miles and miles is a hole, the hole is all there is.

Oblivion all about, and rabbit holes on every side. "It isn't fair," thinks Alice, "it really isn't fair at all!" And it isn't fair, and it's never been fair, and you're in a pretty pickle when you realise that the only thing you ever did that made the slightest scrap of sense was to get lost in Wonderland when you were too young to appreciate it. And know that you had adventures, there was a time there were *adventures* in your life, and they were wild and they were untamed, and you didn't hold on to them hard enough, you let them go, the adventures now are all done. "Bother," says Alice out loud, and she does it so all the holes can hear her too, what does she care any longer what rabbit holes think of her? "I shall go back to sleep. And if I roll over to my left, then so be it, and if I roll over to my right, then so be it too. And if I cough or splutter or snore and by doing so jerk my head upwards, then I hope it'll be quick and painless. I'm not going to worry about death ever again."

The next morning she finds herself alive, and that the holes have vanished in the sunlight. But she is still fierce and determined. And it feels good, it feels almost childlike, it's as if something has been recaptured that she lost years ago. She swings her body out of bed, ready to confront the day. It winces in protest. She ignores it.

She phones Trish one last time. She doesn't know why, she supposes it's to tell her she loves her. But as she starts to do so, it occurs to Alice she's told her this before, and many times into the bargain. If Trish doesn't know already then surely she never will, and there's no more to be said about it. Trish sounds frazzled. "Can I call you back, Mum? I've got my hands full at the moment!" In the background Alice can hear her granddaughter crying, yet another baby that failed to turn into a pig. "Goodbye," says Alice.

Alice tidies the house, she wouldn't want to leave a mess behind her. Then she feeds Dinah, puts on her best blue dress, and leaves, locking the front door behind her. She sets out to find her hole.

But the frustrating thing about holes is, you can never find one when you want one! She goes to Sainsbury's, but there are no holes in stock. She studies the pavement on all sides, she stares up at the empty space just above her head. Alice knows she could go home, and try again some other day—but she doesn't want to try another day, she's had enough of patience, if she's going to yield to the tender mercies of the rabbit hole it has to be now or never. And suddenly she remembers where she's sure to find one.

It's rush hour on the A1, but it's always rush hour on the A1. Alice parks the car, and then tries to cross the road to get to the middle of the roundabout. The central reservation is grassy and the green of it seems to shine out of the grey like a beacon, it's a bit of nature and it looks absurd amidst all the tarmac and all the traffic. Cars slam their brakes and blast their horns as Alice runs towards it; she nearly gets hit; she doesn't.

When Alice can't find the rabbit hole she thinks she'll die of disappointment. She'll just lie down on the grass and die. But it seems to call to her, and she sees it at last, it's grown over with weeds. She picks them away, and there it is, the opening is a perfect circle, she'd never realised that before. The ground is saying "o", the hole's a mouth opening wide in surprise and delight to greet a long-lost friend.

Alice cannot fit inside a rabbit hole. But she's a girl who can do six impossible things before breakfast, and she hasn't eaten that morning. She sits on the edge, and lowers her legs into the void, she leaves them dangling there for a minute or two. Then she wriggles in further, it's a snug fit. She's up to her stomach, she's up to her neck. Little Alice clinging to the side, still not sure whether she wants to commit to this new adventure, whether to let go of the world and all that's within it. She wonders why she thought the hole would be warm. The hole isn't warm.

And she feels a hand grasp hold of her foot. Trying to pull her down.

The shock of it makes Alice kick, but the hand won't let go. It's grabbing on to her, and not she thinks in spite, it's such a little hand, the hand of a little girl. And then she feels another one, and this is on her ankle. And a third hand, pulling at her thigh, and a fourth, and a fifth.

It should go without saying, but not all the Alices survived.

Some fell down the rabbit hole and they just kept falling, and no one knows where they might have ended up.

For just a moment Alice tries to escape, to heave herself back out of the rabbit hole and into the waking world. But this is just a reflex action, surely. She falls, of course she falls—and we mustn't feel sorry for her when she falls, and joins her sisters beneath the ground. This is what she wanted. This is what she always wanted.

5

And this is how the story goes, and how it always goes.

Alice fell down the hole, and she forgot whether she was an old woman or just a little girl. And was there really much difference between the two anyhow? Either the hole was very deep, or she fell very slowly, for she had plenty of time as she went down to look about her and to wonder what might happen next.

But presently she neared the ground, and she could see that there was a table there, with a little bottle marked "Drink Me" standing upon it, and there was a tiny wooden door leading to who knows what. And Alice thought, "I'm quite sure that's a very good adventure, but it doesn't have to be *my* adventure. I shall find another one to call my own." So she refused to land, and just kept falling.

She fell for a very long while. Time dragged by, as time always does, even in Wonderland, even down rabbit holes. "Well," said Alice, "I'll just have to find something to keep me busy in the meantime!" She saw a job centre floating past, and when she went inside they asked whether she could type; fortunately, Alice was an *excellent* typist. And with typing one thing always leads to another, and before Alice knew it she had fallen in love and was getting married.

And that was good, because it's a far distance to fall, and it's so much better to do it with a friend. And before too long, there were three of them falling, they had a little daughter, and sometimes Alice was so very happy with her new family that she nearly forgot she was falling at all.

The daughter kept getting bigger, and getting older, and becoming an adult, and Alice thought that was so very brave, an adult seemed an awfully baffling thing to be! And one day the daughter hugged on to her rather tightly; "I'm sorry," she whispered, "I'm so sorry." And Alice didn't know what she was apologising for, but forgave her anyway. The daughter gave her a smile, and it was the most beautiful smile in the world—and then she fell alone, harder and faster and out of sight, and Alice never saw her again.

When the husband hit the ground it was far too sudden and far too early, and Alice barely had time to say goodbye before he wasn't there any longer. And that seemed a little cruel, and maybe just a little rude. But Alice didn't have time to worry about that, because she was still falling. Still falling in spite of herself, falling all alone—just because he'd hit the bottom it didn't mean she had to. Just because love dies, it doesn't mean you can't go on.

It should go without saying, but not all the Alices died. Yes, some fell foul of the Red Queen and got their heads chopped off. And some fell foul of the big C. But many fell down the rabbit hole and they never quite managed to find the bottom.

They just kept falling, forever and ever, and their lives were sometimes happy and their lives were sometimes sad. But their stories kept on going, and no one knows how they ended up.

There Were No Birds to Fly

M.R. CAREY

"If you follow the rules," the woman said, "you'll live a whole lot longer."

What are the rules, then? I asked her. I didn't know what she meant by that, and it scared me. I don't like things being too rigid. I like them to flow. Everything that's beautiful flows, in and out and round about itself, stopping only for a moment to make a pleasing shape against the sky, then moving on, endlessly.

"You look like you're wearing a dress," the boy said.

It's an apron, I said. And then, to the woman: What are the rules? What did you mean when you said there were rules?

"Later," she said. "If we get out of this."

But...

"Later."

All six of us ran across the bottom of the field, keeping our heads low so the hedge would hide us from anyone standing up on the embankment and looking down. The hedge and its knife-edged shadow, made by a full moon hanging low in the sky. A harvest moon.

There were things much closer to us, of course. On the other side of the hedge, a stumbling, moaning thing muttered, "Poor Tom's a-cold!" and then laughed. The laugh had a crazed, despairing undertone to it. I saw the hedge bend down where the thing leaned against it, and I smelled the stale coriander stench of bedbugs. But the thing had no interest in any of our party, and made no move against us.

Four of us had no idea where we were heading. The woman, Bridget, had suggested a drainage culvert on the bank of a stream where she and the scarred man had been hiding. They had gone out scavenging, she said, and picked up the boy and the other woman—I had heard her name given as Chetna—along the way. Chetna had taken an injury to her head. Her speech was slurred, and she seldom said anything that was relevant or sensible. The other man, who called himself Carter and carried an automatic pistol, was a stranger to all of them, but he agreed to accompany them when the drainage culvert was mentioned.

"That leaves you," Bridget said to me. "You're welcome to come with us, too. We've got a better chance if we stick together, right? Are those weapons in the bag? Tools? What?"

Tools, I said. The tools of my trade. And yes, I'll come.

I wanted to, very much, but it wasn't as though I had a great deal of choice in the matter. Carter was clearly suspicious of me, but the pull was very strong, so I knew I was close to my source. To move away, or even just to stand still while they left, would have been like swimming up a waterfall.

So we ran, and we hid, and we ran some more. And somehow, in the dark, we ended up losing our way. We went among houses, most of them in ruins, and past the remains of a vast, dead thing like a whale with soft, tentacular legs and a mosquito's face, the spear-like feeding tube at least fifteen or twenty feet long.

"There's no stream bed here," Carter said. "I'm sure of that."

"I have to go to bed," Chetna mumbled. "It's getting so late."

"There are shops," the boy said. "Look."

He pointed. A sign ahead of us said SPAR. It might have been a shop sign, to be sure. Or possibly the first four letters of a prayer. *Spare us, Lord. Spare us, O Lamb of God, who taketh away the sins of the world.*

Does the Lamb of God ride in the back of a small rowboat, looking owlishly over its tiny, round spectacles and crying "Feather!" from time to time? Is that the Lamb of God I'm thinking of, or just some random sheep or other? I don't know anymore, if I ever did.

The shop was attached to a petrol station, and it had been ransacked. A trail of blood showed where the assistant had been dragged out from the little serving booth and carried away. Whatever had taken him had left his fingers behind, neatly snipped off and laid along the counter in their original order, with the two thumbs facing away from each other at the centre of the array. I saw the scarred man sweep them off onto the floor of the booth so the boy wouldn't notice them.

"Let's see if there's any food," Bridget said.

Surprisingly, there was. We found tins of tomato soup, baked beans and sweetcorn. We had no can-opener, but at Bridget's suggestion I used my chisel to prize holes in the lids. The chisel came most readily to my hand. There was a completeness to it, a rightness that I liked, though at the same time I instinctively pulled against it. I knew where it had come from, of course, and what it meant.

When I was done, we tilted the cans and gulped down whatever came out. It was quite the feast. There were exclamations of delight and satisfaction.

"I can't shake the feeling that I know you," Carter said to me.

That was significant information, and a hopeful sign. I filed it away. I don't believe we've met, I said. But perhaps I'm wrong. It will come to you in time, no doubt.

"Look at this," the boy said. He had found a newspaper, many months old. The headline consisted of two words: THEY'RE HERE. The adults stared at it in silence for a little while, presumably remembering the time when that had seemed like a cause for excitement or joy. Before we were ruined.

"Is Nurse Delia here?" Chetna said. "I need to go to bed now."

"What do you miss the most?" Carter asked. "I miss driving. I had a Citroën Picasso, with a massive windshield that curved right up over the front seats. I used to take it out into the country on weekends so I could feel how high up the sky was."

"I miss my brother, Robert," the boy said. "He got eaten by this… thing, with great big teeth."

I looked up at that.

What kind of thing? I asked. The woman glared at me, but I ignored her. What kind of creature was it, boy? And what kind of teeth? Do you mean tusks, by any chance?

"It was a bear," the boy said. "My brother always used to have nightmares about bears, so we ran away when we should have stayed hidden where we were. They saw us and chased us."

Perhaps he saw the disappointment in my face, and mistook it for pity or sympathy. At any rate, he went on talking. "The bears were really, really big. Well, most of them were. The size of horses, almost. But one of them had chequered trousers on, and a red pullover. And a scarf. And it was only the same size as us."

"You don't have to talk about any of this," Bridget told him.

The boy rubbed his filthy face with a filthy hand. His eyes were shiny with tears. "It almost wasn't a bear at all, you know? That's why I called it a thing. It was wearing clothes, and it… it was running the same way we were. On its back legs, like a boy. It was right at the front, so we thought maybe it was running away from the other bears, just like we were.

"We got to a wall, and we climbed up it. We thought we'd

be safe, because bears can't climb. But Robert reached down a hand to help the bear with the scarf and the red pullover. And it jumped up and bit his arm." The boy looked down at his hands. "It dragged him down," he said, more quietly. "And the other bears watched while it ate him. I should have come down off the wall and tried to help him, but I was scared. There were other things coming, and one of them was shouting my name. So I climbed down on the other side of the wall and ran away."

The scarred man placed his hand on the boy's arm. "You didn't do anything wrong," he said.

The other things that were coming, I said. Did you see them? What were they like?

"Don't make him relive it," Bridget said. "Can't you see he's traumatised?"

Were any of them—

"And *Taskmaster*," the scarred man said. "I really loved that show."

Nobody picked up that conversational thread, so crudely and determinedly thrown out, but it made it impossible for me to ask again. I looked at the other tools in my bag. One of them was a try square, with a rosewood stock and a six-inch blade. The front end of the blade was a straight line, of course. This was a tool for checking the accuracy of right angles, not for thrusting or stabbing or gouging. I had a saw, too. I liked both of these items very much.

"This is the thing," Bridget said. She was looking at me when she said it.

What? I said. What's the thing? What do you mean?

"You asked about the rules. This is what I was going to tell you."

Oh. Yes. If you must.

"The aliens take the shape of whatever scares you the most. They reach right into your head, and find your nightmares, and then they change to look like whichever is the worst thing there."

"I'm not sure that's true," Carter said. "Yeah, most of them are terrifying. But some of them are just... I mean, they're ridiculous to look at. Ugly, but not horrible. And most of them are not picky about who they attack. They just—"

Bridget swung her savage gaze on him, and he dropped the sentence midway. "They're picky about who they eat," she said. "They'll lash out at anyone, but every one of them is searching for someone. If they're not terrifying to you, that's because you're not their target. They pick their targets. You know that, right? And they can read your mind, I swear to God. If they want you, they reach inside you and grab hold of your fears, and that's what they wear when they come for you. They're chameleons. Predatory chameleon telepaths."

That must be a consolation, I said.

"What?" Everyone there stared at me, except for Chetna. She was looking at her hands, waving her fingers slowly as if to check that she could still control them.

I mean, I said, it's always comforting to have your calamities be someone else's fault.

"What the fuck are you talking about?" the scarred man demanded.

I suppose I'm talking about motiveless malignity. The

predatory chameleon telepaths don't derive any extra nourishment from a meal that's frightened of them. So in that story Bridget just told, their motivation is purely vindictive.

Carter threw down the can he'd been eating from, close enough to me that the tomato sauce spattered my trouser leg as it splashed out. "Well who is eating who?" he asked.

Eating whom.

"Fuck you! You and your crappy suit and your fucking... why don't you take that thing off, anyway?"

The apron? It does no harm.

I met his gaze a while longer, trying to divine what lay behind his anger. I saw nothing, though, or at least nothing specific: only a disconnected, general rage, most likely fuelled by despair.

I turned back to Bridget at last. So, are there more rules? I asked her.

She was still looking at me in perplexity and disapproval. "Yeah. Lots more. But that's the most important thing, right there. If you recognise any of the monsters, you should stay away from them. They're the ones that are most likely to be after you."

Thank you for the advice, I said. But none of that proves—

A hissing sound from the darkness near the door obliged me to break off. We all looked in that direction.

A woman's face hung in the air. There was no body to be seen beneath it. Not at first, anyway. Her skin was deathly pale. White-blonde hair hung straight down, and bright red lips stretched in a wide, welcoming smile.

"Peter," she said. "We've found you. Again."

"You shouldn't have run," said another voice. "When we'd only just begun to eat you." A second face joined the first, at the same height. Then a third emerged from the shadows much closer to the ground. "Get over here, silly billy," it said. "You can't get away now. And we'll hurt you worse if you try."

The three faces were all the same. It was not just that they were similar. Every strand of hair as the wind ruffled it, every expression, every trick of light and shadow was identical. They could have been images made with a stamp of some kind, except that they were moving.

The scarred man climbed to his feet. He took the machete from his belt and raised it in his hand. Carter and Bridget stood, too. Carter drew his automatic, and Bridget her steak tenderiser. For a moment, they made a perfect heroic tableau.

The lamia struck. Its three heads reared up, and darted forward. The three mouths gaped wide, unsheathing slender white fangs. One bit the scarred man's face, on the side that was already scarred. The second sank its teeth into his shoulder, the third into his thigh. Behind each head, a muscular neck many yards long undulated like the body of a snake.

The lamia withdrew with its prize, too quickly for anyone to intervene. Too quickly, almost, for us even to see what happened. The scarred man was there, and then he was gone. A hoarse wail persisted for a second or so, along with the rustling, boots-trampling-through-autumn-leaves sound of the lamia's retreat.

And then we were five.

I realised, with sour amusement, that Carter had shielded the boy's eyes from what had happened. He had been much too slow, though. He was only preventing the boy from seeing the empty space on which that swift predation had inscribed itself.

We should move on, I said. Unless you mean to barricade the door and wait out the night here.

"But…" Bridget said. "He might still be alive. Shouldn't we…?"

"He's not alive," the boy said, with finality.

We packed our things, and a few more cans of food, and moved on. The culvert had been abandoned, now, as a possible destination. It was back the way we'd come, and it didn't seem like a good idea to anyone to try to retrace our steps. We went further into the town instead, the road sloping down more and more steeply as we went, out of the stark white moonlight into a sea of absolute black.

Carter said he had seen a boat, at the marina, that was still intact. He suggested we hide in it tonight and try to sail it out to sea in the morning, across a harbour that was a maze of vessels already sunk. The others agreed to this idiocy, having little else left in which to invest their dwindling hopes.

"I stayed at this hotel once," Bridget said.

"The Phoenix Royale," the boy read, from the sign in the driveway. "Was it nice?"

"The stars aren't coming out," Chetna said, to nobody. "That's a very bad sign."

"It was lovely," Bridget said. She hesitated, scanning the

building's frontage. She was about to suggest that we stay there, in one of the derelict building's many, many rooms. To argue that a desert is a good place to hide a grain of sand, or something of that sort.

But loud, earth-shaking crashes from just inside the hotel's doors dissuaded her. Or perhaps it was the elongated, elbowed limb that was thrust, briefly, through a first-floor window. The Phoenix Royale was incubating something that would have a catastrophic birth. We moved on quickly into Queen's Park, which seemed quiet and safe.

It was not. As we scurried along the path, a shapeless mass rose from behind one of the benches on our left-hand side. It was too dark, now, for any of us to be certain what it was.

Chetna seemed to recognise it anyway. She took a step towards it. She moved slowly, but the rest of us were backing away with haste. Between two breaths, she went from being one of a group to standing alone.

"I remember now," she said. Her voice was a whisper, and it's possible that I, being closest, was the only one to hear it. "I'm so sorry." Her shoulders sagged. She closed her eyes.

I had entertained a hope… but no. The huge maw that closed on the woman's head had not a single tooth, let alone any tusks. The shapeless thing raised her up into the air, and shook her. We all heard the muffled *crack* as her neck was broken.

The thing hauled her over the bench, her feet clattering on the wooden slats, and dumped her down on the grass. Then it dragged her away across the park, its mouth still clamped tight on her neck. Its progress was not rapid. We watched it go for a considerable time. Carter drew his gun and raised it, sighting along the barrel with his head tilted to one side.

"Go ahead," Bridget said. "What are you waiting for?"

But he didn't take the shot. And she made no protest as he put the gun away. Chetna was clearly dead, and it served no useful purpose to remind the giant slug of our presence.

We had intended to detour onto the new, elevated road, and follow it all the way to the marina, but that wasn't possible. We couldn't even get out of the park on that side. There were dogs with the heads of men there, a very large number of them. Two of them were fighting, with incredible ferocity, in the centre of a ring made by the others. They seemed intent on their sport, but we didn't think we could get by unnoticed.

Bridget went ahead to scout the south gate, while the rest of us stayed behind on the steps of the Francis May drinking fountain, which offered us some cover.

"I don't think they're alive," the boy said.

I stared at him, perplexed and perhaps a little angered. What?

"I think they're bio-weapons. That's why they're all different shapes. They're supposed to adapt to the terrain. Hunter-killer drones, with camouflage powers. The real aliens will come later."

I was blunt. Yes, this was only a child speaking, but stupidity has to be challenged and corrected. It's hard to imagine, I said, anything less effectively camouflaged than the things we've seen tonight.

"Maybe their chameleon circuits don't work properly. Like with the TARDIS."

"The TARDIS?" Carter said. "What's the TARDIS?"

They're not hiding, I pointed out. You're the ones who are hiding. They're not even trying to hide.

Bridget came back at this point, and told us that the way to the south gate was clear. We abandoned the ludicrous conversation and quickly made our way in that direction. The dogs were screaming loudly now, either in despair or in elation, so there was no need to be quiet. We just ran, my tool bag and the cans in the others' packs clanking and clattering as we went.

The way was clear, as Bridget had promised, but the gate was padlocked.

Carter rattled the bars. "What the fuck?" he demanded, with weary indignation.

"I didn't check," Bridget said. "Shit! Can you saw through it?"

This was addressed to me. I shook my head emphatically. My saw is for wood, I said. It would be useless on this. We'll have to climb.

We boosted the boy over first. He dropped down lightly on the other side of the gate, straightened.

"Are you all right?" Carter asked him.

"I'm fine," he said.

"Oh, sweetness," someone else said, from out of the darkness. "Oh, my little sweetie pie!"

The boy went rigid, just at the sound of that voice. He didn't turn to face the thing that was coming at him. He ran for the fence, instead, and tried to climb back over. Bridget and Carter took his hands and guided them, lifted him up, but his own movements were jerky and uncoordinated. His hands pawed clumsily at the wrought-iron bars.

An old, old woman, down on all fours, came scampering out of the darkness with inhuman speed. She was naked except for the remains of a filmy yellow nightdress, so torn and tattered it was barely there at all. She scaled the boy's body and clamped herself onto his back, her clawed hands burying themselves deep in his flesh.

"Little darling," she cooed. Her head dipped towards the boy's neck. The back of her scalp was shaved, exposing fresh, puckered scars as though from very recent surgery.

"No!" Bridget yelled. "Get the fuck away from him!" She snatched up her steak tenderiser and struck through the bars, again and again. She was hitting out wildly, but some of her blows connected. They bit deep into the old woman's doughy flesh, leaving indentations that retained their shape. Carter was also attacking her, with the butt of his gun, craning up over the fence so he could bring it down on the top of her skull.

The old woman ignored these indignities, and ate her fill.

"Grandma!" the boy remonstrated, in a strangled, faltering voice.

"Angel!" the old lady cooed, still chewing. "Poppet!" Blood ran freely down her chin.

The boy slumped against the gate, and slid slowly down. After he was dead, the old woman remained seated on his shoulders, looking down at the remains disconsolately. She was out of Bridget's reach, now, but Carter levelled his pistol and took aim.

I seized hold of his wrist, and pulled his arm down.

"The fuck?" he expostulated. "Let go of me!"

No. Wait. Watch.

The old woman's skin began to boil away. There was no flesh beneath, no sinew or bone, only a white substrate that seemed to dissolve on contact with air. She sublimed away into smoke, smiling as she went.

"Why did you stop me?" Carter demanded.

I shrugged. Why hurt her? She was done. When they're done, they leave. You must have seen that before.

"I have," Bridget said. "I'd still have killed it, though. Filthy fucking thing! That poor kid…"

"You go your own way now," Carter said, his face up close to mine. "You're not going any further with us."

There was no fear in him, and no recognition. It was puzzling, and exasperating. It had to be him, surely. I felt no connection to Bridget at all. But then, how could he be so close to me for so long and not know me?

I know a place, I said. Very close to here. Very safe.

"We're heading for the marina. And by we, I mean me and her. Not you."

I turned to Bridget, reading hesitation in her face. "The marina's miles away," she said. "Where's this place of yours?"

Closer. Near the pier.

"He's not coming with us," Carter said. "I don't trust him."

Perhaps she doesn't trust you.

"We've stayed together this far," Bridget pleaded.

It will only take us a few minutes to walk there.

Carter looked from her, to me, to her, down at the ground and back at last to me. “Sod it,” he said, without any heat. “All right. But you walk ahead, and I’m keeping the gun on you.”

That’s acceptable.

“How do we climb over the gate, though?” Bridget asked.

With some difficulty, as it turned out. Bridget went over first. Then Carter made me withdraw about ten yards and gave her the gun to hold. She kept it pointed at me while he scrambled over. As soon as he was on the ground again, he took it back.

“Now you, wood-saw,” he said. “Slowly.”

I climbed over and rejoined them. It’s this way, I said. I set off at a fast walk. I was lying about having a safe place to take them to, but it was obvious where we had to go.

Downwards, following the steep slope of the road. Downwards towards the pier, whose garish lights were not showing, and—much, much more importantly—towards the sea.

Bridget made it almost all the way. As we crossed Marine Parade, deserted now apart from a few strewn bodies, a chance gust of wind brought us the sound of chanting voices.

Bridget froze where she was, then looked around. “What was that?” she asked, but I think she knew. The dull flatness of her voice indicated that despair, or perhaps resignation, had already taken hold of her.

“Nose disease disaster, stick your nose in plaster!” They

were girls' voices, shrill falsettos, raised in ritualistic unison. "Prick it with a safety pin, and throw it in a rubbish bin!"

Bridget growled. It was a deep, animal sound, dragged out of her against her will. There was no threat in it, only raw terror.

Three girls came skipping along the road towards us, congealing out of the deep dark. They wore the school uniform of another era, blue skirts and cardigans and shiny, buckled shoes. They stopped, all at once, and stared at Bridget. They lifted up their hands and pointed.

"Nosy," one of them said. "Nosy parker."

"We'll teach you," the second added.

"Teach you to poke your nose in." This was the first girl again, not the third. The third said nothing, but only opened and closed her hands in front of her face, with the fingers interlaced. She was miming something, but it wasn't immediately clear what that something might be.

Bridget broke and ran. The girls pursued. A moment later, Carter ran after them. All five were swallowed by the deep shadows before they had gone twenty yards. I followed at my leisure. They were all running towards the moonlit beach, which was where I wanted to be. I was content to let them get there first, having no fear now that I would lose them.

Lose *him*, I mean.

Brighton has a shingle beach. I would have preferred sand, for the look of the thing, but the ocean mattered more. Its sibilant surge and retreat filled the air around me like a hymn sung in a thousand voices.

I found Carter at the edge of the sea. He had drawn

the gun again, but his hands were at his sides. He looked bewildered, and exhausted.

"I'm sure they went this way," he said. "But there's no sign of them."

It doesn't matter, I said. Just the two of us now.

I was closer than he had expected. At the sound of my voice, almost upon him, he started as though he had been stung. He turned quickly, backing away, and pointed the gun at my face.

I laughed. I've yet to see you fire that thing, I said.

"Try me," he suggested.

He still was not afraid. Not afraid enough, I mean. Obviously his own imminent death caused him alarm and despondency, but his fear was not focused on me with the intensity that I needed to see, in order to be sure.

"You're one of them, aren't you?" he said. "One of the monsters."

No, I said. You are.

"I'm human, you bastard!"

That's what I said.

Ignoring the gun, which held no fear for me, I knelt and rummaged in my bag.

"Keep your fucking hands off those things!" Carter shouted.

I'm not looking for a weapon, I told him. Not yet, at least.

"I'm warning you."

Yes, I know, I said. I continued to explain, because I needed him to stay still for a little while, until I found what I was looking for. Bridget was right about many things, I told him, but wrong about the most important. My people don't eat yours for sustenance, or sport, or out of any malice.

"You bastard!" Carter said. "You turn around, right now, and walk away." The gun shook in his hand. He still didn't make any attempt to fire it. I was unsurprised. I'd concluded long ago that he had no bullets. The gun was a prop to his sagging sense of self, a comfort blanket he clung to as his options were reduced, one by one, down to this beach. Down to me.

I'm sure you're familiar, I said, with the origin of the handshake. It's meant to show that your hand—your right hand, which is presumed to be the strongest—is empty of weapons. It proves you mean no harm.

In my world, when we meet a stranger, we shake hands with our minds. We open ourselves fully to the other, flow together, two things briefly becoming one thing. Then we flow back to ourselves again, knowing the other as deeply and perfectly as we know ourselves.

"Last chance," Carter said. He took off the gun's safety with his thumb, revealing that—bullets or not—it had never been in any state to do harm to anything we'd met on our journey together.

When we came here, I said, we tried to say hello to you humans in this way. It was... terrible. You're so afraid, you see, of so very many things. Fears are the core of you. Some of them you know about, others you profoundly misunderstand. You're even afraid of the parts of yourselves that are afraid.

Imagine you're staring into the dark. Something might

be moving there, but you're not sure. Mostly, what you see is just darkness, without features, without shape. But then, for just a second, you catch a glimpse of a bone-white face with elongated canine teeth. Or a woman with snakes for hair. A tiger. A cobra. A fiery angel with the wings of a bat. The impression doesn't last long—only a second, or a fraction of a second—but the emotions that go with it are so much stronger.

It's a little like firing a pot. The clay is soft and malleable until it goes into the oven. But afterwards… well. The situation is no longer what it was, you see?

I had found what I was looking for. I straightened up, holding it in both my hands.

You destroyed us, I said. When we said hello to you, you seized hold of us. You swallowed up the parts of us that flowed into you, and what you spat back into us twisted us into a million grotesque shapes. The shapes of your fears; your endless, tedious nightmares. The only way we can get free, now, is to kill you and devour you—taking back the parts of us you stole and closing down the hideous, insistent power of your minds. Then we become ourselves again, invisible and immortal. One by one, we disentangle ourselves and go home. But the cost of our freedom is your deaths.

Carter fired. The reverberation was loud, bringing many of my people out of the dark to watch. The bullet missed me and spent its force on the bodiless air.

You are mine, I said. You made me be this way. But now you don't remember me, and I need you to. I can't break the bond, if you won't acknowledge it.

He fired again. The pain in my side took me by surprise, forcing breath out of me in a loud gasp. But it was only physical pain, and I am not, in any sense that matters, a physical thing.

Here, I said. When I first arrived, I was wearing this.

I put the hat on my head. It was a fragile, intricate thing, made out of a single folded sheet of paper. Its shape was roughly square.

"Oh God!" Carter sobbed. "Oh Jesus!"

Ah! I sighed. At last! That's much better.

Am I late? asked my friend, my beloved. She sidled out of the ocean and dragged her heavy bulk across the shingle, her tusks gleaming white in the moonlight. Their elegant curves were like the brackets around some impossible, ineffable equation.

Carter emptied the pistol in her direction. Some of the bullets no doubt found their mark, but she was colossal, and under her gleaming hide was a layer of fat many inches thick. He caused her but little discomfort.

He would have run, then, but others of my kind were crowded densely around us. This was our feast, not theirs, but they wished us well and they would not let him pass.

It was the poem, then, that had frightened him. As a child, most likely, sitting on his mother's knee, or his father's. That was why he hadn't recognised me, though some familiarity had nagged at him. It was not so much the characters in the poem that mattered, as the atmosphere. The deception, and the devouring.

I had deceived him, and now we devoured him. We had no choice.

The night is fine, my lover said. Do you admire the view?

The butter's spread too thick, I said. And a little later: cut me another slice.

And finally: shall we be trotting home again?

The White Queen's Pawn

GENEVIEVE COGMAN

"Mrs Hargreaves."

"I prefer to be addressed as Lady Hargreaves." The woman sitting on the far side of the desk had her withered hands folded over her handbag. There weren't any guns in it, of course—it had been searched, just as the woman herself had been—but the sheer immobility of her posture somehow unnerved Lucy Hansen. Any normal woman would have been worried by her current situation. Even the woman that they thought she was should have been cautious, prepared, ready for action.

She should be showing *something.*

The afternoon winter sunlight slanted through the window of the anonymous room and lit up its only distinguishing feature—the portrait of the Leader which hung over the empty fireplace. Off-white walls competed with the beige rug for blandness, and both sides lost. Even the furniture—a desk, two chairs—was second-hand. This quiet little house was hidden away in a secluded London suburb so unimportant that even the taxi drivers had to think before they remembered where it was. It had been rented by another Party member specially for this meeting, via a third member's bank account. If anything *did* go wrong, then the police would have no trail to follow.

"Yes, we know that," Mr Walters said. He smiled, pulling back thin lips in a gesture that simulated friendship. "And I think, just between the two of us, that we can agree you deserve that title, madam. Even if the world doesn't acknowledge it. The world's blind to a lot of things."

Mrs Hargreaves—or Lady Hargreaves—inclined her head in a gracious nod. "Thank you. You're a very talkative young man. Perhaps you'll tell me why you've had me brought here?"

"My dear madam! I certainly hope that you didn't feel in any way pressured. Miss Hansen, the lady behind you, was instructed to deliver an invitation. I hope that she didn't confuse her orders."

"I think that Miss Hansen did precisely what she was ordered to do." Lady Hargreaves turned in her chair to look across at Lucy where she stood by the door. She moved with the slow carefulness of an arthritic woman, turning her whole body rather than just her head, a small figure in the large leather armchair. "Didn't you, child? You told me that you represented a private collector who was interested in purchasing some of my literary collection. Your story was very well rehearsed, even if it was obviously false."

Mr Walters raised his eyebrows. "Obviously false?"

"Do you think I don't know the current market, young man? It may be seven years since I sold my copy of *Alice's Adventures Under Ground*, but I've kept up to date with Sotheby's and the other major auction houses. I could have reported her to the police on the spot, but I have always been far too curious. I wanted to see who was behind her."

Lucy kept her face still with an effort, and stared at the window behind Mr Walters rather than meeting his eyes. She knew that she'd be paying for this failure later. Bringing in the old woman for this interview had seemed an easy way to rise in the Party's ranks. Failing at the first step by being recognised as a fraud… now, that was an easy way to fall. Even in the cold room, a trickle of sweat marked its way down her spine.

"And I see that we weren't misinformed." Mr Walters tapped the brown file in front of him on the desk. "So if we're not book-buyers, Lady Hargreaves, who do you think we are?"

Lady Hargreaves flicked a bony finger at the portrait of the Leader. "I recognise Oswald Mosley's face even if I haven't met him in person. What is it that you people call yourselves? The New Party? The British Union of Fascists? The Blackshirts?" Her tone was cut glass, and as she ran through the list of the Party's names, the lines of her face grew more and more disapproving. It was almost, Lucy thought in a flight of fancy, as though the woman was growing younger, as the classic lines of her skull, rigid cheekbones and chin, showed through her elderly softness.

"I have the impression that you don't approve of us," Mr Walters said.

"You are quite correct. I have yet to see anything from your set of which I approve."

"Lady Hargreaves." Mr Walters leaned forward, folding his hands on top of the file. "While I don't like to mention a lady's age, you're eighty-one years old. You've had the chance to see a great deal of the world. You've watched the decline of the British Empire, the pollution of our country..."

"And I've met a great many young men like you. Get to the point."

Mr Walters pursed his lips, unaccustomed to such rudeness. "The point, madam, is that I would like to add your efforts to our cause."

"Out of the question. If that was all you had me brought here for, then I'm afraid you have wasted your time."

"Hardly." He flipped the file open. "I think that you have a great deal to offer the Party."

The old woman's laugh was thin and creaking, the product of ageing lungs and shortened breath. "As you pointed out just now, I'm eighty-one. My time has passed. My finances are devoted to my home and family. I have nothing to offer you except an endorsement—and that isn't going to happen."

"But that wasn't always the case, was it?" Mr Walters' smile was far less pleasant now than it had been earlier. "You were quite an active woman in your youth."

Her voice was colder than a Yorkshire winter morning. "I *beg* your pardon?"

"I'm referring to the White Queen's Pawn." He sat back

in his chair, smile curling to a sneer.

Lucy had been warned to watch Lady Hargreaves carefully at those words; but the older woman gave nothing away. She merely looked vaguely puzzled. She might have been reacting to a *faux pas* by some younger relative, or a bit of ignorant mischief by one of the lower classes. "I don't understand."

"Vienna. Madrid. Rome." Mr Walters gestured to the file. "A number of jobs in the eighteen-nineties. And after the turn of the century, well! Some of your work was so top secret that we couldn't find out any more than the names of the operations. You've served your country well, madam. But that service doesn't have to stop. You're needed more than ever."

"Someone has been talking far too much." The old woman's hands tightened on her handbag, the lines of tendons and bones visible through her sagging skin. "I won't waste time with pretence. You know things that you shouldn't, young man. And you've dragged this girl into it now too. Shame on you!"

"Miss Hansen knows precisely what she's doing," Mr Walters said. "We believe in the emancipation of women. They have a right to serve their country just as we men do. Just as *you* did, Lady Hargreaves."

"And what precisely is it you think I did?" Her words flashed out like a naked knife.

"You killed people." Mr Walters looked her squarely in the face. "You killed quite a lot of people, Lady Hargreaves. And we know how you did it."

Lady Hargreaves sighed. She sounded genuinely weary. "There are a great many ways of killing a person, young man, but none of them alter the fact that dead is dead. If you served in the Great War—as I hope you did—then you would be aware of that."

Mr Walters stiffened in his chair, but Lucy was the one who spoke, bursting in to defend him. "Of course he served! How dare you suggest that he didn't?" He didn't *deserve* that sort of insult. She knew about his war record, just as everyone else in the Party did. She only wished that she'd been old enough and able to serve too: as a nurse, as a farm worker, in any way that she could have done.

"That's enough, Miss Hansen," Mr Walters said, but he gave her an approving nod. "I can answer Lady Hargreaves here. Of course I served. Almost everyone in the Party served—or was too young to fight at the time. Patriotism isn't something that we lack."

"Maybe not." The words were polite enough, but there was no sincerity behind them. Lucy didn't believe for a moment that the old woman had given up. "So what is it that you want from me?"

"Let's go back a step," Mr Walters suggested. "You killed a number of people, Lady Hargreaves. Grown men, some of them with military training. The question one might ask is how a pleasant lady like yourself could do such a thing?"

"And the logical answer would be that I couldn't," Lady Hargreaves snapped.

"We both know better." He flipped pages in the file. "Let's be grateful for the bureaucratic record-keeping instincts of

Great Britain's civil servants, Lady Hargreaves. Even among spies. They began to train you when you were a child. I wonder why you in particular were chosen? We haven't been able to find information about any other girls. Are their records better hidden? Or did they simply not survive?"

The old woman's hands tightened on her handbag again. She seemed to be curling in on herself, settling into position like a statue or a chess piece. Lucy was surprised at her mental image, but then recollected Mr Walters' earlier reference—*the White Queen's Pawn*. That must be why it had come to mind.

Mr Walters waited a moment, giving Lady Hargreaves the chance to reply. "No comment to make? Then I'll continue. Your record says that you were trained to be able to induce what the doctors refer to as hysterical strength." He turned to Lucy. "That, Miss Hansen, is the sort of thing that lets a mother lift a car off her baby *in extremis*, or allows a man to hold up a collapsing building long enough for his friends to escape. It's the sort of strength that would allow a young woman—or even a middle-aged one—to slaughter trained soldiers and walk away unscathed. And according to Lady Hargreaves' records here, this was combined with an altered state of mind that allowed her to view the most appalling scenes of bloodshed and see it as no more than a children's story. Soldiers came back from the Great War unable to bear what they'd witnessed. But Lady Hargreaves here hasn't suffered a single night's broken sleep. Or so she tells her doctors, at least. The perfect assassin."

"And is that what you want from me?" Lady Hargreaves

demanded. "Am I to skip across the diplomatic fields of Europe and cry 'Off with his head' on your orders?" She laughed, and then coughed, and couldn't stop coughing for a minute.

"Of course not," Mr Walters said. "As you yourself know, the spirit may be willing but the flesh is weak. No, Lady Hargreaves, what we want from you is *training*."

"Training?" Lady Hargreaves said slowly. "Who am I to train? And why?"

"Young women who are devoted to the Party. Young women like Miss Hansen."

Lucy's heart leaped: her knees wobbled, and she briefly thought that she might collapse from sheer joy. This, *this* was what they wanted from her! A chance to help rebuild Great Britain, to sweep away the deadwood and remove the communists, the traitors, the enemy... She stiffened her knees and squared her shoulders. She didn't want to look weak.

The light caught the glass that covered the portrait of the Leader, and for a moment she caught her reflection in it. The mirror image seemed to smile at her approvingly.

Mr Walters leaned forward. "You know who trained you, madam. You know how you were trained. England needs that training. England's daughters must be taught to fight, just as you have done. I appeal to your patriotism, Lady Hargreaves. Can you really say no?"

"Two questions," Lady Hargreaves whispered. Her voice was harsher now, torn by her coughing, and each word came in a painful whisper. It seemed to echo in the room. "The first question. Who wrote that in my record?"

"Charles Dodgson," Mr Walters answered. "Or should I say, Lewis Carroll? Another patriot who was hidden by trivialities, just like you. His work as a codebreaker went undocumented by the public. They only remember him for his stories now. Just as they only remember you as the object of those stories. It seems grossly unfair to you both." He smiled triumphantly. "Your second question?"

"Is to Miss Hansen." Lady Hargreaves turned in her seat again. "Young woman, are you listening to me?"

"Of course, Lady Hargreaves," Lucy replied.

"Good. Pay attention." The elderly softness had gone from Lady Hargreaves; there was no gentleness left, only taut skin and rigid bone, and a curious distance in her eyes, as though she were considering chess pieces. "There is no way you can possibly understand the full scope of what you're asking. But I suppose you'd tell me that you're old enough to know your own mind by now. That's what a great many young men said, twenty years ago. So answer me for yourself, young woman, and not for your commander or your Leader or whatever. Is this truly what you want?"

Lucy didn't dare glance over at Mr Walters, in case it seemed that she was looking to him for guidance. But she already knew what he would want and what she would answer. This was all new to her, all unexpected, but she wasn't going to risk a refusal by seeming less than certain. "Madam, it's everything that I want. Please say yes."

"The power to kill people?" Lady Hargreaves demanded.

"The power to make a difference," Lucy answered. "Anyone can kill people. I've learned how to use a gun, madam. I can pull a trigger. But this is something different. This would be helping England—helping Great Britain, helping the *world*. Wasn't it the same for you, madam? Didn't you want to do the right thing?"

"I just wanted to go home," Lady Hargreaves said, very softly.

"But it won't be like that for me, madam!" Lucy pleaded. "I'm older than you were, I understand how *important* this is. I read the news. I've been told the truth about what's going on in the world around us. Someone has to act. Why can't that someone be me?"

"You can see that she's sincere," Mr Walters broke in. "What more do you need, Lady Hargreaves?"

"Nothing." The old woman sighed. "Nothing at all. Thank you both for making my duty clear to me."

It should have been surrender—but it wasn't. Mr Walters and Lucy shared a glance of warning. "Now, Lady Hargreaves, I hope you're not thinking of anything foolish—" he started.

She held up a wrinkled hand, age-spotted and shaking. "What do you think I'm going to do, young man? Leap out of my seat and rip you apart? I'm over eighty years old. The flesh is very weak. No, I'm going to give in to this young lady's demands. She wants to be the new White Queen's Pawn? My dear, the title is yours."

And the light in the room rippled and changed. The glass that covered the portrait of the Leader silvered as though fog was covering it from the other side, becoming as reflective as a mirror.

"Seventy years ago I made a bargain," Lady Hargreaves

said dreamily. "And like any child entering a new world, I didn't realise what I'd done at the time. I only found out later. Dear Charles did his best to cover it all up. He turned what I'd told him into a story, and then told it back to me again until I almost believed it. He lied for me so much that I was employed as a spy and they believed that nonsense about hysterical strength. Those cold men in government were glad to take advantage of me. Just as you said, young man, kings and queens always need assassins."

"Dodgson lied?" Mr Walters asked warily. His eyes moved to the dossier on his desk, as if he was wondering just how much of it was true.

"He was a storyteller. He blamed himself and did his best to protect me. But it wasn't his fault that I had a debt to pay. Once you make a promise over there, you're bound by it for life."

"Over there?" Mr Walters echoed. His hand slipped into a desk drawer and brought out a gun—an anonymous little pistol, the sort that Lucy herself had trained with. "Lady Hargreaves, if this is some sort of attempt to frighten us—"

"Come now," the old woman chided him. "Why so scared, young man? I'm just a frail old lady who can be decoyed off to a quiet back street in London and murdered if anything goes wrong. What is there about me that could possibly frighten you?"

"We know you're not an ordinary woman," Mr Walters snapped. "You're the White Queen's Pawn!"

"I was." She spread her hands in mock benediction. "But now someone else is taking my place."

"Lady Hargreaves," Lucy said, trying not to let her voice shake, "what's going on?"

"The right questions, my dear, but too late." She turned to smile at the glazed portrait. "I always needed a mirror to bring them through. If they couldn't have me yet, then they'd take someone else, and that kept them happy for a while. It put off the final reckoning. Of course, there was some unpleasantness, some violence. They don't see things the way we do. I found that easier to understand as a child. These days... well, one grows old, young man. One wonders if one did the right thing."

"They?" Mr Walters demanded. "In heaven's name, who are *they*?"

"But I did so want to go home..." Lady Hargreaves whispered.

The air shivered with footsteps, soft, invisible, like the footfalls of a huge cat. Lucy looked around frantically; there was nobody else in the room but them. She had no gun of her own. Incoherent panic yammered in her brain, breaking down the pride which had made her so certain she could stand and fight. She thought of running to the door, but instead found herself looking at the portrait. The painting of the Leader was completely hidden now, and the glass showed a clear reflection of the room—all three of them, but also something else.

"Dear merciful God," she murmured, the words coming unbidden and unwanted. The huge feline which leaned on the corner of the desk in the reflection leered at her, huge mouth opening in a toothed smile that never seemed to end. It raised itself to loom over Mr Walters, far larger than any normal cat, as outsize as a tiger beside a human child.

Mr Walters followed Lucy's gaze. His mouth tightened. He waved a hand behind himself, but it passed through empty air. "Pull yourself together, Miss Hansen! We will not be frightened by these party tricks, these hypnotic illusions!"

"Off with his head," Lady Hargreaves murmured.

In the mirror, the great cat opened its mouth even wider and took Mr Walters' head between its jaws. It was like a lion-tamer at the circus, Lucy thought hysterically, and surely any moment now it would simply sit back again and roar at the ceiling...

In the mirror, the cat closed its jaws.

Mr Walters fell to the ground in two pieces. Both head and body dropped behind the desk, so Lucy couldn't see them, but blood gushed out, all over the dull beige rug and the wood and all the way to the walls. She fell to her knees, her hands going to her mouth as she tried not to be sick. This wasn't happening, this couldn't be happening, she was a good girl, she was strong, she was a loyal member of the Party and this was some sort of hypnotic trick and any minute now the hypnotist would snap his fingers and she'd wake up.

But the room was silent, and nobody was snapping their fingers.

"Look in the mirror, young woman," Lady Hargreaves said. While her voice was gentle, there was no sympathy in it, no pity, no human reaction to having seen a man decapitated in front of her. It was like someone telling a story, a very long way away.

Lucy looked up. The cat was still there, sitting on the desk, but as she watched it began to fade from the outside in, till there was nothing but those bloodstained teeth hanging in the air. A moment's held breath, and they were gone as well. Briefly, she dared to hope.

And then in the mirror she saw the figure standing behind her. It was a woman all in white, her skin as pale as her gown, her face all sharp angles, brow and nose and thrusting chin. She wore a crested helmet rather than a crown, and her draperies hung on her like a shroud. Her long nails glittered like diamonds, and her eyes were like holes into molten steel.

"Your new Pawn, Your Majesty." Lady Hargreaves levered herself up from her chair, movements slow and aching. "By her own wish and her own consent. Maybe she'll wish to make her own bargain with you, or maybe you'll keep her for good, but that's not my business."

The woman in white leaned forward abruptly, like a vulture seizing a corpse, her fingers biting into Lucy's shoulders.

And Lucy felt it.

She turned. There should have been nothing there. But the woman was there, she was real, and her hands were still locked in Lucy's flesh like claws. And behind her there were other figures, stretching into the shadows in an expanding wave—a woman in red, a knight, two conjoined men, a long writhing thing, flowers that spoke, things that were wrong in too many ways to be sure, except that Lucy couldn't bring herself to even look at them long enough to be certain…

"And that concludes our contract. I'm free of you." Lady Hargreaves looked around the room. "Dear me, I hope it's not too difficult to get a taxi home. I don't want to have to walk from here. Wherever here is."

Lucy wrenched herself free, blood running down her coat where the creature behind had clutched at her, and staggered forward to grasp at Lady Hargreaves, but her hands met cold glass. Her understanding made the jump before she could piece out the idea in conscious thought, and she clawed at the mirror surface in front of her, seeing the room on the other side, the dead body of Mr Walters, Lady Hargreaves with her hand on the door—everything that was actually *real*. She would not, could not bring herself to look behind her, to see what was waiting for her on this side of the mirror, the side of the unreal and impossible.

The image began to fade. With terror, Lucy realised that the mirror effect on the glass was vanishing, that in a moment it would be nothing more than the covering of the Leader's portrait, and that she would have no way out of wherever she was. "Let me go!" she screamed. "Lady Hargreaves, please, let me out, I'm sorry, I didn't know, I didn't want this!"

The door shut behind Lady Hargreaves with a *click*, and the last of the image dulled and vanished, leaving only bare wall behind it. Bare wall, in a plain house, on the other side of the mirror.

Lucy heard the footsteps approaching behind her, and for

as long as she could she stared at the wall as if she could force it to become the mirror again, unwilling—unable—to turn and look behind her.

But finally she had to turn, and see the Queen who waited for her service.

Dream Girl

CAVAN SCOTT

"Is the White Rabbit late?" the Queen of Hearts inquired.

"Oh yes, Your Majesty," the Hare replied, bowing so low that his long ears dragged across the freshly mown lawn. "I killed him myself."

"I hope the poor thing didn't suffer," the Queen of Spades said, her mount snorting as it pawed the turf.

The Hare smiled up at the most compassionate of the four matriarchs. "Don't fret, Your Maj. He died with a smile on those little coney lips."

The Queen of Clubs shifted in her saddle, her ghoulish interest piqued. "How did you do it?"

The Hare waved a dismissive hand in the air. "Oh, I pulled a funny face, that's all."

The Mad Hatter suppressed a shudder, the memory of the Rabbit's demise still in his mind. The Hare had indeed pulled a funny face; the Rabbit's face, pulled right off the bone when the now ex-bunny refused to talk, a detail the Hare was keeping close to his tabard-clad chest, the jerkin speckled by dried blood and clumps of pink matted fur.

"So, what did you learn?" the Queen of Diamonds asked, her steed gleaming like a precious stone.

"I'm sorry?" the Hare lisped, playing for time, one ear cocked in the direction of the regal playing cards.

"She said…" the Queen of Hearts bellowed, both of her faces scowling down at him, "what did the traitorous cottontail tell you before his untimely demise?"

The Hare shook his head. "It's no good, Your Highnesses. I can't hear a word you're saying, not with Tweedledum bawling like a lovesick banshee."

The Hatter sympathised. Dum-Dum, as his friends and many of his enemies called him, had been crying for days, ever since his twin brother had disappeared. It was a good job the rest of Wonderland didn't follow his example and weep for those they had lost. No one would be able to get anything done.

"Perhaps if you could come down from your High Horses?" the Hare suggested, a proposition that caused outrage among the ruling quartet.

"Come down?" the Queen of Clubs exclaimed from where she sat forty feet in the air, her horse's spindly legs making it look like a giraffe wearing stilts. "Come down?!"

"The cheek of the fellow," the Queen of Diamonds blustered.

"Off with his head," the Queen of Hearts added, which

was hardly a surprise as she had ordered at least twenty-seven beheadings since morning tea.

The Queen of Spades leaned over conspiratorially. "I think he needs his head, dear, if he is to find that wretched girl."

"I do, most definitely!" the Hare agreed, suddenly able to hear above Dum-Dum's boisterous lamentation. The threat of decapitation always focused the mind, even one as addled as the March Hare's. "It's only a matter of time before I complete my task."

"I should think so," the Queen of Clubs said, glancing over her paper-thin shoulder at the tower that dominated Wonderland. "It is almost a quarter past unease. Do I have to remind you what will happen if the Alarm Clock strikes disaster?"

This, the Mad Hatter mused, was part of the problem. No one actually knew what would happen when the Alarm Clock tolled. The tower had appeared the day the Cheshire Cat had vanished. This, in itself, wasn't unusual. The mischievous moggy was always popping off. But this time, the Cat didn't return, and neither did the Eternal Labyrinth, which had disappeared with him. Soon other Wonderlanders were vanishing, great chunks of the Dream Realm melting away like cucumber ice cream left out on a hot summer's day.

No one could even remember the Clock arriving. They were too busy debating what was happening to the rapidly diminishing kingdom. If you believed the rumours—and the Queens certainly did—the dissolution coincided with the arrival of the Dream Girl, a blonde-haired human who had been running amok from one end of the map to the other. The sovereigns had decided that she was responsible and had called for her head, appointing a pack of Jokers to bring her to justice. The blithesome bounty hunters set out, brave in tabards emblazoned with the sigils of all four houses—a heart, a club, a spade and a diamond. None returned. Only the March Hare was left, Wonderland's last line of defence.

Meanwhile, the Clock kept ticking, inexplicably synchronised with every timepiece in Wonderland, from the sundial that rose every morning to the White Rabbit's beloved pocket-watch, which now hung from the Hare's gore-smothered vest.

Tick-tock. Tick-tock. Tick-tock. Tick-tock.

High on her thoroughbred, the Queen of Hearts sulked, peeved that the Hare's head was still on his scrawny shoulders. "Can't we just lop off a bit of his head? Surely he won't miss his brain?"

The Queen of Spades sat back in her saddle, considering this. "A little off the top, you mean? Well, I suppose we could..."

Before the others could agree, the Hare booted the Hatter in the back, sending the smaller man stumbling towards the tetrarchy. The Hatter dropped to his knees in front of the Queens, his back aching and his pride bruised. It hadn't always been like this. The Hatter could remember when they did nothing but eat cakes and drink tea, back when they spent time with the Dormouse. Now the Dormouse was gone, the Queen had somehow split into four separate cards and the Hare wasn't so much mad as criminally insane. The Hatter missed the good old days.

"We have fresh information," the Hare insisted, his ears folded over his straw toupée to protect what little grey matter sloshed around in his skull. "Tell him, Hatta. Go on."

"Well?" the Queen of Diamonds said, peering down at the hatmaker.

The Hatter swallowed. "The Dream Girl has been spotted in the Concrete Jungle."

"The Concrete Jungle?" squawked the Queen of Hearts, the hands on the Alarm Clock shifting to half past consternation. "But the Concrete Jungle holds up the sky!"

"Only on Tuesdays," the Queen of Spades pointed out. "Today is Wednesday... at least, it was the last time I looked."

"Oh, I see," the Queen of Hearts said, her printed face still etched with concern. "But even so, the Jungle can't vanish. We've lost too much already."

"Indeed, we have," the Queen of Spades agreed. "The Dream Girl must be delivered to us to pay for her crimes. Why, only yesterday I heard that the Isle of Flight has fallen from the sky."

The Queen of Diamonds gasped. "Say it is not so!"

"If only I could. One minute the Isle was up where it belonged, and the next, it had dropped like a hippopotamouse who has forgotten how to float."

The Diamond Queen covered her mouth with dainty cardboard hands. "And the people? Our subjects?"

"Gone. Every last one of them."

"That settles it," the Queen of Hearts said, gripping her

reins in fury. "This ends today. It's bad enough that the White Rabbit was colluding with the enemy, but to know that she's still at large..." The Queen's voice trailed off in frustration. "Do we even know what she's doing in the Jungle?"

"Planning a teddy-bear's picnic, if our informant can be believed," the Hatter replied, wringing the brim of his topper.

The Queen's eyes narrowed. "Infiltrate this picnic. The Dream Girl must be brought to justice."

"You can rely on us," the March Hare promised as the Alarm Clock struck a quarter to trepidation.

"I don't like it here," the Hatter admitted as they snuck into the Concrete Jungle, tiptoeing between colourless trees that stretched up to a canopy of slab-like leaves. "It is a screepy place and no mistake."

The March Hare wasn't having any of it. "Don't be so lily-livered, Hatta, old pal, old chum. We're here on royal appointment."

"That won't stop us from being eaten," the Hatter pointed out. "The last thing I want is to find myself sliding down some lolloping monster's gullet, especially dressed like this."

All three of them—the Hatter, the March Hare and even Dum-Dum—were wearing bulky teddy-bear outfits that the Hare had procured from Madame Masquerade's Famed Dressing-up Emporium. At least, that's where he *said* he'd got them. The costumes smelled suspiciously meaty, the insides damp and sticky, with gleaming zippers freshly sewn into the tousled hides. Then there were the flies that buzzed incessantly around them, not the clothes-horse flies that used to flit around Wonderland on delicate fabric wings. These were bloated, with wiry hair and bulging eyes, their scissor-like teeth ready to rend and tear. The Hatter swatted a particularly relentless bug, trying to remember the last time he'd encountered such pernicious pests. The answer, of course, was never. What little was left of Wonderland was changing, rotting around them. Even their current surroundings seemed wrong. Since when did Wonderland have jungles made of concrete? What had happened to real trees, the ones made of candy and jam?

"Will you stop waving your arms around?" the Hare said, snapping the Hatter out of his fly-blighted reverie. "You'll draw attention to yourself."

"It's just so hot in here," the Hatter replied, spitting fur from his tongue. "And so hard to see."

"Just be glad you're not Tweedledum," came the less-than-helpful response. The Hare had a point. Poor Dum-Dum had been forced to squeeze into a bear-skin at least two times too small, a tight squeeze that was exacerbated by the fact that the apparently watertight suit was filling up with the ex-twin's tears. Hatter had suggested putting off their mission to give Dum-Dum opportunity to grieve, but the Hare had merely produced the White Rabbit's blood-smeared pocket-watch which now showed a time of ten past dread.

Tick-tock. Tick-tock. Tick-tock.

Time was running out, and as they trudged through the gloomy trees the Hatter couldn't ignore the voice at the back of his mind that kept repeating the same four words: *It's all your fault.*

That was crazy, of course. None of this was the Hatter's doing. That was the trouble with having so many voices in your head. Hardly any of them made sense.

The same could be said of the scene that greeted them as they drove deeper into the Jungle, stepping over grasping concrete roots and avoiding calcified creepers. The entire forest was carpeted in a thick dusting of snow, flakes streaming down from the branches high above. How could it be snowing within the Jungle? Little could get past the chunky canopy, the interlocking leaves forming an impenetrable umbrella above their heads.

The Hatter shrugged, ignoring the wet sensation of slimy bear-skin against his shoulders. "At least it might cool things down?"

"I'm not so sure," the Hare said, sticking out a tongue to catch a snowflake. It wasn't his own tongue, of course. That was impossible while wearing an oversized teddy-bear head. No, it had belonged to the White Rabbit. The Hare had decided to keep it as a lucky charm when sawing off the bunny's foot proved too much work.

"It's not snow," the Hare exclaimed, peering at the white flake at the end of the lagomorph's severed lolly-licker. "It's cement. The trees are crumbling."

"But what if they crumble away to nothing before next Tuesday?" the Hatter asked, wishing he could give the brim of his hat a good wring to ease his nerves.

"The sky will fall," the Hare replied, stuffing the Rabbit's tongue back in his pocket.

Tweedledum didn't comment. He was too busy gargling with his own tears.

This was worse than any of them had thought. Wonderland was disappearing faster than ever. Just that morning, the Sherbet Dunes of the Dessert Plains had blown away and, according to the Caterpillar, who had heard it from a bellied pig who in turn had heard it from a platypus-billed duck, the seasides of the south coast had collapsed, taking with them the sea-bottoms and most of the sea-tops.

It's not my fault, the Hatter told himself, as they pushed on through the freshly fallen dust. *Why would it be?*

And yet the Clock kept ticking.

Tick-tock. Tick-tock. Tick—

"What's that?" the Hare asked, stopping abruptly.

"It's the Alarm Clock," the Hatter replied.

"No, not the ticking. *Listen*."

The Hatter did as he was told, praying that he wouldn't hear the growl of the dreadfoul Grindlemeer. Of all the monsters still in Wonderland, the Grindlemeer was by far the worst—crueller than the Bandersnatch, sneakier than the Jubjub bird, and, if you could believe it, deadlier than the Jabberwocky itself.

Luckily, he couldn't hear a growl or the sound of gigantuous paws stalking towards them. No, it was the chink of china. The trio peered around a trunk to see the Dream Girl kneeling on a chequered blanket, laying out tea-things from a large wicker basket. She looked up and, catching sight of them behind the tree, beckoned them over with a beaming smile.

"It's about time. I've been waiting for so long."

The Hatter frowned as they approached the picnic blanket, which seemed miraculously free of crumbling concrete. Everyone said that the Dream Girl had fair skin, blue eyes and long blonde hair. And yes, at first sight, the human on the blanket matched the description perfectly. However, now they were closer, the Hatter could clearly see that her skin was dark, her eyes a rich chestnut brown and her hair a glorious swell of tight curls. Instead of the much-reported blue dress, complete with its starched white apron, the girl wore olive-green overalls with rubber-soled sneakers, a collection of strange tools tucked into the pocket on her narrow chest.

The girl placed a small plate in front of him. "I'm so glad you made it. I do so love a party. Any kind of party will do. A tea party. A birthday party. Even a political party."

"Don't forget an injured party," the Hare said, trying to peek in the girl's basket as they sat down.

"Oh, of course," the girl said. "An injured party is a wonderful thing, as long as you bring enough bandages." Her freckled face fell, as if remembering something. "The only party I don't enjoy is a slumber party. If you ask me, everyone around here has had enough of those to last a lifetime. Scrambled eggs?"

"I'm sorry?" the Hatter asked, finding it hard to keep up with the conversation. For some reason, the girl's prim and proper voice didn't match her appearance, as if it had no business spilling out of her mouth.

As he watched, she reached into her basket and drew out a silver platter piled high with steaming eggs.

"If that doesn't take your fancy," she continued, popping them next to his plate, "I can also offer you bacon, kippers, porridge or muffins. I did have toast and marmalade, but I'm afraid I got rather hungry while waiting. Is that awfully rude of me?"

"Not at all," the Hare said, his teddy-bear head wobbling alarmingly. "As long as you have tea..."

"Of course I have tea," the girl said, drawing a bone-china teapot from the hamper. "What is breakfast without tea?"

"Breakfast?" the Hatter asked. "Surely it's lunchtime."

"It is," the girl agreed, the teapot posed in her hands. "But Mama once told me that breakfast was the most important meal of the day, so I resolved to eat nothing but breakfast, morning, noon and night. Shall I pour?"

The Hatter was about to nod, when the Hare interjected. "What about milk? We must have milk with our tea."

The Dream Girl gasped, appalled at her *faux pas*. "Of course, we must have milk. How silly of me. Now, I know I have a jug in here somewhere." Putting down the teapot, she searched through the basket, and when she couldn't find what she was looking for, climbed into the thing so only her chunky sneakers were sticking out from the opening. "I was sure I packed it this morning."

The Hare winked—which was quite an achievement when wearing a stuffed head—and revealed that he had stolen the girl's milk jug and hidden it behind Tweedledum's ever-expanding bulk. Before the Dream Girl could emerge from her search, he threw a small glass vial to the Hatter who, thanks to the increasingly rancid mittens that were covering his hands, nearly dropped it.

"Squeeze a couple of drops of that into the teapot, and for goodness sake, don't take a sip after she's poured you a cup."

"What is it?" the Hatter asked, shaking the vial, the liquid inside slopping lazily around the glass.

"It's a sleeping potion, strong enough to send her to the land of nod. Once she's asleep we'll carry her back to the four Queens and claim our reward."

"There's a reward?"

"Yes," the Hare replied. "We get to keep our heads where they belong."

The Hatter's own head was aching. Lights were dancing in front of his eyes, and his throat felt parched. He could certainly have done with a cup of tea, doped or not.

"Hurry up!" the Hare whispered, but the girl emerged from the basket before the deed could be done.

"I do apologise," she said, looking a little embarrassed. "But the milk seems to have vanished."

"It's going around," the Hatter murmured.

"I did, however, find these," she said, ignoring his comment to produce a pair of juicy lemons.

"Perfect," the Hare said, snatching the citrus fruit from her grasp and jumping to his feet. "If we are to have a picnic, then we need entertainment."

He began to juggle the fruit, adding the eggs, bacon,

kippers, porridge and muffins as the girl applauded, delighted at the spectacle. Her face only fell when he added a bloody strip of muscle to the mix. The girl glanced at the basket, looking rather bemused.

"I don't remember packing tongue," she said, unaware that the Hatter had used the distraction to tip two drops of the sleeping draught into the teapot's bone-white spout. "Certainly not for breakfast."

"Then, maybe you should have a drop of that tea," the Hare said, slinging the plates over his shoulders. "To refresh your memory."

"A grand idea," the girl said, finally pouring the brew into the four cups. "This should wake us all up!"

The Hare picked up his cup, as did the Hatter. Tweedledum just kept wailing, his bear suit now swollen to twice its normal size thanks to all the tears. The Hatter watched expectantly as the girl raised her own cup to her lips. He felt slightly guilty, as the child seemed actually rather nice and not a little familiar, although for the life of him, he couldn't fathom why. He considered swiping the tainted tea from her hands but reminded himself that the fate of Wonderland hung in the balance.

She was just about to take a sip when the concrete trees echoed with the sound of a ferocious roar.

The Hatter's blood froze in his veins. There was no mistaking that sound. It was the roar of the Grindlemeer, whose breath could petrify, and stare befuddle. Sure enough, the beast stalked into the glade, its great mane a riot of impossible colours and its eyes burning like starfire.

"Who dares enter my Jungle?" the creature growled as the Hatter fought the urge to run.

"I dare," said the girl, springing up to face the beast. "And if you don't mind, my friends and I are about to enjoy a lovely, rousing cup of tea, so I would thank you to slink back to wherever you came from."

"*What?*" boomed the Grindlemeer. "I have never heard such insolence. I shall gobble you up without delay."

"Don't you mean gobble me down? Most food goes down to one's belly, after all."

"Up or down, I shall devour you all the same," the Grindlemeer bellowed, closing his indomitable jaws around the slight girl, crunching her bones as one might chew on a particularly crisp biscuit. The March Hare and the Hatter could only watch in dismay. The girl was dead, and if the Grindlemeer didn't kill them, the four Queens certainly would.

The Hatter was just wondering if they should offer the beast a cup of the dosed tea when a voice asked: "Was I tasty?"

The Grindlemeer whirled around to find the Dream Girl standing behind him, a pleasant smile on her not-at-all-chewed face.

"But that isn't possible," the monster gasped.

"Then you'd better kill me again."

"Happily," the Grindlemeer said, bringing a paw the size of a small cow down on her head, snapping every bone in her young body. The Hatter winced as he ground her remains into the dirt just to make sure that she couldn't get up again.

"You're really not very good at that, are you?" the girl said from where she had miraculously reappeared at his side.

"Yes, I am," the monster insisted, proving his point by slicing her into bloody pieces with one swipe of his razor-sharp claws.

"Are you sure?" she asked, resurrecting for the third time in as many minutes.

"How are you doing this?" the Grindlemeer demanded.

"Would you like to know?"

"Yes."

"Are you sure?"

"Yes!" said the Grindlemeer, Hare and Hatter in unison.

"By taking my medicine," the girl said, producing a small glass bottle.

"What kind of medicine?" the monster asked.

With a *pop*, she pulled out the stopper and held the bottle under his nose. "The kind that makes you feel like it's a brand-new day."

His whiskers quivering, the Grindlemeer took a sniff and his eyes went wide. Then the rest of him followed, swelling up like a balloon before exploding. The Hatter threw up his hands, expecting to be splattered by monstrous innards, but the inevitable gush of entrails and vital organs didn't follow. The Grindlemeer had simply vanished.

The girl smiled as the ground shook, the concrete fracturing.

"The Jungle's cracking up," the Hare yelled as the trees pulled themselves apart, the rubble shooting heavenwards as if caught in the pull of a gigantic magnet.

"I know the feeling," the Hatter cried out as the ground beneath him crumbled, great chunks detaching themselves to fly upwards. "We're going to disappear like the Grindlemeer!"

"Not yet."

The Dream Girl hovered in the midst of the carnage like an avenging angel, her form flicking between a freckled black girl with an awesome Afro and Wonderland's blonde-haired bugaboo. "But it will happen soon enough. Tell the Queens what you've seen. Tell them about the Destroyer of Wonderland. Tell them about their waking nightmare!"

The Hare had already turned tail and run, leaping from one rocketing outcrop to the next as the Jungle disintegrated around them. The Hatter yanked at Tweedledum's bear suit, but the weight of the grieving sibling's collected tears was too great.

"Let me go," the ex-twin bawled. "I want to be with my brother."

"You don't mean that," the Hatter said, pulling with all his might as the glade shot into the sky, picnic blanket and all.

"Yes, I do!" Dum-Dum yelled, shoving the Hatter hard in his chest. He tumbled back, his costume snagging on a jagged rock and splitting in two. He fell away from the disappearing forest, screaming as he flipped over and over before landing on his best friend.

"Come on," the Hare said, scrabbling up and grabbing the Hatter by the hand. "We need to get to safety."

But the crisis had passed. The Grindlemeer was gone. The Jungle was gone. Tweedledum was gone. The Hatter looked up into the starless grey sky, searching for any sign of the Dream Girl, but she had vanished too. The only thing that remained was the resounding clang of the Alarm Clock striking half past calamity.

More of Wonderland had been lost, and, this time, they'd seen it with their own eyes.

Tick-tock. Tick-tock. Tick-tock.

"It truly is the end of the world," the Hatter wailed, dropping to his knees. "What are we going to do?"

The Hare pulled off his stuffed head and grinned wolfishly. "What do you think? We're going to throw a party!"

Of all the hare-brained schemes his friend had ever come up with over the years, the Hatter had to admit that this one made sense.

Almost.

"The Dream Girl loves a party," he told the Queens, after explaining what had happened in the Jungle. "She told us herself. So, if we throw the biggest shindig in the history of revelry, she's bound to turn up, especially if we serve breakfast."

"Breakfast?" the Queen of Clubs said, indicating for her executioner to sharpen his axe.

"Don't ask," the Hare replied quickly, and for once the rulers complied.

Within hours, invitations for the mother of all garden parties had been sent to everyone in Wonderland, a task helped by the fact that the kingdom was a fraction of its former size. Only a handful of the Queens' subjects actually showed up, mainly because only a handful were left. They gathered in the shadow of the Alarm Clock, sipping from buttercups and watching a dandelion-trainer place his head in the mouths of various ferocious flowers as the afternoon's entertainment got underway.

Tick-tock. Tick-tock. Tick-tock.

"So," the Queen of Clubs hissed. "Where is she?"

The Queen of Diamonds looked equally displeased. "You said she'd be here."

"Were we wrong to trust you?" the Queen of Spades asked, as the Queen of Hearts floated the idea of cutting off the Hare's quivering ears while they waited.

"There is no need," said a voice from where the dandelion-trainer had been eaten by a petunia. In his place stood the Dream Girl, looking none the worse for dying three times before breakfast.

"What did I tell you?" the Hare crowed, triumphantly. "I have delivered the Destroyer to you. Quick. Off with her head."

"That's my line!" the Queen of Hearts spat, grabbing her executioner's axe and lopping off the Hare's head in a fit of pique.

"That's not very fair," the head said as it bounced towards the Dream Girl.

"What did you expect?" the girl said, stopping his rolling noggin with her foot.

"A thank you would have been nice!"

The Hatter should have been concerned that his friend

had just been beheaded, but he was concentrating, trying to see the Dream Girl as he knew she really was.

Behind him, all four Queens stood to their full heights, which would have been more impressive if their High Horses hadn't vanished an hour or so before. The garden at the foot of the clocktower was all that was left of their kingdom, and they knew who to blame.

"Why are you doing this?" the Queen of Clubs railed.

"Because you're missing it," the girl replied simply, her foot still resting on the Hare's forehead.

"Missing what?" he asked, peering up at her.

"The point."

"You killed the Grindlemeer," the Queen of Diamonds declared.

The girl cocked her head to one side. "Did I?"

"And the Jabberwocky, and the Jubjub, and even the Snark," the Queen of Hearts snapped. "Squillions of Wonderlanders, gone forever. How did you do it?"

"She has a bottle," the Hatter blurted out, his throat more painful than ever. The lights still danced in front of his vision, having now coalesced into three balls of fire, and he didn't care who struck him down for talking, be they playing cards or the Angel of Death. "The Grindlemeer took a sniff of whatever's inside and that was that."

"That was what?" asked the Queen of Spades.

"He was gone," the girl answered, smiling impishly.

"Show us this bottle," the Queen of Clubs commanded.

"Gladly," the Dream Girl said, reaching into her bib. Or was it her overall pockets? The Hatter couldn't tell anymore.

Tick-tock. Tick-tock. Tick-tock.

"Look out," the Hare yelled, still loyal to the Queens despite his recent decapitation. "It's dangerous!"

"Only if you smell it," the girl advised them, holding the bottle above her head.

Tick-tock. Tick-tock. Tick-tock.

"Bring it to us," the Queen of Diamonds commanded.

"No," the Hare shouted, trying to trip the girl with his ears. "It's a trick."

"Of course it is," the girl laughed, drawing back the hand containing the bottle. "Here, catch!"

Tick-tock. Tick-tock. Tick-tock.

The bottle arched through the air, flying over the Hatter's throbbing head and down towards the four Queens.

"I'll get it."

"No, I will."

"No, *I* will."

"You're all off your heads!"

Tick-tock. Tick-tock. Tick-tock.

With a cry, the Queens crashed into each other, the bottle slipping through their cardboard fingers to smash on the table in front of them.

A rich aroma swept out from the broken glass. One by one, the Queens vanished, first Clubs, and then Spades, and then Diamonds and Hearts. They were followed by their subjects, who disappeared the moment they breathed the heady odour into their impossible lungs. The Hare gulped as he watched his body dissipate seconds before his severed head erupted into nothingness.

Only the Hatter was left as the Alarm Clock ticked steadily towards disaster.

Tick-tock. Tick-tock. Tick-tock.

He took in a long, luxurious breath as the bell finally tolled, the earthy aroma sweeping over him. His body lost its shape, the brim of his non-existent hat lifting from a brow that was no longer there.

All he could see were the three lights, and all he could hear was the Dream Girl's voice.

"See you on the other side, Uncle...

"On the other side...

"On the other..."

♥

"Milliner?"

Milliner tried to open his eyes, but the lids were gummed shut. Something was being pulled up from his throat, over his tongue, past his chapped lips.

He coughed, his body racked with pain, muscles in spasm, joints creaking after years of inactivity.

"Hey, take it easy, buddy," the voice said, a familiar lisp softening the words. "The feeding tube's out. Let the drugs do their work."

"Hare?" he slurred, his voice barely more than a croak.

"Yeah, it's me. And don't worry. I had trouble talking when I came around too."

Water sprayed over his face, a refreshing mist that cleared the gunk from his eyes and moistened his lips. He blinked, wincing at the glare of the three LED bulbs above his head.

"Oops. Sorry about that."

Milliner heard the whine of servos as his bed was raised to a standing position. No, not a bed. A pod, the product of Dormouse Hibernation Services.

"Just take it easy, okay?"

A face came into view. Buck teeth. Straw-coloured hair. Milliner smiled, his head still muggy. Hare? Was it really him? He frowned. That wasn't right.

"Haig?"

"In the flesh, buddy-boy. You had us worried for a minute. Thought you weren't going to come around. We're the last."

"The last of what?"

"To wake up, but don't worry—the gang's all here."

Milliner forced himself to look around the pod-bay, full of people he hadn't seen in… how long had it been? Millennia, if the programme had been a success. He smiled as he saw the twins—Dee and Datum—embracing each other as if they never wanted to be apart again. Then there was Glenn, the engineer that had helped design the ship. Some found the lion of a man intimidating, but Milliner knew he was a gentle giant. He just hoped his breath had improved as the years had ticked slowly by.

"Are we there?" he asked, trying to push himself forward.

"For quite some time," a commanding voice rang out to his left. Holding onto the pod to steady himself, Milliner turned to see Captain Delta walking purposely towards him, a steaming mug in her hands. "It appears we overslept."

"By how long?"

Delta smiled. "One hundred and fifty-four years. But

what's a century or two after three thousand years of travel?"

"Apparently the computer couldn't wake us," Haig explained. "She had to construct a special avatar to enter the dreamscape."

"The dreamscape you programmed to keep us all sane," the Captain commented, pointedly. "The first avatar was lost. Corrupted by a faulty line of code, and so the AI entered the 'scape herself, and just in time. The *Liddell*'s power cells are nearly exhausted."

Milliner's head spun and he staggered, Haig catching him before he could fall back into the pod. "It's okay, bud. No one's blaming you."

"Speak for yourself," the Captain said, with a wry smile on her lips. "Heads would have rolled if I'd woken up dead. But I suppose I can forgive you, just this once, especially considering what's outside. Do you want to see?"

Milliner nodded, still holding onto his friend's arm. The Captain tapped a communicator on her sleeve. "Alice?"

"Yes, Captain?" the ship's AI replied, using the voice-print Milliner had programmed a lifetime ago, the voice of the niece who had helped him in his workshop, the niece he'd promised to take to the stars, the niece who had lost her fight against cancer before the *Liddell* had begun its long journey. He smiled, imagining her mop of frizzy hair, her dark freckled skin.

"Will you show Mr Milliner where we are?"

"With pleasure," Alice replied.

A holographic screen shimmered into view, running the length of the room, one of a thousand identical hibernation suites dotted throughout the sleeper-ship. Milliner's breath caught in his throat at the sight of the planet, its continents teeming with life and the oceans cobalt blue, a stark contrast to the dry world they'd abandoned.

The Captain took a sip from her mug, stamped with the logo of the recolonization programme. "Worth getting out of bed for?"

"Definitely," Milliner said, before asking Alice what she had used to rouse them from their slumber.

"A protocol of my own devising," the AI replied. "I call it 'wake up and smell the coffee'."

Milliner smiled, gazing at the globe beneath them.

Their new home.

Their Wonderland.

Good Dog, Alice!

JULIET MARILLIER

In Great-Uncle Bartholomew's opinion, it was a mistake to name my dog Alice. He made that clear from the moment I introduced them.

"Alice? You can't call a dog Alice!" Uncle Bart's moustache quivered with disapproval, putting me in mind of an overexcited caterpillar.

I had known other dogs with names generally reserved for girls and boys: Monty-short-for-Montague, for instance, a British bulldog; and Seraphina, a well-coiffed miniature poodle. "What's wrong with Alice?" I asked.

"My dear girl! Everything! A learned colleague of mine knows a young person of that name, and I gather she is involved in all manner of wild escapades. I once had a gardener whose daughter was an Alice. She would tuck up her skirts and climb trees all day long, and if anyone asked her to descend and comport herself like a lady, she would pelt them with random objects."

That sounded rather fun to me, though I could imagine Uncle Bart being somewhat put out if I hit him on the head with, say, a conker. "What sort of objects?"

"Whatever one finds in a tree, I suppose. Sticks, acorns, squirrels."

"Squirrels?!"

"The slower ones might be caught, then hurled," said Uncle Bart thoughtfully. "The gardener's daughter was a quick sort of young person." His eyes fell again upon the dog, a tri-coloured King Charles spaniel which my favourite cousin, William, had brought for me as a surprise birthday present that very morning. William had not obtained Uncle Bart's permission to give me a dog, perhaps anticipating the answer would be no. He had simply arrived with the puppy in a covered basket. He'd brought his parents too, not in a covered basket but walking behind, all smiles. It had been impossible for Uncle Bart to refuse.

"That's only two Alices," I pointed out. "I believe there is something amiss in your statistical method, Uncle."

"Ah, well," said Uncle Bart, ignoring this comment, "at least the dog will not tuck up her skirts or climb trees. But I fear the wild escapades."

"You could come on them too," I suggested, wondering at what age a person would be too old for escapades. It would do Uncle Bart good to get away from his studies from time to time.

He chuckled. "I am a scholar. A scientist. A man of many

parts. None of those parts is inclined towards escapades. Not to say that scholarship and adventures cannot go hand in hand. I recall a time…" Then, just as he was about to say something interesting, Uncle Bart went off into a dream. This was a frequent habit of his.

"Uncle?"

He snorted, coming back to himself. "Yes, child?"

"I think Alice is missing her mother." I picked the dog up and held her to my chest. "We should make her welcome."

"Why not call the creature Fluff or Spot or… or Rover?" Uncle Bart had not given up.

"Rover is for a boy dog. Spot is for a spotted dog. And Fluff…" There was no denying the fluff; Alice possessed it in abundance. "Fluff is too obvious," I said. "A scientist would not choose that name for his dog."

"Ah," said Uncle Bart. "But she's not my dog. You're the one who had the eleventh birthday."

"And I'm the one who is calling her Alice."

William and his family had stayed only long enough to wish me a happy birthday and hand Alice over. That was disappointing. William and I could have explored or made a snow monster or played shuttlecock. We could have had a proper birthday luncheon: roasted potatoes with rich gravy; tiny cakes with crystallised violets on top; lemonade to drink. Not that our cook and housekeeper, Mrs Manifold, would dream of preparing something so festive. Maybe if I'd still had a mother and a father, birthdays would have been different, but my parents and my brother had been killed when I was three years old. That was why I lived with Uncle Bart.

At least there were no lessons on my birthday. Froggy was away for four days, doing some kind of examination. Froggy was my tutor. I was supposed to call him Master Frederick. He had been Uncle Bart's prize student at Oxford University.

"One good thing, Alice," I told my dog as I put on my cloak and boots and woolly hat. "With *him* away, we have four whole days to ourselves, and nothing to worry about."

Mrs Manifold had decreed that Alice should stay in the scullery, eat and drink from her own bowls and not get underfoot. I saw no good reason to keep to those rules. "You will sleep on my bed, of course," I whispered in Alice's ear as I carried her down the back stairs. "I'll take you for two walks every day, and I'll teach you all manner of tricks. I know you are an exceptionally clever dog."

I gazed into Alice's round, bright eyes, searching for signs of the naughtiness Uncle Bart anticipated her developing, but she was the very picture of innocence. Her face belonged in a painting, the sort where the girls wear white frilly frocks and have their hair in ringlets, and the boys are in satin sashes and knickerbockers. "You won't be that kind of dog, Alice," I told her, "because I'm not a frilly frock sort of girl. You and I will have escapades. At least, when Froggy is away we will."

On the first day I showed Alice the garden. It was winter, but there was not enough snow on the ground to make a snowman. There was not even enough for a snow dog the size of a King Charles spaniel. We made a snow mouse, then another one so the first would not feel lonely. Alice spent most of the time digging a hole under a leafless rose bush. But she was *there*. That was the important thing. I found tiny pebbles for eyes, so the snow mice could watch out for trouble. I made their ears from dried-up leaves and gave them tails of winter grass. I named them Sebastian and Amethyst. When you made something it was right to give it a name, even if it was only a snow mouse that would soon melt away. A name brought a thing to life. A name gave it light. You remembered that light even after the thing itself was gone.

I didn't remember my parents very well. But I remembered Tom. He was my big brother, two years older than me. I spoke to him every day, so he wouldn't be lonely wherever he was. Not out loud; deep down, without making a sound. *Do you like my snow mice? If you were here, we could make a whole army and enact a great battle. But I fear Alice would become overexcited and romp all over the field of conflict, scattering the mouse warriors in all directions.* I imagined Tom smiling, laughing, throwing a snowball.

I spoke to my brother at night, too, when I sat on my bed with my shawl clutched around me, my heart hammering as I waited for the creak of the door. When I whispered his name, the light of it made a little glow in the dark space of my bedchamber. *I wish you were here, Tom. I would be braver then.*

On the second day it was too windy to go out of doors.

I showed Alice the inside of our house. Uncle Bart was in his study. Mrs Manifold was mostly in the kitchen, but as the only live-in servant at Wraithwood Hall she had many responsibilities, so I made a game out of avoiding her. Then there were Molly and Susan from the village, who came in to scrub floors and remove cobwebs and change the sheets. They chattered while they worked, so it was easy to keep out of their way. James, the gardener, had been given the day off.

Alice and I toured the bedchambers. First was Uncle Bart's, with an improbably high four-poster bed and a writing desk strewn with academic papers. We did not go into Froggy's room. After that came two spares, kept in readiness though Uncle Bart rarely had houseguests. Last was mine, with its own little hearth, a tall stack of books—I frequently borrowed items from Uncle Bart's collection—and a window that looked out over the front garden. My room had only one deficiency: the door was without a lock. I had never found the right words to request one. Uncle Bart would be sure to ask why, and how could I possibly answer? If I told him the truth, he would be shocked. He would be upset. He might not believe me. After all, he was a man.

On the third day, Mrs Manifold remarked at breakfast time that a dog should know its place. A disobedient animal, she said, was an insufferable nuisance and not to be tolerated. Alice gazed back at her, eyes bright in anticipation of bacon.

I would train Alice in the old ballroom, I decided. It was cold and dusty and darkish, but had the advantage of being in a tucked-away corner of Wraithwood Hall, visited only by pigeons. There had not been a ball since Uncle Bart was young, and that was a very long time ago.

I taught Alice *Sit* and *Stay*. I taught her *Shh*. And because lessons should be fun, I taught her *Catch*. My breakfast bacon was in my pocket, broken into tiny pieces. Alice was hungry from all the sitting and staying; she learned to catch quickly. I'd been right about her. She was an exceptionally clever dog.

On the fourth day, I lost Alice. We were so busy with our training that I missed the bell for luncheon, and only realised how late it was when I heard Mrs M calling my name. The quickest way back into the main part of the house was through a narrow hallway between the ballroom and the servants' quarters. I was not supposed to use this shortcut. The hallway was barely wide enough for me to pass through; a solid person like Mrs Manifold would be in danger of getting stuck, and a tall one like James would have to stoop, for the ceiling was low. Stranger still was the blue-painted door halfway along, a door just the right height for an eleven-year-old girl, but far too small for grown-ups. Long ago, Uncle Bart had seen me coming out of the shortcut, and I could still remember his stern warning: "Do not go through that passage, child. No good can come of it. And never, ever open the blue door. Do not even speak of it. Promise me, now."

Shocked by the terrible look on his face—it was as if he could see demons—I had squeaked out a promise before I had time to consider. Later, I wished I had asked questions. Why must I never open the blue door? What would happen if I did? And if that place was so dangerous, why didn't they block it up so nobody could go there?

I had never disobeyed the rule about the blue door, though I did use the passage sometimes when in a rush. I had performed some investigations, going around the outside of Wraithwood Hall and trying to work out where the blue door might lead. But it didn't seem to lead anywhere.

That morning, Alice had been learning *Wait. Wait* was short for wait-until-I-say-the-magic-word-before-you-eat. It was a measure of how clever Alice was that before the lesson was over she could wait for a slow count of five without falling upon the scrap of bacon I had placed before her. The magic word was *Crunch.* I thought this might be a useful thing for her to know, should someone offer her comestibles that would not agree with her. I hoped this would never happen, but there was no accounting for the vagaries of humankind, or so Uncle Bart frequently muttered while reading *The Times* over his breakfast eggs.

When I heard Mrs Manifold calling me I ran through the little passage, trying to tidy my hair as I went and hoping I would not be in trouble. Mrs M stood outside the dining room with a covered platter in her hands and a harried look on her face.

"You're late," she said, looking me up and down. "Your uncle has a visitor. Did you wash your face and hands?"

"Yes, Mrs Manifold," I lied.

There followed a tedious luncheon during which Uncle Bart and his guest, a fellow scientist, discussed at length a paper on the topic of phrenology, which had to do with interpreting bumps on the head. I could not imagine why anyone would want to study such a thing, but I knew better than to say so. In fact, I said nothing at all, but worked my way through a somewhat better meal than usual, thanks to the presence of my uncle's learned friend. It was not until I was finishing my stewed apple and custard that I realised I had left Alice in the ballroom on her own.

I set my napkin down and waited for a pause in the conversation. "Uncle Bart, may I please be excused from the table?"

"What lovely manners," commented the learned friend with a condescending smile.

"Go, go, by all means, child," said Uncle Bart, evidently keen to return to the topic of head bumps. I fled. Not through the little passage, since Mrs M was nearby, but the long way, out of the house, around the stone pathway, into the ballroom through the big door that did not quite close properly.

"Alice!" I called. "Alice, come!"

No reply. All was still.

I commenced a search. The ballroom housed a miscellany of old furniture, draped with protective sheets. I crawled under things, I climbed over things, I squeezed behind things. From time to time I called, "Alice!" I had not realised so many spiders lived in the ballroom. As I was pulling the last of the cobwebs from my hair I heard muffled barking. It was coming from the little passage.

I tiptoed over, not wishing to startle Alice into flight. When I looked in, nobody was there, only shadows. But the blue door, the door Uncle Bart had said must always stay closed, stood ajar. A cold draught came from within, making me shiver. Alice barked again. She was in there. In the place beyond the door.

There was only one choice. Alice was my dog. She was my responsibility, and I must bring her back. *Courage*, I told myself. *It's a rescue mission. An adventure.* I walked up to the blue door, pushed it wide open and walked on through.

I had expected a hallway, a chamber or steps to a cellar. Instead, I found myself outside. But this was not the garden of Wraithwood Hall, though here, too, it was winter. Snow lay in drifts around towering trees, enough to make a monstrous snowman. Icicles hung from the branches, shining as if with their own light. I could hear a rustling, as if something was moving about up above, keeping an eye on me. I stared in wonder. This was a place from a strange fairy tale. It surely could not be real. Yet here it was, only one step from home. I had walked into a true adventure.

Alice, I reminded myself. *Find Alice.* There was no sound from her now, but across the carpet of snow was a trail of neat pawprints, heading towards a round bush, all prickles and berries. It looked somewhat like an oversized hedgehog.

"Alice!" I called. My voice sounded monstrously loud. The rustling from above ceased. "Where are you?"

The prickle bush lurched to its feet and began to move towards me. The feet were gnarled and knobby, and the gait was that of an infirm old man. This was becoming odder by the moment.

"Ah, a young person." The bush had a voice to match its

walk. "We are not often graced with such a visit these days. Welcome, welcome! Sit down, make yourself comfortable."

I discerned beady eyes deep in the foliage, and perhaps a twiggy nose. There was nowhere to sit except on the ground in the snow. Fearing to offend my host, I sat. "Have you seen a little dog?" I asked. "Her name is Alice and she came this way. She is very young and will be easily lost."

"It is customary to begin a conversation with introductions," said the creature. "My name is—it is—oh dear. It has been so long since I had a visitor that I cannot remember."

"Oh, how sad," I said, wondering how long it might be before Uncle Bart started to forget his own name. I must make sure I called him by it at least three times a day. "Would you like a new name? I could give you one."

If a bush could blush, this one did so. The edges of his leaves turned pink, and his berries glowed. "Oh, yes!" he said in tones of such awe that I might have been offering a chest full of pirate treasure or *The Complete Works of William Shakespeare* in a collector's edition. "Oh, that would be very fine indeed!"

A name was quite a responsibility. It had to contain the essence of the individual's character, which meant something like Prickly would not do at all. "I'll need to ask you some questions first," I said. The snow was soaking into my skirt, all the way through my undergarments to my skin. I could not hear Alice at all.

"Ask away."

"What is your job here? What is your responsibility in this—this interesting place?"

"I guard. I protect. I keep watch. Small folk hide in me or shelter under me. My fruit keeps them alive in the long winter."

"And in summer?"

The creature sighed; all his leaves trembled. "In summer I rest, so I will be strong when the winter comes. Tiny folk rest in my shade."

This was a very important personage. Clearly the small folk could not survive without him. Such a being could not be given an ordinary name, such as John or Cedric or Charles. "I think your name could be Trusty," I said. "Would that be acceptable?"

"Rusty?"

"No, no—Trusty with a T. Because everyone trusts you, or they would not hide in you or shelter under you or eat your fruit. You are the guardian of the woods."

"Trusty with a T. That is an excellent name. I thank you." The creature seemed to bow; his leaves all tilted a little in my direction.

"Trusty, could you help me to find my dog, Alice? She is about this big"—I motioned with my hands—"and her fur is three colours: white, black and russet. She has long ears and a plumy tail."

Before Trusty could respond, a terrible shrieking broke out, the high-pitched cry of a small animal in deathly peril. I whirled to see an enormous owl seated on a branch nearby. The bird's great eyes were most curious. In one I could see the face of a clock, with a full set of Roman numerals, and in the other was a pair of scales in perfect balance. There was no time to reflect upon this oddity, for the bird held in its beak a tiny struggling creature. It had a tri-coloured coat, long ears and a plumy tail. It was no bigger than a mouse.

"That's Alice!" I cried. "Oh, please don't eat her!" The owl blinked solemnly, making no attempt to reply. If it had opened its beak to do so, I could have dashed across the clearing and caught Alice as she fell. I turned towards Trusty. "Why is she so small?"

"Your little friend has more curiosity than is advisable in one so young," said Trusty. "She has eaten two of my silver berries, and as a consequence has diminished quite considerably. Indeed, she is now too small to furnish a satisfactory dinner for an owl. Let her go!" This command was intended for the owl, and the bird was startled into obedience. Alice plummeted towards the ground; I dived and caught her, rolling to land in a pile of snow. My shoulder hurt, but Alice was safe. Or as safe as a creature the size of a mouse can be. Those silver berries were indeed powerful. I must make sure my dog ate no more of them or she would be shrunk to the proportions of a flea.

Holding Alice between my cupped palms, I took a closer look at Trusty. The silver berries were all on his left side. On the right were berries of rich deep purple. "What happens if someone eats the purple berries?" I asked.

"A foolish question." The owl's voice was undeniably female. "Use your powers of logic and deduction, infant. Tut, tut, whatever do they teach children in school these days?"

"I don't go to school. I have a tutor." I failed utterly to keep the wobble from my voice as I spoke these words. Froggy would be back tonight, and I still had no lock on my door.

"This tutor has not taught you much," said the owl. "Why not feed your animal a purple berry and observe the result? That way you answer your own question."

"Because I love Alice, and I would rather have a mouse-sized dog than a dead one. How do I know those are not poison berries?"

"Did you not name me Trusty with a T?" It sounded as if the bushy creature was smiling. "Feed her one purple berry, as the bird suggests. You may require two, since she took two of the silver. She can eat them safely."

Alice was shivering hard. She'd had a terrible fright. I could only hope this would teach her a lesson. I plucked one purple berry and set the tiny fruit before her on my palm. "Wait," I said, and counted to five. "*Crunch!*"

"Oh, very good!" exclaimed Trusty, as Alice snatched up the berry on command and devoured it as if she had not been fed for weeks. She was immediately larger. But not big enough; she had grown only to the size of a small kitten. I waited a little, wanting to be sure a second berry was necessary. It seemed it was. I put it on my palm. To do so, I had to move Alice to my other hand. I kept her within reach of the fruit.

"Alice, *wait.*"

"One, two, three, four, five," chanted Trusty and the owl in unison.

"*Crunch!*"

The berry was gone, and Alice was back to her normal size again, the size of a puppy just old enough to leave its mother and go to a new home. "Thank you!" I said, curtseying first to Trusty and then to the owl. "It has been good to meet you. I had best take Alice back to… to the place where we live."

"Oh, so soon?" The owl sounded mournful. Yet she had given no sign of taking any liking to me. I eyed her, wondering what life would be like in this world beyond the blue door, and what parting gift might be appropriate for a bird whose meal I had, in effect, snatched from her jaws, or rather, beak. I wanted to leave my new acquaintances on good terms.

"May I know your name?" It had worked before; perhaps it would again.

"My name is Madame Eye." The owl spoke in a grand tone, as if she had been reading too many dramatic plays.

"That is unusual," I said. "But then, your eyes are quite remarkable."

The owl turned her large orbs on me. "I for Inevitability. I am Inevitability J. Moon-Fleet."

"Oh! That is a magnificent name! Does the J stand for Justice?" With the scales in one eye and the clock in the other—is not the passage of time inevitable?—this seemed likely.

An owl cannot smile, but I sensed a softening in Madame I's expression. "That was well deduced," she said.

There was a silence. Both of them were looking at me, expecting something. After a little, the owl asked, "And what is *your* name?"

I really had forgotten my manners. "Dorothea. It means a gift from God. Only… sometimes I think God has forgotten to watch over me. Maybe He has fallen asleep." I held back the words that wanted to spill out. How could these two possibly help? "I must go now. I must take Alice back." My voice trembled.

"Dorothea," said Trusty, "I see tears in your eyes. Why are you afraid?"

The owl shifted on her branch, staring down at me. "Trust. Inevitability. Justice. Now is the time to speak, child."

So I did. About Froggy—Master Frederick—and the strange pictures he showed me late at night when he came tapping on my door, and his clammy hands, and what he had said he would do when I was a big girl of eleven, and how I couldn't tell Uncle Bart or Mrs Manifold or anyone because I couldn't make myself say the words. And how even if I had a lock for my bedchamber it wouldn't be enough because I had lessons with Froggy every day, and sometimes in the middle of a lesson in French or Mathematics he would say something that made my flesh crawl. When I got to the end, I wiped my eyes and said, "Thank you for listening. But there's nothing you can do."

"You could stay here," said Madame Inevitability. "Unless this Froggy is a very small man indeed, he could not fit through our door."

I would have been happy never to see Froggy again. But I would miss William, and I would miss Uncle Bart. And Uncle Bart would miss me. He would be lonely. "I don't think that would do. I need to go back, and so does Alice. Is there any other way?"

"Wait," said Trusty, stretching out his twiggy hand to

pluck a small harvest of his own berries: five of the purple ones and five of the silver. The owl flew down with a large dry leaf in her beak. Trusty dropped the berries carefully into the shallow receptacle. "This task is for you, Dorothea."

"But how…?" I imagined growing so large I would be unable to get out of my bedchamber, or so small that I would fall down a crack in the floor and never be found. That would be a terrible fate, but almost better than waiting for Froggy's tap on the door.

Madame Inevitability passed me the leaf. "The solution is in your hands," she said. "Use your powers of logic and deduction. And take care not to drop these on the way."

I balanced my burdens carefully: Alice supported by one hand, the leaf and berries cupped in the other. In my mind, an idea began to form itself. "You mean…"

But the owl had flown back to her perch and was using her beak to tidy her feathers, and Trusty said nothing.

"Goodbye. And thank you. I am very grateful." The idea was getting bigger. It was getting monstrous.

"Don't mention it," Trusty said. "Just as well your dog is a tidy eater."

♥

Froggy did not come back until the rest of the household was abed. I was watching from my window, with a candle alight on the old chest, and when I saw him come through the gate I took out the berries. The silver ones were in a small china bowl and the purple ones in an eggcup. There must be no confusion in the dim light.

He let himself in by a side door; Uncle Bart had given him a key. When I heard his footsteps on the stairs I spoke to Alice, who was hunkered down on my bed.

"Alice, *wait.*" A count of five. "*Crunch.*" And again. After the second berry, I moved Alice into the shadowy corner near the wardrobe. "Alice, *wait.*" I counted. "*Crunch.*" And twice more. The five purple berries were gone.

A familiar tap on the door. In my stomach, a familiar sinking dread. I blew out the candle. In the faint glow from the banked-up fire, I sat down on my bed and wrapped my shawl around me. "Alice, *ssh,*" I murmured. "*Wait.*"

The door creaked open, and there was Froggy. "Sitting in the dark, my little scholar? You must be lonely all by yourself."

He closed the door behind him, then took two steps forward.

"*Crunch!*"

Alice came out of the dark. Master Frederick's mouth opened wide, but she gave him no time to scream.

The old sheet I had spread over the carpet absorbed much of the blood. When I had bundled it up, along with various oddments of tweed, hair and leather, Alice gave the place a thorough going-over with her large tongue. I stowed the sheet in the wardrobe. In the morning, before anyone was stirring, I would take it outside and bury it in the stack of rubbish James had ready for burning. When all was to rights, I fed Alice the five silver berries. "Good dog, Alice," I said, giving my little friend a special pat. We snuggled into bed together and were soon fast asleep.

♥

For a short while, Master Frederick's disappearance was the subject of local conjecture. He was known to have attended his examination and set out for home. A heavy snowfall overnight had obliterated any clues as to his later movements. The constabulary came to Wraithwood Hall and spoke to James, who was tending his bonfire. They questioned Mrs Manifold and Uncle Bart. But nothing came of it.

I have a governess now. Her name is Miss Flora Buchanan. She speaks four languages and knows lots of games. In her free time she writes stories about monsters. Miss Flora is nineteen years old, but she is a small person: only a little taller than me. I think she might enjoy escapades.

And Alice? She is growing a great deal, but no more than is usual for a King Charles spaniel. She has learned to roll over and to shake hands. I always knew she was clever.

The Hunting of the Jabberwock

JONATHAN GREEN

'Twas brillig, and the sun hung low in the sky as the youth came within sight of the tumbledown tower. It stood alone, isolated atop a rugged crag, as if standing sentinel over the deep, dark forest that filled the wide valley below.

On the far side of that forest he could see smoke rising from the chimneys of the town nestled in a bend of the river. He doubted he could get from here to there before sundown, and considering what dwelt within that tulgey wood—all manner of slithy toves, borogoves and mome raths, and they weren't even the worst that lurked within the wabe—he didn't fancy spending the night within its shadowy depths after nightfall.

And so, following the worn path to the door of the tumbledown tower, he knocked upon the dark wood of that portal three times.

The door was opened by a stooped figure; a scrawny old

man with a shock of filthy grey hair, an unkempt beard, and a gawping peg-toothed leer. His simple robe was as filthy as the rest of him.

He peered up at the youth through one bulging eye, while the other was no more than a twisted squint.

"What do you want?" he snapped, and the youth was treated to a waft of cidery breath.

"Goodly hermit," the youth began, "might I beg of you a bed for the night? Dusk is creeping across the land and I fear I will not make my destination before night falls, after which all manner of manxome foes will be abroad."

"Nobody's spending the night in my tower with me," came the old man's curt reply. "I am a hermit of some repute, and I do not wish to tarnish that reputation. Nobody is welcome here."

"How kind of you!" the youth exclaimed, boldly striding over the threshold, past the bewildered old man, into the tower. "But how did you know my name?"

"What?"

"I am Nobody, good sir. That is my name."

The hermit looked the youth up and down—from his cascading golden locks to his verdant doublet and his crimson hose, taking in the ancient sword at his belt—and then he began to laugh.

"You're Nobody, are you?"

"That's right," the youth said, and the expression on his face could not have been more earnest.

"And what kind of cruel creature thought to call you Nobody?"

"It was my late father, sir," the youth replied, "for he used to say to me, 'Boy, put these notions of monster-hunting from your head. You're not some noble knight galumphing about the place beheading maidens and rescuing dragons. You're Nobody, and the sooner you get used to the idea, the better for all of us. Now get me another drink.'" Lowering his voice he added, "I am ashamed to say that my father was often drunk."

"Out of interest, what career did your father forge for himself?" the hermit asked.

"He was a gong-farmer, sir. But after he fell into a cesspit and drowned, the family business died with him. And so I set out to make my fortune as a monster-hunter."

"And where did the son of a gong-farmer get a sword like that?"

"It's an old family heirloom, handed down on my mother's side."

The hermit regarded the guileless youth for a moment, a wry smile curling his thin lips.

"All right then, why not?" he said with a laugh. Pointing at a pile of logs beside the door, and the axe sunk into a large chopping block sitting amidst a mess of wood shavings, he said, "Chop that little lot for me and I'll give you a bed for the night for your trouble, and I'll even share my supper with you."

♥

And so, as night chased the sun below the western horizon, and the moon rose amidst a smattering of stars, safe inside the tower, the hermit shared the contents of his cooking pot with Nobody.

Warmed from without by the fire and from within by the food filling their bellies, talk turned from cabbages and kings to hopes and dreams.

"So what brings you to these parts?" the old man asked Nobody.

Draining the last dregs from his bowl, Nobody wiped the sleeve of his doublet across his greasy lips. "I'm here to kill the Jabberwock."

The hermit considered the youth's beardless chin, his slim arms, and his barely scuffed boots. "I don't mean to be rude, but are you sure you're cut out to be a monster-hunter?"

"Oh yes," Nobody replied, his face an open book. "And I will prove it to you, just as I will prove it to my late father, by slaying the beast."

"The Jabberwock."

"Has the monster not been terrorising this region for some years now?"

"That is true," replied the old man.

"And always around this time of year, as spring is giving way to summer?"

"That is also true."

"Well, now that I am here, its days are numbered," replied the youth, holding his head high, a beatific smile on his face.

The old man rose to his feet, the flickering flames of the fire growing his shadow on the wall behind him, until it loomed over them both like some legendary predatory beast.

"Beware the Jabberwock, my son, the jaws that bite, the

claws that catch!" the old man challenged Nobody, baring what few teeth he had left and hooking his fingers into claws in a dumb-show mime of a fearsome monster.

"Oh, have no fear, I shall," the youth replied, his determination indefatigable.

"And the Jabberwock is not the only hungry horror that haunts the forest," his host continued. "While you're at it, you'd best beware the Jubjub bird!"

"The Jubjub bird?" parroted the youth.

"It makes its nest at the top of the tallest tree in the forest. And shun the frumious Bandersnatch!"

"I shall have nothing to fear as long as I have my vorpal sword in hand," the youth replied, although his complexion had paled somewhat.

"Then on your head be it," grumbled the querulous hermit.

♥

When dawn came, the hermit hoped that Nobody's youthful boasts and the bravado he had demonstrated the night before would have been seen for what they were in the cold light of day. But the gong-farmer's son would not be dissuaded from his fool's errand and set off once more, giving the hermit a final cheery wave and a beamish smile.

From the tumbledown tower, Nobody descended the crag, where the hermit's home perched at its precipitous peak, and followed an old goat-herder's track that eventually joined with the road that skirted the southern limits of the forest, which brought him at last to the huddle of houses and hovels that had collected at the bend in the river valley.

Crossing a broad stone bridge, Nobody entered the town. The crowded streets were bedecked with bunting and everywhere he looked he saw jugglers, acrobats, fire-breathers, puppeteers and minstrels. The festival had brought a host of entertainers to this place, as well as the monster-hunters and their entourages, not to mention those who had simply come to immerse themselves in the carnival atmosphere, and cheer the hunters on.

Nobody wandered through the streets as if in a trance, mouth agape as he took in all the wonders the festival had to offer this son of a simple gong-farmer.

Beast-slayers, like him, had travelled from far afield in the hope of ridding the town of the creature that had been left to terrorise the town for far too long. There were hairy-armed barbarians from the north, mail-clad paladins from the west, sallow-skinned trackers from the south, and even noble life-liege warriors from the east, wearing red-lacquered armour and carrying tempered steel blades.

But what was clear to even a beardless youth from the sticks, untested by the rough ways of the world, was that the local businesses were doing a roaring trade, providing the hunters, and the cavalcades of hangers-on that followed in their wake, everything they could possibly require or desire, from beer and weapons to trinkets by which to commemorate the occasion of the Hunt and bed companions for a night or two.

The Mayor had declared that a reward of one thousand

crowns would be awarded to the hunter, or hunters, who actually slew the Jabberwock, with only one, small stipulation: anyone hoping to claim the reward had to register with the town authorities first to be granted a licence to hunt within the forest.

Foregoing all that the hot food stalls had to offer, having enjoyed a hearty bowl of porridge that morning courtesy of the hermit, Nobody followed the bands of beast-slayers that were converging on the largest inn that stood at the heart of the town, off the main market square.

Nobody took his place in the line snaking out of the door of The Slithy Tove, and waited patiently until it was his turn to shuffle from the warming morning sunlight into the shadowed smoky interior of the hostelry. And eventually he found himself standing before the table at which sat the town's rotund, rosy-cheeked Mayor and his gaunt, sour-faced clerk.

"And who might you be?" asked the clerk, his words clipped, his tone sharp, his voice nasal.

"Nobody," Nobody replied.

"Anyone can see you're a nobody," chortled the Mayor, taking off his felt hat to mop his brow with an extravagant white lace handkerchief as big as a tablecloth, "but Mortsafe here still needs a name for your licence!"

"Begging your pardon, your lordship," the youth said, and had he been wearing a hat he would most certainly have doffed it, "but Nobody *is* my name."

The clerk adjusted the spectacles perched on the end of his hawkish nose and gave Nobody an uffish look.

"Nobody?"

"Nobody!" the youth said, smiling broadly.

"Nobody," the clerk repeated, carefully writing the name on a fresh permit with a borogove quill pen. Without looking up he said, "That'll be fifty crowns."

"I beg your pardon, sir?"

"Your licence to hunt the beast. The fee is fifty crowns," Mortsafe said irritably. "To cover administration costs, you understand."

"I am very sorry, sir, but I do not have one crown to my name, let alone fifty. I have only the clothes on my back, a handful of copper coins, and the sword at my side. The very same sword with which I intend to slay the Jabberwock!" he declared proudly.

"If you do not have a licence you may not claim the reward, even if you do somehow manage to slay the beast," the clerk snapped.

"Oh, I didn't know that," said Nobody.

"Well, you learn something new every day," said the clerk coldly.

"Be off with you!" shouted the Mayor, making Nobody jump. "And stop wasting our time!"

Disheartened, Nobody turned and headed for the door; he doubted his handful of coppers were even enough to pay for a tankard of the local ale.

"Never mind, lad," came a voice from nearby, "that vorpal sword of yours wouldn't serve you well against a monster like the Jabberwock anyway."

Nobody searched the shadows for the person who had been so disparaging about the ancient heirloom he carried.

Sitting at a table, clad in battered plate and rusty chainmail, was an ageing knight. His white hair hung down to his shoulders, but the dome of his pate was entirely bald. His face was drawn, his nose long and pronounced, and beneath it sat a bristling moustache which hid his mouth when he spoke, although it did nothing to curb his unkind comments.

Crouched beneath the table was a vigilant wolfhound, its ears up, its eyes bright and alert.

"And what would an ancient warrior like you know of hunting Jabberwocks?" Nobody railed, his uffish state causing him to forget his manners.

"I know you need to beware the jaws that bite and the claws that catch!" the white-haired knight countered.

Raising the tankard in his hand, he emptied it in one go. Wiping beer-foam from his moustache, he began drunkenly regaling Nobody, and anyone else within earshot, with the chronicle of his past exploits, finishing with, "And ten years ago, I rid this very town of the Gryphon that was terrorising the farms hereabouts. Of course, that was before my knees gave out, and this backwater wasn't half as prosperous then as it is now." Here he rose unsteadily to his feet. "But I swear Sir Albus will save this town a second time, for I intend to be the one who slays the Jabberwock!"

And with that, the aged knight marched out of the inn, his armour clanking with every wobbling step, his faithful hound trotting after him.

His curiosity piqued, Nobody followed.

"Do you have a licence?" he asked the knight.

"Have it here!" the white knight said, thrusting out a gauntleted hand in which was held a crumpled scroll.

Tethered outside The Slithy Tove was the knight's brave steed. It had doubtless been a mighty charger in its day but, like the knight, the horse was patently past its prime now.

It surely didn't help that the horse's saddlebags were laden with everything from a rusty morning-star and a wooden sparring blade to bellows, a dustpan and brush, and even a bunch of turnips.

"But good Sir Knight, what makes you think you will succeed over the other beast-slayers who have gathered here to hunt the Jabberwock?" Nobody asked, giving the old nag a disparaging look.

"You mean, what do I have that they don't?"

"Yes, sir."

"I have Garm, don't I, boy?" he said, addressing the dog.

The wolfhound wagged its tail enthusiastically.

"And Garm has a sense of smell like no other. Garm will follow the monster's scent, and Tancred and I will follow Garm."

The white knight fixed the youth with a steely stare. "But I know what you're thinking, and you're right. I am not the knight I once was, and it would be remiss of me not to appoint a squire, to join me on my quest."

His bushy eyebrows rose, asking the question for him.

"Me?" gasped Nobody, taken aback.

"Young lad like you should be up to the task, and you might learn a thing or two. And I'll give you a share of the reward."

"Should we actually slay the beast."

"Should *I* slay the beast," corrected the knight, "which, of course, I shall."

"So when do we start?" asked Nobody.

The white knight looked at him askance. "Not now, that's for certain! No, only a fool would venture into that tulgey wood this late in the day. I'll be fighting fit after a good night's sleep. We set off at cockcrow!"

Cockcrow came and went, and it wasn't until the sun was halfway to its zenith that Sir Albus emerged from the hayloft where he had been sleeping off his hangover.

While Nobody made sure that the old nag was fed and watered before they set out, the knight disappeared inside The Slithy Tove again, and didn't return for over an hour.

But when he did, gyring and gimbling unsteadily along the potholed road, it was with a twinkle in his eye, a knowing finger tapping his nose, and the directions to the last place the Jabberwock had been seen.

And so they set off, the knight struggling to remain upright in Tancred's saddle, Nobody walking beside them, and the faithful wolfhound Garm running ahead, sniffing the ground for any sign of the beast.

Passing over the stone bridge and leaving the town, they turned off the track that skirted the southern reaches of the forest and headed north into the deeply wooded valley. They passed from clearing to track, to bog, to escarpment, to defile, to briar thicket, following the knight's directions and the dog's nose, until, upon hearing a commotion ahead of them, they picked up the pace and rushed towards the source of the sound, as a scream cut through the trees.

The screaming brought them to a smallholding within a clearing in the forest, and the discovery of a terrified family of four, as well as several hard, horny scales deposited in the churned-up mud of the yard, and claw marks upon a barn door.

Two pigs lay dead in their pen—"Savaged by the beast!" the farmer told them, picking another armour-like scale from where it had lodged in a fence post—and when they had determined from the man and his wife which way the Jabberwock had gone, the monster-hunters set off again.

♥

Night fell, and for all the knight had said about not wanting to pass the hours of darkness in the depths of the forest—and Nobody's dread of what might be lurking there in the gloom—that was precisely where they found themselves.

Exhausted after their day's hunting, and too far from the town to make it worth turning back now, they made camp, lighting a small fire to keep the cold—not to mention their fear of the dark—at bay, and agreed to take it in turns to watch for frumious Bandersnatches and mome raths.

Warmed by the fire, and weary from wandering through the tulgey wood, Nobody fell asleep as soon as his head hit the pack he was using as a pillow.

He was cruelly awoken from his peaceful slumber by a terrible, bestial screeching. All was still dark around him, but by the wan light of the gibbous moon that bathed the clearing where they had made their camp, he could see that Sir Albus and his dog were gone, while Tancred was stamping his hooves and snorting in agitation.

The horrible screeching continued unabated, as Nobody raced through the bracken and clawing brambles, until he came upon the knight, battling the beast beneath the spreading boughs of a bulbous-bellied Tumtum tree.

It was like a cross between a cockerel, a serpent and a gigantic bat. The creature's wattled head, which was mainly made up of a savage, tooth-lined beak, swayed atop an elongated, snake-like neck; but the beast was still only a head or two taller than the knight.

It wasn't quite the monster Nobody had imagined was terrorising the area. Hopping about on its great, bird-like feet whilst flapping its stunted wings frantically, the Jabberwock certainly didn't strike the youth as being the kind of creature that would give an experienced monster-hunter much trouble. Nonetheless, the old freelancer was making quite the meal of it, every flailing swing of his heavy sword missing the shrieking beast. Garm was barking furiously at the monster, whilst taking care to keep clear of its sharp talons.

Taking his own sword in hand Nobody joined the fray, and swinging the vorpal blade about him wildly, what he lacked in expertise he more than made up for in enthusiasm.

And slowly the tables were turned, and the three of them together—knight, squire and hound—began to overwhelm the beast, blood running from their blades and the monster's body.

Shrieking still, the Jabberwock broke from the fight. Apparently unable to fly, it wasn't able to do any more than take long, leaping hops through the forest as it attempted to flee.

Knight and squire gave chase together, determined not to let the monster escape. But the weary Sir Albus could not maintain the pace as he went clanking through the forest, and exhorted his young companion to press on after the beast, as he began to fall behind.

As the monster performed its hopping flight between the black trunks of the trees, no longer worrying whether Sir Albus was managing to keep up or not, spurred on by the faith the knight had put in him, Nobody sprinted after the Jabberwock and soon caught up with it.

Using the rotting trunk of a fallen tree as a launching-off point, he flung himself into the air as the Jabberwock reached the apex of another half-flying bound. Grabbing hold of one of the creature's large, scaly feet, Nobody hung on as, with an agitated squawk, the Jabberwock found itself suddenly dragged back down to the ground.

The youth clung on, even as the monster tried to kick him free, helplessly beating the bracken with its useless wings, whilst screeching in frustration and fear.

The old knight's clanking footsteps announced his breathless arrival. Tightening his grip on his greatsword, Sir Albus drove it through the beast's body.

Black blood welled up from the fatal wound and the creature let out an ululating death-cry that echoed eerily through the forest.

Tugging his blade free of the monster's body once more, with one clean blow he severed its hideous screaming head from its neck, silencing it.

But as the echoes of its burbling screams faded, a deeper bellow reached them through the tulgey wood, as if in answer to the monster's cry.

Nobody turned in the direction from which the horrible sound had come, and there, rising above the trees, he saw the silhouette of a tower against the lightening sky.

Garm tensed, his hackles rising, lips peeling back from teeth bared in a snarl as a rumbling growl rose from the dog's throat.

Nobody exchanged glances with the knight. The old warrior had never looked older in the brief time they had known each other. He was clearly exhausted after battling the beast.

"Go," he panted. "See what you can find."

Nobody nodded and set off towards the tower, perched atop its rocky crag, picking up the pace again, leaving the knight to recover from his encounter with the Jabberwock, and Garm licking his master's wounds.

Dawn was breaking as Nobody reached the foot of the crag. A mimsy mist rose from a burbling stream that skirted the escarpment and the rock face was thick with ferns and water-worn handholds. The youth began his ascent.

Disorientated by the trek through the forest as they had sought the Jabberwock, it was only as Nobody was scaling the crag that he realised he was climbing towards the same tumbledown tower where he had spent the night before arriving at the town. He'd had no idea that they had circled back to the hermit's home as they wandered through the tulgey wood.

And yet he was sure the burbling bellow had come from somewhere nearby. Panic seized his heart then, his first thought being that the old man was in danger.

Scrambling over the top of the escarpment, he ran to the entrance of the tower. Trying the door, and finding it unlocked, Nobody entered the building.

He was about to call out, to let the hermit know he was there, when he noticed the trapdoor open in the floor of the tower in front of him. He had not seen it the last time he had been here; it must have been closed on that occasion.

Cautiously, he approached the square hole. The suffused glow of early-morning sunlight permeated the chamber beneath.

A stone staircase wound down into the cellar. His curiosity getting the better of him once again, sword in hand, Nobody descended the worn steps. But rather than barrels of ale, or a well-stocked wine cellar, or even an alchemist's laboratory, what greeted his startled eyes was entirely unexpected.

The cellar had been divided into separate compartments by means of a series of wooden partitions. At the foot of the stairs, in the first compartment, were half a dozen straw-filled crates. Sitting within each was an egg bigger than a man's head, their shells mottled green and purple. As he made his way through the cellar, one of the curious eggs suddenly twitched within its warm bed.

Nobody froze.

The egg jerked again, and a crack appeared in its thick shell.

As the youth watched, a tiny beak pushed through the breach and was soon followed by a bulbous head that wobbled unsteadily atop a scrawny neck, and in no time at all, squatting amidst the ruins of the eggshell was what was quite clearly a baby Jabberwock.

It was an ugly little thing, and yet somehow strangely appealing at the same time.

"Who's a manxome fellow then?" Nobody cooed.

In response, the hatchling chirruped at him, fixing the youth with bulbous black eyes that reflected the morning sunlight like a puddle of lantern-oil.

The hatchling's pallid flesh was covered with the prickles of feathers-to-be.

Unable to help himself, finding that he was drawn to the tiny monster—which was currently no bigger than a young borogove—before he knew what he was doing, the youth had put away his sword and picked up the baby Jabberwock, cradling it in his arms as he stroked the drying downy fluff on the top of its disproportionately large head.

Ignoring the pungent smell coming off the creature nestled now in the crook of his arm, Nobody passed from the hatchery into a section of the cellar where a number of larger Jabberwocks were housed in cages.

The youth judged that some of them might be as much as five or six feet tall when up on their hind legs.

The yearlings whiffled and burbled and the hatchling he was carrying gave another mewling chirrup, instinctively recognising the vocalisations of its siblings.

Passing beyond another partition, Nobody felt a gentle breeze on his face and saw that the cellar had been constructed from a shallow cave within the crag. The mouth of the cave opened onto a sheer cliff, looking out over a deep gorge, but was obscured by a screen of trees on the far side, and hence kept hidden from the sight of anyone approaching the tower through the forest.

The hatchling suddenly gave a rasping squawk, which made Nobody start, and which was answered a moment later by the burbling bellow of a much larger creature, right behind him.

Turning, he came face to hideous face with the creature penned there, the brood Jabberwock bringing its huge beaked head close to his, studying him with eyes of burning flame. It was twice the size of the creature he and Sir Albus had encountered in the forest.

His heart racing, the tension in his body eased a little when he saw that the creature was secured to the wall by a chain attached to a brass collar around its neck.

Some innate instinct enabling the hatchling to recognise its parent, the infant gave another squawk. And in a moment of horrible realisation, Nobody saw the monster's burning gaze focus on the baby in his arms.

The mother gave voice to another burbling bellow and Nobody gagged at the fetid stink of rotting meat that assailed him.

It was then the hatchling bit him.

He gave an involuntary cry of pain and dropped the baby, the hatchling having taken a chunk out of the ball of his thumb with its sharp beak.

But the hatchling's bite was nothing compared to the mother's rage at seeing her offspring in jeopardy. The monster opened its huge, beaked mouth and gave a savage shriek of maternal fury.

Backing away from the monster, the young squire slowly drew his sword. But the pain in his thumb and the shock he had felt in the face of the mother's fury were forgotten in an instant, as Nobody was struck violently from behind.

He dropped to his knees, the vorpal sword falling from his fingers.

Dazed, he looked up, fearing another attack might come at any moment. His jaw went as slack as the rest of his body when, through his swimming vision, he saw the hermit standing over him, a shovel held in his hands like a mace. The same hermit whose life he had feared was at risk from the fury of a full-grown Jabberwock.

"I told you not to hunt the Jabberwock," Nobody heard the old man say, his voice sounding strangely distant. "I liked you. You were so full of youthful innocence and optimism. You hadn't been spoiled by the world yet. But it seems like you've grown up a lot in the last couple of days."

The cave-cellar resounded with the cacophonous roars of the mother monster and the distressed squawking of the caged yearlings.

Rolling on the floor, struggling to get up, Nobody reached for his sword, only for the hermit to snatch it up, out of his reach, before he could even get a hand on it.

"I didn't want things to end like this for you." The unkempt Jabberwock-keeper slowly raised the vorpal sword above his head, the shovel discarded. "But now you know too much."

Nobody's gaze met the hermit's cold stare, and so he saw the look of surprise as the old man suddenly lurched forwards, struck from behind himself, by the lashing of the agitated mother's tail.

Losing his balance, the hermit stumbled, landing the sword-blow that had been intended for Nobody against the beast's flank instead, and drawing blood between the feathers and scales.

The monster gave a screech of rage and turned on the old man.

In an instant it was done; the hermit barely had time to cry out himself before the monster's beak-like jaws took his head from his shoulders.

The rest of his body slumped to the ground, as arterial blood painted the rough stone walls claret-red.

The vorpal sword clattered to the floor again. Recovering himself, on his feet again at last, Nobody reclaimed the ancient blade and plunged it into the Jabberwock's throat. The chained beast gave another warbling cry as Nobody struck it again and again—one-two, one-two, and through and through—until the monster's cries were no more than a breathless wheezing. Raising the blade one last time, even though his arms ached with the effort, he brought it down on the monster's neck.

He heard the snicker-snack of neck bones breaking, and

the creature's hideous head rolled onto the floor, a long purple tongue lolling from its beaked maw.

♥

Hearing twigs cracking under Nobody's footsteps, Sir Albus looked up.

His delighted eyes went from the dishevelled youth's face, to the bloodstains soaking his doublet, to the hessian sack his squire cast on the ground in front of him. Opening it, he peered inside, his eyes widening in astonishment.

"You've slain the Jabberwock?" he gasped, as Garm sniffed the sack suspiciously. And then, jumping to his feet, "Come to my arms, my beamish boy!"

He threw his arms around Nobody. Then, putting the youth at arm's length again, he regarded the head of the beast he himself had killed.

"Yours is bigger than mine," Sir Albus said, looking almost disappointed, until a wide grin split his face once more, then he pulled the youth to him and hugged him again.

"Oh frabjous day!" he cried, dancing a jig on his old pins, Nobody having no choice but to join in with the dance.

"Callooh! Callay!" the old knight sang, Garm jumping up at them in excitement, and soon they were both chortling in their joy, as they fell about laughing on the forest floor at the heart of the tulgey wood.

♥

"Good Sir Knight," said the Mayor, eyeing Sir Albus warily, as he entered The Slithy Tove again with Nobody in tow. "What can we do for you?"

The officials still appeared to be taking money from those wishing to go monster-hunting in the tulgey forest.

"We're here to claim the reward," Sir Albus said, and all those present within the inn stopped what they were doing, bringing their conversations to an abrupt end, and turned their attention to what was unfolding in the middle of the bar.

The knight tossed the head of the creature he had slain onto the clerk's table, where it landed with a crash amidst the piles of paperwork, scattering quills and overturning inkwells.

"One thousand crowns, wasn't it?" the freelancer said, relishing the look of shock on the clerk's face.

"Um..." Mortsafe murmured. "Yes, that's right."

Nobody then dropped the sack he was carrying onto the table and upended it, its contents tumbling out.

The crowd of onlookers gasped.

The Mayor swore, while all his clerk managed was a strangled squeal, almost falling off his stool when he met the dead-eyed stare of the mother of monsters.

"And another two thousand crowns for this one, please," Nobody said.

Judging by his reaction, the youth's demand for more money was more shocking to the clerk than the delivery of not one, but two Jabberwock heads, and brought him back to his senses.

"Now wait a minute!" Mortsafe protested.

The not-so-white knight leaned forward across the table and said in a harsh whisper, "You can pay up, or we can expose your little money-making scheme. I killed the Gryphon, remember? I've seen for myself how much attention that brought to your manxome little town. Attention and money!"

"What are you talking about?" spluttered the Mayor, so Sir Albus turned his focus to the portly provost, who was now perspiring profusely.

"With the Gryphon dead, you took stock and saw how much coin all those heroes—coming from miles around, in the hope of killing the beast—parted company with while they were here. And you thought, wouldn't it be handy if we had another monster for all those heroes to come and kill?

"I can see how prosperous your arse-end-of-nowhere backwater has become. I expect the entire economy pretty much relies on people coming to slay the beasts, bringing with them their hangers-on and all their attendant needs: weapons; stabling; saddlers; smiths; prostitutes; beer… I wouldn't be surprised if the whole town is actually in on the plan, seeing as how it benefits everyone."

As the old knight unravelled the workings of their scheme, the Mayor and the clerk listened, their faces reddening with every revelation. And all the while his squire just stood there, a beamish smile on his cherubic face.

"It would be easy enough to fake a monster attack and leave a few scales behind at the scene of the supposed crime. Then all your tame beast-master had to do was release an immature Jabberwock into the woods—one with its wings clipped, I might add—knowing that it wouldn't prove much of a threat and that it would be soon done away with anyway, seeing as how the forest would be crawling with monster-hunters. Then it would just be a matter of who got to it first."

"You can't prove any of this!" the Mayor railed.

"Can't I?" said the knight, thrusting a piece of parchment under his nose. It was a letter Nobody had found in the hatchery, addressed to the hermit. "That's your signature, is it not, your worship?"

The Mayor blustered in indignation but could not actually think of anything to say.

"Are you threatening us?" Mortsafe seethed.

"Yes, it would rather look like that, wouldn't it?" agreed Sir Albus.

At a sideways glance from the Mayor, a pair of rough-looking militiamen stepped out of the shadows. But a fierce, frumious glare from the knight caused them to freeze and reconsider their options, as Nobody put a hand to his heirloom blade—the monster-slaying vorpal sword—sheathed at his side.

"Pay up or we'll tell all and sundry hereabouts about your deception. And there are a lot of armed men hanging around town at the moment. More monster-hunters than you have militiamen, I'll warrant. Hard-bitten men too, used to going toe-to-toe with Snarks and Bandersnatches, and the like. You wouldn't want a riot on your hands now, would you?"

"This is tantamount to blackmail!" protested the clerk.

"No, it *is* blackmail," corrected the knight.

"Very well," said the Mayor, taking three bulging bags of

coin from the coffer hidden under the table, straining with the effort.

"A pleasure doing business with you," Sir Albus said, passing the gold to Nobody, and offering the Mayor his hand. When the Mayor didn't take it, regarding it in the same way that he might look at something he had scraped off the sole of his boot after a visit to the livestock fair, Sir Albus turned the unfulfilled handshake into a sharp salute instead.

"Good day to you," he said.

The knight and his squire turned and started for the door. As they strode out into the brillig sunlight, Sir Albus called back over his shoulder: "By the way, there's now a vacancy for the hatchery job, and you'll probably be needing some new stock too."

♥

Dusk fell, drawing its crepuscular cloak over the tulgey wood, as something both manxome and frumious, with a long neck and the head of some hideous devil-fowl, lumbered through the mimsy air on large, bat-like wings, whiffling as it came.

Eyes of flame helping it find its way through the encroaching darkness, the creature homed in on the cave in the cliff face below the tumbledown tower. Landing heavily at the entrance, it dragged its great bulk into the cellar, horn-toed feet scraping through the half-rotted straw mess covering the rough stone floor.

It hesitated, sniffing the air. Something wasn't right.

Putting its beaked nose to the ground it sniffed again.

Usually there was a ready supply of meat left out for it, but there wasn't anything this night, other than a stringy corpse missing its head. And something else was wrong too.

Following its nose, the snuffling sire soon discovered the headless corpse of its mate.

A burbling rumble rose from inside its huge ribcage and the beast snorted angrily.

With the female dead, and having wolfed down the corpse in one gulp, the bull Jabberwock went galumphing back to the entrance to the cave.

But then it caught another scent on the evening breeze, the smell of roasting raths, and the beast's belly grumbled.

It might have been prevented from sating its desire to mate that night, but it could certainly satisfy another appetite.

Taking to the air again, with powerful beats of its wyvern wings, the Jabberwock set off in the direction of the town, following the mouthwatering cooking smells to the agglomeration of flickering lights in the distance.

It would dine well that night after all. And it was still fearfully hungry.

About Time

GEORGE MANN

Lucy was beginning to wish that she'd never returned.

This was supposed to be her haven, the safest of places, away from all the madness of the real world; a place she'd always been able to escape to. But now... well, now *this*.

And she'd only come here to say goodbye.

Lucy had first discovered Wonderland during a long summer's day shortly after her ninth birthday, when, playing outside, she'd lost her footing and tumbled head-first down a small hole behind the potting shed in her grandma's back garden. Then, she'd been terrified to find herself popping out into such a strange, ridiculous land—and indeed, surrounded by such outlandish company—but she soon developed quite a fondness for the place. She'd decided to explore, searching every nook, cranny and warren of the unusual realm, meeting each of its residents—even the scary ones—until the place became like a second home to her. Adventures ensued, and Lucy found herself seeking any excuse to go and visit her grandma at the weekend, or after school—largely so she could dive with abandon into the secret hole and pay a visit to all of her outrageous friends. She'd never told anyone about it, of course—not even her grandma. Wonderland had been *her* secret, her special place.

Wonderland had been there for her during the difficult years that followed—getting used to having a baby brother, going up to big school, her first broken heart—but in recent years, life had… well, it had started to get in the way. There was so much studying to do, and the other girls were always pestering her on WhatsApp, and then there was the swimming club, and her drawings, and her friend Chris, who also happened to be a boy…

And so she'd let things drift, and although she dutifully continued to visit her grandma—the family had even taken to staying over at the house on a Saturday night, to give Lucy's mum a chance to fuss over the now-elderly lady—she'd not ventured out into the garden for many months. Now, at the age of fourteen, she'd decided that, as wonderful as it all was, it was time she made a break with the childish things of her past. So, her teddy bears had gone into the attic, her dolls had gone down to the Barnardo's shop, and she'd come here to bid a final farewell to the Mock Turtle, the Knave of Hearts and the Cheshire Cat, and all those others with whom she'd spent so much time as a child. She knew they'd be sad, but a grown-up girl couldn't go on spending her life visiting a place like *that*, could they? It was just too… whimsical, too juvenile, and while she would cherish the memories, she had more important things to worry about now.

Only… she hadn't expected to find the place had changed quite so much since her last visit. What was once bright and vibrant had become dull and morose. The very atmosphere had changed. The skies were overcast and brooding, the trees groaned and creaked in the wind, having shed all of their colourful leaves, and everyone seemed to have holed themselves up in their homes. Even the Cheshire Cat's grin had reversed itself into a sulky frown: the creature was looking at her now, peering down from the window ledge above the Queen of Hearts' palace door. She could feel the rumbling footsteps of something moving around inside the castle.

"There's something *big* in there," she said. "Something *mighty.*"

"Oh, mighty, mighty," said the Cat, swishing its tail. "Might he ever forgive you?"

Lucy offered the Cat a sharp glance. "Forgive me? Whatever for? I've only just arrived."

"Exactly," purred the Cat. "You're late."

Lucy sighed and shook her head. The problem—she'd been led to understand—was that a monster had chosen to take up residence here in Wonderland. A monster so fierce, and so terrifying, that none dare oppose it, even when it had swept amongst the pack and plucked a wriggling Queen of Hearts from her throne, taking her prisoner and declaring itself the new king.

"What does it want?" she'd asked the Knave, upon finding him wandering alone in the woods, his heart broken.

"What do any of us want?" had been the Knave's only reply.

Now, she stood before the portcullis door leading into the castle, struggling to find a way inside. Why she'd decided to confront this terrible monster—of whom the inhabitants of Wonderland all appeared to be terrified—she did not know. Only… she supposed it had something to do with her knowing she couldn't say goodbye to them all without at least trying to put things right. She didn't think she could bear abandoning them all to the rule of some terrible tyrant. Or at least, a terrible tyrant they didn't already know.

"Is there *nothing* you can do to help?" said Lucy, glaring up at the Cat.

"I'm *already* doing nothing to help," said the Cat. "But I admit I'm growing somewhat impatient and feel the urge to intercede."

"Well, don't let me stop you," said Lucy, rolling her eyes.

The Cat's lips curled for a moment, hinting at its erstwhile grin. And then the portcullis door vanished, and Lucy—who'd been leaning against it—tumbled through into the forecourt beyond.

She picked herself up, dusting down the front of her dress. "You could have warned me!" she scolded, but the Cat had already gone.

Sighing, Lucy walked across the forecourt towards the open door that led into the castle interior. Noises were spilling out from inside: a hiss, a groan, and the stomping of feet. Whatever was in there was *big*.

Lucy straightened her back, lifted her chin, and strode through the door.

She found herself in a gloomy passageway that encircled the castle's Great Hall. Ahead, the passage opened out onto the north end of the hall, and here, velvet drapes hung from the ceiling, obscuring Lucy's view. She crept forward, confident that—given the clamour being made by the occupant in the hall—she was unlikely to be overheard.

"*You* cannot govern a realm. Just think about it for a moment. All the dreary day-to-day issues of state. All the peasants and supplicants." This shrill voice, Lucy knew, belonged to the Queen of Hearts.

"Yes," said the monster in reply, its voice low and even, "but at least I'll get to lop off their heads."

A moment's pause.

"Well, I don't suppose I can argue with that," said the Queen. Another pause. "Can I watch?"

"I'll think about it," replied the monster.

Still hiding behind the velvet drapes, Lucy frowned. Who was this monster who had so brazenly usurped the throne? Where had he come from? There had to be another way in and out of Wonderland, Lucy decided—one that she wasn't aware of. Yet, in all her years of visiting the place, she'd never once encountered another soul who claimed to have come from the world above, like her. Oh, there were tales of that one girl, years and years ago, but Lucy had always presumed she'd visited via the same hole in the garden—a previous occupier of her grandma's house, perhaps. Yet this creature had found its way in, all the same. Had deposed the Queen of Hearts and cast a morose pall over all of Wonderland.

Now she was here, though, she had no idea what she was going to do. *Reason* with it? It didn't sound particularly reasonable. She couldn't fight it—she was no knight, and she'd never really believed in solving problems with her fists, even when dealing with her troublesome little brother, Peter. Yet she remained adamant—she couldn't allow it to continue. Even though the Queen of Hearts had always scared her—she was, after all, a rather *furious* monarch—Lucy knew that her right and proper place was on the throne.

She took a deep breath, and stepped out from behind the curtain…

…to see a massive, hulking, lizard-like creature lounging on the dais where the throne used to be. It had green, scaly skin, and its fingers ended in sharp black talons—one of which it was using to pick food from between its teeth. It had diamond-shaped bone spurs running along its spine, a bloated pale belly, and huge jaws that hinged open like those of a Tyrannosaurus Rex. Dotted in its skull were a smattering of eyes, reminiscent of a spider's, which all shone a bright, lurid red in the gloomy light of the Great Hall. Finally, its feet ended in massive cloven hooves. Close by, looking furious, was the Queen of Hearts, trapped inside on oversized gilded birdcage that was suspended from the ceiling, close to the monster's head.

"Y… y… you!" blurted Lucy, in stunned recognition. She stared at the beast for a moment, rooted to the spot, feeling the hairs prickle on the nape of her neck. Now that she had seen it, she knew precisely what it was, and exactly where it had come from: it was the monster from under her bed.

This was the creature that had haunted her dreams for so many years, whose glowing eyes had pierced the darkness of her bedroom whenever she was alone. The monster who had tormented her whenever she'd wanted to get up to go to the loo, or when she woke up in the dead of night to find the house was silent, save for its rasping breath, coming from somewhere beneath her.

For years, she'd believed wholeheartedly that this creature had loitered under her bed each night after dark, and if she was truthful with herself (which is a difficult thing for a teenager to be), she had to admit that it was only in the last year she'd recognised her fear for what it was—the overactive imagination of a child.

And yet, now it was here, in Wonderland, fully manifest and larger than life. And what had it done? Taken the Queen prisoner and made everyone's lives a misery. It was pretty terrifying, too!

Trembling, Lucy stepped forward and cleared her throat.

From her perch, the Queen of Hearts looked down, raising her eyebrows in surprise. "*You*?" she cried, echoing Lucy's earlier sentiment.

The monster looked up at Lucy with an air of apparent disinterest, and then returned to picking its teeth. Had it even recognised her?

"Your Majesty," said Lucy, regarding the Queen. "I'm here to help."

"Humph!" said the Queen, with a shake of her head. "I

can hardly see what *you* might do." Her voice was shrill, her tone typically ungrateful.

"Fine. Be like that," said Lucy, turning about on her heel. She made as if to walk away.

"No, no! Do not be too hasty in your retreat," said the Queen, her tone softening considerably. "It's simply that we haven't seen you in such a long while."

Lucy turned again on the spot. She felt a stab of regret at the truth of the Queen's words. "I've been busy," she said.

The Queen nodded, unconvinced. "Busy? Well, as you can see, you're not the only one." She gestured towards the monster, who'd been following the conversation with feigned apathy.

"Busy, yes. Busy!" The monster stopped picking its teeth for a moment, and looked down at Lucy, offering her a wicked grin. Then, looking round at the Queen, it reached over and flicked her cage with the tip of its claw, causing it to rock back and forth wildly. The Queen, clutching the bars, looked thoroughly nauseated.

"Busy making a nuisance of himself," came a familiar voice from over Lucy's shoulder. She turned to see the broad, downturned mouth of the Cheshire Cat.

"So, you've decided to join us at last," said Lucy.

"Kettles and pots," replied the Cat. "Pots and kettles."

Lucy sighed. She'd been racking her brain, but the Queen had been right—although she desperately *wanted* to help, what *could* she do in the face of such a terrible creature? She decided diplomacy would be her first port of call. She stepped closer, peering up at the terrifying visage of the monster. It had returned to picking its teeth, and Lucy saw, with a shudder, that there were bits of what looked disturbingly like playing cards lodged in the gaps between them. "Look here," she said, her voice quavering. "What exactly is it you want?"

The monster seemed to consider this for a moment, its brow furrowing. Then its expression brightened. "More food would be good," it said. "And perhaps some tea."

"Monsters don't drink tea!" said Lucy.

"No," agreed the monster. "But kings do. And I'm the King of Wonderland now." It glared at her defiantly. "So, tea it shall be." It licked its lips. "With a further course of little girl."

"I'm not a little girl anymore," she said, but she could hear the tremor in her voice.

"Oh, but you *are*," said the monster.

Lucy swallowed, but her mouth was dry. All those churned-up feelings were flooding back: the paralysing fear of the *thing* curled under her bed; her worry that her toes might poke out from beneath the bedspread in the night and she'd wake up in the morning to find them nibbled away; her certainty that if she even tried to get up to go to the loo, she'd get dragged under there, to the nether realm where the monster lurked, where all children were dragged to and eaten if they were brave or stupid enough to abandon the safety of their beds after dark.

She forced herself to think more like a grown-up and pressed on with her questioning. "But why would you want to be king? Just think of all that *work* you'll have to do. The meetings. The *admin*. The petitions. The judgements and pronouncements. Governing a realm can't be an easy job. It's not all snacks and tea, you know."

"Hear, hear!" bellowed the Queen, whose cage had finally come to rest again. She was slumped on the cage floor, her knuckles white where her fingers still clung desperately to the gilded bars. "Tea parties are one thing, but what about all the people, hmmm? They're a terrible burden. Terrible."

The monster shook his head. "I'll just eat them all." It hooked a rather large morsel of playing card on the tip of its claw, wiggling it loose from between two front teeth, and then, after peering at it for a moment, popped it back into its mouth and swallowed. Lucy thought she was going to be sick.

"But there are better snacks, surely?" she said. "And besides, if you kill everyone you'll just have even more work to do, because there'll be no one left to command. You don't need to be king to have a full belly. There must be something more you want."

The monster gave a satisfied sigh and rubbed its stomach.

"*Of course* there's something more it wants," said the Cheshire Cat.

Lucy turned to peer up at it. It was curled around the shoulders of a suit of armour, tail lazily describing a figure eight in the air. "Well?"

"What does *anyone* want?" replied the Cat.

"That's just what the Knave of Hearts said."

"A rare moment of insight," said the Cat. "But that doesn't answer the question."

Lucy shrugged. "Power, fortune…"

"Oh, dearie me," said the Cat. "Now we begin to see the truth of the matter."

Lucy frowned. As usual, the Cat wasn't making any sense. Unless… "You can't mean… love and attention?" said Lucy. "Recognition?"

The Cat grinned. "It seems we're not the only ones who've been forgotten, are we, Your Majesty?"

"Oh, no. I think not," said the Queen.

Lucy looked from one to the other, and then back at the monster. Was this really all *her* fault? She'd been so busy growing up, living her life, that she'd barely spared a thought for the people down here, in Wonderland. Let alone the monster under the bed. She'd assured herself it wasn't real—how could it be?—and, as if to prove her point, she'd seen no sign of the creature. She'd slept soundly, safe in the knowledge that she'd put her childish imagination away, and that had been that. And now, to discover that, all along, the monster had been here instead, trying to create a new life for itself, trying to get *noticed…*

Was that really all it wanted? To be believed in again? She supposed the Cheshire Cat was right—wasn't that all anyone ever really wanted?

"Look," she said, waving her arm before the monster to get its attention (it didn't seem particularly interested, she had to admit), "it's all right. You can come home. Back under the bed where you belong. Everything can get back to normal again."

The monster sighed and shook its head. "No."

"No? What do you mean, *no*? Isn't that what you want?"

"*No!*" said the monster, more forcefully this time. Lucy caught a waft of its breath, full in her face, and had to turn away at the sour stench of rotten… card. "I'm staying here. Back there I'll only be forgotten about again. At least here, I can scare people." It offered Lucy a menacing look. "Or eat them," it added, with a lick of its lips.

Lucy tried to remain calm. If the monster had really wanted to eat her, it'd had plenty of opportunity over the years. It didn't seem likely that would change now… did it? Unless it was feeling resentful…

"But if you eat them all, you'll be back to square one. There'll be no one left to be scared of you," she said.

The monster seemed to think this over for a moment, then it waved its claw dismissively. "I'll cross that bridge when I come to it."

Lucy was kicking herself. How could she have allowed this to happen? And why did growing up have to be so hard? All she wanted was to know that everyone was going to be okay. To know that Wonderland and all its denizens—and yes, she supposed, the monster from under her bed, too—were all safe and happy. If she knew that, then she'd be able to go off and get on with things, without having to worry. She needed a chance to grow up, but that didn't mean she had to stop believing, that she wanted to forget about everything, all the wonderful, magical things she'd seen, all the experiences she'd had. Just that there were other things she needed to think about now, as well.

It just didn't seem fair. She'd always kept Wonderland's

secret. She'd always protected them—even when the gardener came around to cut her grandma's hedges back, and had pointed out the hole, offering to fill it in. She couldn't keep it up forever, though, could she? She couldn't be here all the time.

And that's when it hit her. She didn't have to. Not any longer.

"I've got to go," she blurted out suddenly, causing an eruption of frustrated noises from within the gilded cage. "I'm sorry."

"Go? GO? You can't just up and *go*! Get back here at once, young lady, and face up to your responsibilities!"

"Don't worry," said Lucy, "I'll fix everything. I have an idea."

Lucy could hear the Queen snorting in frustration as she turned on her heel and walked from the castle—out into the wilds of Wonderland, along the forest path, across the meadow, and back out through the hole, until, moments later, she emerged behind the potting shed in her grandma's garden.

Here, back in the real world, the light was beginning to fade, and she could see through the window into the dining room, where the rest of her family were busying themselves around the dinner table, setting places and half-heartedly bickering. She glanced back at the hole, certain that she could still hear the echo of the Queen's enraged bellowing, and wondered for a moment if she was doing the right thing. Then, concluding that she didn't really have a choice in the matter, she dusted herself down and went to join the others for dinner.

♥

After dinner—during which her little brother had spent the whole meal waffling on about a new cartoon he'd seen, and accidentally kicking her under the table because of his inability to sit still—she retreated upstairs to read. She liked it here, at her grandma's house, and had always felt at home, although the older she got, the more annoying it was to have to share a room with Peter.

"It's only for one night," her mum would say, stroking Lucy's hair, curling it back behind her ear. "Think of your grandma. You can manage."

For the most part, her mum was right; and besides, Peter was a lot younger, and went to bed earlier, so was usually asleep by the time Lucy got up there. It was this that had given her the idea.

Soon enough, the time came for Peter to turn in. Lucy wished him goodnight and took her book downstairs to sit with the adults for a while. Her grandma was asleep in her chair, the remains of an After Eight mint on her lips. Her mum and dad were watching some awful drama about people-smuggling, and so Lucy kept her nose in the fantasy novel she was reading, although she found it hard to think of anything else but the Queen of Hearts in her gilded cage, and the monster from under the bed, picking bits of foot soldiers from between its teeth.

As soon as seemed reasonable—and after she was certain her brother would be fast asleep—Lucy bid goodnight to her parents and crept off to bed. Peter lay asleep in bed, his duvet tossed to one side, foot jutting nonchalantly over the side of the mattress. Here, she knew, was a child who had never wondered about the monster under the bed. Probably because it had always been too busy terrorising Lucy.

Well, it was time for that to change, because, if there was one thing Lucy was certain about, it was that all children, at some point, have to believe in monsters.

Carefully, working only by the watery light of the moon slanting in under the curtains, she formed her pillows into an approximation of her body and covered these with her duvet, to give the impression she was curled up asleep in her bed. Then, safe in the knowledge that the monster was, in fact, keeping himself busy elsewhere, she lay down on the floor between the two beds, and shuffled herself quietly beneath Peter's.

It was dusty under there—she supposed her grandma wasn't really up to hoovering these days—nevertheless, she shimmied under until she felt the cold wall against her leg and knew that Peter wouldn't be able to see her. Then, steadying her breathing, she reached up and raked her nails across the bottom of the wooden slats.

At first, everything in the room remained silent. She did it again, louder this time, and she felt as much as heard Peter's weight shift on the bed. The springs groaned above her head. She scratched at the boards again.

"H... hello?" Peter's voice was quiet, tentative. "Is there anybody there?"

She waited for a moment, and then scratched again.

"Who is that?"

Lucy made her best "monster" sound, which was halfway between a snort and a groan, and it hurt the back of her throat to do so. She nearly spluttered on a mouthful of dust.

"Lucy?"

Peter shifted again on the bed. She could sense him peering under the bed now, and she turned her face towards the wall, holding her breath and hoping he wouldn't notice her.

"Lucy?"

Her lungs were burning, but she held on. After a moment, she heard Peter lie back in his bed. She reached up and scratched again.

"Whatever you are, I'm trying to sleep, so you'll just have to *stop*," said Peter. His voice was trembling. Lucy felt a sudden surge of affection for the boy, comingling with a sense of guilt. Should she really be doing this? "But tomorrow, we can have a proper conversation, okay?"

Lucy grinned. She scratched again at the wooden slats, more gently this time.

She gave it half an hour, before carefully sliding out from beneath the bed, dusting herself down, and slipping into her own bed, a broad grin on her face—almost as broad as that of the Cheshire Cat.

♥

The following morning, after breakfast, Lucy was sitting alone in the kitchen, drinking a cup of tea and scrolling through her Instagram feed. Her dad had popped out to fetch the paper—she couldn't understand why this was still a thing, when he had a perfectly good internet connection—

and her mum was helping her grandma to have a bath.

She heard Peter sidle into the room. He pulled out a chair beside her and sat down. She could sense him fiddling with his hands, nervously. She looked up. “Everything okay, kiddo?”

He looked at her, opened his mouth as if he was about to say something, and then shook his head. “Yeah, all good.”

“You know you can ask me anything, don’t you?” said Lucy. “It’s okay. I won’t tell Mum.”

Peter chewed his bottom lip for a moment. “Well… um… did you hear anything last night? In our room?”

“What sort of thing?” said Lucy.

“A kind of scratching sound, and some… breathing.”

“Oh, was I snoring again? I’m sorry—”

“No, it wasn’t that! It was coming from under my bed.”

Lucy grinned. “Ohhh! Right. That’ll be the monster.”

“What? Now you’re just being silly. Mum’s told you not to wind me up, Lucy.”

She put her phone down and laid a hand on top of his. “Don’t worry,” she said. “He’s not *that* kind of monster. Not really. Although he can be a bit grumpy sometimes.”

“So you *did* hear it?” said Peter, wide-eyed.

“Oh, I’ve known about him for *years*,” she said. “He’s always been around. Sometimes he’s here, and sometimes he’s at home. But all he needs is a bit of attention—a little chat every now and then. Nothing to worry about.”

Peter was drumming his fingers on the tabletop, excited now. “Seriously?”

“*Seriously*. But don’t tell the grown-ups, because they

don't believe in things like monsters anymore. But we know better, don't we?"

"Yeah!"

Lucy licked her lips. Now the time had come, she wasn't entirely sure how she felt about it. But she knew it was the right thing to do. "There's something else, too," she said. "Pop your shoes on. I need to show you something, out in the garden. You're not going to *believe* it…"

Upstairs, Lucy's mother turned away from the window and smiled.

"Mum, Lucy's taking Peter down to the hole behind the potting shed."

Alice was sitting on the edge of her bed. She met her daughter's eye and gave a long, happy sigh. "It's about time," she said.

Smoke 'em if You Got 'em

ANGELA SLATTER

The church is enormous; blocky, white-washed adobe stark against the red dirt. There are outbuildings, too, making up the compound: a barn, two smaller structures that might be a dormitory and school, cottage, outhouse, chicken coop, a smokehouse, and a well with a steepled roof. Alice is just guessing, of course; she can't know for sure unless she goes down there, which she won't because it's not her goal. All this is surrounded by a high wall.

Alice is up on the tree-covered ridge. A train line, newish, runs beside that high wall. If she turns her head to the right, squints real hard, she can just about spot Queen's Gambit and, further along, the stacks of the smelter that services the silver mine. She'll follow those tracks that link so many little towns together. As she watches, an engine—painted black and silver—clatters past. It draws a single carriage with *Gambit* in green and gold letters on the crimson siding. The sound reaches her, crisp in the autumn-cool air.

Across the square of the compound small figures dash back and forth, all colours, and she wonders at the varied mix. What she's grown used to seeing in this America are children, mostly brown, stolen away from their families to be washed in godliness. To prepare them for positions of subservience in life, as if that's what the god on the cross intended for them, and the men and women in crow's-wing black were put here on earth to enforce that.

Alice glances at her own pale skin; it never burns or tans no matter how long she's in the sun. A boon of sorts from her time in Wonderland, she guesses. She's like Persephone with the pomegranate seeds, only she's not condemned to stay in Hades, but to carry it around with her wherever she goes, a tiny bitter fortress inside her, like the unsuspected poison in the heart of an apple.

Another flash of movement: a tall ebony-clad figure comes out of the front doors of the church. He stops abruptly as if he sees her, even though she's still as a stone up on the ridge. He shades his eyes with a hand despite the broad-brimmed black hat that looks like a dark halo. He calls over his shoulder, words that don't travel up to Alice, and a woman appears, short, stocky, white blouse, light-blue long skirt. She shepherds the congregation of lost and abandoned young like ducklings into one of the smaller buildings. The priest stares a few moments longer, then follows.

Alice thinks how big the church is, almost a cathedral. How many bodies are likely to worship here on this edge of Arizona? Queen's Gambit is over the way, sure, and she supposes folk on outlying farms will travel to make sure their souls are kept clean in case of the unexpected inevitable. She's found that religion is worn here like a raincoat, on and off at convenience.

In the pocket-pouch of her tunic—a weird fawn-coloured melding of linen and fur, draped over dirty-cream canvas trousers and a shirt the colour of old blood—the thing is quiet. The strange fleshy compass, cut edge still pink where it was sheared off in the closing of the portal between worlds; the only thing of himself he left behind. There's just the occasional pulse—a twitch to indicate that what she's hunting came this way, but it's so light, so feeble. Too many years of experience tell her that what she's looking for is no longer around, not even close by.

Yet the trail and her information led *this way*. The stories put her quarry *here* and she's got no other choice but to follow. She gets closer every time, missing him by less at each location. One day she'll catch up. Alice settles her tan-coloured Derby more firmly over the blond hair tucked underneath, the fringe kept back by a black velvet band that's worn bald in parts.

"Hup," she says to the brown horse, giving him the gentlest of urges with her heels, and he ambles on. Alice's stomach rumbles with hunger. She's thinner than she should be, and can't really afford to lose much more weight. Soon, if she turns side-on, she'll disappear like a card-person. Wouldn't that be a joke? To escape Wonderland and end up like that?

♥

Queen's Gambit is kind of big, maybe kind of small. *No*, thinks Alice, *it's neither one nor the other, something in between*. Almost like it's not quite true, but is on the verge of becoming so; *will* become so if given the right chance, whatever that might be. It's precisely the sort of place *he*'d have sought out: porous, unfinished, somewhere he could slip between the cracks.

People are moving across the wide avenues of packed earth: women in dresses with irrationally large skirts; men, the very old and the very young only—presumably the middling are working the mine. Alice remembers London streets from her childhood, from before she was stolen. She thinks of thin, tall houses stretching vertically because horizontally was simply not an option. She thinks of narrow lanes, so tightly woven that there hardly seemed enough room for air, let alone bodies.

She thinks of the lack of true light in that great city, how seldom the sun broke through the industrial clouds. Here it's entirely different: seemingly so bright that nothing can be hidden. That's a lie for sure and she knows it.

The saloon is like any other, maybe a little more rickety with what looks like, from a certain angle, a lean to the left. *The Rabbit's Foot* is emblazoned on the signage in tall red letters outlined in gold; that paint's kept fresh, but the wood of the façade is dry and splintered, bleached back to dead grey. Only superficial touches, then, like too much makeup on an old whore. Alice thinks she'll find some of them inside too, they're like decor that never changes from place to place, but the older they get the less the glamours cast by wigs, cosmetics and corsets adhere to the body.

She hitches her horse to the rail over a brim-full trough, and goes up the steps to the sounds of the beast's slurping.

The floorboards are bare, but the bar itself is made of imposing and expensive polished wood; there is a wall of glasses behind it and a mirror behind that. The curtains are red velvet, with gold tassels, same colour scheme as the paintwork outside and in. But Alice can see wisps of cobwebs from the crystal chandeliers, and dust wheeling away from the drapes as a woman pushes past, taking drinks to a group of dour-looking men.

There's a boy serving at the bar, hardly old enough to sprout a moustache. Three, maybe four hairs bristle across his top lip; he's eleven, twelve at most. Alice weaves towards him between the tables and chairs; clientele is thin on the ground, but it is morning after all. The few women hanging over the furniture look tired, bare-faced, their petticoats and housedresses wilted from age and wear. Apart from the young barkeep, there's an old man at the pianola, chugging out a tune that's too jaunty for his desultory peddling.

"Whiskey," says Alice to the boy who eyes her; he's wearing pinstriped trousers, white shirt with the sleeves rolled up as if it's meant for someone larger, and a fancy vest, navy brocade with golden dragons embroidered on it, so fine that it has to be a hand-me-down. All he needs is a bowler hat and a cigar; in a big city, he'd have both, no question. Alice continues, "The cheaper the better."

The boy doesn't answer. He's got an ancient gaze and she wonders how long he's been working here. Alice bounces a coin on the counter and the boy catches it with one hand, makes it disappear with a magician's dexterity. He produces a shot glass and upends a bottle so generic she doesn't recognise the name. The label looks handwritten. Alice throws the liquor back, finds it doesn't burn any more than usual. She lifts an eyebrow, and the boy refills. Alice takes her time with this one, before she asks her questions.

"I'm looking for someone."

Still, the boy says nothing.

Alice pulls a daguerreotype out of her pocket-pouch—her fingers brush the left-behind furred object, recoiling even with familiarity—and holds the image up where he can't help but see it. It's heavy, a copper-plate image in a neat stamped-metal case. "Little fellow, spruce, white hair, button nose. Snappy dresser, walks with a slight limp."

She came across the simulacrum in Chicago a year or two ago as she followed the pulse of the compass, the trail of missing children. Its creator, a widow with two small daughters, had met the subject in a park, had liked the man's features and fancy dress sense so much she'd invited him for a sitting, hung the portrait on her wall. She had liked him so much, in fact, that she took him in as a boarder then bed-warmer for two months. Then one morning the nattily dressed boarder left, taking the little girls with him. No trace could be found of them by any law enforcement agency; of course, no one but Alice knew of the pattern, the connections. No one else gathered information the way Alice did or kept quite such an intricate network of informants. Word led her to the woman, and Alice heard, for such news travels on swift wings, that the woman had killed herself soon after they spoke.

The boy tilts his head, gaze flat, considers the picture. However, he shakes his head.

"Right," says Alice equably. She knows a liar when she sees one, but she won't pick a fight right now. She hasn't lasted this long, surviving this world and the other, without developing a deep store of patience. "Where might I find a doctor? Must be one hereabouts."

"You feelin' poorly?" The boy speaks at last and his voice is an assault on the ears. Alice doesn't wince, though she wants to. The twang is harsh as a train applying its brakes too fast and hard, the volume unmodulated.

"Nope, just want to talk with them." Alice has invariably found that each time she's missed her quarry, the next most useful port of call is always the local doctor. Physicians always keep more secrets than priests.

The boy gives a long pause. "Doctor Reine's almost at the end of town. Follow the main street, little blue house with a white picket fence."

"Thank you."

"Doc's a good person," he says, as if it might guilt Alice out of any ill intent.

"I'm sure they are." Alice puts her empty glass on the bar. "Thank you kindly."

She leaves the horse tethered at the trough, deciding he deserves more of a rest. People are still milling across the thoroughfare in a kind of dance, no one really paying attention to the newcomer, or at least not appearing to do so.

Alice walks down the street, taking in the buildings: general store, feed and seed, seamstress, a stable and blacksmith, a boarding house, a telegraph office. There's a small church propped between two bigger structures and she wonders why it's there when that great big cathedral is not so far away; then again, faith has its different stripes. There's a jail, too, where she catches sight of a man's florid face pressed against the window, bald head, drooping brown moustache, narrowed eyes, chequered shirt under a black leather vest, gold star shining on his chest. She nods, tips her hat, keeps on pacing; he doesn't acknowledge her. And there are houses, more and more as she gets further away from the saloon.

Alice is careful: she sometimes still looks like a young girl, because time moved differently in Wonderland and she was there long enough for it to affect her, to stop her clock or slow it at least (*I'm late, I'm late, I'm late*). Something she learned, though, on the other side, was how to change her face, make it a little older, just enough to turn aside glances; she doesn't do it all the time, mind, because it's tiring. She keeps a weather eye out, does Alice, always wary of men and women who pay her too much mind, who touch her arm or hand or shoulder or back in a certain way. She carries a Colt Peacemaker in the holster by her hip. Eventually, the crowd drops away entirely and the stretch of street before her is deserted.

So yes, Alice is careful and not stupid, but she is tired. She's been in the saddle for days, weeks, months, she's been hungry and thirsty and sometimes damned near lost. Now she's had two whiskeys on an empty stomach, and she's wandering in a strange town, and whoever is behind her is, to give them credit, impressively silent.

She doesn’t know a thing until that sliver of a second just after they rabbit punch her and just before everything turns to black.

♥

“Fucking hell.” Alice doesn’t swear often, but she figures this is an occasion that calls for it. The base of her skull is throbbing and even her eyes hurt.

“Ah. Awake, are we?” The voice is low, bad-whiskey rough, but somehow comforting. A woman, though that’s hardly distinguishable from the tones. Alice blinks and blinks and blinks but there’s a light above her that’s blinding. She’s lying down on an uncomfortable bed or table or weird concoction of both. An arm goes around her shoulders and helps her to sit a little; a tin cup is held to her lips. “Drink this.”

Something bitter lemon and so fizzy the bubbles almost make her sneeze, but Alice manages to swallow it all down. She starts to feel better pretty quickly, or at least less awful. She swings her legs over the edge of the whatever she’s sitting on and sways.

“You gonna stay upright? If you’re gonna puke or fall, try to let me know. Here, have a bucket.”

The item in question is old and has clearly been used for the purpose before, and washed less well than one might prefer. The smell makes Alice think she *will* puke, thank you very much indeed, even though she probably wasn’t going to before… she pushes the thing away.

"Well, okay then." The woman hands the receptacle to someone standing beside her. Alice gets her eyes to focus, recognises the boy from The Rabbit's Foot, and glares.

"Did you do this to me?"

He nods.

"Then brought me here?"

Again, a nod.

"But you knew I was coming here anyway."

"Didn't want you to hurt the doc," he mutters and looks away.

"Jesus."

"Jesse, you head back to the saloon. Someone'll be looking for you, and you know Old Alston will have told Sheriff Dawkins a stranger was asking questions. You hear anyone's coming this way, you get back here lickety-split. Go on now."

The boy scurries out and Alice takes her first good look at the woman.

She's tall and raw-boned, rangy, and she's lighting a hand-rolled cigarette. Soon blueish smoke is making a halo around her head. A green skirt hangs low on slim hips, and her black shirt is baggy; she could do with the attention of a good seamstress. She's thin in the same way as Alice: too much to do, too little time to do it in, and feeding oneself falls by the wayside. There's an apron over the top of it all, which is white and washed, but there are long-term stains resident in the weave. *Blood*, thinks Alice, and her hand moves for the six-shooter even though she *knows* the woman's a doctor, blood's no surprise. The surprise is that the holster at her hip isn't empty. She takes her fingers away.

The woman grins with a wide mouth; her teeth are very white, tombstone-shaped. Her hair is a mix of red and silver, though for all the age her face shows she might be anywhere from thirty to sixty. In her hand is the daguerreotype, which she shakes as if needing to draw attention. "Ain't never found anything to fear from a woman who's had something to do with this fella. They're always looking for help in one shape or another."

"I'm looking for *him*. I find him and a lot fewer women will be needing help."

"I can believe it." Doc nods, then says, "That's quite the accent you've got there. Not from around these parts."

"Not even close." Alice shakes her head, feels nauseous, regrets it.

"Sorry about Jesse. Wish I could say he doesn't think, but he does, only decision-making ain't his strong point."

"Well, his heart's in the right place, I guess. Pity about his fists."

"Yeah, he's strong for such a squirt." Doc smiles fondly. "Jesse's a good kid, really. He tries hard."

"He's yours?"

"Lord, no. Orphan boy. Started out at the mission, but got hisself a job at the saloon as soon as he could see over the bar." She puts out her hand, which Alice takes, finding the grip firm. "I'm Mehitabel Reine."

"Alice."

If Doc Reine thinks it's strange there's no last name offered, she doesn't say anything. Alice jerks her chin at the cigarette between the woman's long fingers. "Got a spare?"

The doc fishes one from the pocket of her skirt and hands it over, a wry grin quirking her lips. "You look a little young, but then again"—she tilts her head—"maybe not. In some lights, from some angles..."

"I'm older than I look." Alice leans forward, the tip of the rollie dipping into the flame of Doc's Vesta match, and draws breath through it. The smoke zips into her lungs and she holds it there a while, savouring the bitterness.

She takes a second puff, at last looking around the room: a doctor's surgery for sure. She's on a high, leather-covered examination table. There's a desk against which the doctor leans, a chair pushed off to the side, shelves heavy with books, glass cabinets filled with silver instruments, a bench scattered with pestles and mortars, tiny blue bottles, all manner of things for mixing medicines. And there's another bench against the far wall that's lined with specimen jars, the forms inside floating in some sort of fluid.

"That accent," says Mehitabel again. She waves the daguerreotype. "Only heard something like that once before, neat little fella with a limp."

"Really?" In Alice's pocket the compass kicks at her, a protest, something fearful about the motion. She pulls it out, says, "He's missing this." It's a single toe, covered in white fur, large, dangling from a leather thong. "What's he calling himself nowadays?"

Doc eyes the toe, blinks uncertainly. "Jack Hart."

Alice snorts, puts the toe away. "I call him *Rabbit*."

"Rabbit?"

"When I'm being polite."

"And when you're not?"

"You don't want to know. He still around?" But she knows the answer from the trembling thing in her tunic. Alice has figured out, over the long years, that it knows when its owner is in danger of being found, just like it knows when he's close. It can't stop itself from reacting.

Doc Reine shakes her head. "Gone almost two years."

Alice closes her eyes tightly for a few seconds. "If he's not here, then I'd best be getting along."

"Don't be too hasty. He left behind friends." There's a warning tone in Doc's voice. "Left a mess behind, too."

"Always does."

But the doctor's not finished. She pushes away from the desk and paces to where the specimen jars catch sun from the window, gestures for her patient to join her. Alice takes a tentative step, finds she's steady enough, and reaches the bench top without either vomiting or fainting. As she gets closer the toe begins to thud and thump in the pocket-pouch.

"The first girl carried all the way through. Baby didn't live. After that, any girl who'd been with him came to me. Didn't want their parents to know. Look."

"I need to go. I need to get after him before the trail gets even colder..."

But whatever Alice might have said is lost as she *looks*. At first she's confused, then she begins to make out details. Foetuses, curled in on themselves, not carried to term but far enough along that their features are identifiable as mostly human...

It's the ears and tails that set them apart. Rabbit ears, crunched and crumpled to fit in the jars, the fluffy button tails waving like anemones in the liquid, though there's nothing to move them. On some, a line of white fur runs down the spine.

Alice finds her vision swims. She can't count the number of vessels on the bench because they don't seem to be staying still. Turning away, Alice finds by sheer luck the bucket where Jesse dropped it.

As she retches—which is especially painful with an empty stomach—she hears what she at first thinks is thunder. It takes a few moments before she realises it's someone banging on the front door of Doc's little blue house, and Doc's gone pale and is starting to swear.

"Well, that went south quick." Mehitabel Reine has a bloody nose and a split, swollen lip, so when she talks a fine spray of red taints the air.

There's one body on the floor of the surgery. A nuggetty man with a bald head, drooping brown moustache, staring eyes, chequered shirt, gold star shining on his chest. There's an entry wound in the soft flesh beneath Sheriff Dawkins' chin, and one for the exit somewhere in the top of his head. Jesse's covering his ears as if the retort of the gun is echoing still. Kid looks stunned.

Alice, still kneeling, has a smoking Peacemaker in one hand, the other grips her ribs. She'd have preferred not to shoot him, or at least not here and maybe not so soon, but he telegraphed his intentions when he arrived by kicking her as she hunched over the odious bucket. When she gets her breath back, she says, "Would this be one of those friends Mr Hart left behind?"

Doc nods.

"And I'm guessing that, in addition to those"—she points the gun towards the specimen jars and their contents—"that you've got a problem with missing children?"

Doc says, "And I'm guessing you rode past the mission on your way here? Did you wonder why there were so many orphans there? Seem like a large number for such a sparsely populated area?"

Alice half-sits, half-rolls onto her backside, legs bent, arms hanging over the knees. "I did."

"Okay, none of those kids are ever there for long. None ever grow up here. No one gets to adopt from there even though there's plenty of childless couples hereabouts, plenty of farming folk who'd be glad of a helping hand even if it means another mouth to feed." Doc pulls open one of the glass cabinets and grabs a cloth pad to press against her bleeding nose. "Jesse's the only kid ever got out, but that was before Mr Hart arrived and set up his *business*."

"Looks like at least one of the friends isn't prepared to take chances on me asking any more questions."

"You get this sort of thing a lot?"

"Sometimes." Dead men and women littered Alice's trail, either because they wouldn't give her the information she needed or because they tried to stop her from getting it. No point telling the doc that, though; she was a smart woman, she'd have figured it out.

"Jesse, you go sit out front. You holler if you see anyone. And uncover your goddamned ears." The boy goes, eyes as wide as teacups, arms clamped at his sides. "Kid has the worst timing." Jesse'd burst in to warn them just as Dawkins' boot connected with Alice's flank. Doc nodded at the girl on her floor. "Anything broken?"

"Some doctor you are," grumbled Alice, and clambered to her feet, grimacing. "Probably."

"I'll strap your ribs, and while I'm doing that let me tell you about Rabbit's other friends, the priest and the railway magnate."

"Tell me first why you haven't done anything about this before now."

♥

"So, no one complains?"

Doc Reine gives Alice a look like she's a slow child. "What would you do? The sheriff's in on it, the priest's in on it, and the man whose money started the town is in on it. Who else would you complain to?"

"The sawbones. The last responsible adult in town."

"I do what I can. When the first of the girls came to me, those Mr Hart had *favoured*, I thought I was going mad. It took a while, too, for me to realise what was happening at the mission. I almost said something to Mr Gambit one day—I spent a long time trying to figure out who to confide in—but then I saw him and Hart together, laughing, watching a young girl walk down the street." Mehitabel Reine takes a deep breath, pats the neck of the roan she rides. "Who was I going to tell then? And what good was I if I got myself killed, buried in some back tunnel of the silver mine? I could show them the… babies… but that's no proof of either Gambit's or the priest's collusion." Doc shifts her shoulders as if to adjust the weight of the shotgun strapped to her back. She's got a range of scalpels secreted in various pockets of her jacket and trousers too, one slid down her right boot.

Alice sighs. They're heading through the woods out of town, towards the home of the town's founder. They'd left Jesse to dig a shallow hole in Doc's garden for the sheriff's corpse. "Rabbit moves on but the others stay, benefiting from whatever *commerce* he set up. He stays a step ahead. This is how he works: finds likeminded folk, makes promises, then he leaves with his share before things go bad."

"By *things*, you mean *you* arrive?"

Alice nods. She's told the doc what she thinks the woman can bear—she's seen all those little remnants of Rabbit's pastimes, after all, collected them in her specimen jars, but that doesn't mean she'd accept the whole idea of Wonderland as a place you get taken against your will, kidnapped for the amusement of Queen and King and Court. It's enough to say that she, Alice, was taken and bad things happened, and now she spends her time trying to stop those bad things happening to other children. She doesn't mention the land across the way, that she destroyed it for a time, kicking apart the playing-card flimsiness that had done her so much damage; that she made a deal with the Queen of Hearts in order to go home; that now she was honouring that and getting her revenge at the same time. Alice had found most folks can only believe so much.

Doc continues. "There's no mayor here, no council of wise men. There's just Lutwidge Gambit and all his money. He financed the surveys that found the silver seam, he paid for the mining and smelting equipment, he paid for the railway tracks to be laid out here. Hell, he brought half the workers out with their families; shipped in women to make matches for those who wanted them, and the whores for those who just preferred something less burdensome." Mehitabel Reine shakes her head. "And he's smart—*they're* smart. They don't take any child from town, unless they're utterly unwanted. They harvest from around, a long way around so it's hard to see a pattern unless you're looking for it."

"What were they doing before Rabbit?"

"Who knows? Being much sneakier, taking private pleasures and disposing of the evidence. Now... well, now it's a business."

"At least the priest's not going to be a problem anymore."

The mission had been emptied of children when Alice and the doc had burst in, and the woman Alice had seen with the orphans that morning was nowhere to be found. Alice had resisted the urge to pin the priest, Father Eustace, up on his own cross, and just shot him in the head after he'd told them all he could or would. Doc helped her tip him down the well; she also suggested that the woman, Annabelle Foreman, had gone with the children to keep them calm.

The sun's almost set when they rein in their mounts just beyond the treeline that borders Gambit's mansion. The house is a three-storey thing, white with columns and broad verandahs that would look more at home deeper south, surrounded by bayous and cotton fields. Alice takes in the rail lines that lead around the back where, parked as casually as a horse and cart, an engine waits. It’s the one she saw earlier today, but now two cars are attached to it. The first is the luxurious-looking private carriage, the second a windowless boxcar. No steam comes from the engine’s stack; presumably departure won’t be until morning. There’s no sign of an engineer or fireman. From where the women sit they can hear the muted sobs and cries of lost children.

“Where are his men?” Alice takes a breath, scans the area.

“Men?”

“Henchmen, Mehitabel. They’ve all got henchmen.”

“Most of Gambit’s employees work in the mine, live with their families in town, but he’s got a staff here. They must be around…”

“Maybe they’re lying in wait. Or maybe they’ve been given the evening off because they don’t know what he does on the side.” Alice chews at her bottom lip. “You okay with the boxcar?”

“And while I’m doing that, you’ll be…?”

“Making the acquaintance of Mr Lutwidge Gambit.” Alice urges her horse forward. “You watch out for that Foreman woman; there’s every chance she’s in on this, and in my experience women fight harder to avoid consequences.”

“What do you want me to do with any henchmen I might come across?”

“You’ve got a gun. What do you want me to do, draw you a

picture?" Alice gives her a solid stare. "Do you think they're going to be much of a loss to this world?"

"Just checking."

♥

The house is silent and that makes Alice ever more nervous. She'd slipped in through the kitchen door, finding no one there, no housekeeper or cook or maid. There'd been no one in the stables, either, no one in the barn. Then again, she tells herself, if you employ folk to do one thing, but they're not aware of the other things, the bad things you do—and let's face it, the more people know a secret, the less secure that secret is—then you're likely to give them the night off when you're about to ship out a bunch of kidnapped children. So, thinks Alice, maybe this is better. Easier to take out a couple of men rather than a small private army.

The mansion is precisely what you'd expect of so much new money. All the furniture glossy oakwood and mahogany, items designed less for sitting on than looking at. There are inlays of marble and mother-of-pearl, gold filigree, the floors so highly polished they're slippery, the rugs rich and exotic, the curtains thick and velvety. The paintings on the walls are portraits of men and women with high foreheads and receding chins. Alice thinks it all very vulgar. The windows are pristine and the blackness of the fast-falling night is clearly visible, not a single smudge marring the panes.

At the end of the corridor on the ground floor only one door is closed, and she heads towards it. Alice turns the handle and pushes, keeping herself to the side of the frame. Bullets bite at the wood, splinters fly up and flick at her skin. She counts the shots and when the sixth goes as astray as the others, she waits a moment longer, listens to the jingle of panicked fingers trying to reload. Then Alice steps into a library: a lot of chairs, a big desk, shelves filled with books, and behind the desk is a man with an empty gun.

"I'd drop that if I were you," she says and raises her Peacemaker. The man looks at her, sees the cold resolve in her pretty face, then sets his Colt Navy Revolver on the desktop.

He's maybe in his thirties, got thick blond hair, a neat goatee and moustache, and finely shaped eyebrows. He's wearing a masterfully tailored suit in navy pinstripe, shiny shoes, and a bright red brocade waistcoat with golden dragons embroidered on it. Alice thinks it looks familiar but she can't quite place the pattern. He looks flustered, as he probably should; a cigar is smoking in a crystal ashtray on his desk.

"Good evening, Mr Gambit," says Alice, for she was raised well before it all went wrong, and the girl remembers her manners. "May I ask where your staff might be this fine eve?"

"Not here," he answers. "At the moment."

"Don't want them in on your little secret?"

He doesn't bother to answer that. "Who are you?"

"Alice. Didn't Mr Jack Hart mention me?"

"He said only to be wary. Didn't give any names."

"No, he wouldn't. That should have made *you* wary." She smiles. "Where did he go, when he left here?"

"I've no idea."

Alice doesn't even take a breath, just squeezes the trigger and takes off the little finger of his right hand. It's got to hurt, she thinks, and after a moment when he finally realises he's been shot, he starts to swear and scream. She just talks over him. "Now, he may not have told you, but he might. Probably not, but I just wanted to give you a taste of what's coming if you don't cooperate. But he'll have left you bank details, I'd imagine, so you can make sure he gets his cut—and dear Rabbit does love his cut."

She can see in his eyes that he wants to ask about that name, but he's too busy whimpering, holding his hand with a white silk handkerchief wrapped around it. It's not so white anymore, of course, lots of red splotches.

"So, I will ask again just one more time: where did he go?"

"Seattle. Or at least that's where the bank he uses is." He grits his teeth, tells her the name of the institution. "Fuck you, little girl."

"You can dress as a gentleman all you like, but you're still a sewer rat on the inside." Alice takes a few more steps into the room, notices two feet sticking out from under the desk. Very still. She circles around, gestures for Gambit to move.

It's a woman in her forties, rotund, black hair shot with grey, white blouse, light-blue skirt. Her eyes are dark and open and staring at the ceiling, but there's no breath in her. Alice doesn't know her face but surely it's Annabelle Foreman, the clothing's the same as Alice saw this morning. The side of her head's been stove in, there's blood still sliding slowly down her skin. A rectangular grey marble bookend lies on the floor beside her head, one of its corners slick with gore.

"What did she do?" asks Alice quietly.

"Developed a conscience," says Gambit, sneering.

Suddenly there's the noise of footsteps in the hall outside the library, and Alice moves again so she can see both the door and Gambit.

"I do believe the cavalry has arrived," says he with a smug grin.

Alice feels a rush of ice in her belly. Not because of the idea of reinforcements, but because Doc Reine walks through the doorway, slowly, a rueful smile on her mouth. Alice thinks of her own words, uttered not so long ago: *In my experience women fight harder to avoid consequences.* Then she focuses and realises that Doc's got blood dribbling down from a cut at the hairline, and bruising already coming up on the forehead and left cheek. She's got empty hands, too, no sign of her shotgun and the big coat with all the scalpels in its pockets is gone.

Mehitabel gives Alice an apologetic glance and shrugs. The barrel of a shotgun appears behind her, prods her in the back, and Jesse follows it. "You hush now, Doc."

Alice is the one who says, "You little shit."

"You shut your mouth! Coming here, making trouble. Now I hadta go and hurt Doc, all because of you and your interference! Drop your gun." Jesse prods Mehitabel harder and Alice can see from her expression that it hurts a lot; despite his claim, it appears Jesse was enthusiastic in his subduing of Doc Reine. Alice lets the Peacemaker fall and

Gambit swoops from behind his desk to grab it up.

"Jesse—" begins Doc.

The boy talks over the top of her. "I'm grateful, Doc, don't you ever think I'm not. You're always kind but he's done more, promised me more, and kindness will only get you so far in this world. I've thrown my lot in with Mr Gambit here. Look at you: you're a goddamned doctor but you're still scraping for money. Hell, you take bread and eggs as payment! That's no way of living. No, siree. You're always wanting me to improve myself, well, that's what I'm doing."

His voice is just as discordant as before, maybe more so to Alice, seeing him like this. Little rat, little traitor. She must say it aloud because the boy's face hardens.

"You think you're better'n me?"

Alice says, "Very much so."

That makes him angrier but no more articulate. Gambit must see something dangerous in the boy's expression, in the spittle gathering at the corner of his lips, and the man soothes. "Now, Jesse, hold your temper. We've talked about this. You can have your way soon enough, but I need to make sure she's not got anyone else coming for us. After that you can mark her up to your heart's content. But you just be patient, my lad."

Alice has a scar on her right cheek, raised and healed white, and her nose was once broken and improperly set. She likes that it makes eyes slide away from her. Lessens her value. Makes people underestimate her.

Gambit turns his attention to her. "Well? Is there? Anyone else?"

Alice grins, answers obliquely. "Why do you think Mr Hart isn't here anymore?"

"Who? Who's coming?" Gambit's pitch goes up a notch.

"Didn't tell you about me, did he? Why would he tell you about the others?"

Gambit shakes his head, though he seems to regret doing so, telling her more than he wants to. Alice doesn't mention that, as far as she can tell, Rabbit doesn't even know about *her.* He runs because there are others looking for him, others from across the divide between worlds. That's what keeps him moving, making Alice's task both more difficult and a little easier: she's unexpected.

Gambit says, "Now, Jesse, you're going to have to persuade this one. Hurt Doc."

"But, Mr Gambit—"

"Now, Jesse, can't you see? She doesn't care about herself—it's in her face. But she cares about Doc. She cares about children she doesn't even know."

Alice can see he thinks that caring about others makes her weak.

"Mr—"

"You hurt her now or I swear I'll cut you loose! You'll be in one of those boxcars, going to a new home and trust me, Jesse, you won't enjoy yourself."

Alice speaks softly, quickly. "Jesse, did you know the woman at the mission?"

The question is so unexpected that's he's surprised into answering. "Miss Foreman. Sure."

"Have a look behind his desk."

"Jesse, don't." Gambit's tone, the desperate edge to it, tells Alice she's hit a nerve.

"Go on, Jesse, see how he treats his employees."

"Jesse, you don't… she was going to betray me—us! Jesse, don't—"

But it's too late. Jesse doesn't like Alice but he's got no reason not to trust her. He steps away from Doc, takes a few paces to the right so he can see the still feet, the light blue skirt, doesn't bother to go any further 'coz he freezes. Afraid, indecisive.

"Jesse, you shouldn't have—" Gambit doesn't finish the sentence. He brings up the Peacemaker and Jesse swings the shotgun around. They fire simultaneously, then fall at roughly the same speed. The left side of Jesse's head is gone, but Gambit's gut-shot.

Alice scoops up the Peacemaker that's dropped just out of Gambit's reach. She stands over him, aims the gun at him, then reconsiders. "Doc?"

"Much obliged, Alice." And Mehitabel Reine slides the hidden scalpel from her boot and uses it to slice Lutwidge Gambit's throat.

♥

In the darkness of the railway carriage, sixteen children huddle on malodorous sacks and straw, most of them under ten, certainly none over. It takes a while to coax them out, but eventually they trust Doc's face, Alice's grin—maybe they recognise she's one of them. Maybe they see she's survived, and they realise they can too.

"What am I going to do with them?" asks Doc, surveying the gathering.

"The names and details I wrote down? Send a telegram and those folk will come."

"You trust 'em?"

"Oh yes. I've known them a long while." Alice pauses. "I'd stay, but I've got to get after him, after Rabbit."

"I know. I reckon if you raid the kitchen here you'll find plenty to keep you going on the trail."

Alice nods. "You okay to get them back to town?"

"Oh, yeah."

"Anyone left to fear here?"

Doc shakes her head. "Gambit, the priest and Dawkins are all gone. No one's going to go asking questions." She sighs. "Although I'd best make sure that Jesse buried the sheriff before he came after us."

"I'm sorry about Jesse, Mehitabel."

Doc shrugs. "What can you do? You can only teach them right from wrong, whether they choose the one or the other is anyone's guess."

Alice pulls two cigars from her pocket-pouch—souvenired from Gambit's desk—and Mehitabel lights them up. They smoke standing beside the boxcar, while the children sit on the grass and patiently wait.

"Where to next?" asks Doc.

"New York," lies Alice. It's not that she doesn't trust Doc, but who knows what anyone might give up with the right leverage?

Vanished Summer Glory

RIO YOUERS

ROSEMARIE

I know this is irregular, and I feel just awful to have asked, but thank you, David. Thank you for seeing me. As a friend, of course. As Charles's friend, to be more accurate. I just… I didn't know who else to talk to.

Yes, I'm comfortable. Thank you. This is a charming space, and that *view*. Is that Skeffington Hill? I thought so. Charles and I used to walk there, at the beginning, you know, when it was all new and exciting. Charles once climbed a most magnificent elm up on that hill and went so high that I lost him in the boughs.

Oh, I'm blithering. I apologise. Do stop me, I shan't be offended. Charles would stop me in a moment. "I listen to blithering all day," he would say. "I don't want to hear it from you."

Yes, he was often direct. But not unkindly so. He had a good heart.

Has. He *has* a good heart. I'm not ready to refer to him in the past tense. That would be like shovelling dirt on an empty grave. Just because he's gone doesn't mean he's not coming back.

Or at least… oh, I'm sorry, David, I've always been quick to cry. Thin blood, that's what my mother used to say. It's funny the things you believe when you're young. I sometimes wonder if the journey—the adventure—from childhood to adulthood is curtailed by our willingness to discount the make-believe.

There's something else I've been wondering, David. Nonsense, I'm sure, but such thoughts have a way of taking hold, especially in the small hours. And I must be careful how I phrase this, because of your profession. I intend only the greatest respect. But given Charles's… *condition*, I feel it worth examining.

I'm talking about influence.

Yes, I can elaborate. I think so, at any rate. Give me a moment to collect my thoughts.

Okay.

If a person surrounds himself with liars, he is apt to deal in deceit. If a person chooses thieves for friends, he is apt to steal. Does the same rule not apply to psychiatry? Charles was a brilliant doctor, but he delved so frequently into delirium. Isn't it possible that, after a while, he too…?

Ridiculous, I know. I'm so sorry, David. Maybe this has been a waste of your time. And you're right, he was grieving—desperately. He knew he was going to lose his sister and he was scared. Except… except…

Okay, I'm reaching, I *know* I am. But isn't that the point of talking? Isn't that what you and Charles do? People sit in this chair, and they reach, and you help them to grab hold of something. There's more to it, of course, but really, at its core, psychiatry is guidance.

But what if instead of you guiding them, they guide *you?*

Too fanciful?

Forgive me. It's just… well, grief is too convenient an explanation. I believe there was something else going on. In fact, I can state with some confidence that Charles started to fracture when he took on a certain new patient. I have nothing to go on but a wife's instinct, but I can't help thinking that the two are connected.

No, of course not. Charles was a professional. He *did* talk about the man—often, in fact—but divulged nothing of a personal nature. He didn't even use his real name.

He called him Mr Rabbit.

BEFORE

Charles listened.

Mr Southey—a regular for just over a year—sat primly, with his back straight and his hands folded in his lap, just like he always sat, and talked about how his mother devalued him, and how he crossed the road when he saw teenagers walking towards him, because teenagers intimidated him, and sometimes they said things.

"I fantasise about hurting them," he said. "Maybe dragging one of them into the bushes and giving him a right good kicking. Or slapping one of the girls. They're all bitches at that age, you know."

He talked about his philistine neighbours and a woman at work who pulled out a tooth while he watched and a stray cat that frequented his back step, and how he sometimes put down a saucer of milk even though he'd heard that cats were lactose intolerant—that you should give them water, not milk, and what kind of world was it when you couldn't give a cat a saucer of milk?

Charles listened, completely and blissfully. He filled his head with Mr Southey's anxieties and insecurities, to the extent that they consumed everything else, including his own woes. For those forty-five minutes, his brain was full, but his heart was empty.

It was sublime.

"I see progress," he said towards the end of the session. "But I would like you to strive for those common bonds with your mother."

"She's seventy-nine years old," Mr Southey remarked, his nose slightly aloft. "And quite beyond change."

"But you're not."

His three o'clock had cancelled, and Charles thought he might use that newly open time to have a good cry (he'd found such little time for crying recently). But no sooner had he scratched the appointment from his book than the telephone rang again, and a quick, troubled voice inquired as to his availability. Charles was about to explain that he was not taking on new patients, then considered the sanctuary of another man's travails. *I'll cry another time*, he thought, and revealed that he had an opening at three o'clock, and that his office was best reached via the back garden of his house on Havilland Avenue. It was only after he hung up the phone that he realised he hadn't got the new patient's name. A small concern, of course; his name, and his troubles, would be known soon enough.

Charles showed Mr Southey to the door, then checked his watch. 2:47 p.m. He had a little time, so sat at his desk and looked at the framed photograph of him and Alice, the one taken in Daresbury Wood when they were twelve years old. How they'd loved those woods. How often they'd played there, and the wonders they'd imagined.

It will always be our special place.

"Yes, Alice," Charles said to the photograph, and lost himself for more than a moment, remembering the games they'd played, the fantasies they'd indulged. Nothing was too outlandish.

Reflecting on their childhood, it was sometimes difficult to determine the real from the make-believe. Their imaginations—sharp as cats' claws—had left marks. And those marks had remained brilliant throughout childhood, into adulthood. Even when Alice had revealed her devastating news, he had responded with all seriousness, "You must eat tumtum leaves and lucent berries, they'll make you better," as if such flora existed.

His reverie was broken by a loud knock at the door. Charles jumped up. "Oh," he gasped. "Yes. I'm coming." He set down the framed photograph and glanced at his watch. 3:11 p.m. Somewhat flustered, he straightened his hair and his tie, and answered the door.

Nobody there, not at first glance, then Charles registered movement closer to his feet. He looked down, and there on his doormat stood a white rabbit with glittering pink eyes, dressed in a natty waistcoat.

"Dr Lewis," the rabbit said, and fished an ornate watch from the pocket of his waistcoat. He flipped it open and glanced at it with a frown. "My apologies; I do believe I'm late."

ROSEMARIE

He was distant, to begin with. No, not physically. Emotionally. And that was not like Charles. He fervently maintained that a healthy marriage needed only two qualities: honesty and conversation. In all our years together, he had never shied from sharing things with me. I assumed, obviously, that it was because of Alice, and so gave him space. He'd sit in his armchair for hours, not speaking, or he'd wander the rooms of our house with a faraway look on his face. I'd always known him so stalwart. It was heartbreaking to see.

How long was he like this? Oh… weeks, probably, beginning when he first told me that he'd started seeing Mr Rabbit, and deteriorating from there. And yes, David, deteriorating *is* the right word. You might choose something kinder, like "manifesting" or "advancing", but you didn't live with him.

Again, I'll elaborate.

He trapped a sparrow in a birdbox and made a tiny hat for it. A darling thing, really, made from velvet, with a rubber band for a strap. He was quite proud of that hat, having no appreciable needlework skills, and thus grew irritable when the sparrow wouldn't wear it. Now I ask you, David, does that sound like Charles to you?

No.

I discovered him reciting poetry to the roses. Tennyson's "Maud". Do you know it? *Come into the garden, Maud, for the black bat, night, has flown.* Does that sound like the Charles who published several benchmark papers on disorganised schizophrenia and antipsychotic treatments?

No.

I wish for a kinder word, David, but no kinder word will do. He *deteriorated*. And please don't assume that I'm laying this entirely at Mr Rabbit's feet. I believe the thousands of patients before him had tiptoed Charles up the cliff. I believe Alice's illness had led him to the edge, and it was Mr Rabbit who pushed him over. Excuse the violent metaphor, but it was a rather violent descent.

Oh, it's a queer thing, to talk so candidly about this with you, to infer that a psychiatrist might be influenced by his patient. I'd maintain reserve if I didn't know you personally. And yes, Alice's illness was a crucial factor. I would never suggest otherwise.

Did I like her? But of course. She was the sweetest soul.

Jealous?

I'll remind you, David, that this is a *conversation*, not an appointment. But I'll answer your question: no, I was not jealous. Charles was closer to her by far, but they shared a womb, for heaven's sake. Theirs was a togetherness of absolute purity. I was delighted for Charles to have Alice in his life, and heartsore for him to have lost her.

"I'll need to grow again," he'd said to me. This was soon after the cancer had spread to Alice's liver, and not long before Mr Rabbit arrived on the scene. "I'll have new hands, new feet, a new soul. The world will be a new place."

How very cruel that at our most vulnerable, we need to display the greatest strength.

BEFORE

The rabbit hopped across the office and up onto the couch. He twitched his nose, ran his paws across his whiskers, and blinked his startling pink eyes. Charles looked at him for perhaps a little too long, then cleared his throat and took his seat.

"I should have asked your name when you called," he said calmly. "That was remiss of me."

"Not at all," the rabbit said. "I could just as easily have told you, so allow me to do so now: Mr W. Rabbit. Or Mr Rabbit, for short." He twitched his nose again, disagreeably this time. "W is such a cumbersome letter, don't you think? Often longer than the word it begins. And no letter should be longer than the word it begins."

"I couldn't agree more," Charles remarked. "And where do you live, Mr Rabbit?"

"A most wonderful place. A most broken place."

Charles crossed his right leg over his left. His expression was noncommittal. He would not make a great deal out of this. To do so would be to admit that the rabbit was real, and to admit that it was real would be to admit to a neurosis. This was no more than a nonpsychotic hallucination, triggered by anxiety. Quite understandable, all things considered.

"I would normally ask several key questions during the initial appointment," Charles said, speaking with a controlled tone. "To form a road map of sorts, from which to explore and revisit as required. On this occasion, however, I choose only to listen, certain that anything you have to say will be more interesting than any question I might ask."

"As you please," the rabbit said, and struck a thoughtful pose, his little brow wrinkled, one ear pensively cocked. "I can talk for longer than we both have, about our uncertain world, the fragile nature of everything. A flower will wilt. A baby will cry. An iceberg will crumble, Dr Lewis—*crumble*, formed tens of thousands of years ago, miles wide and even more miles deep, yet as susceptible to decay as everything else."

Charles nodded, trying to lose himself in the rabbit's head, and not think about the terrible, ugly, volatile thing charging through his twin sister's body.

"I can talk about time." Mr Rabbit took the watch from his waistcoat pocket again, and regarded its slow, jewelled face curiously. "So fragile, and yet the only unstoppable thing in this or any universe. Time." He tapped the gently curved glass with his paw. "One second is such a tiny measure in the grand scheme of things. Yet one second can change so much. It is the difference between late and not late, between yesterday and today, and between here and gone."

Charles fought the urge to reach over and touch the rabbit. Would he feel his soft white fur, the thin bones beneath? Or would his hand grasp at nothing but air? Certainly, the sound of the rabbit's paw striking the watch glass had seemed real.

Ridiculous, Charles thought. *This is a manifestation of grief… of pain. I've been bottling up my emotions for too long. And I need sleep.*

"It's different when we're younger," the rabbit continued. He cast a fond eye toward the window, where the afternoon sun had started its descent toward the horizon. "Everything is open and unspoiled and possible. I remember being a young rabbit—a kitten." Here he interjected himself, his narrow chest inflating with pride. "Do you know that a young rabbit is called a kitten, Dr Lewis?"

"I do."

"Yes, of course you do. And a young hare is called a leveret. Unfortunate for the hare, but they do lack that kittenish allure. Don't you agree?"

"I haven't given it much thought," Charles said.

"Well, they do. And they're raving mad, to boot. But anyway, yes, as a kitten…" He took a deep breath that whistled through his front teeth. "Oh, I would run, and hop, and the grass had been so tall, the days so long. Time was not a factor in anything, because there was an abundance of it, and nothing to be late for." His pink eyes glazed with nostalgia. His whiskers twitched happily. "I had *such* a time, Dr Lewis, playing with Bill and Pat, waking the Dormouse with my antics, sometimes listening to the wise old Caterpillar. Even the Duchess was cheerier in those days. Goodness, I think everybody was."

Charles couldn't help but think of Alice, and the long, wonderful days they'd shared in Daresbury Wood. It wasn't simply the adventures they'd invented, or the fact that they came to know every tree and wild flower. It was the time as a whole—a period of several years that, when compared to other years, shone with a true, relentless magic. And yes, everything had been open and unspoiled, and the grass had been so tall.

"Then it all changes," Mr Rabbit said dourly. The glimmer left his eyes. His whiskers drooped. "I can talk about that, too, and how, when faced with change, it can feel like falling down an exceptionally deep hole."

"Yes," Charles said. "Quite."

That's exactly how it had felt, looking into Alice's eyes as she told him that she was dying. They had been sitting on her sofa, their hands joined, and Charles remembered how unnaturally silent it was. No traffic noises or planes. No creaks in the radiators. No neighbourhood dogs yapping. It was a moment of eerie stillness. The world had paused for them, awaiting their return—a respite that upset its alignment. It would grind more than spin from that point on.

Charles had nodded at the news, then cried. He had made that inane comment about the tumtum leaves, and then he had fallen and fallen.

"A change," he said to the rabbit, "is often an opportunity."

"Only if *we* change with it," Mr Rabbit said. His left ear cocked in that pensive fashion again, and a grain of the sparkle returned to his eye. "We are told that life is fleeting, that we exist for but a blink. This is true, of course, but it's all relative. Our lives are all we know, and all we will *ever* know. The things we love, believe and trust are also fleeting, which brings us back to fragility and time. It's all so unpredictable."

"Everything changes," Charles said. "It develops, and regresses."

"Indeed," the rabbit said. "Our greatest strength isn't in keeping things the same, but in being able to grow and shrink accordingly."

ROSEMARIE

I recognise that expression, David. Neutral. Is that the word? Or impassive? Inscrutable? I suppose it won't do to show emotion. Did they teach you that during your residency, or is it something you're born with?

A little of both, I suspect. Charles was a master of the neutral expression, even when talking to me. I could never tell if he had a hidden agenda. He was such a clever man.

Is a clever man.

Is.

He talked about Mr Rabbit often, without ever really saying anything. "Mr Rabbit is a warm breeze," he'd say. "A light in the gloom," he'd say. He once referred to him as a "boon companion", which struck me as a rather odd endearment for a patient. You'd think Mr Rabbit, being so special, might have helped Charles in some way, but his deterioration only quickened.

No, I never saw him. I kept to the front of the house whenever Charles was working. I'd occasionally see a patient leaving as I returned from town, or if they came through the front, rather than the back gate. But no, I never crossed paths with Mr Rabbit, which is a touch peculiar, I suppose, given the frequency of his appointments.

Once a week, to begin with. Then twice. And then... well, I remember, towards the end, leafing through Charles's appointment book, and seeing Mr Rabbit's name numerous times in the course of one week. Charles had crossed out his other patients' names and written Mr Rabbit's in their place. I was tempted to call those patients to enquire if they had cancelled, or if Charles had, but I thoroughly lacked the nerve.

BEFORE

They were there for each other, as they always had been, and each drew courage from the other, a harmony in keeping with the colour of their eyes. Charles had always considered himself staunch, but he was nonetheless impressed by the steadiness of his hand when he gave Alice water, and his tone when he read her favourite poems, and how he could kiss the top of her balding head without qualm.

They laughed together. Charles remembered that. They

hugged, joked and listened. They held hands, reminisced and encouraged. It was, in many ways, the most wonderful time—a paradox of everything being perfect, and nothing being perfect.

But Charles also remembered the radiation treatments and compression fractures to Alice's spine and ribs, how she would walk stooped and sometimes scream because the pain was so advanced. He remembered countless medications—the painkillers and anti-oestrogens, and her chemotherapy drugs arranged like soldiers in formation.

He remembered sweeping clumps of hair from her pillow, and how she used hydrogen peroxide to eliminate the odour of her decaying fingernails.

He remembered how the bones in her face collapsed, and how her skin turned papery and old.

He remembered getting stacks of audiobooks from the library because it hurt her wrists to hold a paperback for more than fifteen minutes.

And, of course, he remembered the end…

"One last time," Alice had said to him. "Take me there."

Charles didn't need to ask where, and would never deny this final request. He lifted Alice from her bed and carried her through the bright morning to his car, where he sat her in the front seat and draped a warm blanket over her. He drove through the town centre, past bustling stores and restaurants, through Hatter's Square, then along the B257 towards Daresbury Wood.

"The daffodils are out," she said. "The foxgloves, too."

"Yes," Charles said, even though it was October and

the ground was golden with fallen leaves. The branches drooped, naked of everything but a recent rain. He parked the car in a lay-by, then lifted Alice from the passenger seat and carried her into the woods proper.

"There," she said, pointing, "it's Antoine the Alder. He sheltered us from the Jabberwock. Do you remember?"

Her narrow legs were folded over his arm, her hands looped around his shoulders. She weighed no more than a fawn.

"I remember," Charles said.

They walked deeper, through rusty bracken and beneath skeletal branches, around the greyish hulks of fallen trees—none of which Alice saw. Her eyes flooded with belief and elation. She enthusiastically pointed out the clearing where they'd enjoyed numerous tea parties, the lairs of the Boojum and the Bandersnatch, and the innumerable creatures and colours that weren't there.

Except they *were.*

"Put me down," Alice said.

Charles did… gently, although Alice all but hopped out of his arms. She stood straight and strong, and with every step the woods came to life around her. The leaves fluttered upward, turning green on their passage, the roses and tiger lilies bloomed furiously, the animals peeped from the understory and chattered, the birds filled the sky with song.

It's different when we're younger, Mr Rabbit had said, this memory recurring so vividly that he might have been perched on Charles's shoulder. *Everything is open and unspoiled and possible.*

Alice spread her arms and twirled, and in that moment the fractured, dying woman disappeared, and Charles saw her as a young girl, with her blonde hair whispering, her endless face turned up to the trees.

"Alice," he said. There were tears in his eyes.

In that moment he saw everything.

ROSEMARIE

Thank you for coming to the funeral, David. That was kind of you, and I know Charles was grateful. He was grieving terribly, but you wouldn't know it. He was at his stalwart best. Good old Charles. I think that was the last time he was anything like himself.

And, for all the memories I have, it's how I'm choosing to remember him: dressed so handsomely, with not a hair out of place, not a mark upon his brow.

The eulogy? Yes, he delivered it so flawlessly. A poem—I'd not heard it before, but it felt familiar, somehow, and it stayed with me. Particularly the last stanza.

Yes, of course, but I won't recite it nearly as well as Charles.

And, though the shadow of a sigh
May tremble through the story,
For "happy summer days" gone by,
And vanish'd summer glory—
It shall not touch, with breath of bale,
The pleasure of our fairy-tale

Charles disappeared five months later. A Wednesday afternoon, and a beautiful spring day. All the flowers were showing. He told me he was going to meet Mr Rabbit, and that was it.

I haven't seen him since.

No, nobody knows. Not the police. Not his family in Oxford or Croft-on-Tees. It's quite the mystery, and all the more upsetting for it. I wonder every day if he'll return—if he'll walk through the door and sit in his favourite armchair, newspaper in hand, as if nothing has happened.

His slippers are beside the hearth, just in case.

And Mr Rabbit? The police wanted to question him, of course, but Charles kept no contact information on file. I couldn't even give them a description. He is an unsolved piece of the puzzle. An integral piece, I'm quite sure.

How long has it been? Two years and four months. Sometimes it seems like it has passed in the wink of an eye. And sometimes it seems I could count every interminable hour, every second.

Time is such a clouded thing.

One final note, David, before I leave, and I've never told anybody this before. Oh, a little embarrassed I suppose, but… I looked for him. And I know it's not embarrassing that I *should* look, only that I was so certain I would find him.

Last August. The Sunday of the bank holiday weekend. I was watering the roses in the back garden, when suddenly I dropped everything and ran. Yes, I *ran*, David, like a child. I've never felt so light—so *free*. I ran through Hatter's Square, out of town, and all the way to Daresbury Wood.

It was like Charles was calling to me. I even called back to him: "I'm coming, Charles. I'm coming, my love."

How very foolish.

The woods were empty. I searched for at least an hour, calling his name, my cries becoming more and more hopeless. And all at once the tears came. I fell to my knees and let everything out.

No sign of Charles.

Except...

Indulge me a moment, David.

I *felt* him. In the trees. No, not *in* them, like a squirrel, but within them, in their age and their shape, the way their branches reached and soared. So stalwart. And as I wiped my eyes and got to my feet, I thought I saw, for one second, a young girl with long blonde hair standing beneath those branches, perfectly at peace and forever young.

I walked home with the sun at my back, and it warmed me.

Black Kitty

CATRIONA WARD

I was convinced it was a man, which is embarrassing.

First, I noticed that Snowdrop had started braiding her hair and eating the special dates, the kind that sweeten your breath. She got new slippers of yellow silk as light as air. She looked wonderful—and the shine in her came from inside, not the slippers or the braids. I pretended not to notice anything different. I was buying time until I could figure out what was going on.

Snowdrop and I were born a minute apart. It's too close. We see too much, understand too much about one another. It's like watching your failings and fears acted out over and over by someone who looks just like you, except much more attractive. In theory she and I are identical, and true, we have the same nose, the same cheekbones, and our hair is rich red and brown like the forest floor in autumn. I couldn't put my finger on any difference between us. And yet Snowdrop is beautiful, whereas I seem to just miss being so. I overshoot beauty by a whisker. In the past I tried to make up for this by playing the piano excellently and being interesting in Portuguese and so on. But I found the only thing that brought me level with Snowdrop's loveliness was my talent for villainy. So I decided to focus on that. (Most of the time, villainy is merely making difficult choices.)

Now I watched her from my window, which gave onto the west terrace. Snowdrop looked out over the gardens, presenting a delicate profile. She sat very straight on the balustrade, in that way no one ever sits, unless it is to be watched. But by whom? The terrace was deserted except for the flamingos, which hooted and plucked peevishly at one another, so that the lawns were littered with orange and blue feathers. Now, in general, Snowdrop was not steady of purpose. She was odd-tempered and apt to wander off mid-conversation if distracted. Distracting items included, but were not limited to: bumblebees, clouds, chairs, candy, me, teacups, ribbons and air. But now, hour after hour, she sat patient and still.

On the plain below, beyond the palace walls, the game stretched out in every direction as far as the eye could see, shifting and revolving like a carousel. The game made a sound, a kind of hum, as the land spun at dizzying speed. Trees and houses and rivers whirled. In the game, it takes all the running you can do to keep in the same place.

I saw a small figure stagger across a forest clearing, weeping. It was a young boy in a round hat. As I watched, a tall man strode out of the trees and clubbed him. He struck the boy again and again until he stopped moving. Then the man dragged the body into the shadow of the woods and the game kept turning and they were gone from view again. If you watched the game for more than a few moments, you always saw death. My favourites were the knights with their great horses and gleaming wicked swords. *Snicker-snack*. The boy with the round hat will be back tomorrow, though, running with lips drawn back from his teeth in fear. Death doesn't stick, down there. The game never lets you go.

We don't use the words *magic* or *enchantment* round here anymore. Snowdrop calls it *funny business*. The game is full of funny business. It reeks of it. Snowdrop used to have a touch of it, but she never uses it now, not since Mother.

As the shadows lengthened and dark came creeping in, still Snowdrop sat with that strange look in her eyes, fixed on faraway things—or perhaps she looked inwards at the depths of herself. When night fell Snowdrop at last got up and came inside. She didn't have the air of someone who had been disappointed or stood up. She seemed like she was exactly where she should be, doing just what she wanted. It didn't make sense. I saw then that she held some small object, almost hidden by the curve of her palm.

Straight after breakfast Snowdrop went to the south terrace, arranged herself artistically on a bench, and stayed there. I watched her all morning. The wind made rills in the glassy pond nearby. A gardener trundled a wheelbarrow.

The royal dog walkers took a turn, the dragonhounds panting and straining at the leashes. Below, on the plains, a bishop with eyes of flame cut down screaming children. Snowdrop paid all this no mind. She was watching the object held in her palm very closely.

I was crawling on my stomach to get a better look when I became aware of a burning sensation on my calves, then on my wrists and other exposed places. I saw too late what shared my hiding place under the yew hedge.

"Ssssss," the nettles said in their high voices. "We're sssssleeeeping. Pisssss off." They blinked their yellow eyes and wrapped agonising tendrils about my limbs. I screamed and tore at them until they let go and then I crawled weeping into the light.

That night, after I had soothed my furious red skin with salve, I went to Snowdrop's chamber. She was staring at her reflection in the glass. Her mind must have been elsewhere, because she didn't notice when I came up behind her. She started when I took hold of her throat.

"You're up to something," I said. "I can tell."

"I'm not *up to something*," she said, eyes filling with tears. "Please, Kitty, let me go."

I loosened my grip and released her throat. "Don't lie to me," I said, "I can always tell."

"All right, fine," she said in a different tone, rubbing at my finger marks on her white neck. "I was going to tell you tonight, anyway, after supper. I might have found a way to get out of it, Kit."

Snowdrop was to be married in two months' time, to

the King of Blanch, the kingdom over the mountains. She didn't want to do it.

She looked at my face. I don't know what she saw there but the corners of her mouth turned down in sorrow. "Oh, *Kitty*. Don't be sad. You'll come with me!" She pried my nails out of her arm. "I wouldn't leave you here alone, I swear."

"You can't do it, Snowdrop," I said quietly. "You said you never would again." The last time Snowdrop tried her hand at funny business, she killed our mother.

"I don't have a choice," Snowdrop said. "I have to try, or you know what happens. I'll have to run and scream and die every day. Or kill people, just to stay alive." She was right. When she married she would go into the game. And in due course I would marry and follow her. That's how it worked. I knew she was dreading it.

"What do you have in mind?" I asked, stabbing my palm idly with her nail file.

"Well, it's the most extraordinary thing, Kitty. Come to the west terrace tomorrow morning, and I'll show you what I mean."

It was something to do with a man, I was sure. There was that sheen on her. As I closed the door behind me she was dabbing rosewater on her face.

♥

Three memories.

One: when we were becoming young women the King of Blanch left the game, just once, to come here and choose between us. He had a broad smile and flat eyes. I met his eyes and stared right back. Snowdrop looked down. She was afraid of him, I could tell, and I think he could too because he picked her.

"You'll like Blanch," he said to Snowdrop. "The skies there are diamonds, and the cats are white tigers with coats like silk. You'll like being a queen." Snowdrop nodded and the corner of her mouth trembled, but she managed not to cry.

Two: when we were children I accidentally cut off the very tip of Snowdrop's little finger. Everyone was screaming and running for bandages and the doctor. Meanwhile, I took the bloody tip into my mouth. It was cold and clammy but I swallowed, because all of Snowdrop's flesh belonged to me too, and I didn't want it wasted.

Three: when we were very, very little, Snowdrop killed Mother by drinking her health; Mother shrank and wept until she disappeared. The sound of her bones cracking was sharp on the winter air. It happened in front of all the court, it must have been a feast day. I can't remember which. The courtiers cried, Daddy cried, Snowdrop cried. She had only wanted to drink a bit of Mama in—she wanted our mother's raven-dark hair. Snowdrop hated being a redhead. But she got something wrong and Mama died instead.

Funny business.

♥

The following morning I met Snowdrop on the east terrace, which was filled with tall orange trees. Prisoners hung in cages from the branches. Some were dead and the stench mingled uneasily with that of orange blossom and the cries of the living.

Snowdrop stood in the morning sun, looking very lovely and serious.

"What is this marvellous thing you're going to show me?" I asked.

"Look," she said and opened her hand. In it was a little round mirror, decorated with white pearls and black agate. "I found it in Mother's things. I was looking in her dresser for a ribbon to tie my hair, and it fell out of her button box. As if I was meant to find it, Kitty!"

"Well," I said, "you always did like to look at yourself."

"No," she said. "Keep looking at the sky!"

I watched the still blue image of the sky in the mirror. Nothing happened. At length a bird flew by, lonely and small.

"Did you see it?"

I shrugged.

"Now look up," Snowdrop said.

Overhead, the sky was clear; there was no bird in sight.

"It's another world," she whispered. "Just like this one, Kitty, but better. If I can get us over there to the other place—why, then we don't have to get married ever, or go into the game. I've looked very carefully in each direction and I'm sure—they don't have the game over there. It's full of fields and sheep and mills turning lazily on flowing streams. Oh, Kitty, it's lovely, do look!"

She held up the mirror to the great plains below, where two teenage boys were stabbing one another to death. In the mirror I saw only flashes of cool forest. "And dearest Kitty, there is someone over there who…" Her cheeks flushed prettily. "Oh, I can't spoil it. You will have to see for yourself. It's too wonderful."

No doubt this was the man for whom Snowdrop had put on that shining green belt this morning, for whom she had brushed her hair a hundred times. Some shepherd or miller—when she could have had a king. Honestly.

She laid her hand on mine. "Please, Kitty," she said. "It's our way out. And I couldn't do it without you. Dearest sister."

I don't know if she really wanted me to come. But she was right, she needed me. We're made of the same flesh, and that's powerful magic. She didn't have enough strength to do it by herself.

I took a deep breath. "All right," I said. "I'll come."

"It should be tonight," Snowdrop said. "There's a twin moon, which will help." She bit her nail. "Should we say goodbye to Father?"

"Oh," I said. "Yes, I suppose we should, if we can find him."

♥

We had to search high and low. He had hidden himself well. At last, in the red ballroom, I heard breathing. It came from inside one of the flower vases that lined the walls, each the height of a man. I tugged on Snowdrop's sleeve. We went up close to it quietly and I said, "Papa?"

The vase trembled on its base. "No," a voice said. "Go away!"

"It's us, Papa," Snowdrop said. "Won't you come out?"

"I can't," he said, his voice echoing strangely in the neck of the vase. "It's not safe."

Papa went into hiding after Mama died. Everyone knows that a king is in grave danger once the queen is gone. We had seen him perhaps once or twice in the intervening years.

"Papa," Snowdrop said. "We're leaving here for a better place."

"No!" he said. "Your place is with me! I want you here!"

"It will be fine, Papa," said Snowdrop, with more patience than I could have mustered. "I found a mirror in Mama's bedroom. It's the door to a wonderful kingdom, where there is no game."

There was a long silence from the vase. Eventually Papa said, "You found Mama's mirror? And it still works?"

"Yes," Snowdrop said, "and we have to go, Papa. You must understand that."

"Well, what are you standing here talking to me for?" he asked, which was a very good question.

Snowdrop looked as if she were about to cry. "If you want to come with us," she whispered, "we'll be on the north terrace, at the double moonrise."

"My place is with my kingdom," Father said, spitting the words. "As is yours, you traitorous girls."

"Goodbye Father," I said politely. "I hope no one puts a bouquet of roses on top of you."

We walked the half mile back across the ballroom in silence. At length Snowdrop said, "We need some things for tonight." Her voice had a new, grim note in it.

I helped her gather the necessary items. They were mostly herbs and insects. As we foraged in the garden, the sun bright and the wind bringing the pink to our cheeks, I saw her looking at the castle, at the bright silver doves in the dovecote, the apple tree we climbed as children. I saw her making her silent goodbyes.

I cut a sprig of thyme. “Ow,” it screamed. “Ow, my arm!”

“Oh, do be quiet,” I said.

I didn’t make any goodbyes. I had no intention of going with Snowdrop. I planned to pull back at the last minute, and push her into the mirror world. I knew that alone and without my magic, she would probably die there. As far as I was concerned this was probably the fate she deserved, since she killed Mother. But if by some miracle she made it over, that was fine too. Either way, Snowdrop would be gone. Then, I supposed, King Blanch and I would marry. He should have chosen me—we were well suited. I have always known that I would do well in the game, because I know how to bow to the necessary.

♥

Night fell and the moons rose, one of pearl, the other black like jet, gleaming like the surface of a deep, dark lake. You wouldn’t think you could see a black moon against a night sky, but you can.

We stood on the north terrace, among the graves, the memorials of ornate marble and gold. They all bore the same name. *Queen Dinah of the Raven Hair.* For the short time before he went into hiding, Father kept holding Mama’s funeral, over and over. Since she didn't leave a body to bury, all the coffins were empty.

Snowdrop began. She burned the herbs and insects in a chalice of grey flint. The flame leapt purple and green. She held the little mirror over the flame and whispered, the crease between her brows growing deeper and deeper. At last she stopped, mouth crumpled with distress.

"Come here, Kitty," she said. "I need to use you." We had both known she would—I just wanted to make her ask. I took her hand and we stood side by side, just like the moons above us in the sky.

Snowdrop began again, under her breath, and it happened very quickly this time. The mirror leapt from her hand and into the air where it hung and grew, like a pool of mercury spreading. Soon it was the size of a door.

Snowdrop drew a deep breath. "It's time."

We stepped through together, hand in hand. Ahead, at the end of the shimmering tunnel, I could see a quiet room, with a black cat sleeping on a sofa. There was the sound of a fire crackling in a hearth. I prepared to withdraw my hand and run back down the tunnel, to the castle.

The black cat raised its head and looked at us. Around her neck was a silver tag, which read *Dinah*. She blinked her green eyes. "There you are, children," she said. "Hurry up. Come through."

It wasn't a man that Snowdrop had been preening for, after all. I cursed myself for my stupidity. Whose opinion does a daughter most care for? For whom does she fuss and preen and put on her best finery?

Snowdrop squeezed my hand. "I wanted to surprise you," she said. "Mama didn't want to be in the game either. She wanted to take us away, into this world, but she knew Father would not give us up and she began to fear for her life. So she made it seem like she died, but she came here. Oh, when I first saw her in the mirror, Kitty, it was like I came alive again! I knew we had to go to her."

And what of all those years she let us think she was dead? That you killed her? But at the other end of the tunnel the cat smiled and purred. I couldn't hold on to the bitter thought.

"You're home!" she said. "For a girl's place is always with her mother. Don't just gawp and stand there, Kitty dear. Curtsey while you're thinking what to say, it saves time."

I curtseyed and laughed. "Why not?" I said. I had been planning something very different but there was a crack opening in my heart. It had been sealed shut for many years, since the day Mother died.

We ran towards her, hand in hand. The surface of the mirror was unpleasant and yielding like jelly. We came through it with a *plop* and tumbled out onto the soft blue rug before the fire.

I looked at Snowdrop. She meowed and did a quick turn. She was a kitten now, as white as her name. Whereas I was a kitten the colour of pitch. "Oh, Kitty," Snowdrop whispered. "How wonderful. I hated that red hair."

"You left out many, many details about this, sister dear," I said to Snowdrop.

"All worlds have rules," my mother said. "As you know. Can you accept these ones? I wouldn't dare to try and influence you, but it's actually rather nice, being a cat."

I leapt into the air and batted my two front paws. I couldn't help giggling. It came out as a purr. She was right, it wasn't so bad. I felt very light and playful, quite unlike myself. Perhaps I could be better here. Perhaps there would be no need for villainy.

Dinah leapt down off the sofa. "Come to me, my lovely girls."

A long, thin arm pushed through the mirror. It hung in the air like a dead winter branch. At horrible speed it grasped Dinah's scruff in thin fingers. One of the fingers bore Father's ring.

"Come back," Father said, voice oddly booming. "You belong here."

Dinah screamed and writhed. Snowdrop and I leapt and bit at the arm with our needle teeth. He shrieked in pain and let Dinah go. Then he seized Snowdrop and me by our scruffs and pulled us towards the mirror. Mother was yowling and trying to pull us back into the room.

We went through the clingy surface of the mirror, and then stopped, pulled this way and that by either parent. Then it happened. With a great rending sound we divided. I saw us float back along the tunnel, two girls held by Papa's giant monstrous hand. With a thump, Mama pulled us kittens back through the mirror and into the quiet sitting room.

Snowdrop was screaming. And I understood because I felt it also; the pain was very bad, yes, where our selves had been torn in two.

Mother nuzzled Snowdrop. "It's all right, darling, you're here with me, now."

"I'm there, too. I feel everything she feels." Snowdrop wept. "Father is beating her. Oh, I shall have to get married and be in the game after all, I cannot bear it…"

We were double, now, one of us trapped in each world. I think it could only have happened to twins. Snowdrop and I were divided from a single zygote. And what can be split once can always be split again. Magic is like that. It has no imagination.

Dinah put out a pink tongue and groomed Snowdrop, who continued to weep softly. Mother looked at me. I saw a familiar light, deep in her green eyes. It was triumph.

"Father didn't put up much of a fight about that mirror, or our plan to leave him," I said. "And somehow, you and Father *both* have us now. It makes me wonder if perhaps that was the bargain, all along? A pair of twins each."

Dinah sat up straight. The tip of her tail flicked. "Not now," she hissed. "The girl is coming. Play your part. Remember, you are a cat."

The approaching footsteps sounded like thunder to my new, delicate ears.

"Father didn't close the way behind him," I whispered. I could feel the looking-glass pulsing gently above the mantel.

Mother swore quietly, and then said, "She will never notice."

I sat by the hearth and washed my whiskers.

The Night Parade

LAURA MAURO

Airi sparks up a cigarette. Summer night air lies blanket-heavy across her bare shoulders. She grew up in rural Itakura in a house without air conditioning. On those stifling nights, all you could do was sweat, listless on a stripped-down futon, the futile drone of oscillating fans pushing hot air around. A sluggish breeze through the windows, if you were lucky. Here in Osaka the whirring cicadas compete with main-road traffic to produce the most noise, and the humidity is laced with diesel fumes, the stale heat pumped out by a thousand air conditioners. Sweat-dappled forehead, the persistent cling of damp clothes. The musty scent of unwashed bodies in too-small apartments.

She exhales. It is not yet full dark; the apartment blocks are hazy silhouettes against a sky the hue of a fading bruise. Grey smoke rises from her parted lips, hanging still in the air for a long moment. The complete absence of a breeze feels like punishment, and yet she persists. Summer in Osaka is yet to defeat her, and remaining outside is an act of defiance, breathing smoke into the soup-thick night. To retreat to her tiny air-conditioned apartment would feel too much like failure. Not that she has anyone to prove herself to; her friends are scattered across the city, and the luckier ones are probably embracing the chilly relief of their own air con; skin gleaming rather than glistening, the deliberately cultivated glow of the young and the beautiful, while she sweats punitively on her tiny balcony.

Down on the darkening street, something small and quick darts across the road. Sometimes, in the height of summer, the rats move in. They chew on the electrical wires and cables, build nests beneath the vending machines. They scurry through the children's park, feasting on the remnants of dropped snacks, the detritus of small children. The ripe trash bags left out by her less disciplined neighbours, improperly sorted, marked with lurid red "rejected" stickers and left to rot.

For a long moment, she sees nothing; everything is still save for the maddening dance of mosquitos, insubstantial as heat haze. And then it emerges from behind a parked car. A fox, russet hide blood-dark in the gloom. It is strangely unhurried as it enters the children's park, incongruous against the sand-pale gravel. Every few steps it pauses, looks around, as though surprised to find itself here, surrounded by looming apartment blocks. Airi nestles her chin in the cup of her palm as she watches it, this well-fed beast with its full, thick tail. She has seen foxes before, but never here, deep in the heart of urban Osaka, and never once such a regal-looking creature.

The skitter of sandals on sun-warm concrete, loud in the still silence. On the other side of the road, a small child; a tiny girl clutching something small and white, dark hair cropped short. She is surely no older than three. Airi frowns. The streets are deserted; not even the ubiquitous bicycles are out tonight, and the roads are conspicuously quiet, as though the entire city has collectively and secretly agreed to remain inside. Airi leans over the balcony, scanning the street below. Surely there must be a parent in tow. Perhaps they have been distracted by their cell phone. Perhaps the child has wandered out onto the street while they browse the chiller cabinet in the Family Mart, entranced by the fox. Any moment now some harried-looking mother will burst into view, calling after their little darling.

The child bolts into the road. Instinctively, Airi flinches. The girl does not look before she runs; she is so small, eggshell-fragile in wisteria blue. That there is not a single car on the road does not register to Airi as she stubs her cigarette out on the bricks. She leaps up, pushing the screen door aside and into the apartment, weaving through that narrow, cluttered space, pausing to grab her keys from the dish and tug on her sneakers as she scrambles out the front door. The frantic pitter-patter of her feet on the stairs. Out past the bike racks and onto the pavement, squinting in the serene blue glow of the streetlamps. The child is gone.

Her heart thuds with exertion as she crosses the road—so

empty, so *eerie*. The harsh rasp of her breathing sparks a recurring memory. Mizuki's voice, insistent, exasperated: *You really ought to quit smoking, Ai-chan, you're not supposed to have lungs like an incinerator at our age.* Rich coming from Mizuki, who subsists on the pizzas she delivers on her hellishly noisy Honda scooter, and who swoons at the thought of walking further than two blocks. The child, Airi realises, is not there. Impossible; a child so small could not have disappeared completely in such a short space of time. She turns in a useless circle, peering down the road; small birds sit silhouetted and static on the power lines, gradually blending in with the blooming dark. Into the children's park, where there is no child, no fox, no living thing at all save for the languid summer bugs circling the streetlamps. The swings cast spindle-limbed shadows across the gravel. A breeze kisses the treetops; dry leaves whisper conspiracies. A plush rabbit toy, abandoned.

Scrape marks in the gravel indicate movement. A thin pall of yellow-gold dust lingers in the still air. She has missed the child by mere moments. But this is impossible; there is no path beyond the low bushes, nothing but wire fence and brick wall. A single exit and entrance. But both fox and child are nowhere to be seen. She follows the marks towards a cluster of bushes, a low-hanging tree. She kneels, tentative. "Hello?" Hesitant, so as not to startle. She knows well enough that a cornered fox might bite. A cornered child might, too. There is no sound from the bushes, no motion; a strange, pregnant silence, as though something is holding its breath. As though something is poised and ready to strike.

Ridiculous. She'd grown up on farmland, curious and wary in equal measures of the *mamushi* snakes, watchful for *suzumebachi* nests; there is nothing in the city that can scare her quite so much. She is unfazed by drunks, will glare at subway gropers until they back away, cowed. She reaches a slow hand out, brushing back foliage. The warm-wood scent of temple incense rises up. The space between the leaves is dark. Her hands are wet when she pulls them back, dappled as though with rain. She turns her wrists, examining her skin, the rivulets running down her forearms. And there, inside the bushes, the distant echo of footsteps on stone, the low hiss of rain in the trees. Airi glances back into the still Osaka night, at the cloud-curdled sky and the bone-dry gravel, the perfect stillness of the strange, empty roads. Deserted balconies and darkened windows. The sound of rainfall echoing, impossibly, from deep inside the bushes. A plush white rabbit, abandoned in the middle of the park. All of these things are true.

A firefly flicker of gold catches her eye, a flutter of motion as something turns, disappears into the deep shadow. She follows before she realises what she's doing. She is a child again, chasing frogs into the reeds, incurably curious. Headlong into the bushes, into a darkness so full and profound that it feels, just for a moment, like she may never see the sun again.

♥

The patter of rain shocks her summer-warm skin. Instinctively, she ducks beneath an outstretched bough; her damp hair clings to the curve of her forehead. She blinks slowly, adjusting to the deep, sudden gloom. The rich odour of leaf mulch and damp moss and incense, somewhere close by. The air is thin here, sharp with pine-scent; there is a narrow path creeping steeply upwards, choked with thick foliage, a carpet of ferns. Innumerable torii gates burn vermilion in the moonlight, lining the path, disappearing into the blue-dark wilderness.

She has seen this before, in a different space, a different time. Stone foxes dappled with bright moss, eyes weathered and watchful. A child's tired legs, and the seashore murmur of a thousand tourists, a hundred unfamiliar tongues. The sweet-salty scent of fresh *yaki dango*. But this is not that vibrant, sacred place. These paths are unlit, choked with ferns, untroubled by human feet. A lost, moonlit wonderland. The torii gates are weathered and crooked, listing at broken angles like a long and twisted spine. A severed *shimenawa* rope dangles limp from the lintel, a length of damp, weatherworn twine. The forest has crept in, wrapped lush fingers around pillars, and the paths are engulfed in its mossy gullet.

A sudden rustling in the undergrowth. She turns, curious, afraid. What silent, dark-dwelling creatures might live in this forgotten place? What has scented her strange flesh, is watching her from the shadows? So many places to hide up here. So many places to watch, and to wait. But when it emerges at last—slow, careful, perched in the branches of a black pine—it is only a calico cat, rheumy eyes gleaming jade-green in the dark. A thin creature, pitiful flesh stretched tight over sharp ridges of bone. It regards her with feral suspicion; she remembers these too, the half-wild beasts who haunt the Inari shrine like sleek ghosts. The cat descends; it slips from branch to branch as though half-liquid, all serpentine spine and whiplash tail. In spite of its thinness, it is enormous. It is bigger than any cat she has ever seen, and its claws are half-sheathed sickles, teeth like slivers of bone. Its eyes meet hers, incurious, unthreatened.

"I'm sorry," she tells the cat, quite sincerely. "You look so hungry, and I haven't got anything to give you." Her bare legs feel exposed, vulnerable; the cat could close its jaws around her ankle, drive sharp teeth into the meat, shredding tendon and bone. There are food carts at the bigger shrines—thick, glistening skewers of grilled beef, cloud-soft mochi—but this shrine belongs to the forest, and this cat is nobody's pet. It must sustain itself on the small creatures that scurry and hide, that cower in the long grass, so still and quiet. Pickings must be lean of late; up close she can count each vertebra, see the undulating topography of its ribs.

She thinks of the child, then, wandering deeper and deeper into the twilight forest. Might a hungry cat stalk a lost child? Might it follow them through the trees, into the enveloping darkness, waiting for them to stumble? Might it scent blood, sense the terrified adrenaline, the weakness of exhaustion? There is no sign of the girl here, but she must have come this way, and she cannot possibly have travelled far. She must be within reach.

The cat turns its hungry gaze towards the gate-tunnel, into the distance, where the path is swallowed by shadow.

And in that shadow, a cluster of distant lights like bright eyes, the flicker of flame, white-pale as they pass through the forest. A late-night pilgrimage to the shrine, perhaps, though there is no sound, no sense of motion. It seems the lights are travelling of their own accord, like *obon* lanterns buoyed on a gentle current. Surely a child would be drawn to those lights.

Wet ferns brush at her ankles as she ascends, passing beneath the severed *shimenawa*. The dark unnerves her, the way it bleeds through every gap, every fissure, ebbing like a gentle tide. Like black water at the mouth of an unseen river. The relentless hiss of rain and her exposed skin rippling with gooseflesh. Into the gate-tunnel, in search of the girl-child, alone and vulnerable. A lost and sodden pilgrim following the procession of lights.

♥

The gates are infinite. They are a parade of arthritic limbs held at abject angles, a gallery of dilapidation. Her feet ache miserably; raw skin and damp bones, and still she treads with caution, for *mamushi* make their home in places like this. Uneven ground underfoot, the sway of loose ankles. She is dressed for hot weather, but the sweat in her hair has long evaporated, the weight of Kansai summer cut loose and drifting; the damp cold permeates her flesh like a fever chill. It feels as though she has been walking for days, and still the lights remain maddeningly distant.

She could turn back, still. She could leave the child and return to that quiet threshold, that black and empty space between spaces. It is not too late to go home. But when she turns, footsore and rainslick and tired, the path is swaddled by pale, impenetrable mist, the road lost. She cannot go back. The only way out is through, like a sweltering fever dream; she is all aching bones and empty, growling stomach and the mist mocks her, accuses her: *Did you really think…? Are you actually that stupid…? Would you truly leave that child to die…?*

And no, of course not, of course she would never, but the lights are as far away as ever, and the girl is nowhere. No child so small could have travelled such a distance so quickly. She must have wandered off the path, somewhere. She must be lost in the deep woods, or asleep beneath a persimmon tree, or perhaps she is warm meat in the stomach of something enormous. Perhaps she is close by, weeping softly in the green-black dark. Airi does not particularly like children. She wards off questions of dating and marriage with blunt force, leaving a string of disappointed relatives and nonplussed friends in her wake. This is not some frustrated maternal crusade but a sense of obligation, of responsibility; no other soul saw that child disappear but her. Nobody would ever think to look for her here. She imagines those small bones couched in bright moss. A scrap of wisteria blue like a flag in the breeze.

"You're lost."

She looks up. A tall, thin boy, or perhaps a girl, long in the limb and fine-boned, narrow face and summer-dark skin. Underfed and cautious. Thick hair snarled and knotted as though it has never known a comb, half-hidden beneath the hood of a grey cloak. And those eyes, as sharp and green as sea-ice.

"It can't be."

Lips part in a wide, bright grin. The teeth are needle-sharp. "Can't it?" The voice is half a purr. A glimpse of a thick, heavy tail flickering between narrow ankles. Airi recalls childhood stories of the weird and the monstrous, her *ojisan*'s insatiable love of folklore; tales of *bakeneko*, old and wily cats who shift shape, who dance wild jigs with napkins draped over their heads. Who might lead a man to his doom, if the fancy takes them. "You underestimate what is possible. But then, I'd expect nothing less from a human."

There is no obvious hint of threat in the *bakeneko*'s voice, but cats are capricious beasts; their whims change with the direction of the wind. "You're right," she says. "I don't even really know where I am right now. I came here to find a lost thing and now I'm lost myself." A small, frustrated laugh. "Could you tell me how to get out of here?"

"Well, that depends," the *bakeneko* purrs. "Where exactly do you want to end up?"

"If I can at least find a way out of the torii..."

The grin widens, a flash of garnet tongue. "Why do you suppose I'd help you?"

"Either you've come here to kill me, or to help me." She looks the *bakeneko* in the eye, tries not to flinch at the way its pupils dilate. A bear might let you live if you play dead; a cat will only make a toy of your corpse. Mizuki would call her insane, and perhaps Mizuki would be right, but Mizuki is not here. "If you've decided to kill me, there's nothing I can do to stop you. And I've nothing to offer you to convince you to help me. But I hope you will."

The hollow drum of raindrops on old, rotting wood, a maddeningly familiar rhythm. Somewhere out in the forest an unseen animal calls out, low and eerie. Her heart thrums loud in her ears. The *bakeneko*'s eyes are bright jewels in the shadow of its hood, unblinking, watching her with what might be suspicion, or admiration, or anger. Her heart plummets into the depths of her gut; her body stiffens, taut-muscled, ready to run, but she is so tired, so lost.

"Follow the lights," the *bakeneko* says at last. "And whatever you do, you must not let them see you."

"I've *been* following—" But the *bakeneko*'s grey cloak melts into the surrounding darkness, dissipating with the smooth ease of ink in water until nothing remains save for a hint of pale green iris, watchful even in its absence. She turns back to the path, to the lights, which have progressed no further, drawn no closer. Their steady distance infuriates her. On aching feet she walks on.

♥

The *bakeneko*, at least, is true to its word. Further up, the path forks. One leads upwards, a steep track carved into the hillside, slick mud glistening; the other leads down. Here, the gates grow sparse, blasphemous in their disrepair. The loamy smell of rotten wood. Fragments of red-painted pillar nestle in the leaf litter. And between the trees, glimmering in the near distance, the procession of lights. So close, now, that she can almost make out the shapes of the lantern-bearers; indistinct, a slow-flowing river of half-lit figures meandering through the forest.

The way down is a gauntlet. Thick roots grasp at her ankles; the thin moonlight of the upper slope barely reaches down here, in this deep green gully. If there are snakes down here she will never see them. The forest floor is cut through with shallow streams, rocks gleaming with wet moss. The descent looks endless.

She wonders if they can sense her, if they are possessed of keen hearing, a sharp sense of smell. If her flesh carries with it the sour tang of gasoline and cigarette smoke. The *bakeneko*'s warning nags like an old ache. What will they do if they find her? Their lamplit silhouettes are vague, varied; they look motley, misshapen, but light plays tricks, and so do cats. Are they keen-eyed and fierce-clawed? Are they strange beasts at all, or merely quiet, solemn men searching for some long-forgotten shrine?

Unpainted torii sprout from the mulch as though grown spontaneously from seed. Enormous *sugi* trees marked here and there with *shimenawa*; here the *kodama* dwell, the tree-spirits who, her *ojisan* claimed, would curse any man who dared to fell the trees in which they lived.

"Steady, now." A whisper from the trees. She looks up, startled, but it is no *kodama*. The *bakeneko* peers down at her from a low branch, thin cat-body poised as though to strike. Its ears swivel, tracking sounds too fine for her dull human ears. "You're almost upon them. If you are truly determined to save the child—well, then you're an idiot, but that's no problem of mine. If you must go, go in disguise. If they sense that you are human, they will show no mercy."

Airi frowns. "I never said anything about a child."

The *bakeneko* smirks. "And yet, why else would you be here? Strange enough that one human might happen upon the parade. But for you to stumble in after her on those great, clumsy feet, well… Coincidences are so lazy, aren't they?"

"The parade…?"

"Did you not think it strange, human, that your realm would be so empty, so *quiet*? Didn't you ask yourself why?" The *bakeneko* stretches; sickle-sharp claws graze old bark, and Airi knows this is a deliberate reminder; it could still turn on her, if it wanted to. "The night parade is coming. They will leave this forest and pass through into your world. Any human who looks upon them will drop dead on the spot, such is their power. Did you not feel it? That terrible unease, like a sickness, warning you to stay inside?"

The lanterns hover. The parade has stopped. Her skin prickles. They are so close. "But who are *they*?" she whispers. The sudden stillness unnerves her; even the rain seems to have stopped, and she feels the hush deep in the fibres of her muscles, a terrible pressure like the moment before a storm breaks. They are waiting, she realises, and she is late.

The *bakeneko*'s voice echoes, a faraway song: "Perhaps you should go and find out."

When she looks up—the glow of the lanterns seared pale into her retina, ghostly in the branches—the *bakeneko* is gone, and its cloak hangs from a bough like a shed skin. She pulls it down, slips it on; it is warm against her damp skin. The fabric smells strange; a musty animal odour, yes, but something else. Temple incense and old ash. The sweet-fragrant scent of cedarwood. She pulls the hood up over her head, obscuring her face in shadow. It will have to be enough. The night parade is waiting for her.

♥

The first thing Airi realises is that the lanterns are not lanterns at all, but flickering orbs drifting between the trees, awash with flame. *Kitsune-bi*; fox-lights, red-gold glow and deep shadow, casting the monstrous procession in sharp relief. They are *everywhere*; beside her, a fur-covered beast in scarlet *hakama* trousers, black-lacquered teeth bared in a grin, or perhaps a snarl. Bird-beaked *tengu*, their eyes bright and keen as crows. An elegant woman, long white neck and sleek-silk hair and smooth spider legs erupting from her kimono, splayed and skittering. And there, on the very edge of the parade, the child. She regards the beastly circus with benign curiosity, the way a child might regard a room full of relatives.

Airi moves through them with care, barely daring to breathe as she weaves between the squat, slick-skinned *kappa*, a cluster of chittering *tanuki*. The low murmur of inhuman voices forming peculiar words. They are legion, these *yokai*. They choke the forest path with their numbers, astonishing in their variety; monsters plucked from her *ojisan*'s tales and still others, anomalous but oddly familiar: the corpulent caterpillar smoking a pipe, the raggedy-eared hare sipping deep green *sencha* from a chipped cup;

creatures from another tale, another place, yet they too have joined the procession, and it seems all beasts are welcome here. The night parade, the *bakeneko* had called it: *They will leave this forest and pass through into your world.* And still the child sits among them as though none have noticed her obvious humanity.

The child looks up at her as she approaches, unafraid. Airi kneels; the cloak pools around her, swallowing her feet and ankles. She extends a hand; her exposed fingers feel vulnerable, the slender bones of her wrist, the veins pulsing just beneath the skin. "Let's go," she whispers, and the child's eyes widen a little at the sound; those words, that language, the sound of home. She reaches out, hesitant, one grubby palm unfolding, the dirt-caked crescents of tiny fingernails. The call of familiar skin.

A hand on her shoulder. Rank fox-stink strong in her nostrils, sweet carrion-breath. "She is not one of yours," a voice says, barely a murmur. "If you leave now, I will let you go. I will tell nobody you were here. But if you persist, I will tear off your head and throw your body to the *oni*."

Airi swallows hard. She is aware of the carnival of beasts gathered behind her, around her; of the nervous sweat beading her skin, pungent with adrenaline. The flimsiness of her disguise.

"Do you doubt me?" The brush of skin against her neck, smooth and hot; sharp-tipped fingers tighten around her shoulder. In the corner of her eye, the bright gleam of teeth. "Oh, but you shouldn't. Leave the child and go while you have the chance. You don't belong here, girl. They'll sniff you out soon enough, and they will not show you mercy as I have."

She speaks between clenched teeth, a furious mutter. "She's just a child. What use is she to you? Why won't you let her go?"

"She belongs to *me*." A hand at her throat, now, grasping her chin, the wrench of taut muscle as the *kitsune* twists Airi's head around so that they are face to face, eye to eye. She is beautiful, long-limbed and powerful, skin like burnished gold; dressed all in red silk, an arterial queen. Claws rake Airi's neck, playful as a lover. "Her coward father cast me out. He sent me away from my own child. Ashamed of his fox-wife. But she has my blood. I carried her and I gave birth to her and she is *my* daughter."

The *kitsune* releases her grasp. Airi staggers back, rubbing at her chin, her face, the bright sting of ribbon-thin lacerations. Her breath comes in shallow gasps. The *kitsune*'s eyes are black diamonds; a carnivorous gaze. When she turns back to the child—so soft and vulnerable—there is a glossy beetle caught in her clumsy grasp. Her eyes light up in delight, enchanted by her treasure. She beams at Airi, white pebble-teeth and bright girl-eyes, unmistakably human. The girl crams the beetle into her open, smiling mouth. Teeth crunch against carapace, spraying fragments like black glitter. The hint of a gauzy wing melting on her pink tongue.

"She has my blood," the *kitsune* says, and there is such pride in her voice.

The terminal dance of black matchstick legs as the girl

chews, open-mouthed, unselfconscious. Airi's gut roils; the *kitsune* snickers as Airi backs away, choking down her revulsion. It proves nothing, Airi tells herself, fixing her nauseous gaze on the undergrowth, the lazy drift of a wayward fox-light; children eat worms and dirt all the time, if you let them. It does not make her half a *kitsune*. Somewhere in Osaka a terrified mother and father are searching frantically for their daughter. Isn't that all that matters? Isn't that why she came all this way?

Green eyes bloom in the air before her. "It would be easy to distract them," the *bakeneko* says, disembodied. "Can you run? If they catch you, they will kill you."

They are moving behind her, this seething, monstrous mass; they are a dam on the verge of bursting. The parade is about to begin. "I don't know," Airi says. She is so tired, so hungry. The forest gloom is pervasive, monotone; she dreams of the human clutter of Shinsaibashi, awash with the white noise of a hundred conversations. The neon headache of Dotonbori, comforting in its permanence. It feels as though she has been lost here for weeks. "There're too many of them."

"Chaos makes them stupid." The floating mouth curves upwards, a Cheshire grin. "What other chance do you have? Join the parade? Your disguise won't last that long."

"Why would you do this?" She tries to meet the *bakeneko*'s gaze but its eyes are maddeningly evasive; its grin remains static even as the eyes dance lazily in the dark. "Why help her get away?"

"Oh, it's not for her." The eyes close, blinking out of

existence. "It's not for you, either. They were gods once, did you know that? They were powerful deities. But an unworshipped god decays over the centuries. They still dream of godhood, these *yokai*, even as your kind turn them into mascots and trinkets. I could feed you to them, certainly. They would make short work of your flesh, chew your bones into powder. But it's over too soon. Chaos is so much more fun. Get ready to run, girl. Don't stop until you see daylight." The grin dissipates. "Don't stop until you're home."

The *bakeneko*'s gambit reveals itself in a mad flourish; the manifestation of a human form in among the monsters, screaming as it holds the child aloft. It howls in the language of the *yokai*, a strange and lilting dialect fit for the gods they once were, and never will be again. The child's chin is speckled with beetle shell, her eyes wide and confused as the *yokai* turn, first confused and then enraged; this human intruder in their midst, who dares address them in their own sacred tongue, who dares hold in their mortal grasp the *kitsune*'s own child. The *bakeneko*'s approximation of human skin is uncanny; it is too smooth, too perfect; beautiful and androgynous and utterly false, but the parade converges upon it with ready anger, a monstrous tide sweeping in, engulfing the *bakeneko*'s faux-human body. And Airi, on the periphery of the crowd, watches as the child is buoyed along by hands and paws and wings; one by one, towards her *yokai*-mother, conveying her so carefully;

all must have prizes, she thinks, as they visit their savagery upon the intruder in their midst. How, Airi wonders, can she join the throng, intercept their false fox-child? How can she insinuate herself among them with their blood so high, their senses incendiary?

"Quickly," the *bakeneko*'s voice echoes. "The illusion will only keep for so long."

The *yokai* writhe and thrash, hunting for a trace of the insolent red-garbed human. Airi turns to the *bakeneko*; no floating eyes or half-moon grin, but there, sitting precisely where she had been before, is the child, unruffled by the chaos unfolding around her. Airi scoops her up quickly, tucks her beneath the folds of her cloak; the girl is heavy in her arms, but she is still, and quiet. She does not protest as Airi moves, slowly at first, tiptoeing away from the parade; the irony of skulking fox-like into the forest, the human turned trickster.

♥

Don't stop until you see daylight, the *bakeneko* had said. A pinprick of pale green light glows in the distance, between the trees. That way must be home, she thinks; where the sun rises, the night parade cannot follow. She is exhausted, but she is so close. The girl presses her face into Airi's shoulder, arms too tight around her neck. She runs, and as the air is torn ragged from her smoker's lungs, the burn of acid flooding underused muscles, she realises dimly that the forest is quiet. There is only the sound of her own laboured breathing, the rhythmic thud of feet on wet mulch. Could she have outpaced them so soon? She chances a look over her shoulder, back into the depths of the forest, where no motley shadows lurk in pursuit; but there, close by, three slow-drifting fox-lights burning blood-gold in the gloom, and that is enough. She clutches the girl tighter, forces herself to keep going. To run where they cannot follow, these *kitsune-bi*, these bright, watchful eyes: *I will find you. I will come for you. I will destroy you.* Into the light. Towards the rising sun.

♥

Osaka hits her in the face like a clenched fist. It is barely morning and yet the sheer sensory overload is paralysing; thick petrol and the rumble of engines and people, so many people, like brightly coloured flags in the breeze, smoking and talking and knocking back hot, canned coffee. The sun, migraine-sharp in a sky so blue it makes her teeth hurt. She made it. She is home.

The gravel gnaws at her knees as she sinks to the ground; so warm, so solid and dry. The bundle beneath her cloak is still; sleeping, perhaps, or scared stiff, but safe. With trembling fingers she pulls the cloak from around her shoulders, peeling the wet fabric back like a shed skin. The sun feels so good she wants to weep. It has only been one night, she scolds herself, but it feels as though she has been gone for days; it feels as though she walked those torii-lined paths forever.

"Mummy, is that lady okay?"

She looks up. A young boy in crisp school uniform stands

at the mouth of the park, flanked by his well-dressed mother. She regards Airi with wide-eyed dismay, her discomfort evident in the stiff set of her shoulders. Airi looks down at herself; her grubby legs are tattooed with glistening lacerations, her shoes clotted with thick mud. Wet hair and sodden clothes and skin so cold she almost looks blue. The girl in her arms, so still, so quiet. She must look insane, a mad scarecrow of a parent.

"It's okay," she says, because it *is* okay. There is warmth, and there are people, and the child is safe. The *yokai* cannot come for her here, where the sun burns so brightly. This is not their world. "I just… I need to find this little girl's parents. She got lost and I brought her home, and her family must miss her so much. Please, will you help me?" She holds out her arms, her precious cargo. A flash of wisteria blue. The boy's mother utters a horrified yelp as the child disintegrates into wet leaves, fragments of bark, crushed-twig limbs dangling limp from empty sleeves. A scattering of glossy black beetles disappearing into the bushes, away from the light.

The boy's mother tugs at his hand, urgent, hurrying him away; Airi feels the weight of his gaze upon her as she turns, still clutching the bundle of twigs to her chest, back to the bushes, the infinite forest hidden within. The smell of temple incense filtering up through the leaves; the barest flash of jubilant teeth fading into the dwindling shadows like an afterimage: a grin without a cat. The leaf-girl, scattered and withering in the sun. A plush white rabbit, abandoned in the middle of the park. All of these things are true.

What Makes a Monster

L.L. MCKINNEY

Beyond the world of mortal man lies a place called Wonderland. A place of visions both delightful and dark, where marvels ride the winds and evils claim the shadows. There, humanity's dreams coalesce into a magnificent, ever-changing landscape that is as vast as the imagination. And there, humanity's fears manifest in deadly creatures called Nightmares, with jaws that bite and claws that catch, ever-creeping towards the veil separating the two worlds. It is the charge of Guardians born of Wonderland to train Dreamwalkers born of humanity in the ways of slaying these beasts, for if the monsters are allowed to linger in the mortal plane, the havoc they wreak would leave all in ruin and rot.

♥

'Twas brillig, and the slithy toves
Did gyre and gimble in the wabe:
All mimsy were the borogoves,
And the mome raths outgrabe.

♥

Dusk didn't just settle over London, it fell heavy and thick. All day long, chimneys spewed while furnaces spat, but at the twinkling orange of twilight, the steam and machines sputtered their last. All went quiet as the final plumes of smoke and soot fattened the night sky.

An army of lamps hissed and hummed, stalwart sentinels watching over abandoned streets and boulevards. They did their best, but on nights like tonight, it was all for nothing.

On nights like tonight, a sort of restlessness clung to the air, strangling light from the stars and breathing life into the void. On nights like tonight, shadows chased people into their homes, crawled down alleys, and coiled under bridges. On nights like tonight, the flicker of gassed flames did little to drive back the dark. It was the sort of night Bodie's maman said sent the Devil prowling. The sort of night you heard about in stories, where you couldn't tell if it was the wind or something far more sinister howling. The perfect night for hunting monsters.

The cold clung to Bodie's limbs like a living thing, leaching what scant warmth her layers of clothes provided. The men's coat she wore helped little. Numerous worn holes and poorly patched tears in the wool allowed the winter wind to bite and scratch at her. Granted, the coat was intended to conceal the sword strapped to her back, not to stave off frostbite, but heavens above why couldn't it do both?

"Because nice coats are expensive," Anastasia had said earlier, about an hour before sundown, without looking up from a map of Whitechapel. Five points were highlighted with red Xs, with one X at the center circled twice.

Bodie had snorted a laugh as she fingered the patched and thin sleeve that was part of her intended disguise. "Plan to use it as part of my dowry after we're done?" Bodie lifted one of the cotton shirts and held it up to her chest. She gazed into the nearby looking-glass. Her fractured reflection revealed beige but faintly rosy cheeks that still held a bit of plumpness from her youth. A dusting of freckles covered them and her nose. With her brown coils branded into submission thanks to a hot comb, then pinned into curls atop her head, she made a passable lady. But that wasn't Anastasia's plan.

Anastasia ticked a thin, red brow, but her attention remained fixed on the map. "Expensive coats draw attention, and you need to do the opposite. Can't have anyone figuring you out before you're done."

"And you think the coat is what will give me away? Not..." Bodie cupped her breasts through her shirt.

Now Anastasia did look up. "I think people are suspicious, and someone of possible rapport skulking through these alleys at night will have them assuming the worst, potentially alerting the Yard. Also, I have a way to deal with..." Anastasia gestured at Bodie's still cupped hands. "That." Her slight accent clipped the words in funny places.

Before Anastasia, Bodie had never heard someone with

a Russian accent speak French. In truth, she'd never heard a Russian accent at all, only the nasal way Englishmen chewed on her mother tongue. Anastasia's voice was rather pleasant, where theirs were… decidedly not.

That same voice now called to her from the folds of her breast pocket, the sound muffled against the fabric. "In a moment," Bodie whispered. She glanced up and down the street before ducking around a corner.

Checking to see that the lane was clear, she plucked a small bit of glass from her pocket. A tiny mirror rested in her gloved palm, but instead of looking at her own face, Anastasia's peered up at her from the glass.

"You were supposed to report in three minutes ago." Anastasia's pale cheeks were nearly as red as her hair where it fell around her face. The green of her eyes sparked with anger, and a little fear. "Every fifteen minutes exactly."

"No need to panic." Bodie kept moving. She glanced up from the mirror every few steps, taking in her surroundings. The clap of her heels echoed along the cobblestones. "I'm still in one piece."

"Thankfully. What kept you?"

"There was a bit of a row outside a pub. Crowd had gathered. It wasn't the ideal situation for pulling out and talking to a magic mirror."

"*Otlichno.* Have you seen anything?"

"Not yet."

Of course that was the moment a shadow darted in and out of the corner of Bodie's vision. She stopped as her head whipped around to find herself standing at the mouth of an alley. Darkness poured down the walls and deepened just a few steps from the street.

"Wait a moment." She squinted, waiting for her eyes to adjust.

Gradually, the outline of a few crates faded into view, but beyond that, nothing. She was prepared to move on, but something kept her rooted to that spot. An inkling, a twinge at the base of her skull. Her eyes weren't playing tricks, she'd *seen* something.

"What is it?" Anastasia asked softly.

"I'm not sure."

A sudden gust of wind snatched at her coat and the cloth beneath. She shivered, thankful for the trousers she wore, even if they were a size too large and itched like hell. They offered far more protection than many skirts would have done.

She lowered her arm from where she'd pressed it to her face to stave off the worst of it. That's when the smell hit her, sharper than the constant stench of London's streets, a putrid and pus-filled stink like decayed flesh, stale blood, and shit.

Bodie gagged. "I think I've got something."

"Where are you?"

She glanced around for landmarks or street signs, her eyes lighting on a plaque set in the wall above. "Dorset Street."

"Wait for me."

A scream pierced the air, and the chill that played through Bodie had nothing to do with the cold. "No time." She pocketed the mirror and rushed into the alley.

"Bodie," Anastasia called. "Bodie! Baudelaire!"

Anastasia only called her by her full name when she was angry, trying to *look* angry, or genuinely frightened. Though sometimes, when Anastasia meant for Bodie to be serious, she'd use it then as well.

"Baudelaire," Anastasia had sighed as she adjusted the bindings around the French girl's torso. "Stop squirming."

"Well, it hurts." Bodie had lifted her arms as Anastasia passed yet another layer of gauze across her chest and around her back.

"That's not pain, it's discomfort."

"*Feels* like pain." Bodie wrinkled her nose. "Isn't this a bit much?"

"What did I say before?"

"That I need to blend in. And that means dressing like a man?"

"It means being able to walk the streets without drawing attention to yourself. Things are assumed of a lady out that late, and you can't do your job if you're being propositioned half the night."

The rest of the disguise lay across a wafer-thin cot that looked as if wayward prayers and thread were all that held it together. The rest of the flat wasn't much better off. The walls were more like paper than brick, the glass rattled in the panes of the single, tiny window every time a coach rolled by, and the smell of fetid water and rot soaked the air.

It wasn't at all like the lavish hotel suite they *should* have been occupying, but there was little chance they would be able to sneak in and out of their rooms without drawing attention. That and Anastasia wanted to be nearer the suspected site, but the woman known as the Duchess and her ward could not officially take up residence in such a place.

Arms still in the air, Bodie stole a glance at the map on the nearby table. Stories of the Whitechapel murders had traveled far and wide by the time they reached Anastasia's dress shop in St. Petersburg; tales of a deranged doctor who performed rituals to summon Satan, or a demon who preyed the nighttime streets tearing apart its victims. People had no idea how right they were.

The circled X at the center of the map marked Bodie and Anastasia's current location. The plan was to do a bit of reconnaissance to search for any indication of their target's presence. A fully formed Nightmare left behind clear signs when one knew what to look for, and should your eyes fail you, you could always follow your nose.

"There you are." Anastasia patted Bodie's back. "All done. Get dressed."

Lowering her arms, Bodie rotated her shoulders, and then did the same with her hips, testing her range of motion. Shockingly, the bindings didn't hinder her in the least; not even her breathing was restricted.

"What about you?" Bodie had asked as she climbed into a pair of too-large trousers. "Don't you need a disguise?" She twisted the suspenders twice before she got them to sit right.

"Of course not." Anastasia smiled. "No one is going to notice me. It'll almost be as if I'm invisible." Which she quite literally would be.

After three years, the truth of Anastasia's origins still astounded Bodie. A magical woman from a magical world, here to fight a magical war. What astonished Bodie even more was the fact that this magical woman had needed sixteen-year-old Baudelaire to wage said war.

"Only humans can kill these creatures I hunt," Anastasia had explained. "And only if they're strong enough. Special enough."

Well, born in Arles only to be orphaned at six, and sent to the mills for ten years until Anastasia found her, Bodie was certainly strong. But being born a *négress*, even one with bright skin and eyes the color of sunset—a man had paid her this compliment before trying to force himself on her, for which Anastasia cut off his balls and left them in his pocket—Bodie had never been allowed to believe she was special. But Anastasia did.

And she continued to believe it, through months and months of laborious training with swords, daggers, and all manner of weapons. Bodie found she was a diligent student in the art of taking lives. Monstrous lives, that is.

Helping Bodie pin her hair beneath a bowler hat to complete her masquerade, Anastasia seemed to still believe it.

"There." Anastasia stepped back to look over Bodie. She reached out to adjust the large, ratty coat, like a fussing mother hen. "Do *not* use your Figment Blade unless absolutely necessary." She fastened the buttons and smoothed her hands over the front. "Don't want to draw attention to yourself."

"*Yes, mother*," Bodie said in thick, rounded English, her French accent prominent.

Anastasia huffed in mild annoyance and Bodie smiled. She enjoyed teasing the other woman. They were close in age, at least in appearance, and she'd always wanted a sister. Anastasia was much older than Bodie's nineteen years but simultaneously not. Time was strange where Anastasia came from.

"And above all else." Anastasia drew a slow breath. "Be careful."

Bodie was careful, as careful as she could be, racing through the alley. She vaulted a pair of barrels and barely managed to dodge around a half-closed iron gate before skidding to a stop. Panting, she cocked her head to the side and tried to listen. The stench crawling through the air thickened here. She covered her mouth and nose with a gloved hand, the fabric scratchy.

Another shout, brief before it was choked off. Bodie bolted in that direction, or at least the direction she thought it was coming from. Sound bounced against the stone beneath her feet and the brick rising on either side of her, making it hard to track. She pounded into the center of an alley before drawing up short. The barest hint of light managed to reach in from the nearby street and a few outlines of windows above, but her eyes still strained against the looming darkness.

Her heart thundered in her ears. Anastasia had stopped calling her name, no doubt on her way as quickly as she could manage. Bodie focused on breathing through her mouth instead of her nose, the smell damn near overwhelming now. Her eyes watered and her stomach threatened to empty itself. She swallowed a groan.

"Little one." A low voice slithered through the shadows, the words rumbled in English. "So lost. So alone."

The feeling of dread's frosty fingers that had slid down Bodie's back now dug in like talons. Her hand went over her shoulder and grasped the hilt hidden just beneath the collar of her coat.

"Show yourself," she hissed in French as she drew the sword. Even in the darkness the blade gleamed, a beam of silver and ice in the night, with a razor's edge.

"Hmmmm, Dreamwalker, well this *does* change things." The voice adjusted to French as it floated through the air, but didn't draw near. It skirted along dark corners and shuttered windows. "So, which of them was it that tracked me here? Addison? Like a dog with a bone, that one, aimlessly gnawing and never paying attention to who he's chewing on. Or maybe Romi? No, I don't think she would come this far west."

Bodie knew those names. Anastasia had mentioned them before, others who were like her, who came from her world to hunt monsters in this one.

"The human world was never her favorite place," the voice continued. "And with things like industry defiling the land, I'm sure she stays far away."

It seemed to slink along the walls like a living thing, but Bodie would not be fooled into turning her back. The stench was strongest in the direction of a nearby archway, caught on the bitter breeze pouring through, a putrid perfume. Above the opening carved into brick, a sign was posted: *Miller's Court.*

"Or, maybe, it's Anastasia." The voice rolled the name, tasting it, savoring it. "Yes, she's the only one with the patience to find me out."

Bodie tried not to react, though she couldn't help tensing at the name. She held steady, her breathing slow.

"Or maybe it was Theo. Brilliant Theo, clever Theo." The voice grew heavy, weighty, as something shifted deep in the alleyway. "Too smart for his own good."

Steps thudded against the stone, a shambling gate *clump-sliiiide clump-sliiiiiide*-ing its way toward her.

Bodie lifted the sword and shifted her stance, ready to strike. Nightmares, the monsters Anastasia warred against, the ones she had trained Bodie to fight, could come in any shape or size. They could have one head or more. They could have arms or tentacles, pincers or any manner of limbs. And it could be relatively small or big as a horse. She'd faced many of these creatures over the years, in fights difficult and simple. While she wasn't as experienced as Anastasia herself, she felt she'd been at this long enough that few things would surprise her.

So when the creature finally emerged into the dim light, Bodie thought she was prepared. But then her entire body went cold. Her eyes widened and her grip on her sword faltered. She tightened her fingers, even as her insides quivered.

Fear took hold.

A man stood at the mouth of the archway. At least, it

was shaped like a man, or maybe it had once been a man. Naked, its flesh was mottled with sores and scabs, raw, red, and runny. A tar-like substance oozed from them in the place of blood. It stood on one leg, its knee bent and its ankle twisted where claws extended to tap at the ground instead of toes. The other leg was broken at the hip, snapped out of place and wrenched backwards, black muscle the only thing tethering it to the rest of the body, dragging it along behind it.

Its arms were not arms, but were instead like a spider's legs, gangly and long, much longer than they should have been. It was clear they had stretched, ripped, and the same oozing tissue that held the dead leg in place now seemed to merely wear skin and muscle as a suit.

The head was the most unchanged. The face was sallow, the eyes sunken, the hair falling from patchy, scabby spots on its scalp. It… smiled, and when it did it was as if the man it was wearing grimaced, still somehow alive and in pain.

"So afraid." Lips peeled and split against needle-like teeth. Blood ran watery red and yellow against its chin. It drew a slow breath and its nostrils flapped. "Delectable."

Bodie tightened her grip on her sword to stop the shaking in her hands and arms. There was nothing she could do about the rest of her mutinous body. She inhaled through her nose, the smell the least of her worries. Her breath shuddered, likely betraying her terror. That is if this… this thing didn't smell it on her.

"Bodie!" Anastasia's voice called from the pocket. "Bodie, I'm almost there! Where are you?"

"Oh, so it *is* her." The monstrosity laughed. The muscles of its throat clapped together. Bodie could see them through the tenuous skin stretched where the neck had lengthened. It frayed at the edges.

"M-Miller's Court." The shaking took Bodie's tongue, her words stumbling over it. "It... h-hurry, Ana."

"I'm coming!"

"She won't make it in time." The Nightmare steepled its long, spindly black fingers, stretching out from flesh it wore like gloves. The bones popped as knuckles that shouldn't be there flexed. "But, hopefully, you will prove entertaining until her arrival." It flicked its wrist.

Bodie jolted when something wet and warm hit her in the face. She smelled and tasted blood, swiping it from her cheek and lips, spitting at the ground as disgust roiled through her.

A hunk of flesh lay at her feet, red and fresh, glistening in the low light. Some sort of organ Bodie couldn't identify. Her supper soured in her stomach and crawled toward her throat. She tasted it on the back of her tongue.

"Oh God," she whimpered.

The creature gave a satisfied hiss, then made a clumsy lunge for her. Thankfully the human parts of the body it had possessed still mostly trapped it. She was able to jump out of the way of a swipe of talons, and get her sword up to deflect another as she drew back, but only just. This thing was fast; faster than anything she'd ever faced before.

The monster twisted after her, bearing down as its face split so that rows of pointed teeth were bared. Bodie's body reacted before she could wrap her mind around it, and she parried another swing of claws, angling the blade to drive it at the Nightmare's head.

"Ahhh!" It lurched out of the way just in time, but Bodie stepped into the retreat and brought the sword around a second time. The blade bit into flesh. Yellowed pus and blackened blood bubbled over it and the monster wailed, the sword caught in its side.

A familiar rush started to take hold, adrenaline pushing at the edges of fear folding over her mind, a spindly hand latched onto the sword. But instead of pulling it out, the monster pressed it deeper.

Shock took hold of Bodie just long enough for something long and thick to dart over the monster's shoulder and pierce hers.

Pain erupted white-hot against her nerves. She felt her skin split as it was punctured and she bit down on the scream that tore at the back of her throat.

Chuckling, the monster drew back what she could now see was a tail, tipped in a barb as long and as thick as two of her fingers.

Bodie pulled at her sword. It didn't budge.

The beast readied another strike.

Letting go, Bodie dove out of the way. Her shoulder screamed as she hit the ground and rolled into a crouch. The stone was cold against her knees through the fabric of her trousers. She whirled to face her opponent, her eyes drawn to her useless weapon where it was sheathed in black flesh. If she couldn't free her sword, maybe she could drive it deeper.

As the monster turned to follow her she exploded forward, twisting around to drive the bottom of her foot against the partially exposed blade. The kick hammered it into the beast's body. It howled.

Limbs flailing, it twisted to try and dislodge the blade. Bodie drew back and ducked into a nearby alcove. She bit down on a hiss as she shoved her coat and shirt to the side. She had a hole in her shoulder, and blood ran wet and warm along her arm. The wound looked clear, though her entire arm throbbed, and a feeling like fire burned all the way to her fingertips.

Poison, she realized. Her body would work to naturally expel it, but the wound itself would prove a problem. Throwing off her coat, she tore the sleeve free at the puncture, and then used it to bind her shoulder. The pain sent spots dancing against her vision as she gripped the fabric with her teeth and pulled.

Blinking the world back into focus, she pushed to her feet. The cold air bit at her exposed skin. She could feel her pulse in her neck and her temples.

Steeling herself, she peeked around the corner. The Nightmare was still trying to pull the sword free. It worked the blade back and forth with its own sounds of pain, but the sword cut at its clumsy fingers, some of them now dangling by tendons and bits of bone.

"You cannot hide!" it snarled. "I will find you, and I will feast on you like the others!"

All the others. Anastasia's hunches had been right. Of course they were, she was hardly ever wrong. Those poor women…

But there was no time to think of that. She had to bring this thing down, to end its reign of fear and death over the city. If she could get it on the ground, she'd have the advantage. With a plan forming, Bodie bent to pluck a dagger from each of her boots. Steadying herself, she breathed deeply. Then she stepped out of the alcove and bolted across the lane. Halfway there she launched herself into the air.

The monster tried to turn, but it was too late. She slammed into it from above, driving the daggers into its back. The beast stumbled and roared. It clawed at her, trying to pull her off, but it had severed most of its talons. The remaining ones sliced at her arms and sides. Hissing, she drew one dagger free, holding onto the other where it was still buried in the Nightmare's back, and stabbed at its heart.

Another yowl, this one so loud and sharp her ears rang. She stabbed again, and again, deeper and deeper, trying to reach—

Snikt. Her body jerked as the bared tail stabbed into her back. She screamed.

Snikt, snikt.

Dizzy with pain, she let go. She hit the ground in a tumble, landing on her side. Pain radiated through her. Every breath was like a hammer against her chest and rattled in her ears. The coppery tang of blood coated her tongue.

The Nightmare whirled on her, its tail lifted. Most of the human façade had peeled away, leaving behind an oozing shell of a man-shaped monstrosity of pitch and bone.

"Ahhhh," it sighed as it shuffled toward her. "I will eat well tonight."

Bodie tried to get her arms under her but they refused to obey. So did the rest of her body. She managed to shift just so, but it sent sparks of agony along her limbs.

The thing loomed over her, its wide mouth hung open as it cackled and clacked.

Fear stabbed at her mind, tearing into her thoughts.

The past leapt forward, sewn in with the present. The Nightmare licked at its bloody barb. Her blood.

Bodie's eyelids fluttered and the image of the monster melted into the memory of her maman walking along the dirt road towards their house, her water buckets hanging from a rod over her shoulders.

"M-Ma..." Bodie blinked. The alley rushed back in around her, the cold stone beneath her, and the monster once again above her. It fussed with the sword still stuck in its side. The blade glistened, though it was covered in gore.

Another blink, and Bodie was at her parents' bedside. Maman lay on her back, her brown skin ashen, as her chest buckled with the weight of her croaky breaths. Papa was still and cold beside her.

"Promise me you'll go," Maman had rasped, her teeth rotted and her breath foul in Bodie's face, but her touch gentle as she wiped tears from her little cheeks. "Go. Find yourself a new life."

"No!" Bodie threw herself against her mother's fragile chest, her tiny body wracked with sobs. "I won't leave you."

"We will see each other again. But not before you've lived a good life, so you can come and tell me all about it."

And then, her maman was dead, her jelly eyes staring at the ceiling.

Dead. Like Bodie would soon be.

Bodie closed her eyes and left them that way. She focused on her memories of before, how things used to be. How smiling faces and warm arms used to wait for her. If she was to die, she wanted her maman's laughing eyes to be the last thing she saw before she left this world.

Crack! The monster shrieked.

Bodie's eyes flew open.

Clutching at its face, where one yellow eye dangled by nerves and muscle from its socket, the Nightmare faced off with a figure in the dark.

"Get away from her."

Bodie recognized Anastasia's voice. The woman stepped forward, her arms twirling around her body with a balanced but deadly grace. Pinpricks of light flickered through the air.

Anastasia flung her arm out and the pinpricks solidified then darted across the alley, almost faster than Bodie could follow.

Crack!

The monster barely avoided losing its other eye. While Bodie's vision was hazed by pain and the shadows of the night, she knew Anastasia's whip when she saw it. The woman was a monster herself with that thing.

The Nightmare howled and ducked to the side before darting forward, pausing, and jerking back again. It did this a few times, trying to get inside the continual flow of the whip, which circled Anastasia like a razor-lined cocoon.

But that's all it was, a defense. Why wasn't Anastasia attacking? No, she couldn't kill it, but she could at least put it down for a time. It would rise to terrorize the streets of London, but then they would be ready.

Anastasia's eyes flickered to Bodie, then to something to her left, and back to the monster. She did this three times. A signal, Bodie realized. But what for?

She struggled to push herself into a sitting position. Her body burned and her arms gave twice before she managed it. That's when she saw it.

Resting against the alley floor, her Figment Blade seemed to glow faintly in the dark. The monster must have managed to pull it out while Bodie was dazed.

She struggled onto her knees, then rose unsteadily to her feet. Her legs threatened to give, but held where she tilted heavily against a wall.

Anastasia managed to hold the beast's attention, throwing the whip out to keep it occupied, screaming at it to come at her.

Bodie could feel the life slowly seeping out of her, wet and sticky against her clothes and skin. Her wounds stretched as she moved. One step. Then two. Then three. She somehow reached her sword. Grasping the hilt in shaky fingers, she lifted it. The blade scraped against the ground.

The monster turned and shrieked.

Anastasia flung out her arm. The beast went rigid then started clawing at its throat. The razor whip gleamed where it drew taut around its neck.

"Hurry!" Anastasia cried, digging her boots in.

The Nightmare hissed and gurgled, bending backwards unnaturally with the snap of bone.

Bodie tightened her grip on her sword. She put one leg in front of her, and then the other. Her knees buckled but miraculously held. She pushed into a run. Every inch of every fiber of every muscle screamed.

This was it. This was all she had left. And she would give it.

She drew the Figment Blade up and thrust it forward.

The monster held out a hand to shield itself, but the sword tore through its remaining fingers and bit into flesh with a *slurch*. There was a low *crack* as it pierced the beast's core, the heart of its power, and a muffled rumble like thunder beneath its skin. The Nightmare roared, the sound muffled, distant in Bodie's ears as she dropped to her knees. It toppled over, its body writhing.

So did she, her body falling still.

The creature bucked and flopped in its final moments of life.

Bodie rolled onto her back with the very last of her strength.

"Bodie!" Anastasia dropped to the ground beside her. She smelled like peppermint and roses after rain. "Bodie, can you hear me? *Boshe moi*, hold on, you understand, hold on!"

But there was nothing to hold onto. Everything was gone. The Nightmare fell still as darkness pressed in against Bodie's mind, and everything went black and cold.

♥

"Still lazing about?" Anastasia's voice preluded a rustle of cloth and a rush of light as she no doubt flung the curtains open.

Bodie winced and, minding her still-healing injuries, rolled onto her stomach and buried her face in the silk covering of a down pillow. She groaned in place of an actual retort.

"It's nearly three o'clock. How long do you intend to stay in bed?"

"Forever," Bodie grumbled, before turning her head to peek in the direction of the large bay window.

Anastasia stood at the center of it, her arms folded, her green eyes narrowed. The backdrop of London sky, gray with dust and smoke, set her hair alight, like a halo of fire. White fabric clung to her body, falling in the folds of one of her day dresses. She was an angel of wrath and finery. "We have work to do."

"You just want your bed back." Bodie wriggled in the satin sheets.

After hauling Bodie from the alley two nights past, Anastasia somehow managed to sneak her into the suite, where she cleaned and bandaged her up then waited nearly a day for her to regain consciousness.

When Bodie finally came around, it was breakfast, lunch, and dinner in bed, and all the sweet wine and cakes she could eat. Anastasia tended to pamper her after a bad mission, and that one had been the worst by far.

"I want us to avoid another night like that." Anastasia sighed, her lips pursed. "You need to purge it. Before tonight."

Bodie nodded and winced as a twinge of pain rippled through her when she sat herself up. Multiple stab wounds tended to put one down for the count.

"Also." Anastasia pulled something from the blood-red handbag dangling from her arm. "We made the paper." She fluttered it teasingly then tossed it at the bed. It landed face-up enough that Bodie could read the headline.

MURDER IN WHITECHAPEL,
RIPPER STRIKES AGAIN!

Residents report the sounds, screams
and inhuman howls in the dead of the night.

Bodie pushed the paper aside. "What now?"

"Now? We purge the site, then wait and see if that's the end of it." Anastasia turned to face the window.

Bodie stared at her back before her eyes returned to the paper. "Have you ever seen anything like that before?"

The line in Anastasia's shoulders stiffened. "No. I believed Nightmares had potentially influenced the killer, but never did I imagine…" She fell silent for a few moments more before whirling and heading for the door. "Get up, get dressed, but take your time. Be careful."

"And where are you off to?" Bodie asked as she slid toward the edge of the bed.

"I need to speak with someone."

Though Anastasia acted as if she was in a rush, she gave Bodie enough time to get up, have a bit of breakfast, take a nice, warm soak and then get dressed before they checked out.

The crime scene was relatively empty, and Anastasia managed to distract the officers on duty long enough for Bodie to slip by and drive one of her daggers into the ground, purging the Nightmare's essence from the stone and preventing its resurrection.

After a nice lunch—apparently Anastasia wasn't finished pampering—the two boarded a train bound for Liverpool. Once they were settled in the car, Anastasia sat back against the bench and closed her eyes.

Bodie smoothed her hands against her skirts, picking at an imaginary bit of lint, waiting for Anastasia to look at her. When she didn't for several minutes, Bodie cleared her throat.

"So. Where are we going?"

"Liverpool," Anastasia murmured, eyes still closed.

"I *know*, but what's in Liverpool? Not another job, I hope." She was still barely in one piece after the last one.

"No, not a job. A boat."

Puffing a sigh of vexation through her nose, Bodie pursed her lips. "Is… is it a special boat?"

"Quite special." Anastasia finally opened her eyes, her gaze settling on Bodie. "It's the boat that's going to take us to America. Georgia, to be precise."

The White Queen's Dictum

JAMES LOVEGROVE

"Mind if I sit here?"

I indicated with a nod that I didn't. He set down his coffee and Danish pastry on the table, then pulled back the plastic chair and fell exhaustedly into it.

"Busy, isn't it?" He nodded around him.

Busy the motorway service station café certainly was. It was just gone eleven on a Saturday morning and the place was packed. Families, for the most part, because it was the first day of school half-term and by some unspoken law everyone had decided this was a good time to grab the kids, load up the car and travel. The noise was hellish. Very young children yelled, and their parents yelled at them to stop yelling, and these competing yells bounced off the walls and resounded up to the ceiling tiles, which reflected them back at twice the volume. Older children slumped in their seats, staring at their phones, earholes stoppered with earbuds—as efficient a method of shutting out the racket as any. At a table close to mine, a group of Eastern European hauliers huddled together, heads down, as though under siege, their natural environment having been encroached upon by a horde of interlopers. They reeked of the pungent cigarettes they had been smoking outside a few minutes earlier.

"I wouldn't have stopped here if I'd known," the man continued. "Only, you don't get much of an option on the motorway, do you? You want a break and a bite to eat, it's one of these places or nothing."

"It wasn't my choice either," I said with a shrug. "You end up where you end up. I don't mind too much, though. At least it's lively."

"Lively," he echoed. "Hah. I suppose you could call it that." He took a sip of his coffee and grimaced. "That," he said, "is challenging." He dumped a sachet of sugar into the beverage, tried it again, dumped in another sachet of sugar, and at last seemed to find it drinkable.

He looked over at the three-quarters-empty coffee cup in front of me. "Appears yours has gone cold. It's got that sort of congealed look on the surface. Don't blame you for not finishing it."

"Very observant," I said, glancing down then up again. I half-smiled. "Yes. I should have left ages ago. I've been meaning to but I just can't bring myself to do it. I'm happy sitting here."

"Me, I'm back on the road as soon as I'm done," the man

said. "Refuel myself, refuel the car, then get cracking. Places to be."

"Work?"

"In a manner of speaking."

"What do you do?"

He looked sheepish. "I'm a… well, I reckon you could call me a journalist."

"Newspapers?"

"Oh no. Haven't you heard? Print's dead. No, I'm a television presenter. Actually," he added with some haste, "not *television* television."

"I don't understand."

"I have an online channel."

"Oh. YouTube?"

"That kind of thing. Subscriber-only. I stream videos on my site. These short films I put together."

"Will I have heard of it?" I asked.

"I don't know. Do you watch stuff online much?"

"Not much."

"Well, it's not that popular anyway. Not yet. I get a few hundred views per video. My record's just over a thousand. Here."

He produced a phone, thumbed open the browser and showed me his site.

I read the title aloud. "The White Queen's Dictum."

"Yeah. I'm still not sure about the name. Been thinking about changing it. Bit poncey, and the word 'dictum' might be off-putting. There might be people who don't know what it means."

"A saying. A pronouncement. An axiom. A maxim."

"Yes. Had a feeling *you* would know. You sound educated."

"And the White Queen—I imagine that's a reference to Lewis Carroll. *Alice in Wonderland*?"

"*Through the Looking-Glass*, as a matter of fact."

"And what is her dictum? I feel I should know but I can't remember."

"It's that thing about believing six impossible things before breakfast. Alice and the White Queen are having that weird, circular conversation of theirs, and Alice tells her, 'One can't believe *impossible* things,' and the White Queen replies that when she was Alice's age she did it for half an hour a day and could even believe six impossible things before breakfast. It's kind of become my motto."

"Believing in impossible things?"

"Believing that they're real, against all evidence to the contrary." He tore off a corner of his Danish pastry and munched on it. Judging by his expression, it didn't taste much better than the coffee.

"What sort of things?"

"The paranormal. That's my field as a journalist. That's what my videos are about. I investigate paranormal phenomena. Sounds pretentious when you say it like that, but it's better than 'I hunt ghosts' or 'I hang out in haunted houses'."

"I see," I said. "So hauntings are your speciality."

"Yup." He gave a little, self-deprecating shake of the head. He struck me as a man who felt he ought to be doing something more constructive with his life, but who was incapable of reversing out of the one-way avenue down which circumstance and inclination had led him. He was stuck where he was and couldn't do much now to change the situation. I could easily sympathise.

He said, "And I know what your next question's going to be."

"You do?"

"Same question everyone asks when they find out what I do. 'Have you ever seen one?'"

"A ghost."

"Yes."

"Well, far be it from me to buck the trend. Have you?"

He drummed a brief tattoo on the tabletop with his fingertips. "I'd like to say yes, but..."

"But no."

"No. There's been nothing that's convinced me of the existence of ghosts. No irrefutable proof of life after death. I keep an open mind still. Hence 'six impossible things' as my motto. Every time I look into a haunting, I allow myself to hope that this time, this one will be the one. This time I'll film something, see something, experience something that'll put the matter beyond all doubt. It's the only way to approach the subject."

"Really?"

"Really. If I went in with a closed mind, it'd be counterproductive. Whereas constantly hoping it's going to happen—that makes it far more likely that one day it *will* happen."

"A logical attitude," I said, "but it carries a risk. You might become suggestible, gullible even. You could want so hard to believe in ghosts that you see ghosts where there are no ghosts."

"If that were the case," he replied, "surely I would have seen one by now."

"Fair point."

"I mean, I've been at this for seven years, ever since an uncle of mine died."

"I'm sorry to hear that. Were you fond of him? Is he why you're so keen to learn whether the dead carry on living in some other form?"

"No. No, nothing like that. I hardly knew the bloke. But he was unmarried, no kids, and he left me a bit of money—quite a lot, actually, enough that I could give up my job—and I've been living off that inheritance while I pursue my... I won't call it my dream. My passion project, maybe. At any rate, so far it's got me nowhere. I've been up and down the country, and also abroad, visiting famous haunting hotspots. I've had people contact me via my site and ask me to come and check out a room where they saw a ghost or else had some other sort of spooky encounter. I've spent nights in old rectories and converted monasteries and castles-turned-hotels with multiple digital cameras running, one of them using thermal imaging. I've recorded hundreds of hours of footage. Net result? Sod all."

He spoke without rancour. It was as if he regarded all this effort as just necessary preliminary work, part of the painstaking process towards getting what he wanted, like the prospector tirelessly sifting through riverbed silt for that first glimpse of gold, or the angler casting his line again and again into the water in hopes of a bite.

"You think that if you keep at it long enough, you're bound to hit pay dirt eventually," I said.

"Absolutely."

"I salute your persistence." I illustrated the remark with a touch of forefinger to brow.

"Anyway, hark at me, rabbiting on. You don't want to hear about all this."

"Why not? I'm in no rush."

"But what about you?"

"What do you mean?"

"Well, I've told you about my line of work. What do *you* do?"

"Not much. This and that."

"You on your way somewhere?"

"No," I said. "This is my destination."

"This?" He waved a hand around. "A motorway service station?"

"Yes."

"Not exactly a tourist attraction, is it? Do you work here?"

"No. I'm here because... how to put it? It's my wife and daughters, you see."

"They like it?"

"No. My wife and daughters died here."

His face fell. "Oh God. Oh, I'm so sorry. I shouldn't have pried."

"It's fine, it's fine," I said. "No need to apologise. They were killed. Car crash. Just over there."

I pointed out of the window towards the motorway, where traffic whisked to and fro, intermittently visible through a screen of purpose-planted roadside vegetation. Triple glazing reduced the massed vehicle roar to a low, determined thrum.

"A driver wasn't paying attention," I went on. "They came off the slip road and their car got rear-ended by an articulated container lorry going at eighty-five miles an hour. My wife was catapulted through the windscreen and landed on the verge about a hundred feet away. My daughters were crushed. The car was totalled, of course. Nobody survived."

"That's awful," he said sincerely. "My condolences. So you come here as a sort of pilgrimage, then?"

"Something like that."

"Well, look, I'm sorry to have bothered you." He drained his coffee and wolfed down the last of the Danish, then rose to go. "It was nice meeting you."

"There's no need to be embarrassed," I said. "People never know how to react when I tell them about the accident. You can stay a little longer if you want. I'd be happy to hear more about your ghost hunting."

He hesitated. Conflicting emotions played across his face.

"I could do with another coffee," he said at last. "Even this ditchwater's better than nothing. You want one? My treat."

"That's kind. No, thank you."

He returned a few minutes later after joining the long queue to be served. This time he added sugar to his coffee straight away. There was no point assuming the second cup was going to taste any better than the first.

"You don't mind?" he said.

"Chatting with you a while longer? Of course not."

"It's just, mine's a fairly lonely business. All those all-night vigils in the dark. It's nice to have someone to talk to."

"Same here," I said.

"I've just been on one of those, as it happens."

"An all-night vigil?"

"Yeah, up Sheffield way. An old terraced cottage, classic two-up, two-down. Allegedly the coalminer who used to live there died in a firedamp explosion in the late nineteenth century, and his spirit has lingered around the house ever since. You're supposed to smell methane first. That's what firedamp was, an escape of methane gas in the mine. Then you're supposed to smell burning and hear distant screaming. Then, if you're really lucky, or unlucky, the miner himself appears, all charred and horrific."

"And did he, for you?"

"Take a wild guess," my interlocutor said with a mirthless laugh. "I sat on a badly upholstered settee in that front room for ten hours solid and didn't smell or hear anything unpleasant, except when the homeowner's cat used the litter tray in the kitchen."

"Have you ever come close to seeing a ghost?" I asked. "I mean, has there ever been a moment when you've had just the tiniest tingle, the slightest hint of something unnatural?"

He thought about it. "Maybe once or twice. There was a time when I stayed at a B&B in an old Cornish pub. It was an upstairs bedroom where, supposedly, the ghost of a witch comes to you while you're sleeping and rakes her fingernails through your hair. Around one in the morning, when I was doing my best not to doze off, I thought I heard footsteps. They were in the corridor outside and then they were inside the room itself, or seemed to be. I had the bedside light on and there was nobody in that room but me, and the footsteps got closer and closer, then just stopped. But it was a very old building, and old buildings have floorboards that creak spontaneously. Something to do with the drop in temperature after the central heating goes off."

"So it could just have been that."

"It could just have been that, and most likely was."

"Any other occasion?"

"A glimpse of a shape darting past an open doorway," he said. "This was at a girls' boarding school that had closed down and was due to be demolished to make way for a golf course and clubhouse. The school was said to be haunted by the spirits of three pupils who, back in the seventies, made a suicide pact. They hanged themselves in a dormitory using dressing-gown cords. Girls who slept in that dormitory afterwards always complained they could hear these wet, gurgling, rattling sounds, like people being throttled, and would sometimes wake in the middle of the night gasping for breath, as though someone had been strangling them. The teaching staff dismissed it as hysteria, but eventually the dormitory was turned into a classroom, because no one who knew of its reputation was willing to sleep there."

"And this shape you glimpsed…?" I prompted.

"Could well have been just a shadow. It was a windy

night and clouds were racing across the moon. The windows were all uncurtained, letting in the moonlight. I can't swear it was anything other than that. I certainly didn't hear any throttled-throat noises or feel as though I was being strangled."

"You sound disappointed," I said. "Most people would be relieved."

"But that's just it," he insisted. "I want to see those impossible things. I want there to be unexplainable mysteries and supernatural occurrences and something, anything, other than mundane reality. Look at all this bollocks." He meant the café, the customers, the bad food, the shrieking children, the scolding parents, the whole raucous, teeming mess. His voice grew impassioned. "It's all so ordinary, so banal, so fucking *tawdry.* If this is all there is, then, well, that's pretty rubbish, don't you think? There has to be more. Otherwise what's the point?"

"A rather depressing philosophy."

"Yeah, it is. No wonder I do what I do. It's that or get so despondent about the world that I top myself."

He flapped a hand dismissively in front of him.

"Ah, pay no attention to me," he said. "I'm tired, and I get grumpy when I'm tired. I just want to get home and sleep. Then I'll edit the footage I took at the miner's cottage, stitch it together into a narrative, add a voiceover and a few pieces to camera, and post it. Yet another ghostly non-event. Yet another bit of content for the White Queen's Dictum for subscribers to comment on."

"What do they say, your subscribers?"

"Usually they say, 'Where's the ghost?' They want there to be ghosts as much as I do. Some of them get a creepy thrill out of the investigation itself, even if nothing comes of it. Some of them, the self-professed rationalists, like it that I seem to be debunking hauntings and the whole notion of ghosts. Mixed bag, really, but as long as they keep watching, I don't mind."

"Could it be," I said, "that you set your sights too high?"

He frowned. "I don't follow."

"You expect a haunting to be spectacular, chilling, exciting, full of horror and dread. You're hoping for witch's fingernails and burned miners and hanged schoolgirls. What if hauntings just don't live up to that? What if hauntings are, in fact, just as ordinary, as banal—as fucking tawdry, to use your own words—as this motorway service station and all the people in it?"

He pondered the idea, his eyes narrowing.

"No," he said in the end. "I can't accept that."

"Why not?"

"For the same reason I can't accept the world being as dull as it is. If hauntings are boring, why bother with them? If they're no more interesting than, say, doing up your shoelaces or taking a piss, then they might as well not happen at all."

"I just thought I'd suggest it," I said.

He, however, did not take kindly to my attempt at giving him a new perspective on his vocation. As far as he was concerned I was trying to knock the legs out from under him, or at the very least dishearten him.

"Don't you wish," he said, somewhat peeved, "that the souls of your wife and daughters live on? That they survive somehow, in some non-physical state?"

"What I wish," I replied, "is that they had never been killed."

"You must admit, surely, that part of the reason you're here is that you want a kind of reconnection with them. That's what's brought you to this dismal, godforsaken dump where no one in their right mind would come voluntarily. You want to feel near to them again."

"Your point being…?"

"I'm trying to help you—you and people like you—by showing that there's a possibility of an afterlife. That's the aim with my videos. One of these days I'll capture proof on camera that your instinct is justified, that some residue of your wife and daughters remains in this spot."

I paused, then said, "Maybe one of these days you will." I was reluctant to argue with him any further. Our interaction had soured, and I was eager to preserve the note of cordiality it had started on.

He seemed to feel the same. "Well, I really do have to go now. I've got a hundred more miles ahead of me before I'm home. Thanks for letting me bend your ear."

As he stood, he extended a hand towards me to shake.

I did not take it.

He frowned. "That's how it's going to be, is it?"

"I'm afraid so," I said.

"I see. If I caused offence, I didn't mean to."

"No, it's all right."

But he was ashamed, and hurried off with some mumbled apologies and a curt "Goodbye".

I watched him thread his way between the tables, becoming lost amid the clamour and bustle. I pictured him returning to his car, getting behind the wheel, starting up, heading back out onto the motorway to rejoin the ever-rolling streams of traffic.

"Take care on the slip road," I murmured.

A little later, I myself got up and drifted outdoors. I wandered over to a break in the verge which afforded a view of the motorway junction. Vehicles merged and converged and overtook like dancers in some infinitely complex piece of choreography.

I thought of the driver whose inattention had caused the deaths of my wife and daughters.

I thought, too, of the hapless haulier who hadn't been able to stop his lorry in time and had gone ploughing into the back of our family car.

I wished I had been more careful on the slip road. I wished I had taken a look in the wing mirror rather than pulling out blithely, unthinkingly into the slow lane. I longed to move on from that incident, and from this place.

Perhaps someday I would.

Until then, it would remain a yearning for an impossible thing.

Temp Work

LILITH SAINTCROW

THROUGH THE MIRROR

A small slice of ancient, fly-spotted glass was pasted to the trailer's curved wall, its silvering faded at the edges. On the far end of a small shelf an ancient hotpot and equally tiny T-screen both made soft noises. A slight, long-legged figure moved through the trailer's dim interior, ducking under the small ship-tidy cabinets, knees loose against the wallowing movement of travel, zipping and pressing the hotseal buttons of a scratchy, starched uniform. Short black skirt, tiny frilled apron, the stacked-heel boots—someone had a fantasy, and wanted even the temporary staff to play along.

That was fine. She liked dress-up. Alise's fingertip lingered just over the T-screen's volume button, and a scratchy, tinny talking head's babble rose from the torn speakers.

"*—no word from the East Coast, where containment of the*

Quitasol digiplague is being attempted. At least two cities have gone dark. Martial law has been declared in every corporate city above R-rating, and all civilian travel has been summarily curtailed."

She jabbed at the button again, and the thin, filmy T-screen choked into muteness. A burst of static crawled through the picture from bottom to top, and Alise's oculars picked out a few subtle threads of datapattern in the snow.

Everything was going well. And just as she decided that, there was a shuddering series of blows against the front partition. It was her partner Mocque Tuttle's signal, as he drove peering through a cloud of flying dust, goggles hiding his large dark eyes and his head well wrapped against flying silica particles even inside the sealed cab, his extra limbs tucked out of sight.

It was time to play make-believe. She was extra staff, hired in a job lot for a corporate party. There was a bubbled estate shining among a sea of rust-colored slums, and even the pittance paid for a day's servant-labor could make the difference between survival and starvation for anyone who hadn't been able to buy or study their way into the protective blanket of a corporation's ownership.

The estate was a blister on the horizon, decorative red towers glittering under a hard sun and a very expensive dome-shield holding poverty and the creeping, infectious dust away from sloping green lawns, fantastical white-barked trees with fleecy crimson leaves, and shimmering, jewel-bright ponds.

Alise, humming the soft refrain of a currently popular

vocaloida song about faithless love and corporate-place bling, zipped the dust-shroud over her new, stolen uniform.

THE WHITE RABBIT

The estate's service entrance was in a cavern, a wall of shimmering electroseal zapping dust and other particles from metal and glass; the bubble-truck from Raleigh's walled scramble disgorged a single swathed figure who hurried for two featureless steel doors, not even pausing to glance at the catering company's van. The truck, not waiting to see if its fare would be accepted into the bowels of the red estate, backed out into the howling storm and soon vanished behind veils of flying particles. The slum hunched under tiers of silica dust, every shelter crammed full; any exposed piece of skin would be honeycombed with digiplague within minutes.

Obviously, this latest estate visitor hadn't paid for a return trip. Or maybe she had no means of doing so.

A gloved hand pressed a card-key to the square reader; the light flashed green. One door popped loose with a *chuk-hiss* of sealant and a fog of chembath; she stepped smartly through and the scans began.

A green bar showed over the featureless, steel interior door and she stepped through again, her shroud rustling, into another smaller chamber. On the other side of impact-proof clearpane was a genesplice with thistledown hair in a purple suit with knife-sharp creases, his cleft lip and high, large, pinkish ears all twitching. It was just like a high-rated corporate queen to have a splice as a butler, a flagrant expense much more amenable than even a desperate, fully human employee. And more loyal, too. So far, though, Alise was under-impressed by the estate's security. Still, she held herself stiffly, playing her part.

"You're late." The splice's nose twitched, his voice coming water-clear through round, high-end speakers. His cheeks were almost too plump for him to speak and he'd been built sleek and portly, but those pink-rimmed eyes and pale hair just covering oddly shaped ears could hardly be called aesthetic.

Her dust-shroud hit the floor, and she stepped free in her black-and-white uniform, one leg turned for optimal onlooker pleasure. "Riots in-city." Alise let the scanners tingle over her. The nice thing about military-grade 'ware was the ease with which you could feed corporate-level scanners what they wanted to hear.

Another soughing sound was the new, extremely expensive plague-deterrent, a wave of skin-crawling as a flood of nanobots swarmed her. She stood patiently as they crawled over her face and hands, and her oculars returned a stream of baselines in the lower left corner.

It was a good idea, using the little bastards to search in crevices and taste micro-molecules of sweat. Her own inner colonies, well hidden, tried to come online to deal with the intruders, but she kept them reined in until the tiny, almost purely psychological tickles passed and the invaders withdrew.

"Everyone else is already here." The splice clicked his

tongue against his teeth, the front two prominent enough to peep out behind the perpetual smile his buyer had molded onto plastic flesh during the choose-your-animal phase. "The Red Lady would fire you if she knew."

So this splice was high-status, and liked all the temporary help to owe him something. Alise tried a smile with an edge of desperation. "I couldn't help if the riots closed the South Gate right after the other bus went through. I paid to come out in a bubble, that counts for something, right?"

"Yes, yes. But you're *late*, and the Lady doesn't like tardiness." He scrubbed his white-gloved paws against each other. Most splices were engineered to anxiety, eager to please but wearing out quickly from the strain. You could extend the lifespan of a particularly faithful splice if you had the cash, but most of the time it was just cheaper to arrange transit to a reclamation center for a rebate on their organic matter while you shopped for a new one.

You could even get the new one arriving as the old was shipped out, so there was no lag in service.

"Well, maybe we could not tell her?" Alise did her best not to bat her eyelashes. "I'm all ready, I'm even in my uniform. It's starched, like it said on the job sheet."

"Well, at least you *read* the sheet." The butler hit a button out of sight, and the bar over the innermost door lit with a pale pink glow. "Through there. I hope nobody else is late."

"Me too," Alise murmured, but he wasn't listening. There was work to be done.

After all, in a few hours there would be guests.

THE TEA PARTY

A glass-walled conservatory stuffed with strange gene-spliced fancyplants and nodding crimson-leaved saplings filled with rufuous sunglare. Alise lifted a heavy silver tray of pink-frosted cupcakes, freezing in place as two guests ambled laughingly past. The short round one with a large, floppy, velvet hat and filthy fingernails was Hatter, the head of Oscorp intel; the other listened intently as they strolled.

"I can't do that, Hal," the tall, gaunt man in Banercorp colors finally said, rather gently. "Creighton will never go for it."

"Oh, Creighton's on the way out. Our lovely hostess is on the way *in*." Hatter's cheeks bunched rather like the spliced butler's when he smiled, but the butler in his sober, spotless purple would never look so satisfied *or* well rested. "You heard about Old Wilmington."

"Catastrophic failures in all the estates, who *hasn't* heard?" The Banercorp death's-head made an elderly *tsk-tsk* noise, tongue against the pale pink gum-hill behind expensively veneered teeth. "There's a rash of it. Enough to make you fire all your security."

So, they'd had some success up north. Alise carried the cupcakes to a giant tiered monstrosity meant to hold them before they were shoved into big, moist mouths. She even arranged them prettily for the few seconds they would be unmolested.

It looked like Helena Osbonson's little party was a success. Her brother-in-law, the embattled and putative head of Oscorp, was nowhere in evidence, probably safe in the metallic-glitter high-rises of downtown doing damage control. Maybe he was even oblivious to the vultures flocking to this lovely little country home set among the blasted remains of what was once tobacco or sweet potato fields.

“Idiot splice,” a ringletted and flounced woman hissed at the butler, who turned pink and nose-twitching again, dabbing at a figment of stain imagination on her long skirt. “Leave it alone.” She even aimed a kick at his scuttling retreat, but it didn’t connect because her heels were so high. She wobbled, almost collapsing on surgically clean black-and-white marble squares, and her companion caught her arm, righting her with a slight moue of distaste.

Lean and expensively tan, the companion nevertheless wore a cookie-cutter corporate overall with hotseal sutures and a Banercorp logo on the breast pocket. Security, probably fished out and buffed for a day shepherding a corporate tantrum-thrower. “You should stop drinking, Effie.”

“The fuck I will,” she slurred, and grabbed a champagne flute from a tray held by one of Alise’s temporary coworkers, a skinny dark-haired youth so scared of losing the day’s wages he was perpetually a-shiver. His uniform wasn’t starched, and Alise smoothly exchanged her own empty tray for his full one while making a slight movement with her chin, freeing him to scurry back into the hall leading to the kitchen’s bustle.

The parties were all the same, even this “informal” gathering. The hostess, statuesque in draped crimson plusesilk, smiled benignly as a bald man with wide shoulder-padding on his gray suit lifted his glass in her direction. The baldy was Banercorp's head of acquisitions for the eastern seaboard, and even though the merger had been struck down by an asthmatic regulating agency nobody really expected *that* to be the last word. Certainly Baner and Osbonson were both treating their arranged marriage over the bones of Helena's brother-in-law as a fait accompli.

Outside the dome-shield protecting the estate's velvet verdure and high red towers, the dust storm began its post-lunch hissy fit.

It would exhaust itself near dusk, but by then, Alise would be finished.

THE MOCK TURTLE

Through a veil of vapor, the synthetic in the kitchen moved with sharp efficiency. Its goggled eyes were just the same as Mocque's, but he was an SX-5 for plain culinary use instead of an SX-7e, and it was just like a corporate queen to economise behind the scenes.

Alise closed her hand around the SX-5's arm. Warm skin, vat-grown but indistinguishable from human, dewed with a faint, slippery sheen of steam-sweat—the synthetic looked at her with mild amazement, those large eyes liquid and still as the arms kept moving, subroutines queued and performing perfectly even though the organism was under severe stress.

Data flowed in coruscating streams, and Alise's internal colonies came online, finally free of suppression.

Alise peeled her fingers away. The cook's arms paused for a single millisecond, and a familiar gleam came into those dark eyes.

Often, the splices froze when freedom appeared. The synthetics, free of second-guessing, never did.

The swinging door to the estate kitchens closed behind Alise, and she went back to work.

CROQUET

Crack.

The gunshot echoed, and a soft, helpless, pink-feathered bird fell like a meteor long before it could batter itself on the dome-wall keeping dust-storms and the digiplagued slum crowds out. There was desultory applause, and Hal Hatter lowered his long, penile repeater.

"Good shot." The gaunt Banercorp man—Phil Mosley, rumored to be the power behind the board despite his comparatively lowly status—applauded with just the right edge of dutiful distaste.

"Right between the eyes." Hatter laughed. "Give us another one, Coningham!"

The pink-eyed splice scurried out to open another cage. His butler's uniform was in sad shape; summery heat and the speed required to dart among the boxes and find a long-legged bird to be sacrificed for sport wilting starched cloth. A gap had been torn under his velvet coat's left armpit, and his gloss-shining shoes were scuffed under grass-stained spats.

"Is that what you named him?" Effie Marsh, her mouth a

louche curve and her arm over her companion's shoulders, leered at the hapless splice's puffing and racing. "It's too much, Helena."

"Inherited him from dear old Daddy." Helena Osbonson carried a parasol to shade her from solar radiation even inside her domed estate and wore gigantic heart-shaped sunglasses—crimson frames, of course, top of the line. "But it's rather time for a new one, I should think."

"Hurry up!" Hal Hatter yelled, and the butler flicked a quick-release on one of the low, white cages.

The bird exploded in a puff of pink feathers, but it did not rocket for sky and freedom. Instead, it shrieked and flew straight at the mass of partygoers, who yelped in turn and dispersed with frantic speed.

It was Helena who pulled a darling little chrome repeater from her satin pocket and shot the thing. It didn't die immediately, but flapped weakly and made tiny piping noises until a Baner systems head—one consistently featured on all the society feeds as an *enfant terrible*—stamped on its delicate, bone-carved head.

The assembly cheered, calling for more drinks. Alise moved among them handing out tall, frosted glasses, her own uniform sagging in slow increments.

THE TRIAL

Whirling dust fell flat as the sun sank into a molten puddle, the storm moving toward farmland leached by chemical drought and turned into high rubbish-hills. Agribusinesses were all incorporated now, and too big to fail. Some few of the guests held that the rise in crop prices wasn't a windfall or a corrective but instead the sign of further troubles to come, though the majority found this to be a needlessly pessimistic take.

Business, after all, was eternal.

What was *not* eternal was a splice. The butler hustled furiously, his anxiety standing out in great clear sweat-drops upon his forehead and his purple-gloved paws no longer pristine. There was a dusty bootprint on the left side of his pinstriped pant-seat.

That's what you get for letting a bird attack your mistress, Hal Hatter had crowed before kicking him. *Useless goddamn splices.*

The splice rushed from place to place, fawning-eager to make up for a perceived mistake. Guests laughed except for one or two who traded sour looks, especially when Hatter cornered the poor thing and began telling him, in a low but exceedingly clear and vicious tone, how exactly old splices were processed in reclamation or sold at auction.

Alise should have waited until dinner was brought out, really. There was nothing to be gained by moving the timetable up… but there was nothing to lose, either.

"Another drink," Phil Mosley said, perhaps wishing he hadn't worn his corporate colors to what was proving to be an exceedingly informal event. He wouldn't last long at the top; they would get rid of him for someone more well-bred, if not more ruthless.

Alise smiled, letting him choose from the selection on her

tray. Her ocular streams flashed red for a moment—he had some wetware, this Banercorp man. His nervous system was jacked for speed and muscles injected with highseal, but she was safe enough.

Who, after all, would suspect a *maid*?

Alise waited for him to take a deep, grimacing swallow before dropping the tray with a crash that echoed through the sitting room and brought Hal Hatter's head around, a swivel-motion searching for fresh prey.

Without the suppression protocols dialed down to the low end, her interior colony of nanobots had spawned and spread, almost-invisible motes riding from guest to guest, settling in liquids, decking the food like salt or sugar crystals, burrowing through pores, tiptoeing into orifices and finding congenial homes.

Alise sent out the silent pulse that told the tiny things to begin their own afternoon work.

The screaming was short-lived.

THE RED QUEEN'S GARDEN

Helena Osbonson's body was unwieldy without its inhabitant, but Alise was stronger than she looked and lugged it down a long, shining-sterile corridor. The door at the end wanted both retinal and palm-print identification, so the nanos swarming in Osbonson's fractionally cooling flesh helped as much as they could, a facsimile of biological life pulling a gentle fiction over the passionless mechanical eyes of scanners and other security measures.

The heavy steel door slid sideways with a couth whisper, and Alise hauled the body into Helena's office. Only one of the estate's spires was large enough for internal structures, the rest being only aesthetic, and Alise supposed if she'd been a dyed-in-the-wool sociopath at the helm of a large corporation, she'd put her office up here, too.

After all, the view through tall wraparound crystal panes was spectacular.

The dust-storm was a lowering smudge on the horizon, almost swallowing the sinking sun in a red-and-gold fury. Black dots roamed the edges of the estate, keeping well away from the featureless dome-shimmer. Even the most worm-eaten of the digiplagued knew better than to swarm an *estate.* The truly far gone, consumed by bad wetware or infected implants, might throw themselves onto the shimmer for a quick end to the agony, but nobody had yet today, maybe sensing some feral current kept barely contained by money and technology.

The entire desk was a top-of-the-line Zoylent Apple, its security requiring print, vocal, and retinal lock. Fortunately, Alise had passed close to Helena enough times to build up a reasonably good vocal profile, and she didn't need the whole body for this stage, just an eyeball and the left hand. A kitchen cleaver tucked into the big fluffy black bow at the back of Alise's costume performed separation duty most admirably, and as she settled herself in the ergonomic fauxpleather chair her temples began to throb.

The Red Lady also had a new Zoylent Mini, top-of-the line handheld smart-tech, and Alise's nanos had been busy worming their way into its case, searching and prying. Pressing a rapidly cooling thumb against the Mini's lock undid the encryption, and there, in neatly organized trees, were all the Red Queen's passwords.

Alise turned reluctantly from the windowed panorama, fingers blurring as she watched her ocular feeds and typed with blur-quick fingers. The haul of data was bigger than she expected, so it was a good thing she'd moved the timetable up. Her headache mounted, but she held to her task.

Anything worth doing was worth doing well, after all.

THE GATES

She could have taken Helena Osbonson's sleek red limousine, or even Hal Hatter's sporty, very expensive purple Cyanol. Her gaze alighted instead on a sturdy, dependable SafeControl van, probably the same one that had carried cases of the docile-drugged, pink-plumaged birds from a digirarities supplier earlier that week.

At ground level, a plume of smoke lifted from the shield generator and the estate's shimmerwall was rapidly losing power. It blink-stuttered, and a mass of pink birds, circling restlessly since the locks on their cages had been broken, wisely didn't try to escape just yet. Instead they settled on the taller spires, crying out in musical confusion.

The trash-choked slum seethed. In an hour or so the shield would be down completely. The caterer's bus was gone and the kitchen was empty.

"You!" The pale-haired, purple-clad splice rose from behind a stack of liquor cartons. "What are you doing? That belongs to a *guest*!"

Alise flattened her palm against the SafeControl's driver door, let the proper subroutine take over, and the engine started with a low hum. "You want to come with me?"

"I… I can't…" The splice's cheeks were wet. There was a long furrowed scratch on his fat cheek, where his dying mistress had clawed at him in the commotion as her flesh was riddled with suddenly vicious, feasting nanos. "Who will take care of the house?"

"Do you have to?" Alise's head pounded, rows of steel fangs champing endlessly. It had taken longer than she liked to mine the data-trove and make sure all the security feeds were scrambled. Any corporate security enforcement would assume it was Quitasol and wouldn't know how the plague-carrier got in; the catering company wouldn't be able to tell them since it was a cash-pay operation.

Helena Osbonson wasn't quite a miser, but why would a corporate head actually pay full-time workers? Better to just squeeze desperate temps. Where security and invasive tech failed, greed *always* found a way.

"There's nobody else." The splice's mild, pink-rimmed eyes blinked, a semaphore of confusion.

"That's what everyone thinks," Alise said wearily. "But if you're not coming with me, you'd better look for weapons. The shield's going down."

The splice let out a soft, baffled sound and retreated

towards a servants' door tucked behind a perma-park pylon, still wringing his dirty-gloved hands.

Alise climbed into the van and keyed in the meet coordinates. A thin thread of blood worked down from her left nostril.

She sniffed heavily, tasting copper, and hit the *execute* button. The van slipped its brakes and performed a shallow three-point turn as she sagged in the driver's seat, then bulleted into a dying crimson sunset.

DRINK ME

A SafeControl van rested, in complete defiance of safety and common sense, in the valley between two huge mounds of city refuse. The smell was terrific, titanic, and shapes in the violet dusk were already eyeing the strippable vehicle even before the driver clambered free and vanished around another garbage-mound. It would be picked down to the chassis by midnight, and even the frame's hyperalloy would be cut up and carted off by dawn.

Alise staggered, but the shapes in the dimness didn't approach. They scented danger, though the woman's blood-slicked face was a mask of pain. She looked plagued, and nobody wanted to get close to that, even fellow sufferers.

The sickness made you fast and hellishly strong before it ate you. Better to wait until the body collapsed and strip the bone frame, just like the van. Plagued organs were worthless, but fat deposits and hair could be sold, and sometimes a collection of specialized cells or two would be untainted enough to make the work of pulling them free worth it.

A battered bubble-truck prowled the rubbish mounds, its headlights baffled, dull cat-gleams. It stopped, and the highbeams came on, showing the stark ghost of a woman in the ruins of a once-starched maid uniform bleeding from eyes, nose, mouth. The tops of her almost-exposed breasts were crusted with dried effluvia, and her long legs trembled.

The driver's door slammed, and a synthetic with four big, overbrawned arms caught her as she fell.

In the back of the truck, Mocque Tuttle swept the table free of clutter and laid Alise down. He put a flask to her lips, and the bleeding woman's throat worked slowly.

Military-grade nanos absorbed the venomous green liquid he poured down her throat, and the wracked body eased. The dependence was either a flaw in nanobot design or a way to keep your superpowered troops loyal. Either way, Mocque was an SX-7e model, and fully capable of synthesizing the venom in sufficient quantities. "You cut it close that time, Alise."

"Had to." Color returned slowly to her ashen cheeks as the nanos stopped cannibalizing their host—at least, until the medicine wore off again. "But I've got good news. There's another formula for the green stuff. I'll upload it."

"Rest." Mocque shook his big, lofty-domed head. "We've got a lot of driving."

"How many cities are left?" As if she didn't know.

"Three." The synthetic's brow creased. "We could go west instead, you know. There's nobody tracking our success metrics. You can't build a new world if you're dead." He made a *tsk-tsk* sound, and his dark eyes filmed as she began the upload.

He could drive and collate at the same time, while she lay on the shelf-table jolted by each pothole, and nanos under the green influence repaired what they had damaged by feasting on their hostess.

"Can't build at all with those assholes squatting on the old world." But Alise smiled a slow, sleepy curve of lips and turned on her side, curling into a ball. She might even be able to sleep while they rattled to the next city and began the delicate work of teasing out holes in its corporate security.

Resistance was a low-paying job, sure. But you could fund it by selling the data you mined from each target, not to mention anything else picked up along the way.

And there were, Alise thought as she dropped into a light, healing trance, definite advantages to loving your work.

Eat Me, Drink Me

ALISON LITTLEWOOD

Come, hearken then, ere voice of dread,
With bitter tidings laden,
Shall summon to unwelcome bed
A melancholy maiden!

~ Lewis Carroll

The morning after the tea-party, Alice went downstairs, her hair still in papers and her feet bare, and she knelt in front of the cage where she kept her white rabbit. He peered back at her with pink little eyes, his mouth working—it seemed his mouth was always working, that he could never be still. She lifted the latch and pulled the door wide and took him in her arms, turning him onto his back, wrapping him in her white lacy shawl.

Then she went into the kitchen. She liked to feed Mr Rabbit (for he had no other name) with lettuce leaves, given grudgingly for the purpose by their peppery cook, who was already at her place, leaning over a great cauldron on the range and stirring.

Cook was mean-faced. She kept rat poison in old jars at the back of her highest shelf. She would eye Alice's rabbit as if she were hungry, and she eyed him now as Alice plucked a white bonnet from the laundry and wrapped it about his head, tucking it behind his floppy ears.

"Time." Cook's voice was at her shoulder and Alice jumped; she hadn't realised the sly, wiry woman was leaning over her. "Time you grew out of it."

Alice was certain she felt the wicked woman's chin press into her shoulder before she turned away, back to her soup. "Belongs in the pot," Cook muttered over her shoulder, pointing with her ladle, sending soupy droplets flying across the floor.

Alice followed the gesture but saw only the teapot, knowing that wasn't what she'd meant; then saw the pig trussed ready for their dinner, its turned-up nose and tiny closed eyes, the apple thrust between its jaws.

Alice made to leave, but Cook hadn't finished. She muttered again, something about rabbits doing what they do, and Alice thought that was rather sweet; that she meant the creatures were nothing more than they are, or were yesterday, or would be tomorrow—so very unlike people, so unlike her *visitor*, and then Cook added, "They give us meat."

The woman turned, her eyes as small and narrow as the pig's. "One plus one is four," she said. "Or six, or eight, or however it shall be. Put those together and you shall have forty-two, or a hundred and one, or eight hundred and seventy." She looked Alice up and down as she spoke, then gave a lascivious wink and Alice realised what she meant.

A grin more akin to a grimace formed on her lips. It didn't feel as if it quite belonged to her, just hung in front of her face like a separate thing altogether, but Cook didn't seem to notice anything strange. She put out a hand as if to feel Alice's belly, to see if she was ripe, perhaps—and Alice stepped away, letting her own hands fall, feeling the lithe, warm body of the rabbit slip to the floor and hop away.

She gave a little cry and hurried after it, to the echo of Cook's laughter. As Alice reached out for the rabbit, she noticed on her own hand the ring her visitor had placed on her finger. When he had handed her the gift, she had thought it nothing but a golden thimble; in her confusion she had almost imagined it uncurled in the palm of her hand, stretching like a serpent before wrapping itself about her finger, biting its own tail so that she couldn't take it off again.

Henry wore stiff collars and smelled of Rowland's Macassar oil. His waistcoat buttons were small and black, like a haddock's eyes, and when he looked at her, his eyes were just as bright and shiny. When he'd put the ring on her finger he'd smiled like a fish, too.

She hadn't imagined that the ring would be so heavy, hadn't suspected it would be so tight. And yet she didn't wish to take it off—it made her special. Everyone would want to see it, to look and admire. It shone so much more brightly than Henry's eyes.

Alice had looked away from him and glimpsed her mother peering in through a crack in the doorway, had seen her delighted smile. She could almost hear the words her mother had said to her before the tea-party: "The truest kind of happiness, dear child, the only kind that is really worth the having, is the happiness of making others happy, too!"

Now Alice carried the white rabbit into the drawing room, where she sat in front of the posy of white roses Henry had given her, still tied up in their ribbon. Each time she looked at them she thought a spreading stain was marring their whiteness—as if the roses were gradually being painted red: red like a heart, red like a bloodthirsty queen, or perhaps both together. She reached out, touched her finger to the stem, noticed the blood already beading on her skin. She did not know if she'd pricked herself on a thorn, or if she was just about to; as if her body already knew when it was supposed to bleed.

♥

Alice leaned over her rabbit's cage, watching his long yellow teeth munch. So easy, to be him—so straightforward. There was food and he ate. He had paws and he ran. He had no sense of time passing, of what might happen in the future or what had happened in the past; he had no pocket watch. She let her eyes slip out of focus. The inside of his cage had a dry, earthy smell. It was set into an unused alcove at a turn in the passage and it was shadowed, safe, almost tunnel-like. She opened the latch on the cage, though she didn't lift him out. Instead she leaned in, feelings crowding up inside her: the momentousness of *something*, a decision made perhaps, a path taken that could not be undone. And she found herself falling—falling a long way, though slowly and with time to look about her.

She drifted down past cupboards and shelves laden with little bottles and cakes labelled "EAT ME" or "DRINK ME". They reminded her of a strange story she'd read years ago, where such things made a little girl shrink or grow bigger so that she was never the same size twice. She shuddered at the idea. Only yesterday, her mother had said she must resist eating cake; anyone knew that young ladies must never grow any bigger, must keep a respectable waist. Her sisters had tried but it didn't last; they grew fat eventually, though no one had liked to mention it, nor the squealing and shrieking of the babies that followed. Tomorrow—or was it now today?—her mother had promised to tight-lace Alice's corset. She had joked about snipping off her toes to better fit her wedding slippers.

Alice scowled and without thinking she reached out, snatching a bottle from a shelf, putting it to her lips. The taste that flooded her mouth was of sunshine and childhood: cherry tart and caramel and barley sugar (to sweeten the temper, her mother would have said), and her teeth ached with its impossible sweetness. She flung the bottle away from her, not caring if it struck anyone passing below.

Then she wondered—was the potion changing her somehow? Had she *already* changed? She didn't suppose Henry would like that very much. Was she now taller than him, or did she reach only to his knees? There was no way of telling. And then she was sitting on a soft pile of leaves and twigs and what felt like fur, on the ground in front of a wall with a tiny door set into it.

She stared, wondering if the door really was tiny or if she had become huge: some clumsy, ugly, unacceptable thing.

She turned the minuscule handle and pushed it open, then lay down on the floor so that she could see through it. It was all wrong, everything turned sideways, but she knew at once what she saw. For there *she* was: Alice with her hair neat and golden, wearing a golden crown. She was sitting on a gilded throne next to Henry, whose red face was round and satisfied. Other people were lined up at the table: her mother and father, her sisters and their husbands. She knew at once that this was her wedding breakfast, though she had missed the soup and the fish, for they were bringing out the main course: not a suckling pig but a great roasted rabbit, bigger than the whole table.

Everyone started beating their plates with their fists, setting up a wild cacophony. Queen Alice merely sat as if she were in a world apart, plucking the petals from a daisy, and she heard the words as if they were falling from her own lips: "I love my love with an H. I love my love with an H…"

Everyone raised their glasses in a toast. "Alice! Alice!" they cried, but not in a happy way, not in a pleased way. They screamed the word until it was meaningless, nothing but empty noise spilling from their gaping mouths, and instead of drinking the wine they poured it over their heads, licking it from each other's faces, red like a stain, red like a heart. When they laughed, the wine coated their teeth like blood.

Alice slammed the little door closed and lay staring upwards. A long, long way above her was a tiny pinprick of light, impossible to reach.

After a time she realised there was nothing else to be done but sit up and look around. And she saw that everything had changed: a bank of smooth grass sloped away from her, a neat path wending down towards a little river with sunshine sparkling from its waters. And there, just rounding a bend, was a boat—a gentleman rowed it, and with him were three little girls in white dresses, intent on his words, rapt in some story he was telling them.

Alice leapt to her feet. "Wait!" she called. "I'm coming too!" She started to run towards them, faster and faster. She could still make out the charming cadence of their tale, their merry laughter, but no matter how hard she ran, the path misled her; she ended farther from them than she had been before, finding the little door in front of her instead of the river, so that she had to whirl about to see it. She tried again, ending once more at the top of the hill, staring as the boat rounded the next bend, drifting away. She called out again for them to wait, she was coming, her voice rupturing into a scream, but they did not stop. They showed no sign of having heard her at all.

When she slumped down on the grass, however, something else had changed—a round, black hole gaped in front of her, leading directly into the ground. She leaned over it, seeing nothing. The scent was of damp soil and of the dark. After a moment, she stepped into it.

This time she fell heavily and fast, though not far. The drop could only have been a few feet. She landed on more black earth and saw a circular tunnel stretching away in either direction. The smell was stronger down here, of the earth and time and decaying things, with a hint of sweetness that was not unpleasant. She wasn't merely down the rabbit hole any longer, she realised; she had entered the warren.

It seemed to make little difference which way she went and so she started along the tunnel, feeling earth crumbling into her hair, gathering under her nails as she ran her hands along the walls. It wasn't altogether dark, though she could not tell where the light was coming from, and she realised the walls were not entirely bare. A few sparse flowers clung to them, their stems long and thin, their colours pale.

She paused as she passed a little clump of daisies, thinking she caught some faint sound, and the daisies opened their eyes.

"Where am I going?" Alice asked them.

"You are. You're going," came their weak reply.

"But where?"

"Yes. Going."

"You should leave off asking them. *Hjckrrh!*" The voice that came out of the dark was deep and lugubrious, yet finished on a high rasp that made Alice jump. "They can barely speak any longer, don't you know. They can hardly move on their own. All they can do is agree with everything that is said to them. You'll find them best for looking and admiring, nothing more."

Alice blinked. For a moment the daisies were nothing but golden rings shining in the dark, their heads nodding like ladies bending over their sewing. She pulled a face, snatching at the stems as if to pluck the flowers—didn't they know she would be a *queen*?—but they danced away from her with little squeals.

"Faded," they said, their voices now filled with spite. "You're already beginning to fade."

And the stranger, stronger voice said, "He's coming. You should hurry."

Alarmed, Alice glanced down at herself—*was* she fading? That seemed of greater concern than the warning about the strange *He*, though she glanced behind her anyway, seeing only darkness. She went onward, wondering what had happened to the owner of the voice, then cold air gusted at her hair and she realised there was a side tunnel. A lithe form, almost filling the passage, slunk cat-like away from her, its tail swishing. No, not a cat: a lion, yet as it twisted its head back over its shoulder, she thought she saw the outline of a beak. And were they wings, folded over its back?

The voice echoed back along the tunnel: "You must learn the lessons of the Mock Turtle."

A Mock Turtle—that also reminded her of something she had read long ago. In her childhood book, the Mock Turtle had gone to school in the sea. He had learned Reeling and Writhing, which she had thought meant reading and writing—though an image came to her of the cook, counting in her coarse arithmetic, groping with her rude fingers. The Mock Turtle had learned other things, too: ambition, she remembered, and distraction, and perhaps derision; adult things, things she hadn't been certain she could learn or even wanted to. Those, and uglification: he had learned that, too.

She put a hand to her face, feeling her skin, hearing again the daisies' voices: *Fading.* She shook her head, thought of the cold ring still wrapped about her finger, of Henry's fish-smile. She whispered the words her mother had taught her: "I love my love with an H. I love my love with an H…"

She stumbled onward, seeing only more passageways, one leading into the next or branching into multiple mouths, taking this one or that without hesitation or thought. Sometimes the light grew brighter and sometimes it dimmed almost entirely, leaving behind the faint scent of smoke, like a candle just blown out. She began to see objects scattered across the floor, wasted and broken things: crumpled playing cards, smashed dishes, flamingos with broken necks, hedgehogs' empty skins, a fan with splintered leaves, a soiled kid glove. She stepped over them all and went on until she turned a corner and saw something unexpected and beautiful and bright hanging in the air in front of her.

It was a butterfly. The creature was exactly the same height as Alice. It slowly beat its wings, though it did not fly away, only turning gradually and carefully to hover in front of her. Its wings, little use down here, flashed every shade of the summer sky. They were so bright it hurt to look at them.

"You did tell me," the butterfly said, "that it would all be terribly confusing." Its voice was forlorn—it sounded lost and alone, and with a sigh it added, "It was so much simpler when I was a caterpillar."

She opened her mouth to reply, but no words came; indeed, there was only a void where they had been. She wasn't certain she could even have told the creature her name.

"You must find the looking-glass," the butterfly said. "Mirrors only ever tell the truth. Unless, of course, they get things backward."

She only felt more puzzled. She wished she could tell him how to find the sun. She wished she could see him spread his wings wide, float away on a summer breeze. Why did so many creatures have wings, if they couldn't really fly? But she remained silent as he began to turn from her again, with the words, "Be what you would seem to be."

He started to move away, his wings knocking clumps of earth from the walls and ceiling. They pattered to the floor, but that was not the only sound. A rumbling, low and deep, came from beneath her and everywhere. She tried to cry out, to warn the butterfly—whatever was coming was big, and it felt like trouble—but it was as if she were a child again, waking from a terrible dream, full of all the things she wanted to say and unable to say them. A tear, large and cold, ran down her cheek, just as something like lightning flashed in the distance. For a moment the butterfly's wings gleamed like a winter's night and then one wing was suddenly ripped from the other, parting like the unwrapping of a gift. They fell to the floor, separate, useless.

It had been so quick, and so *quiet*—somehow that was

the worst thing of all, at least until she saw the form that was uncoiling at the end of the tunnel: the flash of a scaly limb, the suggestion of a serpent's back, the flexing of a sinuous tongue.

Jabberwocky. The name was on her lips, coming to her so much more easily than her own, and yet when its face appeared, it didn't look like a monster. It was Henry's face that was balanced on its long and twining neck, Henry's eyes that peered for her along the dim passageway, black and expressionless.

She pressed into the wall, not caring if she dirtied her clothes. Henry's face bobbed and swerved, as if he were trying to sight her like a bird. His nostrils distended, as if sniffing for her. She remained perfectly still, it seemed for an age, until his mouth finally stretched open. She thought of the tone he had used at their last meeting, low and playful, the voice he might have used to speak to a kitten.

But the voice that emerged was high and shrill. "Do let's pretend that I'm a hungry hyena," he cried, "and you're a bone!"

She ran. She ran as a child might, her hands outstretched and her eyes closed, until she felt her heart would burst. The tunnels were all the same; she ran until she could run no further and then she turned, steeling herself to feel the Jabberwocky's hot breath on her skin.

The tunnel was empty.

Time passed. Nothing moved. And eventually, it came to her that she was lost. She did not know where she was or how she had got there or how to get out again. She could wander for weeks in here, or months, or years, and all she would find were more tunnels and more darkness. She closed her eyes, thought of a little blue river with a boat bobbing on its surface, the bright voices of three little girls clamouring for their story.

After a while, she cried.

Then she remembered the butterfly's words about the looking-glass and something a little like hope rose within her. If only she could find it, perhaps she would understand who she was, and what, and where. She would see exactly where she belonged and which way she should go. She would see if she was the same person she had been yesterday, if she would be the same again tomorrow. Maybe she would even remember her name. But she didn't know how to find the glass, had no idea where to look.

Unless, of course, they get things backward.

She caught her breath. Had that meant something, too? She remembered a drop of blood beading on her skin, unsure if she had yet pricked herself on a thorn. Perhaps she should find the mirror first and *then* she could look. After all, wasn't that what one did with a looking-glass?

She felt a sudden certainty that it was close by, that the answers she sought were already waiting. She strode to the end of the tunnel, turned the corner and saw in front of her—

The thing waiting there was not a looking-glass. It wasn't anything she had expected to find, though it was something she recognised, something that made her heart throb painfully in her chest.

She stepped towards it. She told herself that if she didn't truly look at it, it couldn't be real; it would simply melt away, like everything else in this world.

But it didn't melt away. The thing ahead of her was a rabbit. Its fur might once have been white. Now it was soiled and bedraggled and maggots as big as her fist wended through it. Shards of splintered bone had broken through its skin, spearing the tunnel walls. Its teeth were tall as gravestones, twin slabs of dirty yellow smeared with dried blood. They barred the way into the tunnel of its throat. Its eyes were filmy, but had once been pink. Its body was broken and crushed from where the rabbit had—what? Grown? There was no way it could have crawled here as it was, along this tunnel. It was far too large for that. The claws jutting from one out-flung paw were as long as swords.

Then she saw the remains of a bonnet crushed against the ceiling along with its ears, and she knew that this was *her* rabbit. It was Mr Rabbit, always twitching, always nibbling, never still, though he was motionless now. And she saw the little glass bottle that lay at his feet.

Eat Me, she thought. *Drink Me*. Mr Rabbit had come to find her, to comfort her perhaps, and he had reached this place—and found food, a little respite in the darkness. And he had eaten, never knowing what it would do to him. He had grown bigger, and bigger still, hadn't been able to stop himself. He had become the wrong thing in the wrong place, and it had killed him.

But she could also see that the bottle had a label, one in handwriting she thought she recognised. Slowly, she walked towards it, anger building inside her. And she realised it wasn't a bottle at all: it was one of Cook's empty jars, the ones in which she kept all sorts of things.

Time, the mean-faced woman had said. *Belongs in the pot.*

But Mr Rabbit would never go in the pot. She had always known that. She put out a hand and stroked him, the glassy smoothness of claw, the dampness of clogged fur. She snatched back her hand when something wriggled under her fingers.

Time.

The jar at the dead rabbit's feet didn't say "EAT ME". It didn't say "DRINK ME". It was an old label, smudged and faded and finally crossed out, though she could still make out the words "ORANGE MARMALADE". The residue at the bottom did not look like marmalade, however. It looked like something else entirely, and the glass was clouded, as if it had been kept at the back of a high and little-used shelf.

She turned it, making out the marks of fingers pressed into the dust. The cook's? She placed her hands around the jar—her own little hands, the ones that had held Mr Rabbit, had cuddled Mr Rabbit, had loved Mr Rabbit with all her childish love. And the prints fitted exactly. She examined them again, finding the scratch where the glass had been scraped by a golden ring.

She flung the jar from her, heard it shatter in the dirt. She told herself that she could have made those marks just now—or had she only known where to look?

She backed away from the rabbit. She could smell him now, the decay at the heart of him, the decay she'd been able to sense as soon as she entered the warren—no, sooner, as soon as she'd made her decision, to do... what?

She had leaned over his cage. It was so easy, to be Mr Rabbit. He simply was. He had paws and he ran. *Time you grew out of it.* But he had no sense of time passing, of what might happen in the future, and that was a relief, in a way. She had to leave him behind, she knew that. He had become the wrong thing in the wrong place, but he would never go in the pot; she promised him that. The dry, earthy smell of his cage had filled her nostrils—

There was food and he ate.

She backed away, shaking her head.

Alice, she thought, the name returning to her all at once. But who was that?

She knew who she was. She wasn't *this*. She turned and ran. She didn't get far, though, because the tunnel had changed, opening out, the ceiling rising to form a chamber. At its centre, there was the thing she had sought: a looking-glass, framed in ornate gold, an exact copy of the one that hung in her drawing room.

For a moment she saw the reflection of a dead rabbit, its leering, bloody teeth hanging before its face in a grin—and she stepped aside so that she couldn't see it any longer. She circled the mirror. What would she see when she stood straight in front of it? Would the mirror be clear, reflecting only herself? Or would it shatter when she looked into it, fracturing into a thousand pieces? Would it be opaque, revealing nothing? Or would its surface soften, turning to mist, allowing her to slip through to whatever lay on the other side?

She didn't want to look. If she did, and saw only herself, just as she was—would that be wonderful or dreadful? Would it make everything clear or drive her mad?

Still, she continued to move closer, because there was nothing else to be done. And closer still, its gleam entrancing her, drawing her to it until she stood with her nose inches from the glass. She stared into the mirror and she did not blink. She stood there for a long time, looking at the reflection—her home, a fire blazing in the hearth, casting its warming light about the walls; the wing-back chairs; the bureau; the bookshelves. Cook had served a meal, she noticed. A great silver tureen waited upon the table, surrounded by shining dishes. A posy of roses was placed next to it, tied up in a ribbon, though in the firelight Alice could not be certain if they were white or red.

She realised she could hear the crackle of the fire, smell the peppery aroma of soup. The room was behind her too and all around, and so fascinated was she to see her solid, familiar, dependable home again, that for a long time Alice did not notice the strangest thing: that although she stood directly in front of it, she could not see herself in the looking-glass at all.

How I Comes to be the Treacle Queen

CAT RAMBO

When we grimbled, how we grambled, children, down in those treacle mines, with a slow syrup slurry that clung to your boots, your hands, and every bit of skin, so you'd lick your lips, vicious-like, and taste gritty burned sugar and wonder what was happening up in the blue-sky world. And then we grimbled and we grambled moresome, and when we were weary walking, sleep stepping, we came up to the wasty world and tumbled into our flea-scampering blankets, and then in the morning afore the sun came into the sky, we went back down and did it all again.

We were seven sisters then. There had been more, once, but time creeps up on you sometime and snatches a few, leaves others, still grimbling, and pays no attention to your preferences on who or when or how.

And then one day there was eight, because they opened

the door, way up tops, the one we don't come in by, the one where sometimes they lower down a very clean chap in a big oaken bucket, and he looks around and ticks a tricky, ticky mark on the scroll of paper in his hand, and sniffs once, making a fish face, afore they pulls him back up.

This time they don't lower him. They throw the girl in. She's grabbing at the rope and bucket, trying not to fall, but she ain't too far down when she does and then there she is in the darkness with us grimblers, her with her hair like yellow flowers and her dress blue as that sky we'd been told of, and her feet like little white fishes swimming in the treacle and being swallowed whole.

There's one slant of light as falls down from above, and she stands there in its center, looking around with eyes as wide as dish-plates, with us'ems all round, a-looking back.

Salla tilts her head and considers the girl, and she's so worried that her eyebrows nearly knit together. There's a clank and clunk from up above when they close the door, and the light where the girl stands quarters itself, but she don't huddle into it, just keeps standing and looking, with a what-next expression on her face that ain't fear and ain't defiance or hate or even disgust at all that dirty treacle. It's just curiosity.

Selle says to Salla, low and hissing-like, "What is it?"

Salla says back to Selle, "It's a child."

Then there's some silence, as though they expect the girl to talk and yet she ain't.

Sullu nudges up, rubbing at her eyes, because the light hits her harder than most, and says, to the girl, direct as always, "What's yer name?"

"Alice," says the girl, and her voice is like a sunshine that don't burn, or water that ain't got bits of treacle in it.

"What you down here for, Alice?"

The girl shrugs, one shoulder, then the other, and it's like the motion unfreezes us all, and I push forward, just like all the rest, snuffling and sniffing at her. She don't flinch away, stands there all patient-like, and we get our fill of smelling, which is nicer than most, because she smells like green grass and forest shadows—not that I had smelled those in years, back then!

And finally she says, "Take me to where the newest digging is."

None of us ask questions. Sollo and Sullu take her hands in their sticky ones and guide her through the darkness, to where we been tunneling the most recent.

Out in the widesome world, there are birds and butterflies and bees. But down in the treacle mines there are no little friendly things except the nibblemice that live by licking the places where the lamp-oil kegs have rested. But as we went deeper and deeper, I see the mice following us, eyes all a-glimmersome, and then other little things, like glass bottles walking on spindly legs, and a winking lamp that smiles at me, but only when I ain't looking directly at it, and other creatures crossed 'tween imps and insects, their whiskers all a-bristle.

They creeps after us in the dark, and if the others sees them, they don't say nothing, so I keeps my mouth shut and go along.

Fourteen shafts down was the newest digging, and no one

hadn't never dug deeper than that. But Sullu had said she was following the smell of treacle and we'd broken down into there only the day before: a natural cavern, and the veins of treacle rolling along its side and feeding a sticky river that vanished down, down, downest, into the heart of the earth.

There was a candle Sullu had set there and I knew she'd been reading again, or pretending to, at any rate, given that they's no libraries, not down in the mines where we live all our worksome days. But she likes to sit there and imagine turning the pages. I gives her a look now, and she hisses at me, "This is the best place for it I evers found!" then breaks off at a look from Salla.

It was a good new vein of treacle, and you could see it starting to ooze out of the stone, the way it does, even though new treacle's nearly solid, thick as clotted blood or drying clay. Well, you could smell it better than you could see it, that sweet and sour and earthy all wrapped up together in one smell that fills your head and don't leave room for nothing else.

Alice is quiet for a bit. She digs around in a pocket and pulls out a little glass jar, and pours it onto the floor of the mine. As it pours, halfway to the floor it turns to silver light, but one that don't hurt my eyes or anyone else's, even Sullu's, and spreads out like spider-webs all over the floor and then the walls. We can all see the heart of the treacle vein in this end, a big black spot that gleams in the silvery light. All the creatures that have followed us down be lurking in the shadows, watching and wiggling.

The girl walks over to it and sticks her hand in afore anyone can say anything about treacle worms and the way they bite. Maybe she's lucky, because she pulls out her hand again unbitten and unchanged other than being covered in a thin layer of treacle, and held between thumb and forefinger now, she's got a key.

As we watch—and this is startlesome, because some of my sisters do love to grumble and grimble, even when everyone else is being quiet-like—that silvery light burns away all the sticky treacle on it, or makes it vanish at any rate, because what's left behind is no residue, just a shiny silver key with two words written on its face in big plain letters, so plain even I can read them, saying, "Use me."

I looks at Salla and Selle and they looks back at me as though they expect me, by virtue of being oldest, to be doing something about all this strangeness getting in the way of the day's normal treacle production.

I says then, speaking for the first time, "Use me on what?"

Alice turns and looks at me. She says, "Have you never come across a lock down here?"

We all shakes our heads, one after the other, the proper way like our mother taught us. Alice frowns and looks around. She stares at the walls as though she's trying to see through them.

I knows when her eyes light on the treacle river that there's going to be trouble, because you can see the idea flash into her head, even though it's a terrible, terrible idea that shouldn't come to no one.

She jumps in.

We all stares after her, and then looks at each other, and even though this is an even worse idea, we all jumps in after her.

Why does we do it? You could chase me quarrelsome-like or torturous, and I still ain't got the words. It was the way she looked, and the way she spoke, and the way she shone.

She was a queen, like her in the Red and her in the White, even though I'd never seen neither, only heard tell. Down in the darksome mines, we are not part of the Great Fight. We only help furnish its refreshment and provide the gingerbread without which no meal-made accord can come to pass.

Hoity-toity me, maybe you is thinking, tracking everything that my betters is a-doing. But when you're down grimbling and grambling, and scrabbling to see how much treacle you can scrape into a carry-bucket, you need something to think about.

And there was something more than all of this, more than wishy-washy watching and wishing I was elsewhere whilst doing nothing about it all. It seemed to me that if I wanted to change my life and not be grimbling anymore, I needed to follow someone capable of changing things, and if there was one thing I knew about people who looked like her, this Alice girl, it was that they changed things.

I don't know why my sisters jumped in. We all had our reasons, I think.

So there we is, bobbing in the treacle after her.

It's a horrid mess, all that sticky treacle smelling of burned sugar and molasses, and I thinks to myself that drowning is a distinct possibility. But I moves my arms and stays on top of it all, and every once in a while, I collides with a sister and reassures myself that they're still around and kicking just as hard as I am. Maybe harder.

They says that queens are lucksome, and that may be how some time later we comes to be falling down a waterfall, or moving slower than falling, though still not in control. That treacle is thick, and it clings to the cliff-face, and lowers us slowly, stickily, inevitably, and every time I licks me lips, I taste old, old sugar, so hard it'd take a thousand years to lick through it all.

The only light is Alice's key, shining through the sticky layer covering it.

At the bottom, we wades through treacle until we finds ourselves on the shore. The key burns away its coating as Alice holds it out, and it gives enough light to show that we stands at the edge of a vast lake of treacle, which spreads away into the distance so far that we ain't be seeing the opposite side.

Alice looks like she's doing a little curtsey to the lake, but then I realizes she's dipping the key into the treacle, and it doesn't sticky it up none. Instead it writhes and wriggles and moves away from the key, until there's a big wide patch of sand as dry as dry can be.

And that's how we crosses that lake, we does, and it's a fearsome thing, looking up at those walls of treacle all around us, but not pressing inward on the key, just shifting as Alice steps forward, step by footstep.

A lifetime later, I thinks that we are climbing, and then

another lifetime later, I knows that we is, because there's light coming down in big clumps, and as we come up farther, I sees it's snow, big fluffy clots and blots of it and we come out into the light and everything is like it's never been before. We's standing on a hillside, and there's a door in front of us, standing all by its lonesome in the snow, which stretches out all around us. It's cold, but not too cold just yet. The only tracks is ours.

"What's this the door to?" Salla pipes up.

"It leads us further into the story," Alice says, and she turns the knob and swings the door open. There ain't any snow inside, just green, green grass and I see we're at the center of Wonderland, and not at its edges in the treacle mines no more. The air inside is warm and I can feel the treacle falling away from me in a most un-treacle-like manner.

"And here we are, having won through," Alice announces. I squints at her with one eye and then the other. She notices me, and says, "What?"

"Pardon me," I says, and I don't add "my lady" the way I might have, because certain ideas and notions is coming to me. "But ain't you supposed to, you know, defeat something?"

She shakes her head and looks at me in a way that is both patientsome and grating. She says, "The Hero's Journey can be about overcoming internal obstacles too, you know."

I nods, because I can see what's coming up behind her, and it's a Jabberwock.

Long time the manxome foe she fought, and you know, she would have lost, but Salla and Selle throws rocks, and Silli and Sollo throws stones. Sullu does a lot of shouting and waving her arms about—to distract it, she says later, and no one wants to say anything about whether or not it had been successful. Sylly trips it at one point, or tries to, at any rates.

And me? It seems to me the safest spot be where those teeth can't reach me, and so I runs up its back and settles behind its head, and that might have been more distracting than anything that Sullu was doing.

And finally it lies at her feet, or *our* feet being more accurate, and that's how we comes to slay the Jabberwock through collective action.

Alice says to me sister, "Do you want to be a Queen?" and quick as thought, Salla shakes her head no.

So she asks Selle, and Silli, and Sollo, and Sullu, down to Sylly, and then she's to me and instead of shaking me head, I nods but says, quick as a nibblemouse's nips, "But I has Terms and Conditions."

"I would expect no less," Alice says grandly. "But first, though, will you replace the Red Queen or the White? I'll take whoever is left."

"That's the first of it," I says. "We be holding the means of production in trust for the workers, rather than contributing to an outdated system of monarchy."

That makes her blink, but she says, "And so?" She beckons with her hand and a little notebook creeps up on wavering legs, and then a pen creature jumps it and knocks it over and starts writing in it, while the notebook keeps kicking, trying to stand back upright.

"And so if I'm the Queen of anything, it's Treacle Queen,

to remind me an' the others of our origins, and that's as far as any naming like that might go," I tells her.

You see, I does like her, and her style, and the way she holds herself, and how clean she still seems to be, despite all the treacle. But it ain't a model that works for me, not a hundred percent, and so adaptings and adoptings must be made before any agreements cans be come to.

So we's begin, and the pen keeps a-writing and the notebook a-wriggling so sometimes things is more legible than others, but in the end, Wonderland's a different place. Alice's taken a page out of my book for herself, and instead of being Red or White, she's the Blue Knight, because the color scheme and symbology of that suits her better, and each of my sisters has they's own title, and the option to swap around when they like. Salla is in charge of Communications and Deliberations and Selle oversees the roads, because it turns out she's always wanted to go a-wandering. Silli is our General in case of Foreign Invasion and Sollo is in charge of the Ministry of Tourism. Sullu is in charge of the Wonderland libraries, and Sylly, it turns out, wants to go back to the treacle mine and make certain changes there involving management and workers' rights.

All in all, when shove overcomes pushing, we finds out leading a place like Wonderland don't take all the energy that the Queens seems to has thought it did. And maybe they was meddling too much, and steering things their way, because it turns out when everything's sorted, the castle don't need quite so much treacle as it thought, and that frees it up for everyone, upon which occasion they's rejoicings and chantings and general jubilations.

Alice and me, we watches from up in the castle that ain't a castle anymore, but been turned into a university, and all the studentlings and wordbugs and instructor creatures hang out the windows and watch, and cheer, and has ourselves a celebration that be for more than treacle tart for alls that's wants it. We celebrate the new Wonderland, and everything that came about when the Red and the White thought they put our Alice in the darksome treacle mine and keep her quiet.

They forgots all of us there in the darksomeness already, grimbling and grambling so they could have their tarts.

Because with an Alice, it's not that they just changes things, though that's true. With an Alice, they changes you, and that's how things start changing for real.

Six Impossible Things

MARK CHADBOURN

Still she haunts me, phantomwise,
Alice moving under skies
Never seen by waking eyes.
~ Lewis Carroll

"That depends a good deal on where you want to get to," the Cheshire Cat replied. Emerald eyes flickered and a rough pink tongue licked across gleaming teeth.

Alice pressed a finger to her chin. "I believe I've heard that somewhere before."

"Believe whatever you want. That is one of the rules. If you believe hard enough, perhaps it will even be true."

Alice looked around. How on earth had she come to be there? Trees as far as the eye could see, silver birch and ash, lit in a hazy, golden glow. Honeybees droning through sunbeams. The Cat curled on one of the low branches. His smile seemed to be teasing her.

"I don't remember any rabbit holes. Or mirrors, for that matter. How did I arrive?"

"Don't trouble yourself with that! You're here to play a game. That's what matters. Don't you recall?"

"A game?"

"You have to find the Vasteous Shield."

"The Vasteous Shield?" Alice said, her eyes narrowing. "I've never heard of such a thing."

"What does it sound like?" the Cat asked.

"It sounds very much to me like something a knight of old would wear on his arm to protect himself."

"Then that may very well be what it is."

Alice eyed this puss. A talking cat was a remarkable thing in itself, but this one had many other qualities which she found quite astonishing. For one, it had a grin wider than any she had seen on a cat before. There seemed far too many teeth in a mouth of that size. But it appeared good-natured enough.

"Have we met before?" she asked. "I think perhaps we have."

"Have we met before, or will we meet? That is the question," the Cat replied. "I can't quite keep this straight in my head, so goodness knows how you are supposed to."

The Cat frowned, if cats could indeed be said to frown. And a moment later it did something else rather strange. It began to fade away, from the tip of its tail, along its haunches and its back, to its head. And when that was gone, only the grin remained, floating in a sunbeam.

"That's a very extraordinary thing for a cat to do. And for people too," Alice said. "I've always wanted to vanish, particularly when I'm unhappy, or angry, or someone is trying to make me feel bad."

"Over here."

The Cheshire Cat was sitting on a track through the woods. She hadn't seen it before. "I suppose you want me to follow you," she said.

"I suppose I do."

As the puss meandered along the track, Alice glimpsed a flash of movement away in the trees. She felt momentarily blinded, as if she'd been caught by the sun reflecting off the bathroom mirror in the morning.

"Oh! What was that?"

"Those are just the Machine Elves." The Cat's voice floated back. "No need to pay any heed to them. They helped you build this place."

Alice widened her eyes. "Me?"

"Well, not you exactly."

"Did they make you too?"

"Oh no. I've always been here. And always will be, I might say." He looked back and that grin licked a tad wider.

In a clearing, three doors stood side by side. They weren't a part of any building, just a wooden jamb with the doors inside them, panelled like the ones in the grand old houses Alice remembered visiting when she was younger. On the middle door frame, a crow perched. The bird cocked its head, studying Alice with gleaming black eyes. When they neared, the crow soared over the treetops, cawing.

"You scared it off," Alice said to her companion. "It's a well-known fact that birds don't like cats."

"I would be very suspicious of well-known facts, if I were you. Things that you believe are true are very often not. Use your eyes. And ears. And occasionally your nose. And think for yourself."

Alice sniffed. This puss seemed to have a very high opinion of himself. Her thoughts drifted back, across croquet lawns and locked rooms, parks and rivers. Yes, surely she had encountered this odd fellow before, but where, she couldn't quite place. Perhaps it had been a dream.

She wandered around the three doors, looking them up and down. "And what is the meaning of this? A door to nowhere is not much use to anyone."

"Doors always lead somewhere, even when they seem not to. A door is the beginning of a journey. Or the end. And once you set forth upon a journey, you learn a great deal about yourself. In fact, if a journey has any other purpose I can't imagine what it is."

"I know everything about myself. That's how I'm me." Alice stepped to the end of her circuitous route and looked down at her companion.

"But there are so many things about you! How can you possibly tell which of them is important, and which of them is merely butter melting on a hot crumpet."

"I would say hot buttered crumpets are very important indeed," Alice replied.

The Cat clawed his way up a tree trunk and perched on

a low branch where he had a good view of the proceedings. "Here is the game. Choose a door. And once you see what's inside, you might also get a glimpse of the Vasteous Shield."

Alice pressed a hand to her mouth to stifle a titter. *Silly cat!* she thought. *Inside!*

But she'd play along. It would be rude not to. Choosing the door on the left, she tugged on the handle.

"This is very strange," Alice said.

The door opened onto a bookshop. A quiet lay across it, of the kind to be found in bookshops everywhere. People who enjoyed books didn't like to talk very much, Alice thought.

Frowning, Alice peered around the edge of the door. The woods stretched out as they had done. No bookshop to be seen anywhere.

"Curiouser and curiouser," Alice said.

She peered back through the door. A few people browsed the volumes on the shelves, licking their fingertips as they turned the pages with studious concentration. Beyond them, a large glass window looked out onto a city street. A mauve car rolled by, long and sleek, with large lights at the front, and a running board.

"That's not Oxford," Alice said.

"It's a city where people choose to go into holes in the ground without a white rabbit to lead them," the Cat replied.

A bell tinkled, and an elegant woman walked in. She was wearing a long coat of deepest purple edged with black fur. A black hat was perched on her silver hair. Furrowing her brow, she looked around as if someone might ask her for money.

"She has an interesting face," Alice said. "I like her."

The woman edged past the browsers to an area that had been set aside for an exhibition. Pen-and-ink drawings in sable frames covered the wall, and beneath them a glass case contained sheaths of handwritten paper as if they were valuable. Looming over the display was a model of a man with wild eyes and a battered top hat.

"Oh, isn't that—"

"Yes, it is," the Cat interjected.

The elderly woman leaned in to study a drawing of the Cheshire Cat.

"Marvellous, isn't it?"

A man was smiling at her. He was younger, perhaps half her age, and wearing a grey suit and waistcoat with the gold chain of a watch fob dangling from the breast pocket. The woman scowled at him. The man didn't appear deterred.

"Peter Llewellyn Davies," he said, holding out a hand. "I believe we have much in common."

The woman took his hand as if he might be hiding a razor blade in his sleeve. "I wouldn't think so."

"Peter Pan?" he prompted.

"This isn't Neverland."

"Neverland is a place I escape to when the rigours of this world get too much. We all need an escape hatch from reality, eh?"

"I wouldn't know."

The woman turned back to the drawing of the Cat, but Peter leaned in.

"I can understand your reticence. All those stares and

wagging tongues can get a bit much."

The woman began to hum to herself.

"But I understand you," Peter persisted, "and I think you would understand me. I am Peter Pan, but I am not. Sounds nonsense, doesn't it? The whole world is nonsense and we should accept it as such. That way it would make more sense."

"You do like the sound of your own voice. However much drivel spills out of it."

"Prickly as a hedge-pig; I'd heard that! With a tongue that can cut you into pieces and a demeanour like the middle of winter."

"How flattering of you."

Peter stepped past her and waved a hand towards the framed drawings. "The Gryphon. The March Hare. The Mock Turtle. Wonderland. I would imagine, in certain ways, it's like my Neverland. It's hard to find again once you leave childhood behind, as much as you need it—"

"Look," the woman snapped, turning to him with blazing eyes. "If you're looking for money, spit it out and then I can show you the door."

Peter pressed a hand to his chest. "Good Lord, no. I don't need money." He paused, staring into space as he reflected, and in that moment Alice thought how unconscionably sad he looked. "I'm sorry," he said eventually. "What an ass I am. These are my defences, but to other people they often appear as weapons. I'll talk plainly, shall I?"

"Please do."

"Of course you've heard of the esteemed author J.M.

Barrie. Well, he became my adopted father after my parents died and he based his most famous creation on me. I was just a babe in a pram when he first encountered me, in Kensington Gardens. But he befriended two of my brothers, George and Jack. And later he befriended me."

Peter held the woman's eyes for an inordinate amount of time, Alice thought. If the elderly lady saw anything in that look, she didn't show it.

"Uncle Jim only took the name from me, I suppose," Peter continued. "George and Jack were the real role models for the boy who wouldn't grow up. But innocence can be stolen in many different ways, can it not?"

Alice wasn't quite sure what these two grown-ups were saying to each other. They seemed to be having one conversation and discussing something else entirely. Grown-ups were strange like that, she'd long since realised. One thing was certain: that elegant woman looked very uncomfortable.

Peter's eyes brimmed with tears. "May I ask," he said, his voice so low Alice could barely hear it, "the Reverend Charles Dodgson—"

"That's enough of that." The silver-haired woman slammed a hand into Peter's chest and thrust him out of the way. She flew to the door without a backward glance and was gone in the tinkling of a bell.

The door Alice was peering through also swung shut, though slow enough for her to see the fat tears rolling down Peter's cheeks.

"What an unhappy man," she said. "I hope he cheered up."

"Sadly not," the Cat replied. "But he's not really a part of this story."

"There was a drawing of you there," Alice continued, Peter already forgotten. "How odd that you are known in my world too."

"Not odd at all," the Cat replied. "I'm known everywhere."

Alice eyed the closed door, then curled her tiny fists on her hips and tapped her toe. "That wasn't a very good choice at all. No Vasteous Shield there."

"Didn't you see any shields? Anywhere?" the puss asked.

"No. Unless the Vasteous Shield looks nothing like any shield I've ever seen. May I try another?"

"A very good idea."

Alice marched up to the second door. "How about this one?"

This time the door opened onto the nave of a vast abbey. White marble statues of great men peered down at the pews filled with the living dressed in mourning black. Candlelight danced in their moist eyes.

"Why do you keep showing me sad things?" Alice whispered. She wrinkled her nose at the choking aroma of incense.

The Union Flag hung above the benches where the choir sat. Men in military uniform lined up at the back, medals on almost every chest.

"Have I seen this church before?" Alice asked. "I think I have."

The Cat prowled onto the threshold. "Westminster Abbey, that's its name. And a girl very like you came here many a time when her father was headmaster at Westminster School. In fact, she got married here."

"But not me?"

"Not you, exactly."

Alice leaned forward, squinting. "Why, that's the woman we just saw, in the shop. But she looks much younger," she said, pointing. "Is that the one you're talking about? The girl who got married here?"

The woman was hunched on the front row, her hand grasped by a man with a handlebar moustache. He looked quite handsome, Alice thought, but his face was like chalk and he stared through the choir to the altar without blinking.

The organ boomed and the congregation lurched to its feet. "Abide with me," they sang. "Fast falls the eventide… the darkness deepens." Here and there, sobbing punctured the full-throated singing.

"I can't see any shields here either," Alice said.

"Perhaps you're right," the Cat replied.

"Why is that lady crying? Is this what made her so angry in the shop?"

"A part of it. People are made of many things." The Cat licked his paw. "She's mourning her sons. Alan and Rex were killed in a war. The Great War, they call it, although wars are not great, and it was a poor name for this war for other reasons."

"Are all the people here mourning sons?"

"All here, and many more besides."

"Why *do* you show me the saddest things?"

"Her name is Alice, too," the Cat said, as if that was any kind of answer.

"She looks nothing like me, though."

"She *looks* nothing like you. But I look like a cat, and I am nothing like that. You do resemble her sister, or so I'm told."

The hymn droned on.

"Alice's children have always been very important to her." The Cat's tail flicked from side to side. "Indeed, all children are of importance to Alice. Their innocence particularly."

"She sounds like a wonderful lady."

"She is."

"Would she like me, I wonder?"

"Without a doubt."

The grief hung in the air so thickly, Alice decided she couldn't bear it anymore. "No, there's no shield here," she said, thrusting her chin into the air, "so let's not waste any more time. And from now on I would like to see only happy things. Sunshine. And puppy dogs. And a big slice of cake, covered in icing, served on a china plate in front of a roaring fire."

"Your wish is my command."

The second door swung shut and the Cat danced to the third and final door.

"It has to be this one," Alice said. "I shall look extra carefully."

Behind the third door, a beagle puppy bounded around a large, sunlit bedroom.

The Cat glanced at Alice who nodded, pleased. "Understandably, I don't approve," the Cat said. "Dogs can't be trusted, and I'm not wholly sure of their reason for existing. But you're welcome."

It was a girls' room, Alice could see, and there were three beds. One cherubic doll lay spreadeagled on the rug in the centre of the floor. Another one, with a missing eye and straw bursting from its side, was propped up against a pillow on one of the beds. But they were all the toys she could see. Alice turned up her nose. It was actually quite unwelcoming. Not as nice as *her* room.

The bedroom door crashed open and three girls rushed in. The beagle raced around their feet, yapping. Before the third girl kicked the door shut, Alice heard a furious din, a man and woman arguing somewhere downstairs.

The eldest girl stormed to the window, then spun back and jabbed a finger at the middle child. "This is all your fault."

Alice cupped a hand over her mouth and whispered, "Who are they?"

"The Liddell sisters," the Cat purred. "Lorina is fourteen. She has a hunger for all sorts of things, and not just cake. The youngest is Edith. She's nine. Quite bright, by the standards of children, but a little shy."

"Oh. She looks just like me."

"She does, doesn't she?"

Alice watched the tears bubble in Edith's eyes. "Not again." She glared at the Cat. "One puppy dog is really not enough."

"The middle child is Alice."

Alice frowned and studied the third girl. She had brown

hair in a bob and a cherubic face, just like the doll. "Now I can see what game you're playing, Cheshire Puss," Alice said, throwing up her hands. "This is the woman in the bookshop, and the one in the abbey. As a girl."

"Three as one." The Cat grinned wider. "You are a clever girl. But don't call me Cheshire Puss. I have claws. Very sharp ones."

The other Alice pursed her lips, trying to hold back her tears. "It's not my fault."

Lorina snatched the straw doll off the bed and flung it at her sister's head. "Of course it's you. Mother and Father are fighting. Because Charles asked them for your hand in marriage."

"What's that got to do with me?"

Edith began to sob as she watched her sisters fighting.

"Oh, stop being a crybaby," Lorina spat.

"You're only acting like this because *you* want to be Mrs Dodgson," Edith said through a trail of snot.

Lorina harrumphed, but didn't answer, which Alice thought was answer enough.

Downstairs, the father bellowed, "Eleven years old!"

"Eleven years old?" Alice repeated. "That can't be right." She felt gripped by that scene as if she was sitting in the stalls at the pantomime just before Christmas.

"You play up to him," Lorina continued. "All those photographs he took of you. You know the ones I mean—"

Alice Liddell let out a piercing scream, screwed up her face and clapped her hands on her ears. "I don't want to hear about that! I don't want to think about that!"

"Eleven! Years! Old!" thrummed through the door.

"He took photographs of all of us," Edith whispered.

"Yes, but Alice is his *favourite*," Lorina sneered. "He even made up that stupid story for her. And dedicated it to her! Alice, Alice, Alice!"

"It's not a stupid story!" Alice Liddell said. "It's my place. Wonderland is… my place. And… and I can go there…"

Lorina snorted. "Keep spinning your little lies, Alice, why don't you? I suppose everything is Charles's fault? Quite why he chose to fall in love with you, I'll never know. Why don't you admit that you lured him on?" She stamped her foot. After a moment's thought, she eyed her younger sister and said in a voice dripping with acid, "I wouldn't be surprised if Mother and Father got a divorce. Because of you."

Alice Liddell slumped on the bed next to Edith and began to sob uncontrollably.

"ELEVEN! YEARS! OLD!"

"You're cruel," Edith said, looking out of the corner of her eye at her elder sister. She ducked, expecting another missile, but nothing came her way. "Besides, who would want to be a vicar's wife? All that praying. Cold pews. Sermons morning, noon and night, I wouldn't be surprised."

Lorina bit her lip, her shoulders sagging. "Mother and Father won't get a divorce, will they?" she said, almost to herself.

"They're just angry with Charles," Edith said. "Father told him not to come around again. No more trips in the boat on the river."

Now Lorina began to cry, but silently, her shoulders heaving.

"It's not Alice's fault," Edith pressed. "You know that."

Alice dried her eyes. "He wanted some nice photos, that was all. That's what he said. To look at, so he could think of me while he was dreaming up another story."

That wasn't the right thing to say. Lorina glared at her.

"Well, there'll be no more stories now, will there?" the eldest girl said. "Wonderland is gone forever."

There was so much crying at this remark, that Alice clapped her hands over her ears and thrust the third door shut.

"That was yet another waste of time," she said, kicking up little whorls of dust. "This isn't a very good game if you can't win it."

"It's not really the kind of game that you win," the Cat purred. "It's more like a game where you learn."

"How boring. This sounds like those diversions that the governess suggests in the schoolroom when she wants you to remember the capital of Mozambique or how to conjugate a verb."

"Nevertheless, it is the only game we have. So I suggest we play it."

"But we're done," Alice protested. "And there were definitely no shields anywhere."

"Really? I believe I saw a shield once every door was open."

"Now you're teasing me." Alice narrowed her eyes. A notion flitted across her mind and she looked back at the three doors. "What exactly *is* the Vasteous Shield?"

"All will be revealed. Or not. It depends very much on whether you're paying attention."

Alice stamped her foot. Perhaps this was the real entertainment here—to make her seem foolish.

"Why don't you try the fourth door?" the Cat asked. He swayed among the silver birches to where another door stood. This one was white.

"You said there were only three doors."

"Exactly. This is the fourth of three."

"Only a mad person would say something like that," Alice said, following along behind.

The puss looked back at her, a little snootily, Alice thought. "I was sure we'd long since established that we're all mad here."

"I'm not mad," Alice replied. And the moment the words had left her mouth she had the strangest feeling that she'd said them before.

"You must be, or you wouldn't have come here."

Alice shivered, though the afternoon was as warm as any she'd known. "I'm not mad," she whispered to herself.

"That's the spirit. Now, shall we proceed?" The Cat perched in front of the fourth door of three.

Now Alice felt her arms turn to gooseflesh. "I'd rather not," she replied. She wasn't quite sure why, but that white door pulled her belly into knots.

"You don't really have a choice," the Cat replied. His words sounded menacing, but he was still grinning. "The only way out of here is through the door."

"I'd rather not leave, thank you very much." Alice pushed

her chin up, which she'd found was an acceptable way to let people know that she wouldn't be swayed. "This is a perfectly nice summer's day, and I would like to enjoy it with a walk, or perhaps a picnic."

"If you want to stay here, you'll still have to go through that door."

Now she felt the Cat was looking at her in a manner that he had never done before. Perhaps a little sorrowful, though why that should be, she didn't know.

"Very well!" she replied, as indignantly as she could manage. "But… I don't really want to. I'm scared."

"I understand. It is frightening. But it's necessary."

Alice reached out a trembling hand. For a moment, she let it hang there and then she pushed open the fourth door.

Once again it was a bedroom. But this time it was a grand old thing, she thought with a nod, much grander than her own. The curtains were drawn and the only light came from the stub of a guttering candle beside the bed. In the wavering light, she glimpsed a dressing table covered with glinting glass bottles of perfume, jars of cream and a silver-handled hairbrush. How odd, she thought. The mirrors had been covered.

"And no Vasteous Shield here, either," she said.

"But I can see it."

Alice looked round. The Cheshire Cat was staring directly at her, twin candles flickering in the depths of those emerald eyes.

"I'm sure I don't know what you mean." She looked away rather more quickly than she intended. "Oh!" She clasped her hands together.

At first she hadn't seen it, so still it was, but a figure was lying under the thick covers. Arms that seemed little more than skin on bone stretched out beside the body. A head poked above the eiderdown, face like a frozen millpond, hair silver as moonlight. Sleeping, or so it seemed.

"She must be a hundred and fifty years old," Alice whispered.

"Years are only years, and that's no way to measure a life," the Cat purred.

"I can hear you. Step forward." A voice like autumn leaves.

The Cheshire Cat prowled across the threshold and curled up at the foot of the bed, still licking his teeth in that broad, broad grin.

"Oh, it's you. I wondered if I would see you again," the old woman said. "Always vanishing when I needed you most."

"Vanishing?" the Cat said. "I've always been with you."

"Are you alone? I thought I heard another voice."

"Only you and me, as always, Alice."

The puss faded away, beginning with the tip of its tail, until only his smile hung like a wisp of candle smoke. And then that too was gone. Alice blinked, and when she focused again, the Cat was perched on her belly. He stared at her, and she stared at him.

"You like your games," she said.

"If we didn't have games, what kind of life would this be?"

"I'm glad you came to see me one last time, here at the end."

"Every new beginning comes from some other beginning's end."

"I didn't know cats read Seneca?"

"Cats do many things when you're not looking." He licked the back of his paw, but kept those shimmering eyes fixed on her. "Are you ready?"

"For it all to be over?" Alice let out a deep, juddering sigh. "It's been a long life, I suppose. And I have as many regrets as you can heap up in that time. My biggest… I wish I'd been kinder to Peter Llewellyn Davies. I might have been able to help him." She paused. "And he, me. Did he ever…?"

"He threw himself in front of a tube train. Or he will do. I find it hard to get these things straight."

"Oh." A tiny sound.

"I don't say that to upset you. There was nothing you could do. And do you really think he could do anything for you?"

A long silence, then: "No." Her fingernails clawed at the eiderdown. "An escape hatch for reality, that's what he said he wanted. I'm sure he never found Neverland again. And I never found Wonderland. But, you know, I looked everywhere. Searching, searching, searching. In every rabbit hole. In every mirror, until I became sick of my own reflection. That's all I ever wanted. To see you again, and all the others, in a world of nonsense, that made more sense than this world."

"Perhaps you were looking in the wrong places."

"Where is it, then?"

"Where is Wonderland? Everywhere. You walk above it, and below it. But most of all it's inside you."

Alice felt tears well up in her eyes. "I've been searching for that place all my life. Yearning for the magic. For peace."

The Cat said nothing.

Alice closed her eyes, lost to a powerful vision of brilliant colours that was nothing like the world she knew. Of Hatters and March Hares, Caterpillars and Mock Turtles. "I can't remember what happened." To her ears, her voice sounded like it was coming from the bottom of a well. "I can only remember Wonderland. I was there. I was there? I thought… perhaps… it was a dream. That I'd brought everything to life in my head."

"We are all the figments of someone's imagination," the Cat said, in a gentle voice that she hadn't heard before.

"To taste that once," she continued, the visions still playing out in her mind's eye, "to see something so joyous, you can never appreciate this world again. It's too harsh, too miserable, too dark. Too much pain and suffering. This world is supposed to make sense, but in the end you realise it's all nonsense. Where harm comes to those who don't deserve it. Who can't protect themselves. I needed Wonderland then. And I've needed it ever since. I think we all do." She choked back a sob. "But I could never find my way to it again."

"Well, you don't have to worry about that now," the Cat said in a bright voice.

Alice eased open her eyes to look at him, to see that grin. But all that floated in front of her was the deepest, darkest black.

"Peter… Peter…" She heard her voice crack, grow thin. "…'to die will be an awfully big adventure', that was always his message…"

For a while she heard only the silence that came after a bell had been struck. Then…

"Oh," Alice said. "I feel—"

"Reborn?"

Alice felt as light as a feather. Like she was ten years old again, before the summer faded. Somehow she was standing at the end of the bed, and the golden glow of an early July afternoon flooded through the open door.

"Come along, little girl," the Cat said, dancing ahead of her. "Wonderland beckons, and there's an awfully big adventure waiting for the both of us."

The Cat began to vanish into the light, and this time it was his grin that disappeared first.

In a Wonderland they lie,
Dreaming as the days go by,
Dreaming as the summers die:

Ever drifting down the stream—
Lingering in the golden gleam—
Life, what is it but a dream?

Revolution in Wonder

JANE YOLEN

The hounds caught White Rabbit
in a very long chase.
Fought for his watch,
which one kept for his mate.

Humpty was cannonballed
off the high wall.
The Duchess cried foul.
The dogs ate the yolk cold.

Old Caterpillar was skinned
and then fried.
Tasted like chicken,
the sergeants agreed.

The Tweedles were knotted
in a sack for the Jabber.
Left on the field.
Beamish Boy swept up later.

A tribunal then sentenced
both Queens and the Knave.
The executioner's sword
was covered in salve.

Hare turned state's witness,
but Hatter had fled,
off to Amerika
where he was feted.

Dormouse carved up
for an afternoon tea.
His bones into toothpicks.
The last thing he saw?

Alice, in armor,
who publicly wrung
the neck of Flamingo
who had done her wrong.

Dodgson was hanged.
where all Wonder could look.
The world celebrated
one less Carroll book.

ABOUT THE AUTHORS

Jane Yolen, called "The Hans Christian Andersen of America" by *Newsweek* magazine, is the author of over 376 books ranging from children's books to poetry collections, novels, cookbooks, short-story collections, graphic novels, non-fiction, and even a verse memoir of her immigrant family. She lives in both America's New England and St Andrews in Scotland. She writes a poem a day and sends them out to over a thousand subscribers.

Robert Shearman has written five short-story collections, and between them they have won the World Fantasy Award, the Shirley Jackson Award, the Edge Hill Readers Prize, and three British Fantasy Awards. He began his career in the theatre, and was resident dramatist at the Northcott Theatre in Exeter, and regular writer for Alan Ayckbourn at the Stephen Joseph Theatre in Scarborough; his plays have won the *Sunday Times* Playwriting Award, the World Drama Trust Award, and the Guinness Award for Ingenuity in association with the Royal National Theatre. A regular writer for BBC Radio, his own interactive drama series *The Chain Gang* has won two Sony Awards. But he is probably best known for his work on *Doctor Who*, bringing back the Daleks for the BAFTA-winning first series in an episode nominated for a Hugo Award. His latest book, *We All Hear Stories in the Dark*, is to be released by PS Publishing next year.

M.R. Carey is a novelist, comic book writer, and screenwriter. He has worked for both DC and Marvel Comics, on titles such as *Lucifer*, *The Unwritten*, and *X-Men*. He wrote the movie adaptation for his novel *The Girl with All the Gifts*. He is also the writer of the Felix Castor novels, and (along with his wife Linda and their daughter Louise) of two fantasy novels, *The City of Silk and Steel* and *The House of War and Witness*.

Genevieve Cogman is a British author of fantasy literature and role-playing games. She has an MSc in Statistics with Medical Applications. She works for the NHS and lives in the North of England. Her hobbies include patchwork, knitting, and sleeping in at weekends.

UK number-one bestseller, **Cavan Scott** is an author and comics writer who regularly contributes to such popular universes as *Star Wars*, *Doctor Who*, *Pacific Rim*, *Warhammer 40,000*, *Star Trek*, and many, many more. He has two Sherlock Holmes adventures published by Titan Books—*The Patchwork Devil* and *Cry of the Innocents*. Find him at www.cavanscott.com.

New Zealand-born, Australian resident **Juliet Marillier** is the author of twenty-one novels, including the *Sevenwaters* and *Blackthorn & Grim* series, plus assorted short fiction. Juliet is a member of OBOD (the Order of Bards, Ovates and Druids). Her lifelong love of mythology and folklore is a major influence on her writing. Juliet's new novel, *The Harp of Kings*, first book in the Warrior Bards series, comes out in September 2019. When not writing, Juliet tends to a small crew of rescue dogs. More at www.julietmarillier.com.

Jonathan Green is a writer of speculative fiction, with more than seventy books to his name. Well known for his contributions to the Fighting Fantasy range of adventure gamebooks, he has also written fiction for such diverse properties as *Doctor Who*, *Star Wars: The Clone Wars*, *Warhammer*, *Warhammer 40,000*, *Sonic the Hedgehog*, *Teenage Mutant Ninja Turtles*, *Moshi Monsters*, *LEGO*, *Judge Dredd*, and *Robin of Sherwood*. His work has been translated into at least nine languages. He is the creator of the *Pax Britannia* series for Abaddon Books and has written eight novels, and numerous short stories, set within this steampunk universe, featuring the debonair dandy adventurer Ulysses Quicksilver. Steampunk and dieselpunk have left their mark on his latest gamebook publications as well, *Alice's Nightmare in Wonderland*, *The Wicked Wizard of Oz*, and *NEVERLAND—Here Be Monsters!* He is the author of an increasing number of non-fiction titles, including the award-winning *YOU ARE THE HERO—A History of Fighting Fantasy Gamebooks*, which now runs to two volumes, and he has recently taken to editing and compiling short-story anthologies, including the critically acclaimed *GAME OVER*, *SHARKPUNK*, and *Shakespeare Vs Cthulhu*. To find out more about his current projects visit www.JonathanGreenAuthor.com and follow him on Twitter @jonathangreen.

George Mann is a *Sunday Times*-bestselling novelist and scriptwriter. He's the author of the *Newbury & Hobbes* Victorian mystery series, as well as four novels about a 1920s vigilante known as The Ghost. He's also written a *Star Wars* book, *Doctor Who* novels, new adventures for Sherlock Holmes and the supernatural crime series, *Wychwood*. His comic writing includes extensive work on *Doctor Who*, *Dark Souls*, *Warhammer 40,000*, and *Newbury & Hobbes*, as well *Teenage Mutant Ninja Turtles* for younger readers. He's written audio scripts for *Doctor Who*, *Blake's 7*, *Sherlock Holmes*, *Warhammer 40,000*, and more. As editor he's assembled four anthologies of original Sherlock Holmes fiction, as well as multiple volumes of *The Solaris Book of New Science Fiction* and *The Solaris Book of New Fantasy*.

Angela Slatter is the author of the novels *Vigil*, *Corpselight*, and *Restoration*, as well as eight short-story collections, including *The Bitterwood Bible and Other Recountings* and *A Feast of Sorrows: Stories*. She's won a World Fantasy Award, a British Fantasy Award, a Ditmar Award, an Australian Shadows Award, and six Aurealis Awards; *Vigil* was nominated for the Dublin Literary Award. Her work has been translated into French, Chinese, Spanish, Japanese, Russian, and Bulgarian. She is working on a novel set in the fairy-tale world of the *Sourdough* and *Bitterwood* collections, *Blackwater.*

Rio Youers is the British Fantasy Award-nominated author of *Westlake Soul* and *Halcyon*. His short fiction has been published in many notable anthologies, and his novel, *The Forgotten Girl*, was a finalist for the Arthur Ellis Award for Best Crime Novel. Rio lives in Canada with his wife and their two children.

Catriona Ward was born in Washington, DC, and grew up in the US, Kenya, Madagascar, Yemen, and Morocco. She read English at St Edmund Hall, Oxford, and is a graduate of the Creative Writing MA at the University of East Anglia. Her debut, *Rawblood* (W&N, 2015), won Best Horror Novel at the 2016 British Fantasy Awards and was shortlisted for the Author's Club Best First Novel Award. Her second novel, *Little Eve* (W&N), was a *Guardian* best book of 2018. She lives in Devon.

Laura Mauro was born and raised in London and now lives in Essex under extreme duress. Her short story "Looking for Laika" won the British Fantasy Award for Best Short Fiction in 2018. Her debut collection *Sing Your Sadness Deep* is out now from Undertow Books. She blogs sporadically at lauramauro.com.

Leatrice "Elle" McKinney, writing as L.L. McKinney, is a poet and active member of the kidlit community. She's an advocate for equality and inclusion in publishing, and the creator of the hashtag #WhatWoCWritersHear. Elle's also a gamer, Blerd, and adamant Hei Hei stan living in Kansas City. She spends her free time plagued by her cat Sir Chester Fluffmire Boopsnoot Purrington Wigglebottom Flooferson III, esquire, Baron o'Butterscotch or #SirChester. Random fact: Chester is a huge BTS fan, Elle has video proof. *A Blade So Black* is her debut novel, released fall 2018, with the highly anticipated sequel, *A Dream So Dark*, out now.

James Lovegrove is the author of more than fifty books, including *The Hope*, *Days*, *Untied Kingdom*, *Provender Gleed*, the *New York Times*-bestselling Pantheon series, the *Redlaw* novels, and the *Dev Harmer Missions*. He has produced five Sherlock Holmes novels and a Holmes/Lovecraft mashup trilogy, *Cthulhu Casebooks*: *The Shadwell Shadows*, *The Miskatonic Monstrosities*, and *The Sussex Sea-devils*. He has also written tie-in novels for the TV show *Firefly*. James has sold well over fifty short stories and published two collections, *Imagined Slights* and *Diversifications*. He has produced a dozen short books for readers with reading difficulties, and a four-volume fantasy saga for teenagers, *The Clouded World*, under the pseudonym Jay Amory. James has been shortlisted for numerous awards, including the Arthur C. Clarke Award, the John W. Campbell Memorial Award, the Bram Stoker Award, the British Fantasy Society Award, and the Manchester Book Award. His short story "Carry The Moon In My Pocket" won the 2011 Seiun Award in Japan for Best Translated Short Story. His work has been translated into fifteen languages, and his journalism has appeared in periodicals as diverse as *Literary Review*, *Interzone*, *BBC MindGames*, *All About History*, and *Comic Heroes*. He reviews fiction regularly for the *Financial Times* and lives with his wife, two sons and tiny dog in Eastbourne, not far from the site of the "small farm upon the South Downs" to which Sherlock Holmes retired.

Lilith Saintcrow lives in Washington State with her children, dogs, cats, and assorted other strays, including a library for wayward texts. Visit her website at www.lilithsaintcrow.com.

Alison Littlewood's latest novel is *The Crow Garden*, a tale of obsession set amidst Victorian asylums and séance rooms. It follows *The Hidden People*, a Victorian tale about the murder of a young girl suspected of being a fairy changeling. Her other novels include *A Cold Season, Path of Needles*, and *The Unquiet House*. Alison's short stories have been picked for several year's-best anthologies and published in her collections *Quieter Paths* and *Five Feathered Tales*. She has won the Shirley Jackson Award for Short Fiction. Alison lives in Yorkshire, England, in a house of creaking doors and crooked walls. She has a growing collection of fountain pens, loves folklore and weird history, and enjoys exploring the hills and dales with her two hugely enthusiastic Dalmatians. Visit her at www.alisonlittlewood.co.uk.

Cat Rambo lives, writes, and teaches somewhere in the Pacific Northwest. Her 200+ fiction publications include stories in *Asimov's*, *Clarkesworld Magazine*, and *The Magazine of Fantasy and Science Fiction*. She is an Endeavour, Nebula, and World Fantasy Award nominee. Her most recent works include *Hearts of Tabat* (novel, WordFire Press), *Neither Here Nor There* (collection, Hydra House Books), and *Moving From Idea to Finished Draft* (non-fiction, Plunkett Press). She is the current president of the Science Fiction & Fantasy Writers of America (SFWA). For more about her, as well as links to her fiction and her popular online school, The Rambo Academy for Wayward Writers, see www.kittywumpus.net.

A two-time winner of the British Fantasy Award, **Mark Chadbourn** is a *Times* bestseller. His Age of Misrule fantasy sequence has sold around the world and has been translated into many languages. Formerly working as a national newspaper journalist, he is also a screenwriter with many hours of work shown on BBC1. Mark is currently creating new shows for broadcasters in the UK and US while writing historical fiction under his pseudonym James Wilde.

ABOUT THE EDITORS

Marie O'Regan is a three-time British Fantasy Award-nominated author and editor, based in Derbyshire. Her first collection, *Mirror Mere*, was published in 2006 by Rainfall Books; her second, *In Times of Want*, came out in September 2016 from Hersham Horror Books. Her third, *The Last Ghost and Other Stories*, was published by Luna Press earlier this year. Her short fiction has appeared in a number of genre magazines and anthologies in the UK, US, Canada, Italy, and Germany, including *Best British Horror 2014, Great British Horror: Dark Satanic Mills* (2017), and *The Mammoth Book of Halloween Stories*. Her novella, *Bury Them Deep*, was published by Hersham Horror Books in September 2017. She was shortlisted for the British Fantasy Society Award for Best Short Story in 2006, and Best Anthology in 2010 (*Hellbound Hearts*) and 2012 (*Mammoth Book of Ghost Stories by Women*). Her genre journalism has appeared in magazines like *The Dark Side*, *Rue Morgue* and *Fortean Times*, and her interview book with prominent figures from the horror genre, *Voices in the Dark*, was released in 2011. An essay on "The Changeling" was published in PS Publishing's award-winning *Cinema Macabre*, edited by Mark Morris and introduced by Jonathan Ross. She is co-editor of the bestselling *Hellbound Hearts*, *Mammoth Book of Body Horror*, *A Carnivàle of Horror—Dark Tales from the Fairground*, and *Exit Wounds*, plus editor of bestselling *The Mammoth Book of Ghost Stories by Women* and *Phantoms*. She is co-chair of the UK chapter of the Horror Writers Association, and is currently organising StokerCon UK, which will take place in Scarborough in April 2020. Marie is represented by Jamie Cowen of The Ampersand Agency and her website can be found at www.marieoregan.net.

Paul Kane is the award-winning, bestselling author and editor of over ninety books—including the *Arrowhead* trilogy (gathered together in the sell-out *Hooded Man* omnibus, revolving around a post-apocalyptic version of Robin Hood), *The Butterfly Man and Other Stories*, *Hellbound Hearts*, *The Mammoth Book of Body Horror*, and *Pain Cages* (an Amazon #1 bestseller). His non-fiction books include *The Hellraiser Films and Their Legacy* and *Voices in the Dark*, and his genre journalism has appeared in the likes of *SFX*, *Rue Morgue*, and *DeathRay*. He has been a guest at Alt.Fiction five times, was a guest at the first

SFX Weekender, at Thought Bubble in 2011, Derbyshire Literary Festival and Off the Shelf in 2012, Monster Mash and Event Horizon in 2013, Edge-Lit in 2014 and 2018, HorrorCon, HorrorFest and Grimm Up North in 2015, The Dublin Ghost Story Festival and Sledge-Lit in 2016, IMATS Olympia and Celluloid Screams in 2017, plus Black Library Live in 2019, as well as being a panellist at FantasyCon and the World Fantasy Convention, and a fiction judge at the Sci-Fi London festival. A former British Fantasy Society Special Publications Editor, he is currently serving as co-chair for the UK chapter of the Horror Writers Association. His work has been optioned and adapted for the big and small screen, including for US network prime-time television, and his audio work includes the full-cast drama adaptation of *The Hellbound Heart* for Bafflegab, starring Tom Meeten (*The Ghoul*), Neve McIntosh (*Doctor Who*) and Alice Lowe (*Prevenge*), and the *Robin of Sherwood* adventure *The Red Lord* for Spiteful Puppet/ITV narrated by Ian Ogilvy (*Return of the Saint*). Paul's latest novels are *Lunar* (set to be turned into a feature film), the YA story *The Rainbow Man* (as P.B. Kane), the sequels to *RED—Blood RED* & *Deep RED*—the award-winning hit *Sherlock Holmes & the Servants of Hell*, *Before* (an Amazon Top 5 dark fantasy bestseller) and *Arcana*. He lives in Derbyshire, UK, with his wife Marie O'Regan and his family. Find out more at his site www.shadow-writer.co.uk which has featured guest writers such as Stephen King, Neil Gaiman, Charlaine Harris, Robert Kirkman, Dean Koontz, and Guillermo del Toro.

ACKNOWLEDGEMENTS

To begin with, thanks are due to all the authors who kindly contributed to this anthology. Our thanks also to Ella Chappell for taking on this project, Cat Camacho for all her hard work on it and the whole team at Titan Books. Thanks to Jamie Cowen and, as always, our family for all their help and support in bringing *Wonderland* into being. This book wouldn't exist without you.

COPYRIGHT INFORMATION

COMING SOON FROM TITAN BOOKS

HEX LIFE: WICKED NEW TALES OF WITCHERY EDITED BY CHRISTOPHER GOLDEN AND RACHEL AUTUMN DEERING

These are tales of witches, wickedness, evil and cunning. Stories of disruption and subversion by today's women you should fear. These witches might be monstrous, or they might be heroes, depending on their own definitions. Even the kind hostess with the candy cottage thought of herself as the hero of her own story. After all, a woman's gotta eat…

Eighteen tales of witchcraft from the mistresses of magic, including Kelley Armstrong, Sherrilyn Kenyon and Rachel Caine writing in their own bestselling universes!

Available October 2019

TITANBOOKS.COM